BIDDING FOR REVENGE

A DOTTY SAYERS ANTIQUE MYSTERY

VICTORIA TAIT

KANGA PRESS

Cover Design by Daniela Colleo of StunningBookCovers.com
Editing Allie Douglas

For more information visit VictoriaTait.com

CHAPTER ONE

Twenty-nine-year-old Dotty Sayers gulped in a mouthful of air. Without breaking the rhythmic stroke of her arms, she swivelled her head back into the water, seeking the end of the swimming pool through her blue-tinted goggles.

Her hand grasped the concrete-tiled lip of the outdoor swimming pool and she pulled herself into a standing position, breathing deeply. Cheltenham's lido was fifty metres long, and she'd only started swimming front crawl a month ago.

In the neighbouring lane, separated by a red nylon rope with bobbing yellow plastic floats, a lady with a head of auburn coloured corkscrew curls touched the end of the pool with both hands. She brought herself to a stop and stared over the edge of the pool at the small, single-storey white-fronted cafe building.

Apart from the four lanes roped off for adult swimming, the main pool and the smaller family pool, with its red plastic slide, were full of children enjoying England's sunny August weather. Swimming towels, bags and baskets were scattered across the dry yellow grass surrounding the pools, and families sat on benches at round, wooden picnic tables in front of the cafe, or on white plastic chairs under the shade of a semi-circular covered colonnade.

A pair of terracotta plant pots, filled with an abundance of blooms including pink cactus dahlias, small purple petunias and delicate white euphorbia flowers marked the entrance to the cafe area.

Beside one, a woman with a long thin tattoo on her shoulder, and a striped swimming towel wrapped around her waist, who was still wearing her yellow silicone swim cap, sneezed before continuing to talk to a handsome man whose wavy dark hair reached the collar of his white shirt. He flicked his hair back as he laughed at something she said.

"I've had enough," announced Gilly Wimsey from the neighbouring lane. Dotty turned and watched her walk the last few metres of the pool.

"Gilly," exclaimed the woman with the corkscrew curls, who had also turned round when Gilly spoke.

Gilly, who was continuing to move her arms in a breaststroke style as she laboured towards the end of the pool, squinted at the woman. She'd refused to wear her orange-rimmed glasses while swimming, even though she kept her head of orange curls above the water. She'd complained that her hair became an unruly mess when wet.

The woman continued, "It's Molly. Molly Vogt."

"Molly, of course it is. How are you? And what about your girls? How are they?"

"A handful, especially now they're old enough to understand that as twins they can cause an abundance of trouble."

Gilly laughed. "I'm sure they do. And I heard you started working for Cirencester Auctioneers."

"Part time only. I'd have preferred to work for Akemans, but you were quick filling your receptionist job."

Dotty coloured as Gilly looked across at her. "And she's become an invaluable member of the team, even agreeing to take part in the charity team triathlon, haven't you, Dotty?"

"I don't think I'll do very well. I only learned to swim front crawl last month." Dotty had surprised herself, enjoying her swimming lessons, and she'd found she was quite a strong swimmer. At school, she'd been shy and reserved and was always the last to be picked for teams. As a child she'd learned to swim, but only breaststroke, and her parents had refused to pay for additional lessons after the initial free school ones.

Her late husband, Al, had been interested in rugby, not swimming, and the last time she'd been in a swimming pool was during an amazing trip to Kenya when they'd stayed with one of his ex-army colleagues.

She heard Molly say, "We're putting in a team for the triathlon, but it's not really my thing, nor yours I guess, Gilly?"

"I'll stick to breaststroke. I'm only here to keep Dotty company, and because Peter has given me dire warnings about my expanding waistline."

Gilly's husband, Peter, was a doctor and he believed physical exercise and fresh air were the cure for many ailments.

"Mummy, Mummy, have you finished? Can we have ice creams?" Two identical girls of eight or nine, with blonde plaits extending down their backs over the tops of their matching pink swimming costumes, rushed barefooted across the concrete paving stones.

"Ask you father," replied Molly in a bitter tone. She took a deep breath and in a lighter, but slightly forced, voice asked, "Have you both had fun?"

They nodded enthusiastically.

"Then I'll tell you what. I'll get changed and afterwards we can all have ice creams."

The girls screamed with delight and rushed away towards the adjoining family pool.

Gilly smiled as she watched their retreating backs and said, "At least you'll be having a quieter time at work this month."

"Why do you think that?" Molly raised her eyebrows.

Gilly's cheeks reddened, and somewhat flustered she replied, "I assumed that as it's the school holidays, and customers are occupied with children or enjoying the summer weather and events, that you won't be holding this month's sale. We're not, are we, Dotty?"

Dotty shook her head and added, "Everyone's delighted with a quiet month to get other jobs done and prepare for the busy run up to Christmas."

"We should be so lucky," mused Molly. "I'm juggling childcare with work, although Didier is supposed to be lending a hand. But where is he?"

The handsome man with dark, wavy hair and a white shirt, whom

Dotty had seen earlier by the plant pots, approached them. "Looking for me?" he asked.

Dotty felt awkward standing in the swimming pool wearing her tight-fitting swimming costume and purple swim cap which clung to her head.

As Dotty peeled off her cap, revealing her sleek bob of blonde-highlighted hair, Molly smiled sweetly at the man and replied, "Yes, dear. I'm going to get changed, and the girls have asked for ice creams."

"That's a great idea. I'll go and find them." He turned and strode away but paused at the end of the pool as he laid a hand on the arm of a slim woman, said something to her and then walked through a gap in the hedge towards the family pool.

CHAPTER TWO

It was only five o'clock when Dotty parked her green Skoda Fabia in front of her cottage, adjoining the main house at Meadowbank Farm on the edge of Fairford, a small but attractive Cotswold town.

She'd finished her work early and was looking forward to a relaxing, balmy summer evening. Perhaps she'd read a book and savour a glass of chilled rosé wine while sitting in her small cottage garden.

As she climbed out of her car, Norman Climpson appeared, leading a Jersey cow. He called across, "I'm just going to milk Buttercup. Aunt Beanie's in the garden."

Norman was employed as the porter at Akemans but since the auction house was quiet at the moment, he was only working part time, mainly undertaking repairs and maintenance work. He enjoyed the outdoors, having spent most of his life as groundsman for the Duke of Ditchford at Windrush Hall, a large country house in the Cotswolds.

When the Duke died, Norman moved into Meadowbank Farm to help Aunt Beanie around the farm and help her look after her husband, Uncle Cliff, who suffered from dementia.

Dotty found Aunt Beanie and Uncle Cliff in the farmhouse's front garden, which looked out across the approach road to Fairford to the farm's meadows, and beyond to the River Coln.

The previous year, Norman had persuaded Aunt Beanie to lease the farmland to contractors as she was not a farmer and Uncle Cliff was now too ill to manage the farm himself. A herd of a dozen or so cows, black with white stripes like thick belts encircling their midriffs, grazed peacefully in the field.

Aunt Beanie's black legging-clad bottom poked out from amongst thick bushes in the flower border at the edge of the garden. She extracted herself, holding a pair of open pruning shears in one hand and several wilted white philadelphus blooms in the other. She dropped the forlorn flowers in a pop-up green plastic garden bin and turned round.

"Fabulous. You're back early. Time for tea." Aunt Beanie was an intelligent, energetic woman in her seventies. She favoured bright tunic tops and today wore a turquoise one with large pink and yellow roses printed on it. With her sleeves rolled up, she lifted her free hand to tuck a stray strand of long white hair under her yellow headscarf, which was secured with an enormous bow tied at a jaunty angle.

Dropping the shears by the bin, Aunt Beanie approached Uncle Cliff who today was showing signs of his ill health. His lined face was pallid and he slumped in a reclining garden chair supported by green cushions. He wore a vacant expression. She knelt down and touched his legs, asking in a gentle voice, "Tea, dear?"

Uncle Cliff focused on Aunt Beanie and nodded and smiled.

In response, the old woman gently squeezed her husband's leg.

"How is he today?" asked Dotty.

"Calm," replied Aunt Beanie as, with a lopsided smile, she surveyed Uncle Cliff. "I think he enjoys being outside in the sunshine. I suppose it's only natural. He's been a farmer all his life and is used to being outdoors, whatever the weather. Can you watch him while I make the tea?"

Dotty sat contentedly at an octagonal, slatted-teak table and closed her eyes. She listened to the hum of insects and the low moo of a Dexter cow in the meadow field. A car drove steadily along the adjacent road. She savoured the relaxing summer feeling, knowing that, before long, autumn would be upon them, bringing colder weather and lots of work at the auction house.

But it was more than that. A year ago, Al, her husband, had died on a peacekeeping tour in Africa, but she didn't feel any sadness or regret. Was that wrong? So much had happened since his funeral and she knew she'd grown and matured. Life was for living, and that was what she was trying to do. Her father, and then Al, had tried to control every aspect of her life, but now she could do as she pleased.

"Here we are," declared Aunt Beanie plonking a silver tray, which was tarnished black in places and needed polishing, onto the table. As she poured tea from a white teapot with a bunch of pink and blue flowers painted on its side, she remarked, "Norman is joining us soon. And he's bringing his frozen yogurt for us to try."

There was an oink and patter of feet as Aunt Beanie's pet Berkshire pig, Agatha, raced across the trim grass and collided with a water sprinkler.

Streams of water cascaded over Uncle Cliff, who cried out as Aunt Beanie rushed across the garden and stood the sprinkler upright, so its spouts of water fell onto a section of the flower border. Wringing her hands and looking a little damper, she rejoined Dotty.

"I really don't know what to do with Agatha. I can't have her careering about the house this winter, especially as Cliff is getting wobblier on his feet. But I don't have the heart to put her outside with Buttercup."

The wiry black pig, with white socks and a white stripe extending down the front of her face and around her pink snout, trotted across to join them. Dotty's furry grey British blue cat leapt onto the table and sniffed at the plate of biscuits on the silver tray.

"Earl Grey," chided Aunt Beanie as she lifted the large cat off the table and placed him on the grass beside his friend Agatha, "You're spoilt. This food is not for you."

"He can't help it," defended Dotty. "After all, Françoise did send a parcel of his favourite pâté en croute last week."

Aunt Beanie wrinkled her nose and poured tea into white porcelain cups with floral designs which matched the tea pot.

Norman appeared, wearing a khaki-coloured shirt with the sleeves rolled up, proudly carrying a blue-plastic Tupperware box, which he carefully placed on the table. "My frozen yoghurt," he announced. Slowly, he removed the lid and peered inside. His shoulders drooped. "Not again!" he exclaimed. "This is my third batch, and none of them have worked." He tilted the plastic tub and a milk-like substance flowed across it.

"Never mind," responded Aunt Beanie, handing him a cup of tea. "I'm sure you'll get it right in time for Fairford Show."

Norman pulled at his trim beard and Aunt Beanie walked across to Uncle Cliff. She held his cup to his lips as he sipped from it.

"Fairford Show?" enquired Dotty as she picked up her cup and savoured the delicate floral aroma of jasmine tea.

Norman sat down next to Dotty and asked, "You mean you haven't been cajoled into entering a class or two?"

Dotty drew her eyebrows together, and Aunt Beanie looked round, blushing.

"I see," murmured Norman. Turning to Dotty he explained, "The WI, or Women's Institute, run an annual show in early September with a range of classes including handicrafts, garden produce and baking. Beanie is insisting I enter the uninspiringly named 'dairy product' class."

He glanced across at Aunt Beanie, who was fussing over Uncle Cliff. "And I suspect she has entered you for some classes, too."

"What classes?" asked Dotty in alarm. What would she be expected to do?

Aunt Beanie straightened up and rolled her shoulders. "I've only entered you for the traditional Victoria sponge cake class, and one for four pieces of a traybake, such as chocolate brownies or lemon drizzle slices. And I've entered my damson gin in the fruit gin or vodka class."

"It could be worse," replied Dotty ruefully, like agreeing to take part in a charity triathlon and letting her teammates down, she thought to herself.

CHAPTER THREE

Although work at Akemans auction house was relatively quiet, Dotty still liked to arrive on time in the morning to check through her emails, for enquiries about future auctions or requests for valuations of a recently deceased family member's estate.

It was a Monday in the middle of August and the sun shone as she parked in front of the single-storey Cotswold stone auction house, next to the much larger three-storey antiques centre. Gilly Wimsey ran the antiques centre which had originally been a flour mill.

The door to the auction house was kept locked, except during a sale week, so Dotty pushed open the large oak door which led into the high-ceilinged, open plan space of the antiques centre. The vast room was divided into rows of booths, each selling different collections of antiques, bric-a-brac, and collectables. Gilly owned and ran a few stalls, but most were let out to individuals.

It was quiet inside, although Dotty heard a murmur of voices towards the back. August brought an influx of tourists who were vitally important for the continued success of the stallholders.

After contract cleaners had done their work in June, Dotty had persuaded Gilly to paint the internal walls of the old mill. Gilly had reluctantly agreed and together they'd chosen a pale grey paint which brightened up the antiques centre, giving it a less rustic and more elegant appearance.

As a result, three new stallholders had taken prime space in the front corner of the centre, beside the metal staircase, near the interconnecting door which led into the auction house.

Not for the first time, Dotty stopped and brushed her fingers across the soft wool of a green and pink tartan throw which was laid across the back of a cream upholstered nursery chair. She admired a collection of plump cushions arranged on a pistachio green display ladder. Glass vases, cream bowls and a pair of stylish brass table lamps, with pale floral shades, were elegantly displayed on top of a taupe-coloured chest of drawers.

She climbed the stairs to the first floor to check on her own stall before she started work in the auction house. In May, Gilly had suggested Dotty start a bargain stall with items she hadn't room for or couldn't sell on her own concessions.

Dotty's stock quickly swelled as other stallholders donated merchandise, and she'd also received boxes of unsold items from the auction house. As a result, her space on the first floor, otherwise empty apart from a storeroom and Gilly's office, had expanded, and she'd had to sub-divide it into smaller areas.

She'd themed each section with kitchen and dining room objects in one place, living and bedroom objects in another, and a larger, open plan area dedicated to outside furniture, an assortment of gardening equipment she'd recently been donated, and a collection of plant pots from July's auction.

She'd filled some of the pots with flowers and herbs in an effort to brighten up her stall, and customers seemed to like the idea as most of them had already sold. Perhaps she should repeat the idea with the remaining pots.

Fragrant sweet peas with delicate purple, cream and pink blooms filled a large blue vase decorated with peacocks, positioned on a circular oak table at the front of her stand. They would only last a few more days before she needed to replace them, but for now,they still looked attractive.

Satisfied the stall was neat and tidy, Dotty descended the metal staircase and entered the office-cum-reception area of the auction house.

The reception was at the front of the single-storey building with grey tub chairs and a sofa surrounding an oval, reclaimed elm coffee table arranged in the far corner, next to a door which led into the rear auction room.

The small office area had a worn, green leather-topped mahogany reception desk facing the front entrance door, a second desk pushed against the side wall adjoining the antiques centre, and a small kitchenette at the back.

Dotty was surprised to find Marion Rook sitting at the reception desk, reading a magazine. Not a hair of her grey bob was out of place and a pair of amber stud earrings were visible when she looked up and greeted Dotty.

"Good morning, you're looking tanned and fit. Gilly has been telling me all about your swimming training." Marion inclined her head to one side and added, "And the exercise suits you. Your arms have firmed up and your skin is glowing."

Dotty blushed at the unexpected compliment. Usually Marion criticised rather than praised her appearance.

From the rear of the office, Gilly called, "Tea?"

"Please," replied Dotty before turning her attention back to Marion and asking, "I wasn't expecting to see you here. I thought you'd be out on the golf course or tennis court."

"I am playing a round later, but Marcus called and asked David to pop in, so I thought I'd come and see how you are managing without me." Marion was very efficient, and she helped out in the auction house in the week preceding a sale and whenever there were other events or extra work.

Two men walked into the reception area from the main auction room. Marion's husband, David, reminded Dotty of a professor. His large, dark eyes were watchful but intelligent, and he had a high, pronounced forehead and darker-toned skin. He kept his salt and pepper moustache and beard neatly trimmed.

"Dorothy, a pleasure to see you," remarked David.

He was with Marcus Boyd, who Dotty rarely saw at the auction house and antiques centre. Marcus was married to Gilly's sister, Georgina Carey-Boyd, known to everyone as George, who ran the auction house. Marcus was in charge of the small, but exclusive, estate agent side of Akemans, which had a small office in the nearby village of Coln Akeman, and a larger one in the historic town of Cirencester.

Marcus had fair, floppy hair, and he usually wore an impish grin with a sparkle in his eyes. Dotty had heard Gilly and Marion mutter about him being a 'womaniser' and Dotty could easily believe it. He strode across and put an arm around her, squeezing tightly. "Morning, Dotty. I've some exciting news for you."

Marcus let go of Dotty, stepped back and enthused, "Who's heard of Jay Newton?"

"I'm just reading about him," replied Marion, tapping the magazine lying open on the reception desk.

"Isn't he the rock star who bought Windrush Hall?" asked Gilly, as she placed a cup of cardamom-infused coffee on the desk beside Marion and handed Dotty a cup of tea.

"Aged rock star. He's in his fifties now and his group, Spinning Newts, hasn't produced a song for at least five years," responded Marcus.

Marion raised an eyebrow. "It hasn't stopped him attracting the ladies. There's a photograph of him here at a charity event in Cheltenham with an attractive young woman."

Gilly leaned over the magazine and spluttered, "That's Rebecca Randall who works at Cirencester Auctioneers."

"She's quick off the mark. Jay only moved to the area a month ago." Marcus squared his shoulders and continued, "But that's not important. What is, is that Jay has asked to meet our 'antiques experts' as he'd like to buy furniture and items for the hall which are in keeping with its heritage as the former family home of the Dukes of Ditchford. As you know, he bought the house after the contents had been auctioned off, but he is particularly keen to get his hands on some of the original paintings, and anything else from the house which we can source."

"Is that why you asked me to come in?" enquired David.

"It is. George has taken the children to Devon for the week with her parents, so I was hoping you'd come with me this morning and meet Jay."

David pressed his lips together and, like the others, Dotty waited for his reply. "I have a few projects of my own underway this month, as the auction house is quiet, but I'll speak to Gilmore Chapman and see what paintings we can find in London. But I suggest Dorothy do the work down here. She's had nearly a year's training, and it's time she put her knowledge into practice. What do you think, Dorothy?"

Dotty was surprised. She had helped David value private collections, and she organised two sales at Windrush Hall, but to work on her own? She wasn't sure about that. "I don't know. What if I get it wrong?"

"I suggest you start with the auctions," instructed David. "You can request the catalogues ahead of time and do your homework. Then you can attend the pre-auction viewings and take photographs of anything you are uncertain about. I'll be happy to talk through any concerns you have."

Dotty still wasn't sure, but Marion suggested, "Why don't you both go with Marcus and meet Jay Newton? If nothing else, it'll be exciting to meet Cotswold's newest celebrity."

CHAPTER FOUR

Dotty was driven through the winding Cotswold lanes by David in his vintage silver Mercedes, while Marcus preferred to drive himself in his black Porsche 178 Cayman.

They slowed, and David pulled onto the low grassy verge, dotted with white daisies and clusters of purple harebells, to allow a green tractor and trailer to pass. It had emerged from a gap in the beech hedge which surrounded a field of yellow-headed wheat, through which a red combine harvester was making steady progress.

After several more miles, they turned between two stone columns which marked the entrance to Windrush Hall.

Dotty glanced across at the small stone cottage, which Norman Climpson had lived in when he worked for the late Duke of Ditchford, and observed, "It's nice to see someone living in the gatehouse. There are two plant pots beside the front door brimming with flowers."

The drive swept down, between acres of parkland, to a large Georgian-fronted stone house with steps leading up to the front entrance.

Marcus had already arrived and was standing beside his car talking to a shaven-headed man wearing brown moleskin trousers and a fawn polo shirt. As Dotty climbed out of David's car, she heard Marcus say proudly, "And it handles these country roads like it's on rails."

The shaven-headed man, who wore a pair of wacky green glasses, looked across at David's Mercedes and commented, "Now there's a real classic. But personally, I find a Range Rover more practical in the country."

He strode across and extended his hand towards David. "Jay Newton, and you must be David Rook. Marcus has told me all about you."

David turned to Dotty. "And let me introduce my assistant Dorothy."

Jay also shook hands with her, and his handshake was firm but brief. "Come in, come in," he invited them. His voice was deep and gravelly, but still warm and pleasant.

Dotty had grown attached to Windrush Hall and Jay was the third owner she'd known, if you included the old Duke, who'd died before Dotty had first visited.

That was less than a year ago when the hall had been abandoned, with the ornaments and silverware stored away, and the paintings and furniture covered by dust sheets. The Duke had converted the kitchen wing into his living quarters, and he'd locked up the main house.

After his death, a famous opera singer had bought the hall and spent a huge amount of money restoring it to its former glory, including Dotty's favourite room, the blue, peacock-wallpapered drawing room.

Dotty climbed the stone steps, and while the others moved across the stone-flagged entrance hall to the dining room, Dotty glanced into the drawing room. She was disappointed to see it contained a large, flat screen television and an L-shaped settee and a modern desk.

Turning around, she joined Marcus, David and Jay Newton in the dining room, but instead of a polished mahogany table there was a glass-topped one with high-backed black chairs.

"As you can see," Jay was explaining, "my modern furniture sticks out like a teenager at one of my concerts. I need period pieces preferably those which were originally here."

David opened a black leather document case and extracted some papers. "I have the contact details for the purchasers from the sale, although we do have to be careful contacting them. I don't think it would be ethical to call each of them in turn and ask if they'd like to sell us the specific item they bought."

Dotty gulped and ventured, "I could send out a generic newsletter saying that we have a buyer interested in purchasing high-quality period pieces. I don't have to mention Windrush Hall, but the newsletter would be targeted to people on that list, and any dealers who we think might know where the items are."

"Excellent idea," agreed Jay as a solemn, bald-headed man walked into the dining room from the door Dotty knew led into the kitchen. He was dressed entirely in black, from his shoes and jeans to a black jacket over a T-shirt with 'Spinning Newts' printed across the front. His outfit contrasted with his fair, almost white eyebrows and lashes. He carried a plastic tray with five cups filled with foaming coffee.

"Cappuccino, or cappuccino, appears to be the choice," remarked Jay in a matter-of-fact tone. "Tracy likes his new coffee machine, don't you?" The black-clad man took the seat across from Dotty but didn't respond to Jay's question. Tracy seemed a strange name for this rather scary man.

"Tracy?" asked Marcus, trying not to laugh.

"I know it's usually a woman's name, but his mother has Irish roots," Jay replied levelly.

"You wouldn't have survived long at my school with such a name." Marcus shook his head.

"Would you mess with Tracy?" asked Jay, raising his eyebrows.

Marcus turned to the bald-headed man who was staring intently at him and gulped. "No offense intended."

Tracy grunted and turned his attention back to Jay.

"What else do you suggest for acquiring pieces?" asked Jay.

"I'll speak to my contacts in London," replied David. "I heard a rumour last week that the Gainsborough of the second Duke and his family might be coming onto the market. And I suggest Dotty speaks to local dealers and attends the auctions round here. I can't promise you the original contents, but we can find some fitting period pieces."

Jay leaned back and clasped his hands together. "That sounds an excellent idea, but you do understand this has to be anonymous. My name cannot appear as the purchaser. If people hear I'm looking, the prices are bound to rise."

"Is that why you want our help, rather than asking a certain valuer at Cirencester Auctioneers?" asked Dotty.

A shadow crossed Jay's eyes and Dotty realised she'd spoken out of turn. She muttered, "Sorry, that was unprofessional of me."

David coughed. "Jay, perhaps you can give us a tour of the house and provide insights into pieces or styles that particularly interest you?" He pushed back his black chair and stood.

Jay also stood. "I'm not the expert. I'll leave the styles to you, but I'm happy to show you around the house, and the alterations I've made. In fact, let's start outside."

Dotty, David, Marcus, and the silent Tracy, followed Jay through to the kitchen, which was unchanged from when Dotty had helped prepare tea for guests when the opera singer was in residence. Modern units were arranged around the perimeter and a partition wall separated the cooking area from the pantry and storerooms.

Jay stopped on the black and white chequerboard floor tiles and tapped a gleaming chrome cooker. "This doesn't really have the feel of a country kitchen, it's too industrial. What was it like back in the Duke's day?"

David looked towards Dotty so she replied, "This was the Duke's living quarters, together with a bedroom and bathroom upstairs. It was one room back then, with comfy chairs around a log-burning stove, set in a chimney at the far end, and a large pine kitchen table. It had a very homely feel."

Jay nodded his head enthusiastically. "That sounds more like it. Somewhere informal to relax in the evening, especially in winter if there's a log fire. What do you think, Tracy?"

Tracy gave a curt nod of his head.

"Very well. Can you add consulting on the redesign of the kitchen to your tasks, Dorothy?"

Dotty felt the colour rise in her cheeks but she smiled as she replied, "I'd like that, and please call me Dotty."

Tracy suddenly moved towards the open door leading into the pantry and hissed, "Pesky mice."

Jay sighed and explained, "Tracy is at war. But the more traps he sets up for the furry rodents, the more food they take without getting caught."

"You need a cat," announced David. That's what the previous two owners had. In fact, I believe Dotty's cat used to live here, with the Duke."

Jay turned to her and his eyes widened. "You have the Duke's cat? It's still alive? Then it must come home."

"He is home," replied Dotty defensively as she clasped her arms in front of her. "And he came back here to stay, but this is not where he lives."

"But ..." Jay began but was interrupted by David.

"I know how attached people are to their pets, so can I suggest, Jay, that Dorothy also helps find you a suitable cat? One that will happily live here and spend its days chasing mice."

"Curled up on a chair asleep, more likely," grunted Tracy as he trudged across the kitchen and opened the door into the yard beyond.

Jay followed him, grinning. "That's an excellent idea. Now let me show you the recording studio, in the converted stables, and one of these sunny days, Dotty, you must come and swim in my new pool." He led them outside.

CHAPTER FIVE

That evening, Dotty joined Aunt Beanie and Norman in the farmhouse kitchen at Meadowbank Farm.

Norman settled Uncle Cliff into an armchair by the full-height windows at the conservatory end of the kitchen and placed a pair of headphones on his head.

He said, "It's a shame Cliff is no longer interested in rummy. He seemed happier and more engaged when we played cards with him earlier this summer."

Aunt Beanie's voice was flat as she replied, "I thought he was going to rally, but now I fear he is in decline. I'm not sure how long I'll cope, even with your help, when he can no longer feed himself or use the bathroom. But I promised myself he could live out his years here, in the house where he was born and has lived his entire life."

Clouds had started to gather in the afternoon and wind battered against the conservatory windows.

Norman looked out into the garden and commented, "I hope our contractors have finished harvesting. I saw extra combine harvesters working in the field by Robin Wood yesterday, but this wind will lay flat any corn still standing."

Dotty roughly chopped sun-dried tomatoes and scattered them over portions of chicken breast arranged in a white, oval, ceramic roasting dish. She reached for a jar of mixed stoneless olives and grimaced as she struggled to unscrew the top and her oily hands slipped.

Norman strode across the kitchen and took the jar from her, as he said, "Here, let me help." He removed a tea towel from a chrome rail running along the front of the Aga range cooker and wiped the lid of the jar.

Looking across at Aunt Beanie, who was sitting at the rectangular antique pine kitchen table with glossy brochures, newspaper clippings and sheets of papers scattered in front of her, he said, in a comforting tone, "Don't fret about Cliff. We'll do the best we can for him, but I fear a time will come when he won't know where he is, and he'll be better off with proper medical care."

Norman twisted the lid of the jar, which loosened with a pop, and handed the jar and lid back to Dotty, before returning his attention to Aunt Beanie and asking, "What are you working on?"

Dotty started to quarter the olives.

Agatha was curled up in a large dog basket, nestled amongst some of Aunt Beanie's old clothes, including a bright aquamarine printed dress, and Earl Grey was snuggled up against Agatha's tummy.

Norman had become increasingly concerned that hot food or boiling water would be dropped on the pet pig as she'd taken to lying across the front of the Aga, so he'd removed some shelves and built a small open-sided, flat-roofed hut beside it.

Agatha had taken to it instantly, especially with the addition of the dog basket, and Earl Grey often lay or sat on top of the makeshift roof, so he could observe what was happening in the kitchen. Dotty thought he was probably keeping an eye out for tasty morsels of food.

Aunt Beanie sat back on her pine chair, removed her round glasses, and replied, "The Rural, Heritage and Wildlife Unit has picked up reports of stolen and counterfeit antiques being offered to owners of antique shops in Gloucestershire. One man thought he'd been shown a reproduction inlaid Edwardian mahogany occasional table, but he couldn't be sure as the person who brought it in refused to leave it with him and hasn't returned."

"Breaking into people's houses, stealing their contents, and trying to sell them must be commonplace, surely? Isn't that how burglary works?" Norman asked.

Aunt Beanie pinched the top of her nose. She and her brother, Gilly Wimsey and George-Carey Boyd's father, had set up Akemans Antiques and run it for many years.

When Aunt Beanie retired, deciding it was time to hand over to the younger generation, she'd taken a job in Gloucestershire's Art and Antiques unit. But she'd had to leave to help Uncle Cliff on the farm, and the unit was subsequently disbanded.

Now a new division, the Rural, Heritage and Wildlife Unit, had been established under the command of the same police officer, Chief Inspector Ringrose, and he'd asked Aunt Beanie to work as a consultant. Although the new unit's primary purpose was not antiques, both Chief Inspector Ringrose and Aunt Beanie had old cases to solve, and probably scores to settle.

Aunt Beanie mused, "I'm starting to see a pattern. The items being offered are single pieces or a small group of related objects, and the people who bring them in know what they are and have a good idea of their value. That is unusual. Most members of the public have very little knowledge of antiques."

Dotty scattered the remaining quartered olives over the chicken in the roasting dish and looked up, saying, "So you think items are being stolen to order?"

The older woman tapped her fingers on the table. "Possibly, or a house which is known to contain many valuable objects is targeted and its contents stolen, divided up, and sold over a wide geographical region by different individuals, so as not to attract attention."

Dotty tore leaves off a basil plant and added them to the chicken dish. "Wouldn't that take a lot of organisation? And with so many people involved, how could it stay secret?"

"Someone very capable would need to make the arrangements. Someone who has the personality or influence to ensure those involved don't give the game away. Either that, or they have such charisma they've convinced people that everything is above board."

Dotty wandered across to the fridge and removed a tub of crème fraiche, a ball of mozzarella cheese, and a triangular-shaped packet containing parmesan cheese. "So what does your work involve?" she asked.

"I'm reading through statements our friend Sergeant Varma took from the shop and antique concession owners, looking for links or common themes."

Dotty grated the parmesan cheese.

Aunt Beanie looked up and asked, "Do you want to come with me tomorrow? To the viewing at Cirencester Auctioneers? I doubt there will be any quality pieces for Jay Newton, but you never know. And more importantly, I can introduce you to some dealers so you can speak to them about the items you're looking for."

"But we mustn't let anyone know I'm working for Jay," Dotty reminded.

"If you don't tell them, neither will I. And there's no reason for them to jump to any conclusions. It's normal for an antiques expert to buy for private clients."

Was that what she was? Dotty wondered. An antique's expert?

How exciting!

CHAPTER SIX

Dotty drove Aunt Beanie to Cirencester Auctioneers the next morning in her Skoda Fabia. She had expected the auction house to be in Cirencester, but Aunt Beanie directed her along the dual carriageway which passed through the historic town and out onto the road towards Tetbury, another ancient town which was once the site of an Anglo-Saxon monastery.

They drove beside Cirencester's 3,000-acre deer park and past the back entrance to the Royal Agricultural University.

"Turn left here," directed Aunt Beanie. Dotty complied and turned into a narrow lane which led them over a stone bridge, below which she noted railway tracks, and then on past the entrance to Kemble station.

She and Aunt Beanie occasionally used the station for trips to London, as it was on the main line, but in the early morning rush hour traffic they took the back roads and approached it from the opposite direction.

She slowed down as they entered Kemble village and turned right onto a wider road, following the directions of a white sandwich board, branded with Cirencester Auctioneers, with a sticker across it announcing 'Viewing Today'.

Suddenly, Dotty braked hard and swerved.

Aunt Beanie grabbed the dashboard and exclaimed, "What is it?"

"A huge plane," replied Dotty shrilly as she steadied herself and returned to the correct side of the road.

Visible over the top of a hawthorn hedge was the huge white pointed nose cone of a passenger plane and as they drove slowly along the road, a blue and red emblem and then the words 'British Airways' came into view. The Union Jack decorated tail fin rose high in the air.

Aunt Beanie laughed. "The aeroplane graveyard. It gave me quite a shock the first time I saw it, and I was on a horse. A surreal scene in the middle of the Cotswolds."

"There's another one." The hedge finished and a metal mesh fence separated them from the private airport and a long line of British Airways planes parked neatly, one behind the other.

"So many," mused Aunt Beanie. "Kemble's runway is over a mile, one of the longest in the area, so these big planes can land here. I've no idea if they could take off, but they don't. A company on the airfield strips them down and sells the parts. Now, continue past the main entrance to the airfield and take the next right."

They drove past half a dozen modern industrial units until they arrived at an old aircraft hangar, with a large blue semi-circular sign on the end of the building proclaiming 'Cirencester Auctioneers'. The large, double height building was constructed of stone, with solid corner columns, and a curved, black-tiled roof.

The main entrance was along one side, between four oversized metal casement windows, and there was a neat bed of azaleas and rose bushes across the front of the building.

Dotty parked and collected her cream fabric tote bag, with Van Gogh's sunflowers printed on it, which she'd bought on a trip to the National Gallery in London the previous month. Aunt Beanie hoisted her blue-striped straw basket up her arm.

They stepped inside the auction house together and Dotty said uncertainly, "We should find some auction catalogues."

"I already have one," announced Aunt Beanie, pulling a blue-covered brochure from her basket, and, turning away from Dotty, she entered the auction room.

Dotty hesitated. She was an expert now. She couldn't rely on others.

Squaring her shoulders and taking a deep breath, she followed signs to the auction office.

The room she entered had white perimeter shelving which displayed an assortment of lamps, vases, and porcelain figurines. Dotty weaved between tables which bore an array of objects including hatboxes, a set of crystal glasses and decanters, and several colourful collections of bone china dinnerware.

A small queue had formed at the end of the room, in front of an opening in the wall, behind which Dotty presumed was the auction office. The woman at the front of the queue was handed a sheet of paper.

She collected a pen from a pot and shuffled along a white shelf, located beneath the opening, and started filling in her form as the next person in line stepped forward.

When it was Dotty's turn, she looked into the office and was greeted by a smiling Molly Vogt.

Feeling braver, she introduced herself. "Hi, I'm Dotty Sayers, from Akemans. We met at Cheltenham lido, with Gilly Wimsey."

Molly's smile broadened. "Of course. How are you? And what are you doing at our sale?"

Proudly, Dotty explained, "A private client has commissioned me to buy period fittings and furniture. High quality pieces," she added.

Molly raised her eyebrows and leaned forward. "I'm not sure you'll find many of those here. Most of it's junk," she remarked dismissively. She paused, before adding, "Although there is an attractive small walnut sideboard you might want to have a look at." She handed Dotty a blue-covered brochure.

Dotty returned to the main auction room, where she spotted Aunt Beanie talking to a youngish-looking man with jet-black hair pulled tightly into a ponytail.

It was cool in the huge auction room, and Dotty was pleased she'd decided to wear a cropped cardigan over her floral-print summer dress, but she wasn't sure the man's full-length, black leather coat was necessary.

"Sorted?" asked Aunt Beanie as Dotty approached. She introduced the young man. "This is Dani Boy. He and his partner, Patrick, call themselves the 'Fabulous Auction Boys' and they recently started an auction house in an old church at Charlton-under-Cliffe."

"It'sabitofalarkreally," replied Dani Boy.

"Sorry?" replied Dotty in confusion. Dani Boy had a Scottish accent, and he spoke quickly, running his words together.

"I said," he carefully pronounced, "that we started it as a bit of a lark. But it's been surprisingly successful."

"That's because Patrick insists on quality items." Aunt Beanie lowered her voice and added, "Not like the jumble here." Back to her normal tone, she added, "And you've made quite a name for yourself as a music and coins expert."

"Which is why," mused Dani Boy, "I can't understand why this record collection is here and wasn't offered to us." He plucked out a moss-green record sleeve. "This 1972 Glastonbury Fayre LP is worth at least £200, and it's sitting amongst these." He pulled out two broken records.

A confident, athletic looking woman with golden-brown hair and ruby highlights, cut in a long-pixie style, strode past.

"Hey, Amanda," Dani Boy called.

The woman stopped and turned her striking amber eyes on him. "Yes?"

"How come you have these for sale?" He indicated to the two cardboard boxes of records.

She smirked and responded, "The usual way. A client asked us to sell them." She strutted away.

Dotty and Aunt Beanie left Dani Boy as he continued to search through the record collection and approached Molly Vogt's husband, whom Dotty had seen at Cheltenham lido. His dark, wavy hair reached down to the collar of his white shirt.

"Back in the game," he greeted Aunt Beanie.

"Just dabbling, Didier. Can I introduce Dotty Sayers who works at Akemans? She has a commission from a private client, don't you, Dotty?"

With more confidence than she felt, Dotty replied, "Yes, for some quality, period pieces."

"For what style of property?" Didier fished.

"Old, country," replied Dotty, conscious about not saying

something which would give her client away.

"I've not seen anything here that's suitable, but I'll let you know if I do. Excuse me, ladies." Didier hailed the athletic Amanda.

"Liar," spat Aunt Beanie. "He clearly has his eye on something, but he's not about to tell you."

"His wife Molly, who I spoke to in the office, told me about a small walnut sideboard."

"Let's see if we can find it." Aunt Beanie pushed past an elderly couple and started her search.

Dotty realised the wooden furniture was arranged in narrow rows, so she dived in after Aunt Beanie. Most of the items were modern or scratched or had pieces missing. An oak bookshelf stood at an angle and Dotty walked past, turning down the next row.

Aunt Beanie was standing in front of an ornate, heavy, Victorian chiffonier.

"That?" blurted Dotty.

"Don't be silly. On the right, but don't stare. I don't want anyone to register our interest." She opened the auction catalogue and read, "Walnut breakfront sideboard with a pair of central drawers."

"I presume breakfront means that the central section, with the two doors, juts out in front of the side panels, where the drawers are."

"That's right, and it's a useful piece, as it's not too big. It would fit into any room in Windrush Hall."

"But would Jay Newton like it?"

"I don't know. Do you?"

Dotty considered the dirty piece of furniture. "Do you have a tissue or something?" she asked Aunt Beanie.

The older woman rooted round in her basket and produced a white tissue. Dotty looked around before spitting on it and stepping in front of the sideboard, where she quickly rubbed the front of one drawer. A rich orange-brown colour shone through.

Returning to Aunt Beanie, she observed, "What a lovely colour. It just needs a good clean and polish. But I hope it's not damaged."

"I'll make a show of checking this hideous chiffonier while you examine it," suggested Aunt Beanie.

Dotty squatted down and checked the corners and edges of the sideboard. She pulled out the draws and opened the cupboards, and it appeared to be in good condition. She even walked down the row behind to check the back of it.

"OK?" asked Aunt Beanie, joining her.

"I can't see anything wrong with it."

"The catalogue gives an estimate of £300 to £400, but I think it will sell for more. You should speak to your client about it. Good find."

CHAPTER SEVEN

Dotty returned to Cirencester Auctioneers the following day on her own. Aunt Beanie was staying at home to look after Uncle Cliff as Gilly Wimsey had asked Norman to help in the antiques centre, repairing stalls and altering some lighting.

Dotty swam at Cirencester's swimming pool first, continuing her training for the upcoming charity triathlon, before driving to Cotswold Airport and Cirencester Auctioneers.

She was excited and nervous about the day ahead. Jay Newton had agreed she should bid for the sideboard, but he'd left the amount up to her.

Over supper in the farmhouse, she'd discussed it with Aunt Beanie and decided to bid up to £850. That was more than double the estimate, but other people might also have noticed the quality piece of furniture beneath the grime and bid against her.

Auctions were unpredictable. If only one buyer was interested in something, the price would remain low but, add a second person as keen as the first to buy an item, and the two of them would bid against each other raising the price, and the sky was the limit at some international auctions. It was exciting to witness these sales, but she hoped she wouldn't be part of a bidding war.

In fact, she'd never bid for anything herself, and had only taken telephone bids for clients and discretely passed them on to Marion, who assisted George at Akemans on auction days.

Her stomach flipped at the thought of raising her hand to seek the auctioneer's attention. And what if they didn't see her because they were busy with internet bids, or they weren't attentive to the bidders actually in the room?

She'd seen it happen to George and potential buyers had to stand up or call out to get noticed. She wasn't sure she could do that, as everyone would stare at her.

Lost in thought, she realised she'd missed the turning to the front of the auction house, so she followed the road around the side of the old hanger and across the front, which faced the runway.

This end had a series of huge sliding doors which would once have been drawn back so planes could be wheeled in and out. The doors were painted blue to match the auctioneers' corporate colours.

She slowed down and peered through the windscreen, seeking the entrance to the car park, nearly missing the couple huddled in the shadows of the aircraft hangar doors. A man and a woman, she thought, and she caught a glimmer of chestnut hair before they were hidden by the solid square stone pillars at the corner of the building.

The car park was only half-full, but inside the auction house there was a buzz of excited voices. People greeted each other like old friends, although it didn't stop them from bidding against each other for a chosen piece.

"Dotty, isn't it? From Akemans."

Dotty turned as the wavy-haired Didier Vogt approached her. Today he wore a dark-blue shirt and a wide, disarming smile.

"Something catch your eye yesterday?" he asked in a mischievous tone.

"Perhaps." She didn't want to give her interest in the sideboard away. "What about you?"

"I'm here for the contacts and the people," he said, breaking eye contact with her and glancing over her head. Was he being deliberately evasive?

Returning his attention to her, he asked, "Is your 'client' interested in a dining set?"

"Potentially." She realised she was now the one being cagey.

"I know the woman who bought the dining table and chairs from Windrush Hall, but she's not certain she wants to keep them."

To hide her surprise at the mention of Windrush Hall, Dotty replied, in a slightly higher-pitched voice, "The table was large, and wouldn't fit in many dining rooms."

"Exactly, but will it fit in your client's?"

Dotty fought to keep calm and maintain control of the conversation without blowing Jay Newtons's cover. "The table had several leaves, which could be removed to make it smaller." She knew her answer was lame, but also that this was a game she was not experienced at playing.

"Quite. Well, let me know if it is of interest."

As Didier started to move away, she asked, "What's the price?"

"£10,000."

Dotty's mouth dropped open. "What? It only made £3,000 at the sale. It's a quality piece, but as we've discussed, only a few people would have room for it."

"I'm open to negotiation," called Didier airily as he wandered away.

Dotty bit her lip. Buying from dealers was going to be tricky if they all saw her as naïve and inexperienced, which she was.

She entered the side room and approached the opening in the wall to the auction office.

She heard Molly Vogt call, "Bidder registration forms are on the shelf. Fill them in, including your payment details, before giving them to me."

Dotty took a form, but when she handed it back to Molly, it was only partially completed. "I was told to put down Akemans instead of payment information, is that OK?"

Molly looked up at her. "Dotty, isn't in?"

Dotty nodded.

"Sorry, it's always a rush before the auction starts. Akemans is fine. Whatever you win will be billed to the company, but you'll need to come back for a receipt before you can remove your purchases."

Dotty took the number Molly gave her to show to the auctioneer if she had the winning bid. It was 237.

As she returned to the main auction room, Amanda, the athletic woman she'd met the day before, with golden-brown hair and ruby highlights, climbed onto the auction rostrum and said into the microphone, "Ladies and gentlemen. Please take your seats and we'll begin in five minutes."

It had amazed Dotty at the first auction she'd attended, nearly a year ago, that during the sale customers sat on the furniture which was being sold. But she supposed none of it was new and countless other people had sat on the chairs and sofas over their lifetime.

Her mouth was dry, and she looked around for someone selling drinks, but she couldn't find anyone. Instead, she squeezed between a floral-printed sofa and a claret-coloured wing-backed chair and sat down at a dining table, two-thirds of the way back from the auctioneer's rostrum. She removed her catalogue from her cream tote bag and found a pen to make notes.

A woman with tight steel-grey curls sat down next to her and whispered, "I do love a good auction. Don't you work at Akemans?"

Dotty nodded.

"So do I. I have a small stall in the antiques centre. The last couple of weeks have been great with all the tourists, but my stall's a bit bare now, so I need to stock up. What about you? What are you interested in?" the woman gushed.

"Furniture," replied Dotty.

"You'll find some real bargains here, although the quality isn't great. I sell porcelain bowls, figurines and trinkets on my stall. There are a couple of boxes full of assorted items near the beginning of the sale but I won't pay more than £30 for any of them. Most items I sell are less than £10. They're an impulse buy for someone."

Dotty's head was beginning to spin as the woman continued, "And I buy hat boxes and sell them on eBay. There's a large collection in one of the early lots."

"Lot 1," said Amanda into the microphone, and Dotty leaned back in her seat with relief.

Lot 9 was the hatboxes, but the enthusiastic woman sitting next to her was disappointed when the price rose over £80. "Too rich for my taste," she lamented.

She had better luck with the boxes of porcelain trinkets and statuettes, picking up four of them for a total of £45. With a satisfied smile, she tapped Dotty's hand and remarked, "A good morning's work. I'll see you around."

As the auction continued at a slow pace, Dotty considered the other customers. There was an elderly couple who seemed to be constantly arguing, sitting on a threadbare pale-blue sofa in the front row Every time the man, with wisps of grey hair, raised his hand to bid, the woman beside him snatched it down.

Over to Dotty's left, sitting on two upholstered dining chairs, was a young couple who whispered constantly, looking up at the auctioneer and back down at the catalogue they were sharing.

Dotty glanced behind her to a group of men, dealers, she thought, by their nonchalant or indifferent expressions. Was the auction business like a giant game of poker? But then, not everyone was trying to win the same hand.

"That is the end of the first section of the sale. I'll pass you over to my colleague, Rebecca Randall, for the sale of the furniture."

Amanda stepped down from the rostrum, making way for a younger woman, who was slim, and the copper highlights in her sleek brunette hair glinted in the light of the screen erected behind her. Dotty recognised her as the woman Jay Newton had been pictured with in Marion's magazine.

"Hiya," called a familiar voice, and Sergeant Keya Varma slid into the chair beside Dotty. "Aunt Beanie said I'd find you here and Chief Inspector Ringrose suggested I join you and familiarise myself with some of the faces of the auction world. Have you bought anything?" she asked enthusiastically.

"Not yet. Are you undercover?"

Keya was wearing an ink-blue and white tunic top with red detailing and a pair of bright red leggings, rather than her black and white police uniform. She grinned. "Isn't it great? Chief Inspector Ringrose says there are times to wear uniform and times when we should be ourselves and mix with the local community."

She ran a hand through her long black hair and turned towards Rebecca Randall who said, "Lot 100. A three-seater pale-blue upholstered sofa."

The elderly couple at the front jumped when they realised the picture on the screen was the item they were sitting on, but they soon settled down and the woman shook her head fervently at the man as he tentatively raised his hand.

The auction continued.

"Lot 115. A Victorian Chiffonier," announced Rebecca. The sideboard was next.

There was no interest in the chiffonier. All the wood, time and workmanship which had gone into making it, but heavy, Victorian furniture was not in fashion and a piece like that was too large for modern houses.

"Lot 116. A walnut breakfront sideboard with a pair of central drawers. I've a number of bids on the books, so we'll open the bidding at £360." The price was already close to the top of the estimated value.

"370, 380, 390, 400," said Rebecca, clearly but calmly.

Keya looked around the room and then whispered in a confused tone, "Why is she bidding against herself?"

"Either it's two internet bidders, or someone on the internet bidding against a higher bid she's already received from someone who's not at the auction."

"£410, on the internet, and I'm out," announced Rebecca.

Dotty leaned towards Keya and explained, "That means the price has exceeded the amount that the absentee customer agreed to. Once the internet stops, she'll look for bids in the room."

Aunt Beanie had made it clear to Dotty that she should wait and let others play their hands. Dotty felt her body quiver, and she fought the contradictory desires to raise her hand, so as not to miss her chance, against the compulsion to sink deeper into her chair and avoid bidding altogether.

Rebecca looked over Dotty's head and said, "420, 430." She looked behind Dotty again and nodded. "440, 450, 460." She raised her eyebrows to the bidder behind Dotty and nodded curtly. The bidding stands at £460 on the internet."

"There's an attractive-looking man at the back staring at you."

"Shush," hissed Dotty. She gathered her strength and raised her hand.

"New bidder. 470. 480." Rebecca looked at Dotty, who held up her number as she'd seen other bidders do, until they no longer wanted to bid and lowered their piece of paper. "490. 500. 510."

There was a pause. "Are you finished on the internet?" Rebecca asked nobody in particular. The price on the screen remained at £510. Rebecca steadily ran her eyes over the people in the room. "Any advance on £510." She continued to scan the room, but the price on the screen did not change. "Sold for £510. Bidder number 237."

Dotty grasped Keya's arm and whispered, "I won."

CHAPTER EIGHT

"Well done," cried Keya, bouncing up and down on her chair beside Dotty. "Is it for you?"

"No, for J … a client." In the shock of being the winning bidder and actually purchasing the walnut sideboard for Jay Newton, she'd nearly given his identity away.

"You look as if you need a cup of tea. Or are you bidding for anything else?" asked Keya.

Dotty shook her head and hesitantly got to her feet, her legs wobbling beneath her and she steadied herself by leaning against the dining table.

"Are you OK?" Keya asked in a concerned voice.

"I will be. Just give me a minute." Taking a deep breath, Dotty calmed herself before picking up her catalogue and pen and returning them to her cream tote bag. "I'm not sure we can buy refreshments here."

"Yes, we can. I saw a sign on a door pointing to a cafe on the first floor. Look. Up there. You can see people sitting at tables." Keya pointed to a window in a breeze block wall, which was part of a two-storey structure built inside the old hangar.

Dotty followed Keya as they climbed the concrete steps to the first floor. She sat down at an empty table near the counter, while Keya ordered their drinks and returned carrying two mugs of tea and a KitKat on a brown plastic tray. Opening the chocolate bar, Keya snapped it in half and offered one stick to Dotty, commenting, "Hot tea and chocolate does wonders for shock."

Putting her hand back on the table, she knocked the plastic tray which clattered to the floor. "Oh, toda!" she exclaimed, leaning down to pick it up.

As Dotty munched the KitKat and sipped her tea, she felt herself returning to normal, although she was still shaking.

"Congratulations," said Didier Vogt as he approached their table. "I'm impressed you managed to find the diamond amongst all this rough. I was interested in it myself, but once the bidding rose above £450, there was no profit in it for me."

Dotty felt the heat rise in her cheeks but thought she better not tell Didier his wife had suggested looking at the sideboard. But why had she done that? And did she know her husband was interested in it?

"Let me know about the dining table," he said before striding away to a corner table.

"Who's that?" asked Keya in awe. "He was the one staring at you earlier."

"That's Didier Vogt. His wife works in the office downstairs."

"And what does he do?"

"I believe he's a dealer. But how are you?"

"OK, but we might have to cancel the charity triathlon."

"Why?" asked Dotty, her eyes widening. What about all the training she'd done?

"It's our sleepy colleagues in Cheltenham. They've only just realised the triathlon's on August Bank Holiday Monday. They're already stretched covering other events, and if they insist on closing roads for the running and cycling, we'll definitely have to cancel."

"Can't you find somewhere else?" implored Dotty, surprised by her own disappointment.

George had flatly refused to do the swim leg of the triathlon and although Gilly had offered, her husband, Dr Peter, had kindly, but firmly, turned it down.

He and Marcus were resigned to missing the event until Gilly suggested Dotty should take part and agreed to join her for some training sessions. When Dotty admitted she couldn't swim front crawl, Keya had arranged lessons for her.

Although she had only been training for a month, she felt much fitter and far more confident with her swimming. She realised she'd been looking forward to the triathlon. To representing Akemans. To being part of the team.

"Where else is there?" responded Keya. "Everywhere else is booked up or busy over the Bank Holiday weekend. We'd need a private venue and who has their own swimming pool and acres of land to run and cycle around?"

"Jay Newton," cried Dotty. "I was at Windrush Hall on Monday, and he showed David, Marcus and me the swimming pool he's built. It would be perfect. It's undercover, built in a wooden pool house, but the whole of one side opens up and a canopy extends out. That could be the transition area."

Keya grabbed Dotty's wrist. "That sounds perfect." Her initial enthusiasm ebbed, and she pulled her hand away.

"Famous people like him move to the country to get away from people and publicity. He won't want us locals using his pool and running around his grounds. And we need changing rooms, and refreshments, and medical facilities. If we can't hold it in Cheltenham, I think we'll have to cancel."

She pressed her lips together, looking dejected.

Dotty's stomach clenched. She knew how excited her friend was about the triathlon. Chief Inspector Ringrose had persuaded her to join the committee as part of her role in the Rural, Heritage and Wildlife Unit and she'd dived enthusiastically into organising the event.

Dotty gently laid a hand on Keya's arm and said reassuringly, "Let me speak to Jay. I have to call him, anyway."

Keya jerked her head back. "Why?" Then she leaned closer to Dotty and whispered, "You're not involved with him, are you?"

It was Dotty's turn to be surprised. She stared at her friend and replied, "You must be joking. He's way older than me."

"So is Gilmore Chapman," replied Keya, her good humour returning as she grinned at Dotty.

Dotty bit her lip as the heat rose in her cheeks.

"It's business, not pleasure."

Keya rolled her eyes.

Dotty placed her empty cup on the table. "Talking of business, I better sort out a receipt for the sideboard and work out how to deliver it to Akemans. It won't fit into my car."

As Dotty entered the auction room she noticed the image of records on the screen behind Amanda, who must have taken over from Rebecca as auctioneer.

Dotty stood and watched. Two men were bidding for the records. One of them she recognised as the black-coated, pony-tailed Dani Boy, and the other was hidden behind a double-height shelving unit holding various boxes and auction items. She just caught a glimpse of a bald head.

The price on the screen increased, and she watched Dani Boy, his mouth open in concentration, nod his head firmly each time Amanda looked at him. Only when the price hit £1,000 did he hesitate.

He scribbled on the catalogue he held and reluctantly agreed to an increase of £50. The partially hidden bidder immediately increased his offer. Dani Boy shook his head.

"£1,100," Amanda stated. "Do we have any advance on 1,100?"

The room was quiet and the price on the screen remained unchanged.

"Sold," announced Amanda, as she looked towards the back of the room. Dotty followed her gaze, but instead of finding the winning bidder, her eyes fell on the wavy-haired Didier who nodded back at her.

"£1,000 for some old records?" remarked Keya, beside Dotty.

Dotty continued to watch Amanda as she replied, "Some of them are valuable collector pieces these days."

"Yesterday's junk," muttered Keya as she glanced at her black-strapped watch. "Time to head back to the station. Inspector Ringrose has a new case to discuss with me."

"That sounds exciting," said Dotty, returning her attention to her friend.

"I doubt it. Probably some Neighbourhood Watch scheme or an anti-litter campaign." She sighed. "Let me know if you do speak to Jay Newton about the triathlon." And with her head bowed, Keya turned and left.

Dotty looked back into the auction room as the black-clad, bald-headed Tracy, Jay Newton's man, stepped out from behind the shelving units. So he'd bought the records.

She followed Tracy towards the auction office, wanting to ask if he could take the sideboard back to Windrush Hall, but she was too afraid to speak to him.

As she joined the queue in front of the opening in the office wall, Tracy turned and looked at her. His eyes narrowed as he asked, "Don't I know you?"

"Yes," she stammered. "I visited with Marcus Boyd on Monday."

"Of course," he grunted and made to turn away.

Wanting to continue the conversation, Dotty asked, in a slightly shrill voice, "Congratulations on buying the records. Are you a collector?"

"Only of the Spinning Newts. Their first LP is in that collection."

"So that's why you bid."

"Yeah, I paid over the odds, but they rarely come up for sale."

"And what about the rest of the collection?"

"I'll give it away or something."

"Really?"

"It's no use to me," he said dismissively.

Dotty had a sudden insight and suggested, "Why don't I take the records and sell them for you, and in return, can you take the sideboard which I bought today back to Windrush Hall?"

"Why do I want your furniture? Can't you take it yourself?"

"It won't fit in my car, and I presume you have the Range Rover?"

Tracy nodded.

"Anyway, it's not for me." And she raised her eyebrows in a rather melodramatic gesture.

"Oh, I get it. Sure, I'll take it with me."

Tracy paid for the records and walked away as Dotty smiled at Molly Vogt through the opening to the office wall.

"Lot 116," said Dotty.

Molly tapped her keyboard and then looked up, grinning. "The walnut sideboard?"

"Yes. Thank you for your suggestion. It's a lovely piece."

"Would you like me to bill Akemans?"

"Yes, please."

Dotty found Tracy squatting beside his two boxes of records in the main auction room. He held a black record cover in one hand as he flicked through the other record sleeves. He removed a red and black cover, grunted, and returned to his task.

"I'll be back in a minute," Dotty told him, although she doubted he heard her.

She found a blue polo-shirted porter and gave him her receipt. As he left to locate the sideboard, she looked round for the black pony-tailed Dani Boy. Had he already left?

The door to the stairs opened, and he walked into the auction room. Dotty approached him and asked, "Are you still interested in those records?"

"Why?" His eyes narrowed.

"I know the winning bidder and he only wants one or two of them. Are you interested in buying the others from him?"

Dani Boy's face brightened. "Aye."

She and Dani Boy returned to Tracy as he stood up, holding three record covers in his hand. The two black-clad figures eyed each other as Dani Boy asked, "What you got there?"

"Spinning Newts' first LP. Bob Dylan and …" Small blotches of colour appeared on Tracy's cheeks. "And Pentangle. They were my mum's favourite folk-jazz group."

"Well spotted. I missed that one, but there are a few avid collectors of their music. And the rest?" Dani looked down at the two cardboard boxes.

"Not interested," replied Tracy.

The two men were silent.

Dotty looked from one to the other and said boldly, "You bought the whole collection for £1,100, Tracy. You've taken what you want, so how about splitting the price? £510?"

Tracy considered the suggestion.

"£500 cash," offered Dani Boy.

"Done," replied Tracy.

Dani Boy turned to Dotty and asked, "And what's your cut?"

"My cut?" replied Dotty in confusion. "I don't expect anything. I'm just glad I could help you both and make sure the records aren't thrown away as rubbish."

"I owe you,' said Dani Boy as he removed an envelope from a pocket in his long black coat and peeled off £50 notes, which he handed to Tracy. He picked up the first box of records and walked away.

Tracy asked, "Where's the sideboard?"

Dotty and Tracy walked across the concrete car park to the black Range Rover, followed by two porters wheeling the sideboard on a trolley. When it was safely stowed in the car, Dotty waved at Tracy, who'd already climbed into the driver's seat and pulled away.

As she wandered back to her own car, alone in its section of the car park, she glanced across at the entrance to the auction house. A figure ducked inside.

CHAPTER NINE

"Are you sure Jay Newton doesn't mind meeting me to discuss the charity team triathlon?" asked Keya for the umpteenth time.

Dotty was driving them both to Windrush Hall, and it was a beautiful summer's day, although the recent rain and wind had caused havoc for those farmers who hadn't finished harvesting.

As Dotty slowed to take a bend in the road, she glanced through a gap in the hedge at the field beyond where the flattened wheat formed craters at intervals across the field, like a giant's footprints. In the adjacent field, large golden bales of straw stood like oversized children's building blocks.

She drove cautiously, her view of the road obscured by tall grasses and an abundance of wildflowers on the verges. Purple pointed foxgloves stood behind strands of wild oats and clusters of white yarrow.

As they passed the entrance to a wood of wide-canopied ancient hornbeam trees with short, twisted trunks, Keya tutted.

"What is it?" asked Dotty, concentrating on the road ahead.

"Someone has dumped an old bath, a sink and sagging armchair at the wood entrance. It's amazing how much fly-tipping there is once you start looking. It's why the Rural, Heritage and Wildlife Unit have been asked to tackle it. That's the job Chief Inspector Ringrose wanted to talk to me about, but where do I start? I can hardly patrol all the lanes in the Cotswolds or watch the entrances to all the woods and fields."

Dotty smiled sympathetically. It did sound an impossible job.

Keya continued, "I've set up an online group so people can post when they spot rubbish which has been left, and we can start clearing it away. But that doesn't stop people doing it. In fact, it might encourage them."

Dotty turned off the road and drove between the two stone columns and down the sweeping drive to Windrush Hall.

She said, "Please don't worry about that now, or about meeting Jay. Remember, I called and he's happy to meet you, although he made no promises."

A dark-silver convertible BMW was parked at an angle in front of the large house with its roof down. Dotty parked her Skoda Fabia and Keya jumped out and walked across to the BMW. She reached forward, as if to touch the leather headrest, but snatched her hand back.

She was not wearing her police uniform and looked relaxed and summery in a sunflower-yellow, short-sleeved tunic over white leggings. She joined Dotty as they climbed up the front stone steps, and said, with a note of awe, "I wonder who owns that car?"

The front door was ajar, so Dotty called, "Hello?"

There was no response. Stepping inside the stone-flagged hall, beneath the glass chandelier which hung lifelessly in the summer brightness, she looked through to the empty dining room before crossing to the drawing room.

She turned round and bumped into Keya, who had followed her.

"Sorry," apologised Keya, jumping back, "but where is everyone?"

"I think only Jay and his man, Tracy, live here, but there'll also be the visitors who own that smart car. Let's see if they're in the morning room, or they could be in the garden or using the pool. I wouldn't mind a swim myself." Dotty pulled the top of her sticky dress away from her sweaty skin.

The morning room was empty but the full height alcove doors stood open and Dotty led Keya out into the garden. The previous owner had remodelled a section of it and trim box hedges enclosed neat borders of delicate pink and white cosmos and purple zinnias.

Further along, she noted that the mounds of purple lavender were less abundant than earlier in the summer, but their aromatic fragrance still filled the air.

She heard a woman's raised voice and looked to her right, beyond the formal garden and tidy green lawn, to a raised decking area at one end of a single-storey wooden cabin-style pool house.

"Oh, is that the swimming pool?" Keya asked in a wistful tone. The side of the pool house was open and they could see the inviting blue water shimmering inside.

"Why are you so dull?" yelled a slim woman wearing a strapless black bikini top and a pink sarong wrapped around her waist. The sun glinted off the copper highlights in her bob of brunette hair, in which she'd secured a pair of sunglasses. She was standing in front of Jay Newton who was seated at a white, ornate cast iron table.

Keya stared at the woman and asked, "Is that a tattoo on her shoulder?"

"It could be," replied Dotty distractedly.

"What shall we do?" whispered Keya. "Sneak back inside until they've finished their domestic? And who is she?"

"I'm not sure. She looks vaguely familiar. But I think we should just wait here. Moving will only attract attention."

Jay regarded the woman and nodded his head slowly as he spoke calmly to her.

She stepped closer to him, in what appeared to be an aggressive manner, and said something Dotty could not catch. Then she threw her head up and stalked into the poolhouse. She stopped before disappearing inside and shouted, "Don't push me."

Dotty hesitated but Jay looked across at her and Keya and beckoned with his hand for them to join him. He stood up as they approached across the vibrant green lawn, and he greeted Dotty with an air kiss on both cheeks.

Rather taken aback, she stammered, "This is my friend, Keya, who I mentioned to you."

Keya grinned, and replied, "I like what you've done to the place. What an amazing swimming pool."

"Thank you. It's perfect for days like today, although I prefer to swim first thing, and work up an appetite for breakfast. But you must be thirsty. Sit down while I fetch you drinks. How about some homemade lemonade my daily brought me?"

"Lovely," purred Keya as she took a seat.

Jay disappeared inside the pool house and Dotty followed him to the edge of the pool, whose water lapped against blue and white mosaic tiles. A door opened at the far end and for an instant she locked eyes with Rebecca Randall, the young auctioneer from Cirencester Auctioneers whose sale she'd attended two days earlier, at Cotswold airport.

Rebecca turned away and left through an exterior door in the direction of the house.

Dotty remembered the article Marion had shown her in the office at Akemans. Rebecca and Jay were an item. So why had she been so angry with him, almost threatening?

"Here we are," called Jay, and Dotty returned to the cast iron table and chairs on the decking. As she sat down, she was grateful for the cream canopy which extended out from the side of the pool house and provided welcome shade.

As she sipped the sweet but sharp lemonade, Jay pronounced, "I love the walnut sideboard you bought. I've put it in the morning room for now. It's so much warmer than the dark furniture you generally see."

Dotty made a note to herself not to buy too much mahogany furniture, although the original contents had mostly been made from that wood.

Keya looked from Jay to Dotty and exclaimed, "So, this is your secret client?"

Dotty bit her lip.

"I am," responded Jay, "and I'd like to keep it that way. I presume you can keep a secret."

Keya nodded enthusiastically and replied earnestly, "Of course."

Dotty glanced across at her friend. Secrets and Keya did not go well together, and she wondered how long it would take before her friend inadvertently gave Jay's identity away.

She remembered the dining table and said, "A dealer told me the lady who bought the hall's dining room table and chairs might be looking to sell them. They are a darker mahogany, so would you be interested?"

"The original ones? Certainly. And I don't mind darker wood in the dining room. It sort of fits the formality."

"He's asking more than double what it sold for in the house sale."

"Money's not a problem." Jay gestured with his hand. "It would be fantastic to have the original dining table. And David Rook assures me his friend Gilmore can find me some of the Duke's paintings. In fact, he's coming over today to discuss them with me." He turned to Keya, "So we better talk about this event you're organising."

Keya brightened as she replied, "It's a charity team triathlon. One member of the team swims 500m, another runs 3km and the third member cycles 8km. And each team must be a mix of men and women."

"It's soon, isn't it?" enquired Jay.

Keya nodded. "Bank Holiday Monday, so only ten days away." She bit her lip before adding, "Sorry for the short notice."

"That's not an issue to me. I'm not organising the event. So who's entered?"

Keya's eyes sparkled. "Only a company, club or organisation can enter, but lots of local ones have. There's a team from a nursery school, one from a garden centre, two from a builders' merchants, another from a butcher in Bibury, and there's even one from St Mary's Church, Fairford."

"Really," queried Dotty. "Aunt Beanie never said anything about it."

"Yes, they entered several weeks ago. And three of the local auctioneers have entered teams, including Akemans," Keya glanced across at Dotty and back to Jay, as she continued, "and we have two teams from Cirencester police station."

Jay leaned back. "This is more like it. An event run by local people for local people, not a crowd of incomers from London who care nothing for the area."

Dotty wondered where that remark had come from.

Jay grinned. "I'd be delighted to host it. What do you need?"

"The swimming pool, which we'll divide into two lanes, and use of your grounds to mark out the running course. The cycle route is more problematic as we don't want too much of it on the roads, for safety reasons, but we can have a shorter course and competitors will complete two laps."

Jay tapped his finger against his glass of lemonade. "The driveway will make a challenging start, but if riders turn right at the top, there's a mile or so of relatively straight road before a turning into the woods which'll bring them back here. I'll go out with Tracy tomorrow morning and we can measure the route and check it's usable."

"That's brilliant, thanks so much," gushed Keya. "And we'll also need changing rooms, first aid facilities, space for the scorers and refreshments. One of the companies involved hires out marquees and although their best ones are being used over the holiday weekend, they've promised us some of their older ones. And some of the companies involved have offered gazebos."

"I'm happy for gazebos on the lawn, but I'd prefer tents to be erected down by the woods. If the scorers need somewhere quiet, they could use the dining room."

"You wouldn't mind them being inside?"

"Of course not."

Dotty had been listening to the conversation with relief. The triathlon would go ahead. She asked, "Keya, are there prizes? If so, it might be nice for Jay to present them." She looked across at the green-spectacled rock star and continued, "If you're happy to do so?"

"I'd be delighted. In fact, why don't I present a trophy to the winning team, and we can make it an annual event?"

"Brilliant," exclaimed Keya, knocking against the cast iron table. Dotty and Jay snatched the glasses of lemonade before they wobbled off.

"Sorry." Keya sat back in her chair and bowed her head.

"Don't apologise. I'm as excited as you are," grinned Jay. He turned to Dotty. "Can I add finding a silver trophy to your list of tasks?"

"Of course," agreed Dotty, thinking that it would be fun choosing the triathlon prize.

"We've lots to do," enthused Jay as he jumped up. "Keya, why don't you join me tomorrow to check the cycle route? And we can discuss the running track."

"That would be great."

"Fantastic. Can you be here for half-past eight?"

"Yes," Keya agreed, as she and Dotty stood up.

"I'll show you out," offered Jay.

Rather than walking across the lawn, and past the formal gardens to the morning room, Jay led them around the back of the pool house and along a gravel path to an arch in a high stone wall. They passed through the arch and entered a large courtyard with stone buildings on three sides, which Dotty presumed had originally been a barn, stables, and storerooms. The fourth side was the entrance to the drive and what Dotty thought was the kitchen door.

Rebecca was standing outside this door, once again acting in an aggressive manner. Her face was close to Tracy's, as she looked up at him, and whatever she'd just said had a profound effect. The blood drained from Tracy's already pale features and he visibly shrank away from her.

As Rebecca strode off along the drive without a backwards glance, Jay rushed across to Tracy and laid a hand on his arm.

Dotty heard a car skid to a halt on the tarmac outside the front door, but she ignored it as she hesitantly approached Tracy, who was crying.

What had Rebecca Randall done or said to reduce this man, whom Dotty had been more than a little frightened of, to tears? Without looking at her or Keya, Jay led the distraught Tracy inside the house.

"What was all that about?" asked Keya. "Who was that man?"

"That's Tracy, who lives here with Jay. But he comes across as the strong, silent type, so I've no idea what Rebecca said to upset him."

Glumly, they walked round to the front of the house and Dotty covered her eyes as sunlight glinted off a car windscreen. She heard laughter, a man and a woman, and both voices were familiar.

As her vision cleared, she saw Rebecca Randall touch Gilmore Chapman playfully on the arm as she said something to him.

Gilmore smiled ruefully and watched as she climbed into her car and drove away.

CHAPTER TEN

The following week, the last before the triathlon, Dotty arrived at Akemans' auction house on Monday after an early morning swim at Cirencester pool.

She was beginning to enjoy the routine of getting up early three times a week to swim and wondered if she'd be able to keep it going after the triathlon, or whether she'd stop as the days shortened into September and she'd be getting up in the dark.

She took a sheet of paper from a pad on her desk, placed there so whoever answered the phone could write messages, and jotted down her tasks for the week. She needed to buy a trophy for the triathlon. Would she find one in the antiques centre, or would she need to look further afield?

Her stall needed cleaning and the contents rearranging, with any gaps being filled from items she'd stored. She sucked her pen. And she needed to expand her search for items for Windrush Hall.

The next auction in the area was being run by The Fabulous Auction Boys at Charlton-under-Cliffe at the end of the following week, and she hadn't yet received a catalogue. But she did have one for an auction near Oxford this week, and for another auction further north, at Malvern, in Worcestershire.

She was also waiting for Didier Vogt to call back after she'd left a message at the end of last week about the dining table and chairs.

But first she had a triathlon meeting. She walked to the back of the office, filled the electric kettle and switched it on. As she did so, her phone rang.

Picking it up, she didn't recognise the number, so she answered formally, "Hello, Dotty speaking."

"Good morning, it's Didier. I'm so sorry I didn't return your call last week, but work got in the way. Were you calling about the dining table I mentioned?"

Dotty took a deep breath to calm herself. "I've spoken to my client who is interested, but I need to be sure it's the one we sold at the Windrush Hall sale." What proof would she need? "I need to see the original invoice from the sale."

"I can get you that, although my client is away until the end of August. Is that too late?"

"No, there's no rush."

"I'll be in touch, and I'll let you know if I find anything else which might interest you … or your client."

Dotty ended the call and wondered if Didier suspected her client was Jay Newton. After all, during the quiet summer months, how many clients were Akemans likely to have who had room for a large dining table?

The adjoining door to the antiques centre opened and Gilly and Dr Peter Wimsey entered the office.

Dr Peter greeted her in his usual foolish fashion, which Dotty suspected hid a sharp brain. She also thought his manner was a shield against the highs and lows of his role as the local doctor. However competent his diagnosis and treatment, a proportion of his patients still died. "Ah, Dotty darling. Were you up with the larks for a splash around?"

"I did swim this morning," she replied politely.

"Good girl, that's the team spirit."

Gilly walked past Dotty's desk to the kitchenette at the back of the office.

Dotty turned and said, "The kettle's just boiled."

"Then I'll play mum." Gilly hummed as she cheerfully reached into the cupboard above her head for cups.

Dr Peter leaned towards Dotty and confided, "My wife has an unusually joyful disposition for a Monday morning."

"That's because," called Gilly, "last week was the busiest in the antiques centre for over two years. It helped that two busloads of tourists stopped on their way to Bibury. I wonder if we'd attract more of them by opening a small cafe?"

Dr Peter rolled his eyes. "I know the devil finds work for idle hands, but my dear, haven't you enough on your plate?"

Gilly carried two cups towards them and placed them on the reception desk, before fetching her own cup of coffee.

She leaned back against the spare desk and said, "I know, but I'm supposed to 'manage' the antiques centre, not run around restocking shelves, and half my time I spend in the auction house, helping George prepare for the monthly auctions."

"More staff," announced Peter.

"I know, but they're expensive and people like Dotty don't just walk in off the street."

Dotty raised her eyebrows. That's exactly what she had done. She'd been waiting in the auction house and Gilly, who had been busy again, had asked her to answer the telephone. Then she'd helped with last September's auction before being offered a full-time position.

"Well, you know what I mean," replied Gilly, in a strained voice. "And what happens if we get no visitors in September and October?" She sighed. "I'll just have to manage for now."

The door to the antiques centre opened again and Marcus Boyd stepped through, flicking his fair hair out of his eyes.

"You need a haircut," remarked Dr Peter. "That's the problem when the women in our lives are away. Standard's slip."

"You've never said that about me," quipped Gilly.

Dr Peter turned to look at her and raised his eyebrows.

Dotty enjoyed the playful banter between Gilly and Dr Peter and she knew they held a deep affection for each other, even though Gilly had a tendency to be scatterbrained and was far from a domestic goddess at home.

Gilly returned to the kitchenette, as Marcus admitted, "I am missing George and the kids. I thought I'd enjoy the peace and quiet. No bickering."

"And that's just the children," interjected Peter.

Gilly handed Marcus a cup of coffee as he smiled ruefully at Dr Peter. She pulled the chair out from under the spare desk and sat down as Marcus leaned against the desk. Dr Peter looked at each of them in turn, and then at Dotty and announced, "Let's begin. The triathlon is a week today, at Windrush Hall."

Marcus did a double take. "I didn't know that. Why isn't it in Cheltenham?"

Dr Peter explained, "The local police couldn't manage it on Bank Holiday Monday, so Dotty and Sergeant Varma persuaded Jay Newton to host it at Windrush Hall instead. Personally, I think it's a smashing venue, although my cycling leg will be gruelling. There are bound to be hills in the course, and I suspect some off-road sections as well."

Dotty licked her lips and said, "Keya and Jay were marking out the course on Saturday. I think it starts up the drive and comes back through the woods."

"As I suspected." Dr Peter clasped his hands in front of him.

"Can't see it'll affect you, Peter. You're always dashing about the country lanes on that bike of yours. I should know, I've nearly run into you plenty of times," admitted Marcus.

Dr Peter tilted his head to one side and responded in an impish tone, "That's because you drive too fast in that toy sports car of yours."

"Boys," interrupted Gilly. "Some of us have work to do. I'm not even in the team, so I don't know why you need me here"

"Quite so. Back to business. You are here, my dear," Dr Peter maintained eye contact with his wife, "because you will be the first aid responder when I'm pedalling like fury around the Windrush estate. Fifty teams have entered, so if they all take part, that's a hundred and fifty competitors. I expect the main injuries to be falls from bikes. If you clean and patch the competitors up as best you can, I'll deal with any serious strains or broken bones when I've finished."

"Isn't it a statistical probability that at least one runner suffers a heart attack during a marathon?" remarked Marcus.

"When there are over 50,000 competitors, not a hundred and fifty," replied Dr Peter, "but you raise a good point and I always take my portable defibrillator with me."

The topic of conversation was alarming Dotty, who asked, in a shrill voice, "Does that prevent a heart attack?"

Dr Peter touched the tip of his fingers together as he explained, "In a manner of speaking. It actually shocks the heart into stopping."

"What?" cried Dotty. She knew there was a defibrillator on the wall by the entrance to the antiques centre, but she'd never thought about using it.

"Heart attacks are fatal when the heart beats irregularly, either too slowly or, often, far too quickly. The defibrillator delivers an electric shock to the heart, through the chest, which stuns it and causes it to stop. This gives the heart a chance to restart or for a trained responder to perform CPR."

"CPR?" enquired Dotty.

"Cardiopulmonary resuscitation."

"Oh, mouth-to-mouth," cried Dotty.

"That's what it was termed, but it is more important to start the heart than fill the lungs with oxygen during a heart attack. But don't worry, my dear wife is trained to perform heart compressions. Besides, I'm sure there will be no need for her at the triathlon."

Marcus added ruefully, "Let's hope not."

CHAPTER ELEVEN

After the triathlon meeting, Dotty answered emails asking for the date of the next auction, and responded to requests for valuations of household contents, which George was not undertaking until her children returned to school in early September.

Dotty's next task was to sort out her stall on the first floor of the antiques centre. Her enterprise was a test to see if customers could be enticed up the metal staircase to the first floor and it appeared to be working, as there were some glaring gaps on the shelves and tables.

Her source of new stock had dried up during the summer months as Gilly and the owners of the ground floor concessions were successfully selling their wares and had no excess stock for her. She still had some items packed away in the first-floor storeroom, which she'd fetch once she'd dusted everything on the stall.

Dotty was contentedly daydreaming when Gilly called out to her, as she climbed the metal staircase.

"I have the team T-shirts for the triathlon. Do you want to see them?" Gilly reached the top of the stairs and balanced a cardboard box on top of a collection of brightly coloured costume jewellery, arranged on a white linen tablecloth.

Opening the box, she removed and held up a light grey T-shirt with

'Akemans Antique Heroes' printed in the company's corporate maroon. Smiling, she asked, "What do you think?"

Dotty was pleased they were grey rather than white. "Antique Heroes. It makes us sound as if we're all over sixty."

Gilly's face fell.

Hastily, Dotty added, "Oh, I get it. Very clever." She still thought it made her and her teammates sound old, but she wasn't sure she could have thought of a better name.

With a shaky laugh, Gilly responded, "That's a relief. Anyway, it was all I could come up with." Folding the T-shirt, she returned it to the box and said, "The girls on the till say you've had a steady stream of sales, and it certainly looks as if stock's been selling. Do you have any more?"

"I still have a couple of boxes in the storeroom."

"Have you considered buying from other auctions or at car boot sales?"

"Keya and Aunt Beanie have both suggested car boot sales, but I'm not sure. Actually, I've only been to one, and that was a charity event organised by the regiment. The large public ones Keya visits sound rather daunting."

Gilly mused, "I suppose they are, but they're also fun. You should go with her." Gilly picked up the box of T-shirts. "I'll put these in the office and then head home. One of Peter's receptionists has been keeping an eye on the children, so I need to get back to relieve her. It's a pleasant day, so we might go for a walk round the Cotswold Water Park. Do you want to join us?"

"No thanks, I'll finish here."

Dotty retrieved the last two boxes from the storeroom, unwrapped their contents, and displayed them on the shelves and tables. She rearranged items until she was satisfied the stall looked neat and inviting. She must remember to bring fresh flowers the following morning.

Descending the staircase, she decided to look around the ground floor stalls in the antiques centre for a suitable trophy for the triathlon.

She found a stall selling horse racing memorabilia with silver cups and rose bowls, but they were all engraved with the name of a race, and some also had details of the horse, owner, trainer and jockey who had won it.

Dotty wandered on. She discovered a small stall she hadn't noticed before, with a sign stating that the owner cut keys and engraved trophies, as well as selling them. She leaned towards a glass display case of weird and wonderful keys. Some were small and plain, while others had intricate designs or were made from gold or silver.

"Makes you wonder what treasures and secret rooms they opened," remarked the young sandy-haired stall owner.

"Yes," replied Dotty politely. "I'm looking for a trophy, a large one, to be presented for a charity sports event next week."

"Take your pick," replied the man, stepping back and using his hand to indicate four shelves on the opposite side of the compact stall where a collection of trophies was displayed. She picked up one with a lid, but when she turned it around, she noted it was engraved with '1938' and the name of a tennis tournament.

"I'm looking for something plain, so we can engrave the donor's name on it."

"How about this?" suggested the man, reaching to the bottom shelf and removing a large silver trophy, with two curved handles, and a wooden base with a silver plaque. "The trophy is plain, and I can replace the plaque."

Dotty examined it. She liked the slight dent near the top, and that one handle was higher than the other, as it gave it an authentic feel. "This is perfect," she replied.

"And the engraving?" the man asked.

"Something simple." She paused to think and added, 'The Jay Newton Trophy'.

CHAPTER TWELVE

On the morning of the charity team triathlon, Norman drove Dotty and Aunt Beanie in the farm's Land Rover Defender.

"What a glorious summer's day," Aunt Beanie remarked, as they chugged along the Cotswold lanes. "But one of the last, I suspect. There's a taste of autumn in the air."

"I've the taste of bacon. Thanks for my sandwich, Beanie," acknowledged Norman, "although another one might have helped. We could have a long day ahead."

"But you ate Dotty's," responded Aunt Beanie in an indignant tone.

Dotty's stomach churned even though she hadn't been able to face food this morning. At least her team was in an early heat, and her swim was the first leg.

White vertical banners, topped with Cirencester Auctioneer's blue logo, advertising the charity triathlon, were located beside each of the stone columns at the entrance to Windrush Hall.

As Norman drove down the sweeping drive, Dotty realised access to the front of the house was blocked off by yellow, triangular, police traffic cones.

A sign directed Norman to park on an uneven grassy area, to the left of the main house, marked out with blue and white police tape.

A handful of vehicles were already there, including Sergeant Varma's, new-to-her, Ford Focus, with its distinctive blue and yellow squares on the sides, and a strip of blue and white lights across its roof.

Keya had proudly told Dotty it had belonged to the traffic division, and the turbocharged engine could reach sixty miles per hour in six seconds. She prayed Keya didn't test drive the theory on the narrow Cotswold lanes.

Dotty wore her navy and turquoise swimming costume beneath her blue and white stripped jersey T-shirt dress. Goosebumps prickled her arms as she stood outside the Land Rover, so she grabbed her navy cardigan as well as her pink sports bag containing her towel, swim cap, flip-flops and goggles.

Aunt Beanie hoisted her blue and white striped straw basket up her arm and, after locking the Land Rover, Norman joined them as they strode towards the garden, following large yellow traffic diversion signs.

Dotty noted several white, slightly tatty tents erected at the bottom of the garden, where it bordered the woods, and a blue and white gazebo at the entrance to the garden branded with Cirencester Auctioneers.

Molly Vogt greeted them as she arranged fragrant sweet peas and dahlias with green foliage in a cut-glass vase. "Good morning. How are you all today?"

"Grand," replied Norman, doffing his flat cap. "I'll find Keya and see what last-minute jobs she needs doing."

He was about to walk away when Molly called out, "I think she's in the courtyard at the side of the house. Didier is helping her sort through the road signs which need putting out along the cycle route."

Aunt Beanie joined Norman, and they strode away.

"Those smell lovely," said Dotty politely, as Molly placed a final piece of green myrtle in her arrangement. "Did you grow them?"

Molly beamed with delight. "Thank you, the sweet peas and some of the dahlias are mine, but Jay said I could also take some from his garden. I thought they'd freshen up the ladies changing tent as it's going to be a hot day and you competitors will be exerting yourselves."

"I'm only doing the swim," replied Dotty, shifting from foot to foot.

"Only. I know you've been training hard. Remember, I met you at Cheltenham lido." Molly picked up a small vase and placed it in front of her. She unwrapped tissue paper from around a bunch of colourful pansies.

"Do you wish you were taking part?" Dotty asked.

Molly tilted her head to one side and smiled ruefully. "It's good to be part of a team, a partnership where each member relies on the others. But I don't get a look in, not with sporty Rebecca and athletic Amanda. It's like working with two female gladiators."

Dotty thought Molly looked very feminine and attractive in her blue and yellow floral sundress. She was petite and almost doll-like with her auburn ringlets which reached down to the nape of her neck.

"Do you enjoy working at Akemans?" Molly asked.

"Of course. As you say, it's like a team or a family and we all look after each other."

Molly picked up a yellow pansy with a rich purple centre. "Even George?"

"She's very good at what she does, as an auctioneer. She just gets nervous before a sale." Dotty could understand why, and her stomach churned as she looked past Molly, through the open gazebo, to the wooden chalet style pool house.

"And do you have a man in your life?" Molly asked in a gentle voice.

Dotty's cheeks burned as she replied, "Not at the moment. Besides, it's only a year since I lost my husband." She bit her lip. She'd forgotten last week was the anniversary of Al's death. She must visit his grave tomorrow and lay some flowers. But what a year it had been.

Molly mirrored her thoughts by asking, "Do you miss him?"

Dotty hesitated before replying, "Not really. And I know that sounds awful, but I now realise how much he controlled and … restricted my life. Since he's gone, I've done so much and learned to stand on my own feet. I've grown up."

It was true. She did feel as if she'd developed from a young girl suspended in marriage, to a maturing woman who made her own decisions.

“Good for you,” said Molly, in a choked voice, as she leaned towards Dotty.

“Dotty,” called Aunt Beanie. “Can you help set up the swimming lanes and transition area?”

Molly smiled at Dotty and said, “And I must get on, too. Nice talking to you and good luck today.”

CHAPTER THIRTEEN

"Hello, Dotty," said a rich, masculine voice.

She was standing outside the wooden pool house. Tracy, Jay's man, had shown her how to retract the side panels, but rather than have an issue just before the triathlon started, she'd asked him to leave them open.

There was still a slight chill in the air, but the morning was warming up and there wasn't a cloud to spoil the crisp blue sky.

She turned to face the handsome, mature face of Gilmore Chapman, but instead of his usual collared shirt, often worn with a woollen waistcoat, he sported a black T-shirt with 'Fabulous Auction Boys' stamped across the front of it. She glanced down and noted his dark trainers and baggy shorts.

Her eyes widened, and she asked, "Are you competing?"

"You'd think I'd have better things to do on a bank holiday Monday, and I do, but somehow Dani Boy and Patrick persuaded me to join their team."

"Are you swimming?" Dotty asked hopefully.

"I wish," Gilmore replied dryly, "but Patrick's doing that. I have to cycle. I'm used to pedalling on roads and along the tarmac paths of London's parks, but the countryside is quite a different proposition. London has its potholes, but the route through the woods and around the park will be rough and uneven. At least I get it over with. We're third to go."

"I don't think I'll be able to watch you start," Dotty responded with regret. "We're in the fifth heat."

Gilmore looked up as a plane, high above their heads, cut across the sky, leaving a white line in its wake. "Just what I need. The human dynamo that is Dr Peter lapping me."

Dotty couldn't help giggling at Gilmore's resigned expression.

"Teammate, here you are. Fancy a pick-me up to get you into the mood?" A stocky man with tight-brown curly hair and a ruddy face clapped Gilmore on the shoulder and offered him a tarnished hip flask.

Gilmore rolled his eyes and shook his head.

"More for me," the man said in his Gloucestershire burr.

"Steady on, Patrick," reasoned Dani Boy, his black hair hanging loose around his shoulders.

Both men wore black 'Fabulous Auction Boys' T-shirts and Patrick had on baggy, cargo-style shorts, while Dani wore a pair of black Lycra running shorts, from which his skinny white legs protruded.

"Dotty," a female, Indian voice called.

"Excuse me," muttered Dotty, but she doubted the Fabulous Auction Boys team heard her as she walked across the lawn to join Keya.

"One of the teams is running late, so we're in the same heat as you. When you've finished your swim, can you man my radio?"

Keya must have noticed Dotty tense, as she added, "Just until I've finished my cycle."

"But I've no idea how to use it."

Keya smiled. "I'll set it up for you. Just press this button at the top and speak slowly and clearly."

"But who's listening?"

"Those at the start and finish of each phase, the officials at the furthest points of the running and cycling courses, the scorers in the house, Norman, and the medical officer, either Dr Wimsey or Gilly. And I gave one to Jay's man, but he looked at me as though I was an irritating fly he'd like to swat, so I've no idea if he'll bother to use it."

"But why do I need a radio?"

"In case there's a problem or a medical emergency. If someone needs picking up, say a competitor's fallen off their bike and can't continue, then Norman will collect them in his Land Rover."

"I'm not sure," Dotty replied hesitantly.

"It won't be for long. I hope." Keya grinned. "I think it's nearly time to start."

The first two teams to start were from a butcher in Burford and a children's nursery in Cirencester. Their runners were ready, although they still wore lightweight, waterproof jackets over their Lycra tops, and the lady swimmers wore corporate T-shirts over their leggings.

An official-looking man Dotty didn't recognise, stepped onto the decking in front of the open-sided pool house and consulted a clipboard. "Are the first swimmers ready?"

The two lady swimmers peeled off their T-shirts and Dotty realised they both wore triathlon suits, and they looked very professional as they pulled on their silicone swimming caps and adjusted their goggles.

"Come this way," the official instructed, and the two women followed him.

Dotty looked across the garden as Didier Vogt left another gazebo, inside which was a white-clothed table with the vase of pansies Molly had been arranging, a microphone on a stand, and the silver trophy which gleamed in the sunlight. She regarded the trophy proudly, pleased she'd polished it.

Didier asked, "Please can everyone leave the transition area, apart from the first two runners? The pots of flowers mark the boundary." Dotty had helped position the pots, which were blooming with colourful flowers, including pansies, dahlias, petunias and red-flowering begonias.

It was time to change.

She walked down the slope towards a white tent with a 'Ladies' sign tilting at an angle beside the entrance flap.

Inside, there were white plastic chairs and two trestle tables. Protruding over the edge of one table, where Molly had placed her beautiful arrangement of dahlias and sweet peas, was a plastic water container with a spout and, beside it, white plastic cups. There were packets of fruit juices and bottles of water and energy drinks. There was even a bowl of fruit and a basket containing energy snacks. She wondered if it was Molly who had thought to provide everything.

The flap of the tent opened and Amanda, from Cirencester Auctioneers, and Rebecca Randall walked confidently inside and deposited their bags on the second trestle table.

They ignored Dotty, who poured herself a cup of water and walked across to the furthest corner of the tent. She pulled her T-shirt dress over her head and replaced it with her grey Akemans team T-shirt. As she wrapped her towel around her waist, she heard a voice remark, "It's the opposition."

Hesitantly, Dotty turned round. "Weren't you at our last auction? You outbid Didier for that attractive walnut sideboard." Rebecca Randall's eyes widened. "The one in the music room." She stepped towards Dotty and, narrowing her eyes, demanded, "Has Jay commissioned you to buy furniture for the hall?"

Dotty's mouth was dry, and she didn't reply.

"That's supposed to be my commission. I'll have words with him after I've finished. I've warned him. This is the final straw." She turned and sneezed.

"And whose idea was it to put flowers in the tent?" Rebecca reached into her bag and removed a white plastic bottle. Removing the cap, she stuck its elongated top up each nostril and inhaled.

She sniffed, grabbed a bottle of water, and strode angrily out of the tent.

Amanda had already removed her top and as she stepped out of her linen trousers, Dotty noted her triathlon suit.

"Ignore her," Amanda said. "She's wound up about today. We're all competitive and like things to go our way, but Rebecca has to win."

CHAPTER FOURTEEN

Dotty felt self-conscious as she trod up the garden towards the pool house wearing her blue flip-flops, with her striped towel wrapped around her waist and her grey Akemans T-shirt covering her blue and turquoise swimming costume.

Carrying her purple swim cap and blue-tinted goggles, she had everything she needed for her swim.

A small crowd had gathered outside the pool house and as she approached, a runner broke away and ran across the garden, starting his run leg of the triathlon.

Dani Boy remained outside the pool house, desperately glancing inside for his teammate Patrick to emerge. His black hair was neatly tied back in a ponytail.

The tension in the crowd mounted, but after a minute a dripping and panting Patrick appeared. Dani Boy ran up to him, they clapped hands and Dani Boy was away on his run. Patrick doubled over, gasping for breath.

As another team was called to the start of the swim by the official, Keya joined Dotty, looking tense. She kept glancing around, so Dotty asked, "What's wrong?"

"Chief Inspector Ringrose has been called away to Poulton. We can't change the start times again, and I'm not sure what we'll do if he's not back soon." Keya walked back towards the house, still glancing around.

Dotty was joined by her teammates, Marcus Boyd and Dr Peter. Dr Peter couldn't stay still, bobbing from one foot to another or swinging his arms back and forth.

"Ready, Dotty?" asked Marcus.

"I think so."

"Remember, you have to climb out of the pool and tag me in the transition area so that I can start my run."

The small crowd around the transition area cheered as a swimmer appeared and tagged her teammate.

Within seconds, the second swimmer appeared.

"Ok, we're on," announced Marcus. "Good luck, Peter."

Dotty pulled her T-shirt over her head and when she opened her eyes, she was looking into the face of a grinning Sergeant Unwin.

Stepping back, she noted his branded running kit, down to the black Nike flash on his yellow running shoes.

"What no tri suit, Dotty? Isn't that a bit amateur?"

Dotty wasn't sure if he was teasing or belittling her, but she tried to ignore him as she concentrated on the swim ahead and pulled on her purple swim cap.

"Can we have Akemans Antique Heroes and the Trois Amies?" called the swimming official.

Keya jogged towards them and exclaimed, "We can't start without Chief Inspector Ringrose."

"No fear. I'm here," boomed a deep Welsh voice.

Keya froze, and Sergeant Unwin stepped back, his eyes bulging. They all turned towards the approaching figure of Inspector Evans. His white tummy flopped over the top of a pair of baggy, mango-coloured shorts.

"You're doing the swim," Sergeant Unwin gasped.

"Well deduced Sergeant Onion. You'll go far."

Dotty grinned as she felt the sergeant tense beside her.

"Chief Inspector Ringrose sends his regrets and asked me to substitute. Besides, how difficult can it be to swim 800m? And my opponent is Miss Meddlesome, is it?" He grinned at Dotty.

"Swimmers, please," called the official in an exasperated tone from the open side of the pool house.

Dotty strode purposefully inside and stood at the end of the first lane, as directed by the official. She looked up the length of the pool at the inviting, clear water and slowed her breathing as she prepared herself.

She mustn't start too quickly, but if she was too slow, she might not make up the time. She needed a strong, determined swim for the first twelve lengths, after which she should steadily increase her pace, building up to a sprint at the end.

"Twenty lengths of the pool," instructed the official, "and you must climb out when you've finished and tag your teammate."

"Twenty lengths," repeated Inspector Evans uncertainly. "Can you manage that, lass?"

Was he speaking to her? She tried to ignore him as she concentrated on what she had to do.

"I doubt I'll climb out after twenty lengths. I'll need to use those steps at the far end, I will," the Inspector grumbled.

"Take your marks," called the official.

Dotty pulled her goggles on and checked they were in place. She stepped to the edge of the pool.

"Get ready."

She moved her arms behind her.

"Go."

Swinging her arms, Dotty flung her body forward and dived into the pool. As soon as she surfaced, she pulled her arms up and began her front crawl strokes. She found a pleasing rhythm, breathing every three strokes until she reached the end of the pool. Here she took a deep breath, turned and pushed herself away from the wall.

She had no idea what the inspector was doing as she counted off her laps. She felt strong at the halfway point and increased her speed.

"Four laps to go," said a lady as she made a turn. She pushed off and started pumping her arms and kicking her legs as she sped on. At two laps to go, she went for an all-out sprint.

Approaching the end of the final lap, she slowed slightly to gather her breath for the climb out. She pulled herself up and swung her legs up and over the edge of the pool.

Stumbling forward, she picked herself up, ran out of the pool house and clapped hands with Marcus in the transition area.

As she collapsed to the ground and sat with her head bowed, Keya put something on the ground beside her, laid a hand on her shoulder and murmured distractedly, "Well done."

Close by she heard Sergeant Unwin mutter, "When did he learn to swim? Surely he can put his head in the water, even if he is doing breaststroke."

It was several more minutes before she heard the sergeant grumble, "At last," and Inspector Evans dropped down beside her.

"That was harder than it looks, but you were crackin' lass. You've obviously been training rather than poking your nose into police business."

Dotty's jaw clenched.

The inspector added, "Let's hope it stays that way."

CHAPTER FIFTEEN

Beside Dotty, a radio crackled into life and a muffled voice said, "The cyclist for the 'Fabulous Auction Boys' team had a fall, but he's back on his bike and heading through the woods towards the finish."

A voice Dotty thought was Norman's replied, "Thank you."

Fabulous Auction Boys. That was Gilmore. Her mouth felt dry.

"I'm not being funny, but someone's dropped their police radio," remarked Inspector Evans. He leaned over to pick it up, but Dotty snatched it off the grass.

"It's Keya's. Sergeant Varma's. She asked me to look after it while she's cycling."

"Please, can I have the next swimmers?" called the official.

Dotty stood up as Amanda from Cirencester Auctioneer's pulled on a yellow swim cap with 'Cheltenham Triathlon' printed on it. She clasped Rebecca's arm and said unemotionally, "Good luck."

Rebecca sneezed, before replying, "And you."

A woman Dotty recognised as the vicar of St Mary's Church in Fairford stepped forward and removed her T-shirt with the team name 'The Holy Trinity' printed on it.

The sun had risen high in the sky and Dotty felt its warming rays as she dried off. Should she change? What if she was needed and was standing in the changing tent in her bra and knickers? No, she'd wait with Keya's radio until her friend returned.

From the pool, there was a splash as the swimmers dived in.

Rebecca rubbed her eyes before reaching down to re-tie the laces of her running shoes. She spoke to someone in the crowd and Molly stepped forward, pulling a tissue from a small hand packet. Rebecca blew her nose, but she still appeared agitated, shifting her weight back and forth from one foot to another.

The radio in Dotty's hand crackled, and a voice said, "This is the scorers. Can someone bring the time sheets from the swimming?"

Dotty was at the swimming pool. Should she get them? Examining the black radio, she pressed down the switch-like button at the top and tentatively said, "This is Dotty. I'll ask for them after this heat has finished."

"Thank you," came the curt reply.

Rebecca appeared even more agitated and kept alternating between pulling at her throat and taking sips of water from a plastic bottle. The area around her eyes looked puffy and blue.

Molly ran up the bank from the direction of the changing tent and handed Rebecca a white plastic bottle. "Thanks," said Rebecca, removing the top and sticking the elongated top up her nose. She pressed down on the bottle and sniffed.

"Are you OK?" Molly asked.

"Just a touch of hay fever. I'll be fine now I've had an antihistamine shot." She handed the bottle back to Molly and added, "But keep this for me. I might need it after my run. There's something in the air that's really irritating me today."

The dripping wet but athletic figure of Amanda appeared at the edge of the pool house, and she clapped hands with Rebecca, who started her run. Rebecca looked strong as she ran with smooth, long strides across the garden and out into the parkland of the Windrush estate.

After the second swimmer had emerged from the pool house, Dotty found the official and collected the swim time sheets.

Keya had told her the scorers were working in the house, so she walked through the formal gardens, inhaling lavender from the few remaining sprigs on the bushes, and pulled at the French windows in the alcove of the morning room.

The door opened, and she stepped inside the cool house, padding across the floor in her blue flip-flops. She found the scorers in the drawing room.

A lady sat at Jay's desk with an open laptop in front of her, and a man and woman sat on the L-shaped grey sofa surrounded by paperwork. They thanked her for bringing the swim sheets before returning to their tasks.

Uncertain what to do next, Dotty heard cheering from the front of the house where the finish line was located. Had Peter finished his cycle?

Clutching the radio, and still feeling self-conscious wearing her team T-shirt over her damp swimming costume, with her stripy swim towel wrapped around her waist, she opened the front door and stood at the top of the stone steps at the front of Windrush Hall.

She tried to make sense of the people milling about below. The cheering continued as a Lycra-clad figure pedalled furiously across the front of the house, in a lane marked by a blue rope, and braked to a stop after passing under a finishing banner opposite the stone steps. His supporters surged forward to congratulate him.

Beyond the finish line was the transition area between the running and cycling.

Several people stood next to their mountain bikes, their colourful aerodynamic cycle helmets either strapped on their heads or hanging from their bike's handlebars.

A runner entered the transition area from the parkland of Windrush estate, and high-fived a cyclist who stood up on his bike, pushing down on his pedals, as the wheels of his bike turned slowly forward. He turned towards the drive and remained standing out of his seat as he pedalled up the slope.

Dotty realised just how steep the drive was. A tough start for the cyclists.

"Come on Gilmore," a man in the crowd shouted.

Dotty looked to her right as a figure cycled past the front of the temporary car park.

"Go, Gilmore, go." The two men shouting encouragement were his fellow Fabulous Auction Boys' teammates, Patrick and Dani Boy. Patrick was jumping around enthusiastically, his head of curly hair bobbing up and down.

Gilmore's finish was more sedate than the last competitor, and he stopped quickly after the finishing line, placing his feet on the ground and leaning against his bike's handlebars. Dotty ran down the steps as Dani Boy and Patrick clapped Gilmore on the back.

Dotty saw Gilly's bright orange hair ahead of her and she heard her exclaim, "Boys, give him some room. Gilmore, are you OK? Did you fall?"

As Dotty joined them, she heard Gilmore reply, "I'm fine. Just sore, and my arm and leg stings."

"I'm not surprised with those scrapes. We need to get you cleaned up," instructed Gilly, in a motherly tone.

Gilmore did not look his usual sophisticated self. His plastic cycle helmet, with its moulded holes, resembled an alien's head and the whole of his left side was covered in soil, leaves and blood.

There was another cheer from the crowd and someone called, "Here comes Peter."

Gilly looked towards the park and then back at Gilmore.

"I'll be fine, go and cheer on your husband," encouraged Gilmore. "At least he didn't lap me." He looked up at Dotty and smiled sheepishly. "You too. I'll be fine. Go and support your teammate."

Gilly was desperately trying to see over the heads of the crowd.

"Come with me," called Dotty, above the noise, and she grabbed Gilly's arm and led her back up the stone steps. They stopped part way up and turned to watch Dr Peter, whose head was bent low over his handlebars as he sped towards the finish. It was Gilly's turn to grab Dotty's arm, and she bounced up and down on the balls of her feet, calling, "Come on, Peter."

The Lycra-clad figure swept through the finish line and didn't stop until he nearly reached the entrance to the courtyard. Gilly ran down the steps and as Dotty slowly made her descent, she watched Gilly throw her arms around her husband.

Dotty returned to Gilmore as Patrick was handing him his tarnished hip flask. "Surely you want a swig now. It's medicinal."

"Are you sure there's any left?" quipped Dani Boy.

Patrick shook the flask. "A bit, but if you don't want it, I'll finish it."

Gilmore reached up for the flask, took a swig and choked. He handed it back to Patrick, who lifted it up to his lips and tipped his head back.

Gilmore shook his head and turned to Dotty. "That does feel better." He finally climbed off his bike and asked, "How did you get on?"

"I've no idea. I beat Inspector Evans in my heat, but I don't think that's much of an achievement."

"Come on, Rebecca," someone in the crowd beside the run-cycle transition area called.

"Shall we?" suggested Gilmore, and he pushed his bike across the tarmac towards the edge of the parkland. Dotty fell into step beside him while Patrick and Dani Boy ran in front, cheering and enthusiastically shouting encouragement to Rebecca Randall.

Her strides were not the smooth, flowing ones Dotty had noticed earlier, and she tripped, caught herself and staggered forward.

"Something's wrong," whispered Dotty.

"She's probably just tired. It's really hot out there, but she'll soon be finished."

Dotty wasn't so sure. Rebecca stumbled again and collapsed to her knees. Her teammate, Amanda, ran forward, her green and yellow swim towel wrapped around her waist.

Rebecca waved her away and pushed herself up, staggering forward two more steps before once again collapsing to the ground. She mouthed something to Amanda, who leaned over her as Rebecca appeared to repeat her request.

Amanda rushed back to the crowd and called, "Molly, Rebecca's spray."

Molly stepped forward and threw a white plastic bottle to Amanda, who easily caught it and dashed back to Rebecca, who was kneeling on the ground. The crowd was silent, as if holding its breath, as Rebecca pushed the elongated end of the bottle up her nose, pressed down and inhaled.

Dotty was also holding her breath as she waited for Rebecca to stagger to her feet, but instead she slumped down on her knees, clutching her heart.

"Doctor," someone in the crowd shouted.

"What's wrong?" Dotty asked Gilmore. "Why didn't her medicine work?"

"I've no idea. I think she's having an asthma attack."

"Out of the way please, I'm a doctor."

Dr Peter was still wearing his cycle helmet as he pushed forward through the crowd and ran towards Rebecca, who was gasping for air. He dropped down beside her, and Dotty couldn't hear what he said.

Gilly, sweat running down her face, rushed past Dotty and Gilmore, carrying what Dotty presumed was Peter's medical bag. As soon as she dropped it beside her husband, he reached in and removed his stethoscope.

Out of the corner of her eye, Dotty noticed a figure cycling slowly towards the finish line, but nobody was cheering or shouting encouragement.

"It's Keya," blurted Dotty and she turned and ran across to the finish line calling, "Keep going."

Hers was a lone voice amongst the subdued mutterings of the crowd.

Keya came slowly to a stop after the finish line and Dotty ran across to congratulate her as she climbed off her bike and unclipped her helmet.

"That was tough," panted Keya, "and I'm the one who set the course." She looked around. "What's the matter? What's happened?"

"Defibrillator," called Dr Peter.

"What!" cried Keya, dropping her bike on the ground and running across the tarmac. The growing crowd had moved to the edge of the parkland and Dotty had to skirt round them as she rushed after her friend.

Keya joined Gilly as they stood beside Dr Peter, who leaned over the prostrate figure of Rebecca Randall. Gilmore pushed his bike across to Dotty and muttered, "This doesn't look good."

"What do you think is the matter?"

"From my experience, I'd say she's having a heart attack."

CHAPTER SIXTEEN

The kneeling Dr Peter rocked back on his heels and tilted his head back, looking up into the clear blue sky.

The still figure of Rebeca Randall lay on her back in front of him.

The crowd, standing respectfully at the edge of the parkland, was silent as Amanda ran forward, but Gilly grabbed her arm. When Amanda tried to wrench it free, Gilly shook her head and whispered something Dotty didn't catch.

"No," cried Amanda. It was a heartfelt, primeval sound.

Gilmore placed his arm around Dotty's shoulders and pulled her against his chest. She had not known the dead woman, and what little she'd seen she hadn't really liked. But Rebecca was young and fit and had no reason to die. No more reason than she did. Tears welled in her eyes.

Gilmore smelled earthy and metallic, and she remembered he had fallen from his bike. But that was nothing compared to watching Rebecca Randall die in front of her.

"My radio," cried Keya, grabbing it from Dotty's hand.

"Sorry," sobbed Dotty, letting go and removing her face from Gilmore's chest. She turned and watched Keya twiddle the knob on top of the radio and, holding it to her mouth, she said, "This is Sergeant Varma. Please send an ambulance to Windrush Park."

Keya turned the knob again and said, "Norman, I need you at the front of the house. Do you have a screen?"

"Excuse me," called another runner, pushing through the crowd into the transition area. Soon after, her teammate started cycling up the drive. The competition continued even though one of the participants was lying dead on the grass.

"You're shivering," murmured Gilmore. "Go and get changed. There's nothing more you can do here. I'll see if I can find Jay or Tracy and grab a shower to wash this dirt off, and then we'll see what we can do."

Avoiding a fast-finishing cyclist, Dotty wandered around the side of Windrush Hall and back to the changing tent. She felt numb, and as she stepped inside the tent she stopped and stared at Rebecca's bag, lying on the trestle table.

She felt better after she'd changed. Someone had placed a flask of hot water and some tea bags in the tent, and she carried a disposable paper cup of tea back round to the front of the house.

A blue, yellow and pink striped beach windbreaker had been secured around the body, hiding it from people standing on the tarmac in front of the house.

The crowd had dispersed and although there were still cyclists waiting to compete, and competitors finishing the run and cycle phases, there was no shouting or cheering.

Dotty walked across to the small group gathered by the screen comprising Dr Peter, Gilly and Norman. Inspector Evans was standing several metres away, talking to Amanda and Molly, and Keya was speaking into her radio.

Keya finished her conversation and walked past them, saying, "The ambulance is here." She continued towards the entrance to the drive and waved her hands at the ambulance. People moved out of its way as it backed towards the temporary screen.

Inspector Evans, who had changed into a pair of brown trousers and a short sleeve beige shirt, approached the group and said, "Dr Peter. I'd like a word, I would."

Although they both stepped away from the group, the inspector's deep baritone Welsh voice was clear as he asked, "What is your opinion of the cause of death?"

Dr Peter replied, in an unusually serious tone, "It was definitely a heart attack, but I couldn't say what caused it. She was young and fit, but she was seen using a nasal spray."

"Which suggests what?" the inspector pressed.

"That she had asthma, or an allergy. Recent studies have shown that the number of heart attacks increases in hot weather. And strenuous exercise may also have been a factor."

"So there's nothing suspicious about her death?'

"Not that I can see. But that will be a matter for the pathologist."

They all turned as a man and woman wearing moss-green uniforms emerged from the ambulance and opened the rear doors. They pulled out a stretcher and wheeled it across the uneven, grassy ground and around the side of the temporary screen.

The group of people standing with Dotty increased as Molly Vogt, a clean Gilmore with damp hair, Jay Newton and Tracy, joined them.

As the stretcher was mechanically lifted into the back of the ambulance, with the covered figure of Rebecca Randall strapped to it, the inspector announced, "A tragic accident."

Dotty's grief was pushed aside as she felt another emotion from those standing around her. There seemed to be a collective exhaling of air and a feeling of … relief!

CHAPTER SEVENTEEN

As the ambulance drove away up Windrush Hall's long drive, and manoeuvred around a cyclist who was standing up on his bike, pedalling slowly up the incline, Inspector Evans announced, "Here comes my sergeant. He can question you all, he can."

"Question us?" repeated Amanda in an indignant tone.

"Yes, madam. There has been a suspicious death and just as the body has to be examined by a pathologist, witnesses and those close to the deceased have to be questioned."

"Why is the death suspicious?" Amanda continued, her voice rising in pitch.

"Because a perfectly healthy young woman just dropped down dead. I'd have thought you'd want to know what happened, and that you'd be happy to work with the police to clear this matter up and provide closure for her family and other friends."

Ouch, thought Dotty. The inspector was not pulling his punches today.

The remarks appeared to have hit home as Amanda's shoulders drooped and she started crying. Between sobs she muttered, "Of course I want to help, and find out why she died."

Gilmore stepped across and wrapped his arm around Amanda,

who turned and buried her head in his chest. Just as Dotty had done earlier.

"Mr Newton," called the inspector in his deep baritone voice. "Perhaps there is somewhere we can go? And is it possible to get a cup of tea?" He looked across at Dotty, eyeing her paper cup.

Tracy whispered something to Jay before turning and striding back to the hall.

"Of course," replied Jay. "You can use the dining room."

As the group weaved their way around competitors, spectators, and the blue-roped cycle lane, to the front steps of Windrush Hall, Didier strode across to Molly and asked, "What's happened? I saw an ambulance leave. Who's been injured?"

She looked up at him and in a disbelieving voice replied, "Rebecca. Rebecca was in the ambulance. But she's dead."

Didier froze and Gilmore, who was guiding the crumpled figure of Amanda, nearly bumped into him.

"Rebecca," Didier murmured. "Dead."

The inspector appeared interested in his response as he turned and looked at Didier, his eyes narrowing, and then moved across and asked, "You knew the deceased, did you?"

"Of course. We all did." He looked from Molly to the slowly retreating figure of Amanda. "We worked together."

Keya's radio crackled and Aunt Beanie's voice said, "I've stopped one of the cyclists for heat exhaustion. Norman, can you come and collect her? And can you bring some more drinking water with you?"

Norman changed direction and walked towards Keya, who said, "Inspector, we're needed elsewhere. And Aunt Beanie's right, it's very hot, so we need to make sure all the competitors and officials stay hydrated."

Inspector Evans nodded. "I'm sure Sergeant Onion can collect statements from this bunch. You do what you need to do."

Surely the inspector knew his sergeant's name by now. Sergeant Unwin had been with Cirencester Police for nearly four months, or was the inspector deliberately winding up his ambitious young sergeant?

Sergeant Unwin walked slightly apart from the group, still wearing his designer running kit.

When Dotty had first met him, she was intrigued by his dark looks and confident manner and he had appeared to reciprocate the attraction, but she had been dressed up for a television show.

Now, he usually ignored her, either because of her lowly role at Akemans or because she didn't spend hours on her hair, makeup and appearance. Or both.

"Dotty," called Jay as she was about to climb the stone steps. "I know this sounds very chauvinistic, but can you organise drinks for everyone? Tracy has an aversion to the police. And the fridge is full of food if anyone is hungry. I'm not sure I am after what happened, but it might help the shock." He joined her at the foot of the steps and asked, "And who is that woman with Gilmore?"

"That's Amanda, from Cirencester Auctioneers. She worked with Rebecca, and they were in the same team today."

"And the doctor?"

"That's Dr Peter, and his wife Gilly is the one with the bright hair. She runs the antiques centre at Akemans."

As they climbed the steps together, Dotty said, "I'll be happy to help." And she was. Being active would help keep her mind off Rebecca's death. Besides, it gave her an excuse to listen in to the police interviews.

She walked into the dining room, where the rest of the group were standing around uncertainly. She hesitated as Jay went ahead of her and when she left the dining room and entered the kitchen, she heard him say, "Your secret's safe now."

She hesitated in the passageway, created when the kitchen was divided by the previous owner, and heard Tracy reply, "As is yours. You should never have brought that scheming witch into this house."

"I know, I know. But I was flattered. She was a beautiful woman," replied Jay regretfully.

"But one who continued to cause trouble for both of us. I thought that episode of my life was finished. I've done my time. Unlike you."

Dotty felt extremely awkward, hovering in the passage. She started whistling and emerged into the kitchen.

A flush spread across Jay's cheeks but he said, in an even tone, "Tracy, can you show Dotty where the cups and glasses are, and how to use the coffee machine? Dotty, sparkling water and juices are in one of the fridges through in the pantry."

Dotty stepped inside the pantry, noting the two large fridges and a long, white chest freezer.

As she backed out, she heard Jay mutter, "Well, it is over now. And you know you have my gratitude and my friendship."

She turned and saw Jay and Tracy clasp hands.

CHAPTER EIGHTEEN

Dotty carried cups and glasses on a plastic tray through to the dining room, placing them on the glass-topped table.

Inspector Evans had seated himself on one of the black, high-backed dining chairs in the corner of the room from where he was observing the other occupants.

Sergeant Unwin sat at the foot of the table, closest to the entrance hall, with Dr Peter and Gilly seated on one side of the table and Molly, Gilmore and Amanda on the other side. Didier stood behind Molly, his back turned as he stared out of a large sash window.

"So, doctor, in your opinion Rebecca Randall died from a heart attack?" concluded Sergeant Unwin.

"Yes. One that may have been brought on by intense physical exercise in this heat."

Dotty returned to the kitchen. Tracy placed a cup of coffee topped with frothy milk on a round metal tray next to several others. There was also a flask of hot water, tea bags, sugar and a small white jug of milk. Dotty picked up the tray and carried it through to the dining room.

Amanda was speaking. "I didn't think Rebecca had asthma, although I know she suffered from hay fever. But she used a nasal spray when it got too bad." She turned to Molly and asked, "Didn't you give it to her this morning?"

"Oh, yes," stammered Molly. She reached into a cotton shoulder bag and removed the white plastic bottle she'd given Rebecca earlier, outside the swimming pool and when she collapsed at the end of her run.

Dotty poured the inspector a cup of tea, remembering he liked it milky with two sugars. She carried it across to his corner as the sergeant picked up the bottle and read, "Non-drowsy antihistamine nasal spray. Pretty harmless, wouldn't you say, doctor?" He pushed the white bottle towards Dr Peter as Dotty returned to the kitchen for cold drinks.

She placed bottles of sparking water and fruit juices on the table beside the small, white plastic bottle.

"Coffee for me, black," instructed Sergeant Unwin.

Dotty looked down at the coffee cups. "I'm afraid there's cappuccino or cappuccino."

"Ok, that'll do," replied the sergeant dismissively. "As long as it contains caffeine."

Gilmore reached over for a cup of coffee and Amanda poured herself a glass of sparkling water. As she did so, she reflected, "Rebecca was sneezing this morning. And complaining about the flowers."

"Flowers can't help where they grow," interjected the inspector.

"No, not the garden flowers, the ones in the vase in the ladies' changing room."

"We better have a look at them. Dotty, isn't it?"

Dotty sighed. The inspector knew her name.

"Make yourself useful and fetch the vase of flowers from the ladies' changing room."

"I'll go," said Molly, pushing back her chair.

"No, you stay here. Miss big-ears can go, rather than listening in to this interview."

Dotty felt the blood rush to her face, and she bowed her head as she fled from the dining room. She passed through the morning room, out of the French windows and down to the ladies' changing tent.

As soon as she walked in, she spotted Rebecca's bag. She might as well bring it too, to save the inspector sending her on another errand.

She hoisted the black canvas sports bag over her shoulder and looked at the trestle table, expecting to see the vase of sweet peas and dahlias, but it wasn't there.

She dropped Rebecca's sports bag to the ground and conducted a thorough search of the tent, but there was no vase of flowers.

As she walked into the dining room and dropped the sports bag by Sergeant Unwin's chair, Inspector Evans demanded, "What have you got there, lass?"

"It's Rebecca's bag," cried Amanda.

The inspector, still seated in the corner, looked up at Dotty and enquired, "Is it?"

"Yes, I saw her with it this morning and as it was still in the changing tent, I brought it back with me. I thought you might want it," she ended lamely.

"I do. That was astute of you. And the flowers?"

"They've gone. I searched the tent, but I couldn't find them, or the vase they were in."

"My vase," exclaimed Molly.

The inspector glared at her and she shrank back on her chair. "Is that all, Sergeant?" he asked.

"I just need everyone's contact details. And I'll take the nasal spray for testing, as a precaution." Sergeant Unwin looked across the table. He stood up, walked around the table, and then stared accusingly at Dotty. "Where did you put the white plastic bottle?"

She cleared her throat and in a small voice replied, "I haven't touched it."

"But you must have. It was on the table."

She dropped her gaze to the floor. A small voice inside her head whispered to her. Who was the sergeant to blame her just because she was sorting out refreshments? She wasn't a servant. It was his fault the bottle was missing. Not hers. Besides, she'd been sent away to the ladies' changing tent.

She looked up and locked eyes with the sergeant as she felt her heart race. "Sergeant, you're the policeman. Maintaining evidence is your job, not mine. I'm only trying to help."

She picked up the tray of unwanted cappuccinos and returned to the kitchen. Jay was leaning against a marble-topped counter, reading something on his phone. He turned as she appeared and raised his eyebrows. "What happened? What's the matter?"

"Sergeant Unwin. He's jumping to conclusions and blaming me for losing evidence. And all because I agreed to help organise refreshments."

"Take no notice of him. Anyway, what evidence did he have?"

"The nasal spray Rebecca used for her hay fever."

"Do they think that contributed to her death?"

"I've no idea. But I was sent to get the flowers from the ladies' changing tent."

Jay raised his eyebrows and then dropped them as he narrowed his eyes and stepped towards the open door leading into the pantry. Dotty followed his gaze as a furry brown mouse scuttled out of sight.

"Right. Never mind antiques. What I need your help with is remodelling this kitchen and getting rid of the pesky mice."

CHAPTER NINETEEN

Later that afternoon, a subdued group of competitors, supporters, and officials stood in front of the stone steps at the front of Windrush Hall. Norman and Tracy had removed the finishing banner and ropes which had cordoned off the end of the cycle route.

Didier Vogt announced, "And the third team is Akemans Antique Heroes."

Dotty didn't feel a hero. She hadn't done anything to stop Rebecca Randall dying. But she climbed the front steps and smiled politely at Jay Newton as he handed her a bronze medal attached to a red, blue and white-striped nylon ribbon.

The winning team, from a garden centre on the outskirts of Cirencester, proudly held aloft the silver trophy Dotty had excitedly polished the previous day.

"Let's go home," murmured Norman. "Jay has agreed that Keya and I can come back tomorrow to finish tidying up, and he mentioned something about you, and the kitchen, and mice."

"Mice?" asked Aunt Beanie as she joined them.

"Jay Newton needs a cat for Windrush Hall. But he's not having Earl Grey."

Earl Grey sat up on Dotty's lap, munching flakes of fish Dotty dropped onto a newspaper. It had wrapped the fish and chips Aunt Beanie suggested they buy on their way home from Windrush Hall.

Dotty was grateful, as she didn't feel like cooking and doubted she'd have had anything more than a slice of toast if left to her own devices.

She, Norman, and Aunt Beanie were sitting at the pine table in the kitchen at Meadowbank Farm. Uncle Cliff was also seated at the table and appeared to be enjoying his fish and chips as he watched a small television mounted on a bookcase.

Earl Grey's large yellow eyes fixed on the piece of fish Dotty held, from which she extracted an inch-long opaque bone. She dropped the fish onto the newspaper and Earl Grey greedily attacked it.

"At least someone's hungry," observed Aunt Beanie as Dotty dissected another piece of fish.

"I'm famished," retorted Norman, dipping a chip into a blob of brown sauce at the side of his plate. "It was a long day, and despite the obvious tragedy, it passed without too many incidents. And you and the Akemans team did well, Dotty."

"Yes, but it feels rather an anticlimax after all that training."

"Start running," suggested Aunt Beanie. "Every town and village hosts fun runs these days and both Cirencester and Cheltenham hold half marathons."

"I'm not sure that's my thing, but I might start running."

"Couch to 5K," added Norman.

"What?" demanded Aunt Beanie.

"It's an NHS initiative. Someone was talking about it on a radio programme I was listening to with Cliff last week. You download an App on your phone and each day it gives you running instructions. Apparently, the distance and times increase each week, and the aim is that you can run five kilometres by the end of the course."

"I'll see," replied Dotty dully.

"Give it a try," pressed Aunt Beanie. "You did so well with the swimming. There's a glow about you, and you look fitter and stronger. Besides, it's depressing getting up to swim in the winter when it's dark and cold outside. But you could run during a break at the office. And there's a shower in the antiques centre."

Dotty didn't know about the shower, and she might consider running. But she'd need some new running shoes, as her flimsy trainers wouldn't provide enough support.

"I'm meeting Chief Inspector Ringrose tomorrow. What's everyone else doing?" asked Aunt Beanie.

"Dotty and I are returning to Windrush Hall, aren't we?" Norman looked back at Dotty for confirmation.

She nodded her consent.

"Anyway, where was the chief inspector today?" asked Norman. "He was supposed to be competing."

"He had a tip off about a stash of stolen items that had been discovered by kids in a shed in Poulton. That's the reason I'm meeting him tomorrow. There are several pieces of furniture he has concerns about."

Dotty pushed her plate away and stroked Earl Grey, who curled up in her lap, purring.

"Fakes, you mean?" asked Norman.

"The chief inspector's not sure. They are either exquisite pieces of antique furniture or excellent forgeries."

CHAPTER TWENTY

Dotty and Norman arrived at Windrush Hall on Tuesday morning. The weather was much fresher than the previous day, and gusts of wind swirled around their legs and plucked fallen flower petals from the grass, dancing with them in the air.

Dotty was glad she'd worn a fleece, and she stuck her hands in its large pockets.

Keya met them beside the pool house, and she had large bags under her eyes.

"Bad night?" asked Norman.

"I barely slept a wink," she replied. "I spent the whole night going over what happened and thinking I should have been able to prevent it."

"You couldn't, and you know that, so don't be so hard on yourself." Norman's voice was kind but firm.

"I'm not sure we'll run the triathlon again next year. Nobody will want to enter." Keya's voice was glum.

"By next summer, the tragedy will be forgotten, so I wouldn't worry too much," Norman replied reasonably.

Keya still sounded dejected as she muttered, "They're performing the autopsy this morning."

"That's good news. It'll put the matter to bed. Now, what needs doing?" Norman asked.

Dotty left Keya and Norman and walked along the gravel path, between the mounds of lavender with their few remaining flowering sprigs.

A spark of light caught her eye, and she stopped and stepped back. There it was again. She bent down and parted two lavender bushes. Beneath them were the shattered remains of Molly Vogt's cut-glass vase, and the scattered stems of greenery, sweet peas and dahlias.

This was the missing vase of flowers from the ladies' changing room. She reached down and collected the stems, being careful not to cut herself on the broken glass.

There were also two discarded small plastic water bottles. One was empty, but the other was partially filled with a cloudy liquid.

Stuffing the bottles in the pockets of her fleece, and clutching the haphazard bunch of flowers, she continued along the gravel path to the morning room, pulling open the French windows. She heard loud music.

"Hello," she called.

There was no reply.

She followed the music to the drawing room, but was shocked to find papers scattered across the floor. Jay was emptying the contents of a desk drawer onto the grey L-shaped sofa as he cried, "Where is it?"

"Can I help?" shouted Dotty, above the noise of the music.

Jay dropped the drawer. "What? No. Sorry." He walked across to an expensive-looking music system and twisted a knob. The music stopped and Jay apologised, "Sorry about the mess. But you know what it's like when you can't find something, yet you're certain you knew where you put it. It's so frustrating."

Dotty knelt down and reached for a piece of paper with her free hand, but Jay blurted, "Please, don't worry. I'll do that later. Besides, it'll give me a chance to go through them. I need to have a good clear out."

Dotty thought he would have done that before moving, but perhaps he hadn't had time.

"Do you enjoy living here?" she asked, standing up. "It must seem so quiet after your life in London."

"It's wonderful and peaceful. And if people want to visit, they have to phone up rather than pop round, so I can say I won't be in. The life of a country gent is very appealing and, despite yesterday's tragedy, it felt gratifying to be able to lend the house and gardens to the local community. I think we should organise other charity events. What do you think?"

"Events and parties aren't really my thing." Dotty was surprised by Jay's upbeat manner. She had expected to find him in mourning for his dead girlfriend, even though Rebecca had been angry and had threatened both him and Tracy when Dotty had seen her at the hall.

And yesterday, after Rebecca's death, they had appeared relieved, rather than upset. But to talk of organising events at such a time ...

"Nonsense. You'd make an excellent hostess. Speaking of which, tell me how we can create a wonderful English kitchen." Dotty saw his eyes flash behind his green-tinted glasses.

Still clutching the flowers, Dotty followed Jay through the hall and dining room into the kitchen.

"I'd like a country feel," declared Jay. "Rustic and homely rather than designer. You said there's a fireplace somewhere?"

Jay was wearing a pair of blue corduroy trousers and a short-sleeved fawn polo shirt and he leaned against the marble worktop, facing into the kitchen. His sockless feet were pushed into a pair of brown sheepskin mules.

"It's at the far end, so if you do want a large kitchen, like the Duke's, you'll have to remove the pantry and storerooms. Where would you put the fridges and chest freezer?"

Jay looked around. "There'll be room for two fridges in the kitchen, and the freezer can go in one of the outbuildings. What about the floor? These black and white chequerboard tiles give me a headache."

"You should find the flagstone floor underneath, like the rest of the house." Dotty walked across to the industrial stainless steel range oven and commented, "I bet this was expensive and it's probably a good oven. Would you like to keep it or replace it with an Aga range cooker?"

"An Aga. That's what all country kitchens have, with a rail above it for drying things."

Dotty turned and leaned against the cooker, the flowers hanging from her hand. "What about installing an electric oven and hob as well?" she suggested.

"Agas can be temperamental. And a pine dresser and kitchen table would add to the homely feel, but the main units will need to be installed by a professional kitchen designer. Would you like me to look around for one, or would you prefer to?"

"You look, and bring me a shortlist, or your preferred option."

The back door of the kitchen opened and Tracy walked in with soil covering his hands. "Some people have no respect. They've paddled over the borders in the formal gardens, squashing pansies and dahlias, and someone smashed a glass bottle."

"I think that was a vase which held these." Dotty lifted up her disorderly bunch of blooms. "It disappeared from the ladies' changing room yesterday."

"Why would someone want to hide it amongst the lavender?" Tracy crossed to a stainless-steel double sink and nudged one of the tap levers with the back of his hand.

As water cascaded out and washed away the dark soil, Dotty thought the butlers sink by the back door would be more suitable for the purpose, rather than the one used for food preparation.

There was a knock on the back door.

"That'll be for you," grunted Tracy. "Your friends have finished. Thankfully."

Dotty walked across the chequerboard kitchen floor and opened the back door. Keya stood outside, smiling. "How much longer will you be?" she asked.

"I think I'm nearly finished." She turned round and waited as Jay and Tracy were speaking in hushed tones by the sink. Through the running water she caught the words, "Not here," "Need to find it," and "I'll do it."

She wondered what they were talking about and if the item to be found was the one Jay had been searching for earlier.

In a slightly forced raised voice, she asked, "Is there anything else?"

Jay turned to her. "Keep a look out for furniture for the house, and for this kitchen. I want to sort it as soon as we can." He glanced across to the pantry. "I'll get some builders in to tear down these walls and then we'll know what space we have."

A furry face twitched its nose and whiskers in the pantry doorway. Jay picked up a plastic tub from the draining board and threw it at the mouse. "And find me a cat."

Dotty and Keya left the kitchen and at her car, Dotty removed the water bottles from her pockets and stuffed them in the pouch at the back of the driver's seat. As she lay the flowers on the back seat, Keya commented, "Nice flowers. Are you laying them in remembrance of Rebecca?"

Dotty shook her head and in a mournful tone replied, "No, they're a reminder that I need to buy some fresh ones and visit Al's grave."

CHAPTER TWENTY-ONE

On Thursday morning, Dotty drove steadily down a steep winding road and what she presumed was the edge of the Cotswold escarpment, to the village of Charlton-under-Cliffe, the home of the Fabulous Auction Boys' auction house.

A temporary black sign with 'Auction today' printed in white writing was secured to a short post in the grass verge at the entrance to the village.

Dotty followed a series of signs as they led her through the village, past a small shop and post office, and the local school, which was still closed for the summer holidays, to a church on a road which began to climb back up the escarpment. Another sign instructed her to park in a field behind the church.

She grinned to herself. There was nothing normal about Patrick and Dani Boy. They were an unusual partnership with the farmer-like Patrick and the Scottish goth figure Dani Boy. And their auction house was an old church.

At least there would be plenty of space, and it was probably cheap to rent.

As she followed yet more signs, she was directed to the auction office in a two-storey Victorian brick building next to the church, which had probably been the church hall.

The first people she saw were Amanda, from Cirencester Auctioneers, talking to Didier Vogt beside a blue-covered noticeboard. She was surprised to see Amanda at this auction but maybe, like her, she was buying for a private client.

Didier and Amanda joined the queue and Dotty crossed the hall and followed their example, standing behind an elderly man and woman who started arguing.

Dotty recognised them as the couple who had been sitting on a sofa at the front of Cirencester Auctioneers' auction. As the woman scolded her husband, Dotty wondered if she ever let him buy anything and if that was the reason they had to attend so many auctions.

The man turned away from his wife to study the auction catalogue and Dotty heard Amanda say, "The police came yesterday to question me again."

"Why?" asked Didier.

"They're still investigating the cause of Rebecca's death. The autopsy found high levels of histamine and her airways were inflamed."

"Which means what?" prompted Didier.

"That she was struggling to get air and oxygen into her lungs, and the high levels of histamine increased her heart rate, perhaps fatally."

"But what was the nasal spray for?"

"Apparently, antihistamines work to lower histamine levels, which is why the police are suspicious. Her levels should not have been that high and as her nasal spray mysteriously disappeared, the case remains open."

Amanda sniffed and rubbed her eyes. "We can't hold her funeral or say our goodbyes."

"What about this one?" the old man in front of Dotty asked, bringing her thoughts back to the present.

"Don't be daft. Where would we put it?" rebuked his wife.

Inside the old church, furniture was arranged into narrow rows, often with one piece stacked on top of another. Dotty turned the corner of one row and spotted Didier at the far end, squatting down and examining an open drawer in a piece of furniture.

He smiled and made a note in his catalogue.

Dotty cast her eye over the assortment of furniture as she slowly made her way along the row, but really she was interested in what Didier had found.

He'd ducked around the corner, leaving her free to inspect an attractive walnut side table. The front of the table curved gracefully in at the centre and the three brass handled drawers followed the line.

In typical Queen Anne style, the four cabriole legs, with the upper sections curving out, away from the table, and the lower sections curving in, creating an elegant s-shape. The legs ended in claw-and-ball feet, so named because they resembled a bird or animal claw grasping a round ball.

Overall, it was an extremely attractive piece of furniture, but it was likely to be a reproduction piece. Dotty pulled out a drawer, as she had seen Didier do, and was satisfied that the wood used for the back of the drawer was not walnut, but a cheaper type, probably pine. And the front and back of the drawers were attached with dovetail joints.

There was a slight crack on the side of the table, but that was not a bad thing. Wood shrank with age and cracks across the grain were a sign of a genuine antique, as was the lighter coloured wood visible in the crack.

She looked at the sticker on the table. Lot number 87. Opening the catalogue, she noted it was described as Queen Anne style, which meant a 1920s or 1930s reproduction, but what if this was a genuine Queen Anne side table from the 1720s to 1750s?

She felt her pulse quicken. A reproduction would make up to £1,000, but a genuine table would be worth three or four times that.

She stood up and appraised the delicate, graceful piece. The mellow walnut was in keeping with Jay's preference for lighter wood over darker mahogany. She would see what interest there was in it.

Mentally congratulating herself, she turned into the next row and found a large antique pine dresser. As she bent down to inspect the bottom cupboards, two people walked past.

She heard Didier say in a hushed, excited voice, "Come and look at this."

From the row behind the dresser, where the Queen Anne table was located, she heard Amanda reply, "It's beautiful. But is it the real thing?"

"I think so," replied Didier. "Look at the delicate carving on the leg."

Dotty smiled to herself. Didier did think the Queen Anne table was genuine.

An amplified voice announced, "Ladies and gentlemen. Find somewhere to squat. The fun and games are about to begin."

Dotty sat down on one of four dining chairs lined up facing the auctioneer's rostrum, which was actually the church's stone pulpit. Dotty hadn't realised the church had raised wooden balconies extending around all four sides, supported by carved wooden columns.

On three sides, people leaned against the edge of the balcony, waiting for the auction to begin, and on the far one she spotted Amanda.

From the front balcony, a screen hung down, which displayed a picture of a small mahogany clerk's desk with dark green leather covering its sloping top.

As Patrick climbed the steps to the pulpit, Didier slid onto a wooden chair at the end of a row in front of Dotty.

The first Lot Dotty was interested in was the antique pine Welsh dresser. It was a large piece, with four drawers over two double-fronted cupboards, and she hoped there would be limited interest as it was too big for most modern houses.

A picture of the dresser appeared on the hanging screen as Patrick announced, "We have a telephone bidder for this Lot."

A bespectacled lady held a mobile phone to her ear. After a minute she shook her head at Patrick, who leaned towards a small microphone mounted on the top of the pulpit, and said in an irritated tone, "If you ask to bid by telephone, have the courtesy to answer our call. Try again," he instructed the assistant, his face reddening.

This time, her call was answered. In a slightly bored voice, Patrick said, "Ask the caller if they are willing to bid up to the estimated value of £350, which, after all, is a condition of securing a telephone bid."

The lady spoke into her phone, listened and then said something to

Patrick whose face took on a deep red-purple colour. "Why do I have to deal with such idiots? Sorry, I know that is not professional, but when you request a telephone bid, you agree to bid over the reserve. Otherwise, please leave a proxy bid. Is the caller prepared to bid £300?"

The assistant spoke into her phone and then shook her head.

"Then tell them to stop wasting my time." Patrick shook his head of curly brown hair and addressed the room. "We'll start with an opening bid of £270."

He looked up at the balcony above Dotty and said, "280, 290." He looked up at the balcony again. "300. I'm out. Any advance of £300?"

Dotty raised her bidder number, feeling more confident than she had at Cirencester Auctioneers.

"New bidder. 320." Patrick looked up at the balcony again. "330." Dotty and the unseen bidder raised the price to £390. It was Dotty's bid, and she thought the price was modest for such a large piece of furniture. Besides, Jay did want to remodel his kitchen quickly and the dresser would be a central piece. She raised her bidder number again.

"400," announced Patrick. "410, 420. Any advance on 420?" He looked up at the balcony but did not raise his price. Had that bidder finished? Patrick looked around the room and held up his gavel. "Selling at £420. Going once. Going twice. Sold." He dropped the gavel and peered at Dotty, who held up her number.

Didier turned round and gave her the thumbs up. She had bought her first item at an auction without anyone else's help. She sat up taller. She could do this.

CHAPTER TWENTY-TWO

Dotty sat back on the wooden dining chair inside the large stone church of the Fabulous Auction Boys' sale.

After securing a large Welsh dresser, with a bid of £420, she needed a cup of tea, but she didn't want to miss the Queen Anne table. Excitedly, she drummed her foot against the stone floor.

Lot 77. Only ten more to go. Lot 86. The table was next. She rolled her shoulders back, found her auction number, and composed herself.

In front of her, Didier looked up at Amanda, who nodded. Was he bidding for a client of hers?

"Lot 87," announced Patrick. "An attractive Queen Anne style walnut table. There has already been some interest in this piece, and I'll open the bidding at £860."

Dotty's enthusiasm waned. If that was the opening price, where would the bidding go? Other people must also think it was a genuine piece. But wasn't that good news?

She sat still and waited as Patrick looked down at the front of the stone pulpit and turned his head from side-to-side, presumably alternating between the internet and the bids he'd written down from proxy bidders.

"£1,250," he stated, still looking down. The price on the hanging screen at the front of the old church did not change. "If there are no more internet bids, I'll ask the room." He looked up. "Any advance on £1,250?"

Dotty hesitated.

In front of her, Didier raised his catalogue, which he'd curled into a tube shape, and nodded at Patrick. The price continued to increase to £1,800. "I'm out," announced Patrick, which meant he'd reached the top price of his proxy bids.

Dotty bit her lip. Should she bid?

Didier looked up at Amanda, who grinned back at him.

Her heart thumping, Dotty raised her hand. She wasn't going to let Didier and Amanda win this one.

"New bidder. £1,850."

Didier and Dotty pushed the price to £2,400. Dotty was sweating, even though it was cool inside the old church. The audience was hushed as they waited for her next move. She'd never felt such power. What an adrenaline rush. Her heart pounded as she raised her bidder number again.

"£2,450." Patrick declared and looked at Didier, who turned to Amanda on the balcony. Her mouth was fixed in a thin line, and she shook her head.

Didier declined to bid.

"Sold for £2,450," declared Patrick, bringing his gavel down. Around her, Dotty was aware of excited whispering and people muttering and glancing in her direction.

Didier stood up and approached her. He held out his hand for her to shake and said, "Well done."

As Dotty had two pieces of furniture to transport, one of which was the large Welsh dresser, she had called Norman who told her he'd come with the Land Rover and trailer and be with her in an hour and a quarter, maybe an hour and a half. She hoped he'd be OK, towing the trailer up the steep escarpment road with its load of furniture.

She queued up at the auction office and asked them to bill Akemans for her purchases.

When she'd been handed her stamped receipt, she went in search of a cup of tea and found another room in the hall, set out with wooden classroom tables with tubular metal legs and matching chairs. At the far end there was a hatch through which a woman was handing a customer a mug.

She wondered where Didier and Amanda were as they had left the auction room immediately after the Queen Anne table had been sold. Perhaps there was nothing more of interest to them and they'd left.

After drinking her tea, she returned to the auction room, waiting for Norman's call.

Her phone vibrated in her hand and when she answered it Aunt Beanie announced, "We're out front."

She stood up and walked outside, finding Norman and Aunt Beanie standing by the lowered ramp of a two-horse trailer, which was parked on the short drive at the front of the church.

"I couldn't resist accompanying Norman," declared Aunt Beanie. "This is so exciting. What have you bought?"

"A large antique pine Welsh dresser and a walnut Queen Anne table."

"A reproduction table?"

"No, I think it's the real thing," replied Dotty, feeling a little less certain than she had when she bid for it.

"What, here?"

"Ladies, shall we collect the items, rather than standing about discussing them?" suggested Norman.

Dotty found a porter and handed him her receipt. He returned several minutes later wheeling the dresser on a trolley, although it hung over the back and was being supported by his colleague. With Norman's help they lifted it into the back of the trailer, protecting it with old blankets.

"I thought we'd need those," stated Aunt Beanie. "Now, this table of yours."

The two porters returned carrying the table which they placed on the ground beside Dotty and Aunt Beanie.

"Thank you," called Norman from inside the trailer where he was securing the dresser with ropes. "We can take it from here."

Aunt Beanie prowled around the table, her lips pressed together.

Silently, she opened a drawer and examined it. Pushing it closed, she stood up and pronounced, "It's a forgery."

"What?" cried Dotty, her stomach clenching. "You mean it's not genuine but a reproduction?"

"No, I mean it's a modern forgery. Exactly like the ones Chief Inspector Ringrose discovered with the stolen house items earlier this week. We hadn't realised pieces were already on the market."

"But how can you tell? There's a crack on the side where the wood has shrunk, and the wood underneath is a lighter colour. The drawers are backed with pine, I think, and there are dovetail joints."

"That's the first indication," explained Aunt Beanie. "In an eighteenth-century piece the dovetail joints would be fewer and less uniform as they were created by hand. These are machine-made with a few marks from a chisel to make them look hand cut. And feel underneath."

Dotty did as instructed.

"It's smooth and has been sanded by a machine, not by hand."

Aunt Beanie stood back and sighed. "Someone with great talent made this and, in the future, it may well be worth something. Quality wood has been used and the detailing on the legs is intricate, but I'm afraid you cannot pass this on to Jay Newton as a genuine Queen Anne table."

Dotty looked down at the broken concrete driveway and felt the tears welling up in her eyes. She was a failure.

CHAPTER TWENTY-THREE

On Friday morning, the 1st of September, Dotty drove to work passing through the village of Coln Akeman and following the River Coln for half a mile to Akemans converted mill buildings.

She pulled into her usual parking space, feeling less like a member of staff and more like an imposter.

The gathering clouds and prospect of rain did not help her bleak mood. She had hoped to accompany Aunt Beanie on a walk over the weekend to visit the Uffington White Horse, a prehistoric figure carved into a chalk hillside, but the weather forecast didn't look good.

She picked up her bundle of pink, white and purple alstroemeria wrapped in an old newspaper, and her wicker basket, and walked towards the antiques centre.

Her first job was to check her first-floor stall and change the flowers in the large, blue, peacock decorated vase. As she reached the top of the metal staircase, she was both pleased and concerned about the obvious gaps.

It was great to be selling items, but as supplies from Gilly, the auction house, and other vendors had dried up, she had nothing left to fill the gaps. Still, the school holidays finished next week, so the antiques centre should be quieter.

Dotty found Gilly in the auction house office making herself a cup of tea, and as she placed her basket on the worn, green leather top of the reception desk, Gilly asked, "Did you have fun yesterday? The sale at the Fabulous Auction Boys is quite an experience, isn't it? Did Patrick have a rant about anything? I think half the people who attend that auction do so for the theatrical aspect."

Despite her sombre mood, Dotty couldn't help smiling at the recollection of Patrick berating the telephone bidder. "He was annoyed that a bidder had asked to be called and bid by phone, but then declined to bid up to the reserve price."

Dotty removed her retro-style metal sandwich tin, with an image of a chicken on the top, and a metal handle, like a suitcase, and she stowed it in the small under-counter fridge.

Gilly handed her a cup of tea and asked, "Did you buy anything?"

"A large antique pine Welsh dresser and …"

"Good morning, Gillian, Dorothy," remarked David Rook brusquely. "Is Georgina about?"

Without waiting for a reply, he strode across the reception area and through the door into the auction house.

"David didn't look very happy," observed Dotty. There had been no playful gleam in his dark eyes, which had been more watchful and hooded than usual.

"Probably had one of his mystery trips cancelled," responded Gilly, picking up her tea. "Well done at the triathlon, by the way. Peter was very impressed by how much your swimming has improved."

"What's that doing here?" exclaimed David in a shaky voice as he returned to the office. He was blinking rapidly and Dotty thought his naturally tanned skin was a shade lighter.

"What?" asked Dotty. The only items in the auction room were those Norman and Aunt Beanie had brought back from yesterday's auction. "The Welsh dresser or the Queen Anne style table." She emphasised the word style.

"Yes, the table. Who brought it here?"

Dotty was upset and annoyed with herself for thinking she'd bought a genuine table, and no doubt the cost would be deducted from her wages, but she didn't know why David was so upset. Was he worried about Akemans' reputation?

"I'm sorry," she blurted. "I didn't know it was counterfeit. I honestly thought it was a real Queen Anne table."

"Oh dear. How much did you pay?" asked Gilly.

"£2,450," replied Dotty, with a bitter smile.

Gilly winced.

"I know, but I did check it. Obviously not well enough, but Didier Vogt was interested in it. He was the underbidder, and I thought if he was willing to pay that price, it must be the real thing."

"Didier was the underbidder?" growled David.

"Yes. I thought he was buying it for a client of Amanda's, from Cirencester Auctioneers."

"Amanda was there?" This time, David sounded alarmed.

"Yes, I think she was with Didier."

David was silent and appeared to be thinking over what she had told him.

Gilly laid a hand on Dotty's arm. "Don't worry. It isn't always easy to tell genuine period furniture from early twentieth century reproductions."

"But it's not a reproduction. Aunt Beanie says it's modern. That it's a forgery."

"She does, does she," stated David flatly.

"Why?" asked Gilly.

Dotty sipped her tea before replying. "Because the Rural, Heritage and Wildlife Unit found similar items with a collection of stolen things."

"But this item isn't stolen, is it?" Gilly's voice rose in pitch.

"No," replied Dotty dully. It might be better for her if it was.

Gilly pushed her orange-framed glasses up her nose. "Then why don't we enter it in this month's auction and describe it as 'in the style of' and see if we can recoup some of the money you paid? We've all been duped at some point or another."

"No," declared David sharply.

Dotty and Gilly looked at him.

He added, "We can't sell it here."

"Because of the reputation of the auction house?" asked Dotty.

David ignored her as he drew his lips together in thought. "I'll contact an auctioneer I know who holds weekly auctions in one of the London suburbs. He won't ask any questions."

David took a deep cleansing breath as he composed himself and then asked in a polite tone, "And did you also buy the Welsh dresser? It's a nice piece, but a large one. I presume it's for Jay Newton's kitchen."

Dotty was relieved to move on from discussing the Queen Anne style table and replied, "Yes, he's organised builders to rip out the internal partition walls and return the kitchen to the single room it was when the Duke lived there. He wants a country style, so I thought the dresser would make a lovely centre piece."

"It certainly will," confirmed David. "And how much did you pay for it?"

"£420."

"Good girl. We can charge Jay £1,000 and recoup some of our losses from the table. Now if you'll excuse me." He left through the door into the antiques centre.

"I'm sorry about the table," repeated Gilly. "But at least David suggested a solution. Now, what are you working on today?"

"I've put together a list of people who might have items to sell at this month's auction. I'm going to contact them and see if they're still interested. Then I'll organise deliveries. September's auction will be here before we know it, but at least with the end of the school holidays, it'll be quieter in the antiques centre."

Gilly laughed. "Don't you believe it! Once the children go back, retired people have their holidays. We can expect them to arrive by the busload."

Dotty's shoulders drooped. She would have to find more stock for her stall.

CHAPTER TWENTY-FOUR

Dotty was satisfied with her morning's work, and she'd put the fiasco of the Queen Anne table out of her mind as she contacted people about September's auction.

She already had items from two house clearances, and office items from a firm of receivers who used the auction regularly to sell the various assets they found themselves with when they took over a failing business.

She was sitting at the reception desk when the door to the antiques centre opened and Keya walked in, wearing her black and white police uniform.

"Hiya," greeted Keya as she placed her black hat, with its black and white chequerboard band and a large metal badge, on Dotty's desk. She leaned forward and whispered, "I know I shouldn't, but can I trade some juicy police info for a cup of tea and one of your yummy sandwiches, which I'm sure you've brought to work today."

Dotty narrowed her eyes but as her friend smiled back mischievously, she couldn't help laughing.

She made fresh cups of tea and removed her sandwich tin from the fridge, placing it on the green leather top of the antique mahogany reception desk. As she opened the tin, she asked, "So what's your news?"

Keya peered into the open tin and enquired, "Which are the vegetarian ones?"

"The white bread sandwiches are tuna, sweetcorn and mayonnaise. Can you eat those?"

"Yes," replied Keya, picking one up and biting into it.

Dotty sipped her tea and waited.

Although still chewing, Keya spluttered, "First, I think you know about the hoard Chief Inspector Ringrose found on the day of the triathlon. Well, actually some children found it when they were playing explorers and one of their mums called it in."

Dotty signed. "I know he found some modern furniture forgeries. I was duped into buying something similar yesterday at an auction."

"Really?" Keya's eyes bulged.

"Yes, but I'd rather not talk about it."

Keya's mouth drooped, and she looked disappointed, but Dotty narrowed her lips and refused to say anything further.

"The forgeries weren't the only items he found. There were also some stolen items, which have been linked to a house robbery in Kent."

"Aunt Beanie mentioned stolen items, but not where they came from. What's the chief inspector doing about them?"

"He's gone to Maidstone today to see the Kent police and visit the owners whose house was burgled. They've just returned from holiday and didn't know anything about the break-in."

"Does the chief inspector suspect a gang?"

Keya bit into her sandwich and appeared to be considering Dotty's question as she chewed. Dotty picked up a roast beef and horseradish sandwich.

"I overheard the chief inspector and Aunt Beanie talking about it," Keya admitted. "They do think a gang is involved, and they kept talking about old cases and selling items at auction to raise money."

Dotty thought of the table she'd bought and felt miserable again.

"You better watch out. You don't want to get into trouble with us for handling stolen goods." Keya grinned and added, "But the chief inspector didn't think Akemans would be affected."

"I wonder why." Dotty drew her eyebrows together.

"Maybe because of Aunt Beanie's connection, and I bet David could spot a stolen item a mile away."

Or a fake one, thought Dotty.

Perhaps Keya noticed Dotty's glum mood as she leaned forward and said in a conspiratorial tone, "I've more news. As the chief inspector is away today, I'm in charge and I was called to a suspected burglary this morning."

"Suspected?"

"A neighbour noticed a light which shouldn't have been on."

"How did the neighbour know that?"

"Because the light was in Rebecca Randall's cottage."

"Oh," replied Dotty, understanding.

"And the neighbour was right. Someone did break into Rebecca's cottage. It's a lovely house, by the way. Picture postcard with mellow Cotswold stone, a thatched roof and a small garden leading down to the river on the outskirts of Upton, near Burford. I dream of a place like that but there's no way I could afford it on my salary."

"What had been taken?" asked Dotty.

"Well, that's the funny thing. I couldn't see that anything had. All her jewellery was still in a drawer in her bedroom. And she had some lovely pieces. But the cottage was a real mess. The cupboards and drawers had been emptied, books had been pulled out of bookcases, and the cushions pulled off the chairs and sofa. Even the air vents in the kitchen had been unscrewed. I've no idea what the thief was looking for."

"Or if they found it," muttered Dotty.

"I called Sergeant Unwin, and he came straight over. He was probably bored or just wanted to get away from Inspector Evans. Anyway, he said the break-in supports his theory that there's something suspicious about Rebecca Randall's death. That it might not be from natural causes."

"But what else could it be?" asked Dotty, although she also had a nagging feeling she was missing something.

"The autopsy results showed high levels of histamine."

"Amanda from Cirencester Auctioneer's said that."

"When?" asked Keya sharply.

"At the auction yesterday. She was talking to Didier Vogt and said

Sergeant Unwin had interviewed her again. But I still don't understand why high levels of histamine are important and, if Sergeant Unwin is right, how someone could deliberately manipulate them."

Keya sat up and explained, "When the body has an allergic reaction to something, say pollen - we know she had hay fever - the body produces histamine and this causes the membranes of the nose to inflame and produce a protective mucus lining. That's why people sneeze. But they can struggle to catch their breath if the inflamed lining obstructs their airways."

"You know a lot about it."

Kaya's cheeks flushed. "I recently did a first aid training course with the unit. Ambulances can take up to half an hour to reach some areas of the Cotswolds, so I might be a first responder and need to know what to do while I wait for an ambulance."

As Keya picked up her cup of tea she added, "But I just think it was an unfortunate accident, made worse because it was a warm day and Rebecca was running hard. But the sergeant's in trouble because Inspector Evans blames him for losing Rebecca's antihistamine nasal spray, even though Inspector Evans was in the same room."

"So what is Sergeant Unwin going to do?"

"I've no idea. But I'm sure he'll be told to close the case unless he turns up evidence to support his theory."

Keya's radio crackled.

She unhooked it from her uniform and, holding it close to her face, spoke into it. "Sergeant Varma, over."

"Can you return to Lilac Cottage? The neighbour has reported someone acting suspiciously. Over."

"I'm on my way. Out." Keya hooked her radio back on and took a last swig of her tea.

"Thank you for lunch but that's Rebecca's Randall's cottage. I better go back, even though the intruders are bound to be gone by the time I get there. But at least it's better than chasing my tail trying to identify people who are fly-tipping. Do you know, this week someone dumped a load of sawdust, offcuts of quality wood and bits of plywood."

She shook her head as she pushed back her chair, knocking it over as she stood. "Oh toda!" she exclaimed.

Keya dashed out of the office, through the door leading to the antiques centre, but returned a minute later.

Dotty stood and held out her friend's police hat.

"Thanks," said Keya, smiling ruefully.

Dotty shouted at Keya's retreating back. "Let me know what's happened."

Dotty finished writing an email to a client, telling them Akemans would be delighted to sell the furniture from their spare bedroom in September's auction, and asking if they would be organising its delivery or if they would like her to do so and add it to their bill.

Her mobile phone rang and, seeing Keya's number, she picked it up and answered excitedly, "Hi, what did you find?"

"As suspected, whoever was here has gone. I don't think they went into the house, but I found a garage up a small lane at the back of Rebecca's cottage and the side door had been forced open."

"Was anything missing?" asked Dotty quickly.

"Some boxes from a shelf. There are dust marks where they used to be, but that could be thieves, or Rebecca could have moved the boxes herself. Anyway, at least they didn't leave a mess like they did in the house. It's almost as if it's different set of intruders."

Dotty replied, "Or they found what they were looking for."

CHAPTER TWENTY-FIVE

As forecast, Saturday was wet and blustery but Sunday dawned bright and clear, and weak sunlight seeped around the sides of Dotty's daisy-patterned bedroom curtains.

She was sitting up in bed, reading a book about an amateur sleuth attempting to solve a murder in a fictitious Cotswold village. With a cup of tea on her bedside table and Earl Grey curled up on the white duvet cover beside her, Dotty was content.

"Cooee," called Aunt Beanie from downstairs. "Can I come up?"

Before Dotty had a chance to reply, she heard the creak of the old wooden staircase and Aunt Beanie pushed open her bedroom door. "How about that walk to Uffington's White Horse? It's a lovely fresh day and I feel like getting out. Norman will sit with Cliff once he's milked Buttercup."

"Oh." Dotty knew her response sounded weak, but she was enjoying lounging in bed with her book and Earl Grey. But Earl Grey uncurled himself and jumped off the bed. He glanced up at Aunt Beanie before disappearing through the bedroom doorway.

Dotty yawned. "I suppose I should go with you. I haven't been swimming or done any exercise since the triathlon."

Aunt Beanie beamed. "Good girl. I'll make you a bacon sandwich and see you in the kitchen in twenty minutes." She retreated back down the stairs and Dotty heard her call, "Come through, Earl Grey. Agatha's in the kitchen."

"There's no need to walk all the way up the hill," Aunt Beanie exclaimed as she turned the farm's Land Rover Defender onto a single-track road. She drove up a steep hill and turned left into a small muddy car park with puddles filled by the previous day's rain.

It was busy but unperturbed, Aunt Beanie pulled onto the end of the row, parking half on the parking area and half on the grassy bank. With the car tilted at an angle, Dotty struggled to climb out of the passenger door, and she used the side of the vehicle to guide her to flatter ground.

A springer spaniel bounced over and jumped up, depositing its muddy paws on her jeans.

"Jasper," a man called, and the dog bounded away.

They climbed over a wooden stile, next to a white metal sign warning them of grazing sheep and that all dogs must be kept on their leads. In front of them, Jasper bounded around, seemingly oblivious to his owner's calls.

They crossed a narrow road, passed through a green, lichen-covered gate, and strode along a well-worn grassy track which stretched out in front of them. It followed the contours of the hill and Dotty could see miles of Oxfordshire and Gloucestershire countryside spread out below them.

It was a fantastic view and Dotty stopped to admire it. Clusters of trees and the dark outline of villages with protruding church steeples broke up the patchwork of green, fawn and brown fields.

"You used to be able to see the towers of Didcot power station until they were demolished," commented Aunt Beanie. She was wearing her multicoloured wool jacket, and she tightened the bow of her yellow headscarf against the blustery wind on top of the hill.

They continued to follow the path up a steady incline until they reached another metal sign asking them not to walk on the white horse. Dotty peered down the hillside at the outline of a horse which resembled a child's pencil drawing.

Standing next to her, Aunt Beanie explained, "The white horse is thought to be a prehistoric figure created by carving trenches in the white chalk. And do you see the hill that's in its shadow?"

"The lone, flat-topped one, beside the road?"

"That's Dragon Hill. So called because of the legend that St George slayed the dragon on it with his sword. It's a lovely story, although many other places claim to be the location of that mythical event."

The grassy path curved to the right, and Dotty felt she was walking on ancient ramparts with a wide grassy ditch below her and a raised central section.

"Uffington Castle was one of several Iron Age hill forts built along The Ridgeway and there have been settlements of some kind here from Neolithic through to Roman times. And here," Aunt Beanie tapped the top of a faded white, waist-high concrete column, "is the highest point in Oxfordshire."

The grassy footpath continued its large circle around the mound of the ancient hill fort and as they turned back towards the car park, it ran alongside a wider chalk track along which a group of four mud-splattered cyclists rode.

"I wonder if they're cycling the whole Ridgeway," mused Aunt Beanie.

"What is The Ridgeway?" Dotty asked. She'd heard people talk about it and thought it was something to do with Stonehenge and the druids.

"It has been described as England's oldest road and was popular because of its height, which meant travellers could see attackers, and also avoid wet lowland ground. I think the official trail is about 85 miles long, starting between Aylesbury and Luton and ending at Overton Hill, near Ogbourne St George, on the way to Marlborough. But it was originally thought to link the Dorset Coast to the Wash in Norfolk."

"And Stonehenge?" asked Dotty.

"Ah," grinned Aunt Beanie. "Although there is no visible track, probably because roads and canals have destroyed it, many consider a path branched off the main Ridgeway at the standing stones of Aylesbury and linked them with those at Stonehenge."

As they stopped and watched the retreating cyclists heading westwards, the older woman added, "Just think, this track could have been taken by King Arthur's Knights of the Round Table and it's highly likely that King Alfred's Wessex troops tramped across it between battles."

Aunt Beanie drove back around the outskirts of Swindon, along the dual carriageway towards Cirencester.

"Oh look," she exclaimed. "There's a sign for a car boot sale. You're not in a rush to get home, are you?"

Dotty wasn't, although the thought of sitting by the warm Aga in Aunt Beanie's kitchen or curling up in her favourite high-backed chair was appealing. But she hadn't visited a public car boot sale before. And she needed stock for her stall, although she only had the twenty-pound note she'd hastily stuffed into the pocket of her jeans.

Aunt Beanie turned off the road into the car park of an empty retail unit which stood forlornly at the far end, its once bright store signage faded and broken. She fished around in the unused ash tray for some pound coins to pay the man on the gate.

"Oh good, there are some catering vans. I'd love a cup of tea, but first we should look around. How about I meet you at the refreshment area in half an hour to compare notes? And remember to haggle if something catches your eye."

They climbed out of the Land Rover and Dotty watched Aunt Beanie's retreating back. She slowly wandered along the first line of stalls.

There were a variety of vehicles, including white vans, smart 4x4s and smaller saloon cars, all parked nose in with their rear boots open facing the public. Some had clothes hangers secured to their open boots from which hung jackets, scarves and shirts, but in front of all of them were plastic or wooden tables piled high with an assortment of items.

She passed a lady selling baby clothes and items including a potty and even a Moses basket on a stand. Several were selling children's toys and games. A young boy looked hopefully at passers-by, his various Lego creations laid out on the white plastic table in front of him.

She stopped at a stall selling porcelain figurines, bowls, and delicate decorative trinket boxes. Such items were popular in the antiques centre as long as they weren't too expensive.

"Hello," said the stallholder, a lady with frizzy white hair. "They're all part of a lifetime collecting, but my Sid says I have too many and I need to get rid of some."

"That's a shame," replied Dotty sympathetically.

"I suppose so, but they've been hidden away in the spare room for the last five years, gathering dust."

"How much are they?"

"£5 a piece," announced the woman.

Dotty felt for the £20 note in her pocket. At £5 each, she was unlikely to make a profit.

She smiled apologetically. "Too much for me."

"I'm open to offers, particularly if you buy a few."

Dotty hesitated and picked up a round trinket box with purple pansies painted on the lid.

"Pretty, isn't it?" the stallholder said. She reached across and picked up a figurine of a shepherdess. "And what about this one?"

"I prefer these." Dotty reached across for a pair of decorative shell-shaped dishes, edged with gold and painted with individual flowers.

She also found a figurine of a black and white cat, and a blue and white Chinese style rectangular dish.

"That's five items in total," calculated the stallholder. "I could sell you those for £20."

Dotty did have twenty pounds, but she didn't want to spend it all at this stall.

"Would you take £15?" she asked tentatively.

The woman looked around as people passed her stall without interest. "Go on then. And I'll wrap them in some old newspapers Sid was complaining to me about. He said they were gathering dust, but do you think he did anything about them?"

The lady carefully wrapped each piece and placed them in a sturdy plastic bag. Dotty would have brought her own if she'd known she'd be visiting a car boot sale. She received her change in five £1 coins, thanked the white-haired stallholder, and moved on.

On a row near the front of the car boot sale she spotted a record cover protruding out of a cardboard box, beneath a while plastic table displaying hand tools and what she thought were car parts.

She bent down and removed the record sleeve as one of the three youths, who were manning the stall, remarked, "Bit before your time, isn't it?"

Feeling the heat in her cheeks, Dotty tried to ignore the comment. She turned the record over and was surprised by an image of an oversized green newt on a dark street background. The title was, "Cries of the Street," written by Jay Newton and performed by the Spinning Newts.

This was Jay's band. She had no idea if the record was worth much, or if Tracy, who she knew collected the band's records, would want it, but she asked, "How much is this?"

"A tenner," replied the youth nonchalantly.

"I only have £5." Dotty fished the pound coins out of her pocket and held them up to the young man.

"That'll do." He grabbed the money out of her palm. She turned to walk on, but he called, "And the rest of the box. It's all together."

Dotty wasn't sure she wanted the contents of the box, but rather than get into an argument with the young man, she muttered, "Thank you," and slotted the record back into it.

She balanced her plastic bag of porcelain on top of the box, lifted it up, and carried it away. It wasn't as heavy as she had expected and the refreshment stalls were close by.

"You've been busy," remarked Aunt Beanie.

Dotty peered around the side of the box and saw Aunt Beanie sitting at a lightweight metal table with two paper cups of tea on it.

She placed the box carefully on the ground and sat down, picking up a cup of tea.

"Thank you," she said.

"So, what's in your box?"

"I'm not sure. It came with a record of the Spinning Newts. But I also bought some pretty trinkets for my stall at Akemans, so now I'm spent up."

"That's a shame. There's some glassware I wanted to show you. But I can lend you some money if we find anything else you want to buy."

CHAPTER TWENTY-SIX

On Monday morning, Dotty placed her rattan basket on the worn green leather top of the reception desk in Akemans auction office. Careful not to damage the porcelain items she'd bought at the car boot sale, she removed her metal sandwich tin and placed it in the under-counter fridge.

She returned to her desk with a cup of tea, placed the basket on the floor, and switched on her computer.

"Good morning, Dorothy. I was hoping to catch you." She hadn't noticed David enter the office, and she jumped in surprise. He held out an auction catalogue.

"This is for Hall, Edgar and Seabrook's auction near Gloucester tomorrow. The blue upholstered gilt wood sofas and chairs, which Zenobia Richardson reupholstered for Windrush Hall, are in the auction, together with a pair of brass standard lamps and the round mahogany hall table, all of which we sold in June."

"Do you want me to go to the auction?" Dotty wasn't sure that was a good idea. Not after her mistake at the Fabulous Auction Boys' sale.

"Yes. I've marked the items, and a wardrobe which might also be of interest. Check they are the ones we sold and that they're not damaged or repaired in any way. I've spoken to Jay this morning and written down the price he is willing to pay for each piece."

Did he not trust her to speak to Jay? Probably not.

"And my contact in London sold the table you mistakenly bought at last week's auction for £1,500. With the transport costs, we are out of pocket by just over a £1,000, but I expect we can make that back with the Welsh dresser and tomorrow's purchases, depending on how much you have to pay."

David left the catalogue with Dotty and she spent an hour answering emails. After that, she picked up the plastic bag and carried her porcelain purchases through to the antiques centre and up the metal staircase to her stall on the first floor.

She felt conflicted. She was pleased David still trusted her to attend the auction on her own, but he had been careful to mark the items she should buy and also the maximum price she should pay. But in a way, that was a relief.

At her stall, she removed the newspaper wrapped items from their bag and placed them on a table as she continued to think about the auction the next day. What if there was something else she liked? Could she bid for it, or did she need David's permission?

She unwrapped the figurine of the black-and-white cat and smiled at the fun character as she stood it on the table. Maybe this was what she was best at. Buying and selling attractive but low value items.

She unwrapped the shell-shaped dishes from a double piece of newspaper, but as she lifted the first one, a black-and-white photograph caught her eye. She stared at the image in the old, yellowing newspaper.

She was looking at a man's face, which was familiar, despite having plenty of hair instead of his now shaved head. Underneath the caption read 'The accused Tracy Ivers'. Accused of what?

She removed the second shell-shaped dish revealing a photograph of a girl and man standing in front of a modern-looking brick building, with the caption 'Becky Randall speaking emotionally outside Birmingham Crown Court'.

Dotty smoothed the yellowing newspaper and read the headlines. 'Spinning Newts' Assistant Manager Convicted of Underage Rape'.

The article started with a quote from Tracy Ivers, which read, 'I am truly sorry about what has happened, but I don't believe I have done anything wrong. Miss Randall told myself and other members of the band that she was seventeen and we had no reason to doubt her. I never forced her to do anything against her will."

Dotty read on. Becky Randall had been a groupie of the Spinning Newts following them on their UK summer tour. There was a photograph of her scantily dressed in the front row at a concert.

She had become friendly with the band members who believed she was seventeen, but she had been only fifteen years old. Tracy Ivers, who was clearly the same Tracy who lived with Jay Newton at Windrush Hall, had been convicted and jailed for three years.

Wow. So there was one person with a motive to harm Rebecca Randall, but what would Tracy achieve by killing her? If he kept quiet, nobody would know about the case, unless Rebecca had threatened to tell people.

Dotty carefully rolled up the newspaper article, fearing that folding the old paper would damage it.

She unwrapped the remaining items and arranged them on a table at the front of her stall. She'd bought them for £3 each. The cat she'd price at £4, the blue and white dish at £6, and the trinket box at £8.

She picked up the shell-shaped dishes which were very attractive. Although hers was a bargain stall, she didn't want to let the dishes go too cheaply. She'd price them at £20 for the pair.

After moving other items around on her stall, to make the gaps less obvious, she returned to the auction office and found Sergeant Unwin standing in front of the reception desk, reading something on his mobile phone. He wore a dark suit with a grey tie tied in a fat knot, and a dark shirt.

"Can I help you?" Dotty asked him politely.

She was wearing a long-sleeved navy dress with large pink spots and a V-neck, which was cut lower than she was entirely comfortable with.

The sergeant's gaze lingered on her as he drawled, "I hope so."

She really couldn't make him out. One day he was eyeing her up and the next he dismissed her. But was she really that bothered? He was attractive, with his dark hair and rugged looks, and he certainly kept himself fit.

But he had a materialistic approach to life and seemed more concerned with how he, and those associated with him, looked, or at least how other people perceived them. She supposed she thought him rather shallow.

She placed the rolled-up newspaper on her desk and asked the sergeant, "Coffee?" She walked to the back of the office and switched on the white plastic kettle.

"Please, strong and black," replied Sergeant Unwin.

As she prepared the drinks, Sergeant Unwin remained silent, until he suddenly asked, "Where did you find this? And why haven't you informed us about it?"

She turned and nearly dropped his cup of coffee. He'd unrolled and flattened the old piece of newspaper on top of her desk.

In a shrill voice, she replied, "It was used to wrap an item I bought at a car boot sale yesterday. I've only just unpacked it." But she hadn't been sure she would have informed him. She'd probably have spoken to Keya about it instead.

Dotty handed the sergeant his coffee and sipped her tea, not wanting to offer an opinion on the newspaper article.

"You realise this gives Tracy Ivers a motive to murder Rebecca Randall?"

"Does it?" she replied. "Why would he want to reopen something like that? I'm sure he'd prefer it stayed buried so he could continue his quiet life in the Cotswolds."

The sergeant tapped the green leather on top of the desk. "Rebecca drove a new BMW 8 series convertible and wouldn't have received much change for £100,000."

"That much for a car? What's the point?"

Sergeant Unwin frowned at her and she remembered Keya had once told her he was a car buff. Her dismissive approach to expensive cars was bound to disappoint him, but she only needed a car to get from one place to another, quickly and safely.

There was so much more she could do with £100,000. Like help other people, but clearly Rebecca hadn't thought so.

"The point is," repeated the sergeant, "that she couldn't afford that car on her auctioneer's wages. She might have bought and sold some antiques to supplement her salary but expensive items, not like the stuff you sell here. More Sotheby's and Gainfords."

The sergeant's derogatory attitude irritated Dotty. She was proud to work at Akemans and sometimes they did sell expensive antiques, like those which had been at Windrush Hall before Jay Newton bought the house.

But perhaps it wasn't antiques per se that Rebecca had been involved with, but the counterfeit furniture and stolen items from the house in Kent. Perhaps there had been other robberies.

"But I suspect her game was blackmail," announced Sergeant Unwin.

That had been Dotty's initial thought when she'd read the newspaper article, but she doubted Tracy had £100,000 to pay Rebecca.

"There was the break-in at her house," continued the sergeant, "which might have been one of her victims searching for whatever evidence she held against them. For that amount of money, you have to think of someone rich, or famous, or both."

"You mean Jay Newton, don't you?"

"That is who I was thinking of. He could have paid the blackmail money for his man, Tracy."

"But they were going out, Rebecca and Jay. Perhaps the car was a gift, or something ..." Dotty's voice trailed off. It was a very expensive gift, and Rebecca and Jay had not looked a loving couple when she'd seen them together at Windrush Hall. And she was sure Rebecca had threatened Jay and Tracy. Perhaps there was something to Sergeant Unwin's theory.

Sergeant Unwin remarked, "I heard Rebecca was bored of the former rock singer and was moving on to an antique dealer or two. One of them you might know. Now what would I do if I was an attractive, yet unsophisticated country girl working in a provincial antiques centre and a debonair valuer, from one of London's top auction houses, started paying me attention? And then another provincial female auctioneer muscled in and stole my admirer's interest."

He stared intently at Dotty.

Flustered, she stumbled over her words. "I don't understand. What do you mean?"

"I think you know exactly what I mean."

"You think I had something to do with Rebecca's death because you say she was involved with Gilmore Chapman?"

"It's a theory." The sergeant crossed his arms.

"But I had no idea they were together." It was Amanda she'd seen Gilmore put his arm round at the triathlon and he hadn't seemed particularly upset about Rebecca's death. Was Sergeant Unwin just trying to goad her?

Anyway, what had Gilmore to do with the sergeant? He often paid her compliments when he saw her, and he had asked her to join him for dinner when she visited London, but he hadn't gone out of his way to pursue her romantically. He was just being polite.

She was fed up with the sergeant's jibes and the way he looked at her, which was either admiring but rather crude, or disdainful.

"Sergeant, I've been a widow for just over a year, and I've spent that year settling into a new job, a new home, and a new life. Gilmore Chapman has been very supportive and whilst he is an attractive man, there is nothing between us."

She added with a sweet smile. "Not that I'd turn him down if he asked."

CHAPTER TWENTY-SEVEN

That afternoon, Dotty accompanied Norman to Windrush Hall. He drove the Land Rover, which towed the trailer containing the large Welsh dresser. Despite wearing her dress, Dotty helped Norman, Tracy and Jay manoeuvre the heavy piece of furniture out of the trailer and through the back door of the house into the kitchen.

After they stood it upright, she tugged her dress back into place, realising how much lighter and airier the kitchen felt.

Jay must have noticed her look as he remarked, "When we removed all the internal walls, we realised a window had been covered up. It's so much brighter in here now. And this dresser," he stood back admiring the piece of furniture, "will look fantastic beside it. Come on, let's move it over there."

The fireplace had also been revealed and the Duke's wood-burning stove still stood inside it. Norman walked over and patted the stove.

"This is just what you need on a chilly winter evening. But I'd start collecting fallen branches and logs now and store them in one of the outbuildings to dry out."

"Any thoughts on kitchen units?" asked Jay as he leaned against the marble worktop.

"Sorry, I haven't had a chance to look," apologised Dotty. "And I'm going to the auction near Gloucester tomorrow. I think David spoke to you about it."

Jay's eyes shone. "He did, and I'm very excited about buying some of the hall's original pieces. Be bold and don't let the other auction-goers intimidate you."

He gave her a steady, but well-meaning, look. She wondered if David had told her about the fiasco at the Fabulous Auction Boy's sale.

They heard a car approach the house.

"Are we expecting anyone else?" asked Jay.

Tracy shook his head. Dotty noticed his usual all-black attire had been broken up with a bright white T-shirt. He crossed to the window above the sink and looked up the drive. "It's a metallic grey Mercedes."

Dotty heard the car brake to a stop and then Tracy groaned, "It's that young policeman who was here last Monday."

He and Jay exchanged a look which Dotty could not decipher.

Jay pushed himself upright and sighed. "I'll see what he wants."

"And we better get back," remarked Norman, clasping his hands together.

Dotty followed Jay and Norman out of the kitchen while Tracy continued to stare through the window.

Norman untied the ropes inside the trailer and started to coil them up as Dotty watched the greeting between Jay and Sergeant Unwin.

Both men behaved civilly, shaking hands, but they were both stiff and wary of each other. As they walked towards her, she heard Sergeant Unwin ask, "Where is Tracy Ivers?"

"Why do you want to see him?" countered Jay.

"I need to ask him about his police record and his conviction for the underage rape of Rebecca Randall." Inside the trailer Norman dropped the front bar he was about to reattach.

"Sergeant, you have to understand. He had no idea she was only fifteen. None of us did. The way she dressed, the way she acted, the language she used. I couldn't believe she was so young. Besides, Tracy's done his time, so why bother him about it now? Rebecca is dead and she can't do us any more harm."

"Exactly," responded Sergeant Unwin, narrowing his eyes at Jay.

Dotty had the impression he was enjoying having the upper hand, and she wasn't impressed by his supercilious attitude.

The sergeant stopped and stood with his feet wide apart. "I repeat, where is Tracy Ivers? I'm taking him to the station for questioning."

That was unfair and uncalled for. She pressed her lips together, stepped in front of Jay and Sergeant Unwin, and demanded, "On what grounds?"

Sergeant Unwin raised his eyebrows. "For the underage rape of Rebecca Randall."

"That's finished with. He was tried and convicted. He can't be tried again." She crossed her arms and widened her own stance.

"What's it to do with you, anyway?" The sergeant narrowed his eyes at her.

"It's my fault you found out about the conviction and hounding a man for a crime he has already served time for is wrong. Anyway, what grounds do you have for investigating Rebecca Randall's death?"

"I don't have to justify myself to you. I'm perfectly within my rights to take him to the station and question him about the suspicious death of Rebecca Randall."

Dotty felt the blood flood her cheeks as she demanded, "Your rights. What about Tracy's rights, or any other person who has the right to be considered innocent until found guilty? We all know that taking him to the station will guarantee his previous conviction comes out. Is that what you're hoping for? That the press will find out and condemn him for Rebecca's death."

Sergeant Unwin was really winding her up today, but she needed to calm herself, and the situation, down. In a level tone, she added, "I'm sure Mr Ivers will answer your questions here."

What right had she to tell him what to do, or to assume what Tracy would or would not do?

She was about to back down and apologise when Jay Newton clapped and proclaimed, "That's absolutely right. Come inside, Sergeant, and both Tracy and I will willingly answer all your questions, but you'll have to arrest us both before we take one step inside your police station."

Norman chuckled as Dotty helped him lift the trailer ramp and he asked, "What's the sergeant done to rattle you?"

"I'm not sure," she replied, but she wasn't thinking about the sergeant.

Why had Jay Newton said he and Tracy would answer questions? Was he just offering moral brotherly support or was it something more? And why say 'arrest us' rather than 'arrest Tracy'? Had he something to hide?

CHAPTER TWENTY-EIGHT

Dotty arrived at Hall, Edgar and Seabrook's auction on Tuesday morning in a purposeful mood. She wasn't exactly sure why.

It might be the need to prove to David that she could find, bid, and buy quality furniture on her own. Or it could be the result of her encounters with Sergeant Unwin the previous day, when a more tenacious side of her had taken hold.

Either way, she walked confidently into the converted Cotswold stone barn, with a steep-sloping grey slate roof, that was Hall, Edgar and Seabrook's auction premises.

She picked up a bidder's form from a pile on a circular table beside a vase of pretty yellow, blue, and purple pansies in the entrance foyer. Once completed, she handed the form to a lady standing behind a glass screen, through which Dotty could see two other ladies sitting at computers in the office beyond.

She was handed a printed number. 133.

Small items of furniture were on display in the entrance corridor which led to a high-ceiling barn with exposed elm roof timbers. Stepping inside, she noticed a large group of people gathered around the glass cases to her right.

She was here for larger items than those inside the cases, so she walked into the barn where tables, sofas, desks, and other pieces of furniture were displayed.

Her eyes were immediately drawn to the peacock-blue upholstery of two delicate gilt wood sofas and matching chairs, which had originally graced the drawing room at Windrush Hall.

Several customers were admiring the drawing room set, and she mingled with them, trying not to draw people's attention to her interest in the items.

The sofas and chairs appeared to be in good condition, which they should be as the previous owner of Windrush Hall had repaired, re-gilded, and reupholstered them.

The blue satin seats were bright and vibrant. Accompanying another couple, she moved closer to a sofa and bent down to examine its legs and frame for nicks, scratches or other damage. Excellent, she couldn't find any. The drawing room set was the main item she was to bid for, but there were others.

Consulting the catalogue, she noted David had put a mark against a large wardrobe. She looked about the main barn space but couldn't see any wardrobes.

At the far end, someone entered another space, separated from the main area by temporary, shoulder-height partitions, over the top of which she spotted larger pieces of furniture.

She weaved a path around tables, desks, and chests of drawers, and entered the partitioned space, which seemed to be used for items either too large, or too dirty for the main room.

A pair of huge white marble planters in the shape of trophies mounted on plinths, which reached Dotty's waist, still had soil clinging to the cobwebs surrounding them.

She noticed a wardrobe and, stepping closer, opened one of the doors to peer inside. Disappointed, she observed a large crack running down its wooden back.

Opening her catalogue, she read the description beside the mark David had made. 'Vintage 1950s Cotswold School English Oak wardrobe'. This wardrobe had an oak frontage, but she didn't think it was the right one.

Just then she heard Didier Vogt say in an agitated tone, "Hello," and then, "You want what?" His voice rose in volume, but he whispered the next words. "For your silence?"

It sounded as if Didier was speaking to someone on his phone, and they were threatening him.

"Not today. I'm at an auction."

Dotty gasped when she heard Didier demand, "How much?"

Was he being blackmailed? And if so, for what? Was he responsible for the counterfeit furniture? It made sense if he was, and that he'd bid against her to force up the price of the Queen Anne style table. She couldn't help feeling that with his experience, he should have known it wasn't authentic.

"I can't get my hands on that much … OK, OK, tomorrow evening … Yes, 7 pm, in the rear car park at The Axeman. But where should I leave the money?"

There was a longer pause before he replied in a resigned tone. "Yes, I understand. And no, I won't involve the police. How can I?"

Dotty thought he finished the call, but she waited several minutes before peering around the edge of the open wardrobe door. There was no sign of Didier.

So someone knew about Didier and the fake and stolen furniture. And they were blackmailing him.

An amplified voice announced, "Ladies and gentlemen. The auction will start in ten minutes."

She'd better find the right wardrobe.

She peered down two more short aisles of furniture before spotting an attractive wooden wardrobe with a wonderful golden-brown colour which highlighted the grain of the oak. It had a simple central full-height mirror between a pair of wardrobe doors. It was an elegant piece, and Dotty loved it.

"Oh, that's nice," exclaimed Aunt Beanie. "Are you bidding for it?"

"Shush. I don't want everyone to know. Anyway, what are you doing here?" asked Dotty. Was Aunt Beanie checking up on her?

"Checking out the auction and seeing if I can spot any stolen or counterfeit furniture after your experience and the items the unit discovered recently. Are you bidding for anything else?"

"Ladies and gentlemen. Please take your seats, we shall begin in two minutes," proclaimed the amplified voice.

"Yes, several pieces, although I still need to check some of them," replied Dotty, looking past Aunt Beanie into the main auction room.

"Let's find somewhere to sit and then you can look for them while I watch the auction."

Dotty stopped and grasped Aunt Beanie's arm. "And I've something important to tell you. But not here where we might be overheard"

"That does sound intriguing."

Dotty and Aunt Beanie found seats at the end of a row, so when the auction started, Dotty stood and moved as quietly as she could around the perimeter of the auction room. She recognised the circular hall table which used to stand in Windrush Hall.

The auction catalogue described it as a 'circular regency table with a flame segment and cross banding'. She presumed the cross banding was the ring of lighter wood around the perimeter and the flame referred to the attractive natural pattern in the wood which resembled flames emanating from the centre of the table.

It was a lighter shade than most mahogany, which suited Jay's taste, but unfortunately there was a large scratch across the top. Reaching forward, she touched the scratch with her finger. It wasn't deep.

"Still looking for a table?" a voice whispered.

She snatched her hand back and look round at Didier Vogt.

"If you're thinking a skilled furniture restorer could remove that scratch, you're right. But it means the price should be lower than its actual value."

Dotty drew her eyebrows together. Was Didier going to bid against her again?

He must have noticed her expression as he raised his arms and whispered, "Don't worry. I won't bid against you. I've been told." That was a relief, but told by whom?

"Now the dining table I told you about for Windrush Hall."

"From Windrush Hall," corrected Dotty.

"I'm no fool. I know who your client is. And so did Rebecca, and she was furious Jay hadn't commissioned her to buy antiques and furniture for the hall."

Oh dear. If Sergeant Unwin heard that, he'd probably return to question her again as a possible suspect.

"Sold for £450," called the auctioneer.

Didier continued, "I've negotiated with the owner, and she'll sell the tables and matching chairs for £4,000. With a £1,000 commission for me and another £1,000 for you, that's £6,000 in total. I'm sure Jay will pay that, especially to replace that hideous glass topped thing he has in the dining room. And those black chairs are so ugly."

"I'm not sure I should charge my client £1,000 commission or agree to pay you, but let me think about it and discuss it with David Rook."

"You do that," agreed Didier.

"Lot 17. A Regency mahogany hall table with a flame segment and cross banding. A very attractive piece, although I have to disclose a large scratch across the surface. Nothing a furniture restorer couldn't clean up."

The auctioneer was an elderly man wearing a tweed suit, and he peered at the assembled audience over the top of his brown-rimmed glasses. "Who'll start me at £450? 450. 400. 350. 300."

"£100," a lady called.

"This is your piece. Good luck." Didier walked steadily away before stopping and turning towards the auctioneer.

"The internet has woken up," revealed the auctioneer, and the price rose on the large screen behind him by £10 segments to £250. "All done on the internet at £250. Do we have any advance in the room on £250?" The auctioneer asked, staring around at the people seated in front of him.

Nobody moved.

Dotty stepped forward and raised her arm.

"Thank you, miss. £260."

Someone on the internet was clearly still interested in the piece and Dotty bid against them to £310.

"Your bid," the elderly auctioneer looked over his glasses at her.

She nodded her head.

"£320," confirmed the auctioneer.

The price on the screen remained at £320.

"£320. Going once. Going twice for £320." The auctioneer looked around the room for the final time before announcing, "Sold."

Dotty held up her bidder number, as Aunt Beanie looked round and smiled at her.

She was relieved to buy the table and at a fair price, despite the scratch. She'd arrange for that to be fixed before the table was delivered to Windrush Hall. But she still had to find the floor lamps, and they were scheduled for sale in five Lots.

She found the lamps which were a pair of standard lamps with gilt Corinthian style tops on reeded mahogany columns, with gilt stepped bases and lion's paw feet. They weren't to Dotty's taste, and neither were the Damask gold and cream shades with tassels hanging from them.

But David had marked them, and he'd told her to bid up to £600, so she'd follow his instructions as the lamps were in good condition.

She secured the standard lamps for £450, which was a reasonable price. Next were the peacock blue sofa and chairs, and after those the oak wardrobe.

CHAPTER TWENTY-NINE

"I wasn't sure you were going to be successful with the drawing room sofas and chairs. I think the man bidding against you was a dealer also buying for a client," remarked Aunt Beanie.

"I think you're right." Dotty had been pushed close to the generous limit David had set her of £2,600 for the peacock blue upholstered drawing room set.

"But I'm sorry you didn't win the wardrobe," consoled Aunt Beanie. "It was an attractive piece of furniture, but I wouldn't worry, wardrobes are regularly entered into auctions. Fewer people need them these days, as modern houses have built-in cupboards. But I wonder who bought it?"

"It was an internet bid," explained Dotty. She thought she'd secured the wardrobe for £650 until a new bidder on the internet had pushed the price above £800, the limit David had marked in her catalogue.

She'd been tempted to bid more, but didn't want to get in trouble again, so she'd left it. Someone else in the room had joined in the bidding and the wardrobe had sold for £1,100, which was way more than she would have paid.

Still, she was satisfied with her other purchases. "We have the hall table, which will be beautiful after it's been repaired, and the standard lamps."

"You will get new shades for those, won't you?"

"I hope so. But that's not my call."

She and Aunt Beanie were queuing for refreshments at an old-fashioned van which had been painted black and converted into a food truck which claimed to be the Cotswold's Mobile Deli.

Dotty heard a phone ring and, realising it was hers, she removed it from the small black bag she'd secured over her head and across her body.

She stepped out of the line to answer it. "Hello."

"Dotty, it's Jay. Are you at the auction?"

"Yes, and I've bought you the drawing room furniture, the hall table and a pair of standard lamps."

"Ah." Jay sounded despondent.

"Didn't you want me to?" Oh, no! Had she made another big mistake?

"It's not your fault. David and I agreed to bid for the pieces, but I'm not sure we'll need them now."

"Why not? What's happened?"

"It's Tracy. He descended into such a black mood after the sergeant's visit that he's refusing to speak to me. I appreciate your intervention yesterday, but I don't think it's enough. Poor Tracy, it doesn't matter where we move to, he can't seem to get away from that case. And he's so ashamed of the stigma it brings. If his mental health doesn't improve, we might have to sell up and try living abroad."

That sounded drastic, especially as Jay seemed so happy at Windrush Hall. Tracy obviously meant a lot if he was willing to give it all up for him. A small voice in her head added, or Tracy had some kind of hold over Jay.

She mentally shook her head. This was the trouble with getting involved with the police and their cases. She started to doubt everyone's motives.

She said in a small but hopeful voice, "I've also been offered the dining room tables and chairs, which were originally at Windrush Hall."

Jay's voice remained forlorn as he replied, "I can't commit to buying anything else. Not until this issue with Tracy is resolved."

Dotty heard Aunt Beanie raise her voice and say, "Two teas, a pulled pork sandwich and a brisket Philly."

"I understand," sympathised Dotty.

"Dotty, can you pay for these and claim them as expenses?" Aunt Beanie called.

"I'll let you go." Jay ended the call abruptly.

Dotty found a £20 note which she handed to the girl in the food truck, and received a receipt and few copper coins of change.

"What was that about?" asked Aunt Beanie.

"Some dirt the police have dug up." Dotty didn't think it was her place to tell anyone, even Aunt Beanie, about Tracy's criminal record, or admit her part in discovering it.

They carried their lunch across to a pair of white-painted wooden chairs with rattan seats positioned either side of a small, circular wooden table.

Aunt Beanie sat down and sipped her tea. "That's better. But it's a fascinating auction with some interesting pieces."

"Did you find anything?" asked Dotty.

"No, but I'll speak to Jeremy, the auctioneer, later. I suspect he's too savvy to accept attractive period pieces without some provenance or history, but we can all be duped by stolen items."

Dotty bit into her intriguingly named brisket Philly sandwich. Cheese oozed down the side of her mouth, and she wiped it away with a white paper napkin before sipping her tea.

There was a fieriness in her sandwich, she wasn't sure about. Opening it up, she spotted and removed three slices of green jalapeño chilli.

The next bite was perfect and the sweetness of grilled peppers was no longer overpowered by the heat of chilli.

"So what did you want to tell me?" asked Aunt Beanie.

During the adrenaline rush of bidding in the auction, Dotty had forgotten about Didier's earlier conversation, which she'd overheard.

She finished her mouthful, wiped her lips with the napkin, and leaned forward. "I think I've found someone involved with your counterfeit furniture racket."

"You have?" Aunt Beanie's eyes widened as she asked, "Who?"

"Didier Vogt."

Aunt Beanie leaned back. "That would make sense. He knows lots of people in the industry, both honest and disreputable, and he can come and go as he pleases."

"And he bid against me, when he probably knew the Queen Anne table wasn't genuine."

"That's true, but it's not conclusive. He might not have known, or a client might have instructed him to bid for it."

Dotty pressed on. "Then there's the conversation I overhead this morning. I think someone is blackmailing him. It sounded as if he's going to pay them for their silence. And he's meeting them tomorrow evening, in the car park at the back of The Axeman pub."

"Are you sure?" asked Aunt Beanie dubiously. "I can't see Didier as the type to linger in dark corners, waiting to pay someone off. In fact, I would expect him to call them out and tell them to go to the police rather than ask him for money."

"Well, there's only one way to find out. Wait for him in The Axeman car park tomorrow night," Dotty enthused.

"Norman won't like that. He'll tell us to leave well alone and speak to someone in my unit, since I do work for the police."

"That's a great idea. Let's call Keya." Dotty fished her phone out of her bag.

"Hiya," said Keya when she answered Dotty's call.

"Aunt Beanie suggested I contact you."

"Not exactly," the older woman muttered.

Dotty clarified, "Or at least I should speak to someone in your unit, because I think I've identified someone involved with the fake furniture. But I think they're being blackmailed and meeting whoever is threatening them tomorrow evening to pay them off."

"Hang on. Say that again," Keya requested.

Dotty repeated her story and what she'd overheard Didier say to his mystery caller.

Aunt Beanie ate her pulled pork sandwich in silence.

"So you think," summarised Keya, "that Didier is crooked. And someone else knows that and they're using it to their advantage. And you think we should wait in The Axeman's car park tomorrow evening to find out what's going on?"

"Yes, and if nobody turns up, we can just have a drink," suggested Dotty cheerfully.

Keya responded hesitantly, "I suppose it can't do any harm."

CHAPTER THIRTY

"I don't think you should go," declared Norman. "Leave it to the police."

"I will be with the police," reasoned Dotty. "I'm meeting up with Sergeant Varma."

Norman drew his eyebrows together.

He, Dotty and Aunt Beanie were sitting at one end of the pine kitchen table at Meadowbank Farm.

Uncle Cliff was content, sitting in an armchair and illuminated by the last of the day's sunshine penetrating the full-height windows in the conservatory section of the kitchen.

It was late afternoon on Tuesday, and Dotty had arranged to park her Skoda in the car park at the rear of The Axeman pub at half-past six. Keya didn't want to leave her car nearby in case she spooked Didier Vogt and whoever he was meeting, so she planned to park on one of the side roads in Coln Akeman and walk to the pub.

Norman pressed on. "Sergeant Varma is certainly enthusiastic. I can't fault her for that, but she's not who I'd choose to be with if things turn nasty. What about Sergeant Unwin? He keeps himself in shape, and he's professional."

Too professional to include Dotty in a stakeout. If Didier was responsible for the counterfeit furniture, and he'd deliberately bid against her at the Fabulous Auction Boys' sale, then she had a score to settle.

She replied, "This case is with the Rural, Heritage and Wildlife unit, of which Keya is a sergeant."

"And I'm a consultant," muttered Aunt Beanie.

Norman pressed his lips together and turned to Aunt Beanie. "We've already agreed that stakeouts are beyond your remit. I'm not happy with Dotty being part of it."

He turned back to Dotty and insisted, "But promise me you'll stay inside your car and don't do anything stupid or courageous, like trying to arrest the suspects."

Dotty was about to say she rarely did anything courageous, but bit her tongue. During the past year, not one but two murder suspects had injured her, and one incident was entirely her own fault.

"I promise," agreed Dotty.

"Good." Norman crossed his arms and Aunt Beanie seemed about to continue the conversation, but she glanced across at Norman and remained silent.

Keya slid into the front passenger seat of Dotty's Skoda Fabia at twenty-five minutes to seven. "Hiya. Isn't this exciting?"

"Norman didn't think so," replied Dotty as she handed her friend a bottle of bitter lemon and a packet of crisps.

"Thanks. I'm starving. Do you have any yummy sandwiches?" asked Keya.

"No, sorry. But why don't we go into the pub for supper after this?"

"It depends if I have to arrest anyone and take them back to the station."

Keya pulled at her packet of crisps, but the top refused to open, so she yanked it hard. The packet tore and crisps scattered across her lap, the car seat and down into the footwell. "Oh toda!"

She picked at the crisps on her lap and mused, "At least this is better than waiting in country lanes on the off chance someone comes along and dumps a load of builder's rubble or an old mattress."

"How is your case progressing?"

"Frustratingly slowly, although local people are getting the hang of reporting incidents, and I've set up several online groups. Yesterday I marked all sightings on a map and there are patterns, but so many people are involved, I can't stop them all. In fact ..."

"Shush," interrupted Dotty. "I think someone's standing in the shadows. There, against the wall by the back door."

"Did you see anyone come out of the pub?"

"No. But then I was distracted by you trying to open a packet of crisps."

"Sorry," said Keya as she popped a crisp into her mouth. "Yum. Cheese and onion."

As her friend munched away, Dotty stared through her windscreen into the pub car park. A car turned in and its headlights lit up the stationary cars. "Someone's coming," she said, feeling the adrenaline rush through her veins.

The car slowed, pulled into an empty space close to the pub's back door, and stopped. A middle-aged couple emerged and, chatting to each other, they entered the pub through the back door.

"False alarm," noted Keya as she struggled to unscrew the plastic top of her bottle of bitter lemon. When she finally forced it open, yellow bubbles foamed over the rim and some dripped onto her seat. "Not again. I'm sorry. I'll clean it up ..."

"Not now," cut in Dotty. "Someone's definitely standing in the shadows at the back of the pub." She narrowed her eyes as she searched the darkness. "Look, it's a man with dark hair. Did you see him by the light of his phone?"

"Only a glimpse. Didier has dark hair, doesn't he?"

"Yes," replied Dotty. "And whoever's standing there is speaking into their phone."

A movement caught her eye. A figure skulking by the entrance to the car park. A figure with a headscarf and large bow.

"What's Aunt Beanie doing here?" she cried.

"Shush," chided Keya. "You don't want to spook our suspect. Anyway, what do you mean? Where's Aunt Beanie?"

"She shuffled around the wall at the entrance to the car park and I can't see her now. There's a van in the way."

Didier stepped forward into a pool of light cast by a fitting mounted on the wall of the pub and looked sharply across to the van parked beside the entrance.

"I hope she doesn't give the game away," groaned Keya.

"Norman is going to murder her, or me, for suggesting tonight's adventure," complained Dotty.

"Oh look, he's moving."

They silently watched the figure of Didier Vogt stride into the centre of the car park, which was clear of cars, and drop something on the ground. He turned and swiftly returned to the pub, the back door swinging closed behind him.

"Now what?" asked Dotty.

"We wait."

Nothing moved in the car park.

After several minutes, a head appeared around the back of the van.

"No, go back," mouthed Keya, but Aunt Beanie looked furtively about before tiptoeing across the uneven earth and gravel surface to the centre of the car park, where the packet lay on the ground.

"No," cried Keya, as Aunt Beanie reached down.

The car park was suddenly lit up by the headlights of a car parked in the far corner. They couldn't see the driver.

"Is that the person collecting the money?" gasped Dotty. "Have they been here the whole time?"

"Yes," replied Keya, leaning forward and grabbing the dashboard. Her open bottle of bitter lemon hissed as it spilt on the floor.

Ignoring it, she muttered, "Leave it," but Aunt Beanie couldn't hear her. "Get inside the pub," she urged.

Surely Aunt Beanie would realise the danger she was in and dash to the safety of the pub or hide behind a parked car.

But Aunt Beanie remained frozen to the spot. She looked down at the packet, across to the nearest car, and back to the packet. She seemed to make a decision and reached for the packet, but as she did so, the headlights of the car sped forward.

CHAPTER THIRTY-ONE

Dotty gasped at Aunt Beanie's terrified expression, and then the older woman somersaulted through the air. The car stopped and Dotty was aware of a figure jumping out, but by the time she'd opened her own door, the other car was accelerating away.

She and Keya ran across the dimly lit car park to the prostrate figure of Aunt Beanie, whose leg was splayed at an awkward angle. Keya turned on a torch, but Aunt Beanie did not flinch or move when the light was turned on her.

There was a small pool of blood seeping from beneath her head.

"Quick, call an ambulance. I'll see what I can do," instructed Keya as she bent over Aunt Beanie.

Dotty ran back to her car for her phone and called the emergency services. When she was assured that an ambulance was being dispatched, she made a second call.

"Hi Dotty. How are you?" answered Gilly Wimsey cheerfully.

"Is Peter there?" asked Dotty briskly.

"Yes, I'll get him. You can tell me what's happened later."

"Dotty?" enquired Dr Peter.

"It's Aunt Beanie. She's been knocked over in the car park at the back of The Axeman and she's unconscious." Dotty hoped that's all she was.

Peter broke into her darkening thoughts. "I'll grab my bag and be with you in a few minutes. See if she'll respond, but don't move her."

Dotty returned to Keya and with trepidation asked, "Is she …."

"Breathing. Yes."

Dotty gasped for air and her legs felt wobbly, but Aunt Beanie was alive.

A figure wearing a head torch ran into the car park. Blinded, Dotty wasn't sure who it was until the person dropped a bag to the floor and asked, "Have you called an ambulance?"

"Yes," replied Dotty, in relief. It was Dr Peter.

"Good, but it won't be here for at least another ten minutes. Right Bernadette, let's see what the damage is."

Dotty stepped away as Peter examined Aunt Beanie.

Keya joined Dotty and, placing a comforting arm around her shoulder, said reassuringly, "She's going to be all right. It's not your fault."

"But it is. If I hadn't told her about the call I'd overheard, or our plans to meet here, she'd never have come."

"You said she was staying at the farmhouse."

"She must have slipped out when Norman wasn't looking. She probably wanted to be part of the action." Dotty smiled weakly at her friend.

"The package," announced Keya. "Where is it?"

Dotty and Keya searched the ground around Aunt Beanie and Keya flashed her torch across the brown earth surface of the car park but there was only a scattering of gravel and an occasional empty crisp packet or chocolate wrapper. There was no sign of the packet Didier had left.

"Is it under Aunt Beanie?" Keya asked and they turned back to Peter, who was supporting the back of Aunt Beanie's head.

"Did they get away?" Aunt Beanie mumbled.

Peter looked up at Dotty and Keya and, rubbing the back of his neck, asked, "What's all this about?"

"We'll explain later." Dotty blurted. "Is she lying on anything? A packet of some description?"

"No, I dropped it over there." Aunt Beanie inclined her head towards the pub.

Keya shone her torch over the ground in the direction of the pub, but there was no packet.

"Just a minute," exclaimed Dotty. "The car stopped, and the driver jumped out. They must have grabbed the package."

Keya groaned.

"But what about Didier? We can still arrest him, can't we?" asked Dotty eagerly.

"What for?" Keya's shoulders slumped dejectedly. "Loitering in a pub car park? Speaking on a mobile phone? Without the evidence inside that packet, there's nothing we can do."

"Oh, I see what you mean." Dotty felt numb with disappointment.

Keya placed her hand on Dotty's arm and said, "Look, why don't you go into the pub and explain that Aunt Beanie has been knocked over and tell the landlord not to be alarmed if he hears an ambulance. And while you're there, see if you can spot Didier and watch what his reaction is to the news."

Reluctantly, Dotty left Keya, Peter, and the injured but conscious Aunt Beanie, and ducked as she entered The Axeman through the low stone archway of the rear door.

Inside, it was warm and noisy. The first room she entered was small and frequented by men from Coln Akeman and the surrounding villages who were regulars to the pub.

She squeezed between them and entered a larger room at the front whose exposed soot-blackened beams were decorated with horse brasses and farm implements. At the far end, a fire was smouldering in the large inglenook fireplace.

Glancing around, she couldn't see Didier.

As she approached the bar, the landlord asked, "What can I get you?"

She scratched her neck and replied, "Actually, there's been an accident. Someone's been knocked over in the car park."

The portly barman turned and reached for a telephone attached to the wall beside upturned bottles of spirits, mounted in a chrome and black rack of dispensers.

"It's OK," called Dotty. "I've called an ambulance, so don't be alarmed if you hear sirens. And Dr Peter is with her now."

The barman turned back and leaned forward across the bar, asked, "Do you know who it is?"

"Yes, Aunt Beanie. I mean Bernadette Devereux."

"She's not one of my regular evening customers. Was she with you?"

Dotty dropped her gaze to the bar counter and replied, "Not exactly." She gulped and raising her head asked in a slightly strained voice, "I was supposed to be meeting a colleague here, Didier Vogt. Do you know him?" She crossed the fingers of one hand behind her back.

"Didier, sure. He was here, but it was strange. He rushed in from the back, looked around and left by the front door. Were you late?"

"Something like that," Dotty muttered.

"I thought he was the one who was late. His wife was in here earlier having a drink."

"Molly?"

"Yes, that's the one. Sweet lady, although she did seem rather anxious. Perhaps she was supposed to be meeting her husband before you, but he didn't turn up."

Hanging around outside the pub, thought Dotty.

"I better get back," said Dotty, excusing herself. "The ambulance should be arriving soon."

She shivered as she crossed the car park to Dr Peter and Keya. The evening air was chilly but fresh compared with the stuffy pub.

Dr Peter had found a blanket to keep Aunt Beanie warm and she appeared to have regained some of her vigour. When she saw Dotty, she called, "Did you see him?"

"Didier. No. He must have left as soon as he deposited the packet. The landlord saw him rush out of the front door."

"Bernadette," chided Dr Peter. "You must keep calm. Whatever antics you three were involved with are finished now. We need to settle you into the hospital and get you checked out. The pain killers I gave you will only last so long, and that leg needs looking at. I'll also be ordering a head scan, as you were unconscious and probably have a degree of concussion."

"I'll be fine. Stop fussing," insisted Aunt Beanie. "Now girls, what about the car? What make and colour was it and did you take down the number plate? I don't suppose you recognised the driver?"

Keya and Dotty exchanged glances.

"I didn't see anything, I'm afraid," admitted Dotty. "The car's headlights blinded me and then I was focusing on you. I do remember the driver jumping out, but I couldn't even tell you if it was a man or a woman."

Keya added, "I don't remember any details about the car either. I was too worried about you."

Aunt Beanie smiled up at them and then winced. She breathed deeply in and out several times and then said, "I'm sorry to cause so much trouble. Norman will be furious."

Norman, thought Dotty. He was stuck at the farmhouse looking after Uncle Cliff. She'd better call him.

Norman answered before she'd even heard her phone ring. "Dotty, have you seen Beanie? She vanished and I can't find the Land Rover." He sounded frantic.

"I'm with her now. With Keya and Dr Peter."

"Dr Peter? What's happened? What's she done?"

Dotty turned and walked several steps away from the others before replying. "I'm so sorry. It's all my fault. I should never have told her about the conversation I overheard. She came down to The Axeman and got knocked over, and now we're waiting for an ambulance to take her to hospital," gushed Dotty.

And she broke down in tears.

CHAPTER THIRTY-TWO

A bright yellow ambulance, arrived and Aunt Beanie was manoeuvred onto a stretcher which was wheeled over to a ramp at the rear of the ambulance and mechanically lifted into the vehicle.

"I'll go with her," directed Peter, "to keep an eye on her and explain what treatment and painkillers I've given her." He climbed in after Aunt Beanie but turned and asked, "Can one of you pick me up from Cheltenham Hospital? Gilly has to say with the kids."

Dotty shuffled from one foot to another, and replied, "I better go home and explain what has happened to Norman, but if he wants to go to the hospital, there'll be no one to look after Uncle Cliff."

"I don't mind driving you," said Keya. "And I have to write up a report anyway. I'll be able to finish it when the hospital tells me the extent of her injuries."

The ambulance departed quietly, with no sirens or flashing lights. A few drinkers from the pub had come outside when it had first arrived, but they didn't hang around for long.

Keya touched Dotty's arm again and reassured her, "I'm sure she'll be OK. I'll call you with a progress report."

Keya followed the ambulance on foot, out of the car park, leaving Dotty all alone.

Dotty's eyes travelled to the corner where the unknown car had been parked. It must have been there before she arrived as only one other car, with the middle-aged couple, had entered after her.

She shivered, wrapping her arms around herself. The driver had watched them all. She might have been hidden inside her car, but Keya had walked, Didier had stood around outside the pub's back door, and Aunt Beanie had made her furtive, but obvious entry.

What would have happened if Aunt Beanie hadn't tried to rescue the package? She flinched as a replay of Aunt Beanie flying through the air played in her mind.

Would she or Keya have received the same treatment if they'd waited a little longer and then, thinking the coast was clear, tried to retrieve the packet? Or would the driver have risked being spotted and collected the package themselves?

There was no point going over it. She'd never know. The package was lost and Aunt Beanie was seriously injured. She prayed Aunt Beanie continued her recovery and didn't deteriorate in the ambulance or on her arrival at the hospital. She'd never forgive herself.

And neither would Norman. She took a deep breath. It was time to face him.

She slid into the front seat of the car, wondering what the sickly-sweet lemony smell was. Glancing across at the passenger seat, she noted the scattered crisps and an empty bottle of bitter lemon in the footwell.

Inwardly, she groaned. It would take ages to clean up the spilt liquid. She'd be best taking her car to a hand car wash on the outskirts of Cirencester when she had time. Starting the engine, she drove out of the car park.

CHAPTER 33

As Dotty gently braked to a stop in front of the gate leading to her cottage at Meadowbank Farm, Norman rushed out of the main house.

As she climbed out, he blurted, "How is Beanie? Has she gone to hospital?"

Dotty clasped her hands in front of her and looked down at them, as she replied simply, "Yes."

"I need to be with her," insisted Norman. "But you'll have to stay with Cliff. I hope he's OK. He's been quite agitated this evening. Probably picked up that I was worried about Beanie." Norman's words came out in a rush, as if he was speaking his thoughts out loud.

He seemed to collect himself and asked, "Can you go to your cottage and collect what you need for the rest of the evening and then come through to the farmhouse? I'll get Cliff ready for bed and show you what you need to do."

Dotty nodded her acceptance and opened the door to her cottage. She stopped in the hallway and the tears flowed down her cheeks again.

What had she done? She'd been so excited about overhearing Didier's call and thinking she could solve the case of the counterfeit furniture. But she was no police officer.

Why had she persuaded Keya to let her join her in the car park? If she had remained at Meadowbank Farm, so would Aunt Beanie.

She looked down at the brown hessian welcome doormat, printed with the silhouette image and paw prints of a cat, which Norman had given her for Christmas.

Beside it was the box she'd bought at the car boot sale containing the Spinning Newts' record and other oddments. She picked it up as she might as well sort through it while she looked after Uncle Cliff and it would keep her mind off … other matters.

In the kitchen of the farmhouse, Dotty placed the box on the table and absent-mindedly stroked Earl Grey, who jumped onto the table to examine it.

Norman led Uncle Cliff by the hand back into the kitchen and said slowly, "I have to go out and meet Beanie. I might not get back until after your bedtime but Dotty is here to help you. You know Dotty?"

Norman stopped in front of Dotty and said, "Introduce yourself to Cliff."

Wondering why this was necessary as she saw Uncle Cliff most days, Dotty did as directed and said, "Hello, I'm Dotty."

"Shake hands," instructed Norman.

Dotty reached forward and Cliff limply shook her outstretched hand.

"Good, we're all friends now. Let's settle you down to watch the TV and Dotty will make you a lovely cup of Ovaltine in an hour."

"Is that like hot chocolate?" asked Dotty.

Norman gave her a warning look as he joked, "No, it's not hot chocolate, is it Cliff? You don't like hot chocolate."

Uncle Cliff's hands moved jerkily as he stood waiting for Norman to push an armchair over so he could sit in it to watch the small television, mounted on the bookcase. Normally he sat on a dining chair, but the armchair was probably more comfortable.

As Norman settled Cliff in the chair, he reassured him. "Ovaltine. Dotty will make you a warm cup of Ovaltine and maybe she'll even let you have a chocolate biscuit as a treat. You like chocolate biscuits, don't you?"

The slumped figure in the chair nodded his head.

Dotty wondered if she would end up like Uncle Cliff one day. But who would look after her? She had no husband now or family.

She dropped down beside Uncle Cliff's chair and said softly, "I like chocolate biscuits too. We're going to have a fun time together, aren't we?"

"And bedtime is half past ten, isn't it, Cliff?"

"Half past ten," the older man repeated in a thin, reedy voice.

Norman left for the hospital, calling, "I'll phone if I'm going to be late back."

Dotty reached for the cardboard box and pulled it across the table. As she sat down, Earl Grey jumped onto her lap but did not lie down. He began kneading her jean-clad legs with his paws.

"Ow, steady boy," admonished Dotty as he pricked her skin with a claw. She stroked the top of his head, which he raised towards her, purring loudly.

She'd never had her own pet before. Al, her husband, had Banff, a loyal black Labrador who she'd enjoyed taking for walks around the golf course and through the woods surrounding their last military house, but he'd never completely taken to her.

After she'd been attacked by a suspect and ended up in Cheltenham Hospital, like Aunt Beanie, Banff had gone to live with Al's ex-wife and children.

She'd been reticent about taking in Earl Grey as she'd been unsure where she was going to live, and if her new landlord would accept pets. But Aunt Beanie had offered her the cottage and welcomed Earl Grey with open arms.

She'd lost him earlier in the year - well, someone had catnapped him - and it made her realise how much she missed his silent company. She supposed that now there would be no need to look for a cat to live at Windrush Hall if Jay was thinking of moving on.

Earl Grey settled down on her lap as she reached for the Spinning Newts' record. It had a dark street scene overlaid with the image of a green newt on the front cover.

She turned it over and began to read the lyrics printed in green on the back. They were haunting and clearly written by someone trying to find their voice and way in the world. It was something she could relate to.

She realised that someone had written on the back in black pen. She rotated the record and read, 'To Becky. I couldn't have done this without you. Jay.' Was Becky a young Rebecca Randall?

Placing the record on the table, she reached into the box and felt around until her hand touched a spiral bound, cardboard covered book. She wriggled it free from the other contents and placed it on the table, but when she opened it she realised it was a scrapbook.

Fascinated, she flicked through it. The cream pages were filled with concert tickets, flyers and even faded polaroid photographs of a younger looking Jay Newton and his fellow band members. An attractive young woman, with a bouffant of permed blonde hair, heavy blue eye make-up, and bright red lipstick appeared in many of the photos.

Dotty noted that she always wore either hot pants or a very short rara skirt with a strappy top and several long strands of beads. Squinting, she examined a head shot of the woman. Was it a younger Rebecca Randall?

She turned another page of the scrapbook and was confronted by a black-and-white photograph of Jay which he'd signed in large, scrawly writing, 'For Becky, our favourite fan'.

If the scrapbook, and the other contents of the box, had belonged to Rebecca Randall, how had they ended up at a Swindon car boot sale? Then she remembered the break-ins at Rebecca's house and the tools on the stall where she'd bought the box. Tools were easy targets for thieves. Was she handling stolen goods?

She placed the scrapbook on the table beside the record and regarded the box. She should give it to Keya, but what harm could she do by looking through it first?

She lifted Earl Grey off her lap and he looked indignantly at her when she placed him on the terracotta-tiled floor. As he walked away, his tail erect, she stood, pulled the box closer and tipped it upside down.

Items cascaded across the table and Uncle Cliff turned to her with wide, shocked eyes. She smiled reassuringly, and said, "It's OK. I'm just sorting through this box."

There were badges, backstage passes, concert tickets and two bundles of stapled sheets. She picked one of these up and thought the front sheet was a poem. But looking closer she realised it was the lyrics from the record she'd bought, but that song was called 'Cries of the Street' whereas this was titled 'Who Can Hear Me?'.

Glancing down at the bottom of the lyrics, she saw the name 'Becky Randall'. Confused, she turned over to the second page with the song's chorus written below a hand-drawn music score.

There was a series of musical notes, some of which were crossed out and others marked beside them. It looked like the beginning of a song. Again, 'Becky Randall' was scribbled at the bottom of the page.

The rest of the pages were music scores with printed notes and lyrics. At the top of the first page were the words, 'Music by Jay Newton and Becky Randall' and 'Lyrics by Becky Randall'.

Dotty placed the stapled sheets on the table and sat down. Rebecca, or Becky as she had been known back in the 1980s, had clearly been a huge fan of the Spinning Newts. But had she been something more? Had she written this song for the band?

She picked up the record again and looked closely at it, front and back, but there was no mention of Rebecca's name. Instead, it clearly stated that copyright for the words and music belonged to Jay Newton. Had Jay paid Becky for the song which the Spinning Newts recorded?

Her thoughts were interrupted by a hammering and she looked across at Uncle Cliff, who was thumping the arm of his chair. The programme on the TV had changed and a tank rumbled across the screen. Clearly, this programme was not to Uncle Cliff's taste.

She found the TV remote control on the pine table, beneath some of the contents of the box and flicked through the channels until she found one with a man cutting a hedge. Uncle Cliff slumped back in his chair.

Dotty squatted down beside him and asked, "Shall I make you a nice hot cup of Ovaltine?"

CHAPTER 34

On Thursday morning, Dotty walked into the kitchen of Meadowbank Farmhouse.

Uncle Cliff was seated at the pine kitchen table with a white linen napkin tucked into the collar of his green shirt. He appeared relaxed as he ate his porridge, the brown sugar scattered on top turning golden as it melted into the thick oaty mixture.

Norman pulled the chrome kettle off the Aga hot plate as it reached boiling point and its lid rattled and steam escaped from the spout.

"Tea?" he asked.

"Yes, please," replied Dotty. "Did you hear any more from the hospital last night? Did Aunt Beanie lapse back into unconsciousness?"

"I don't think so. Sergeant Varma called to say she had returned from her MRI scan and although there was some swelling on her brain, it was not serious enough to need surgery. They think her losing consciousness in the ambulance was just her brain needing time to rest after the post-accident excitement. The doctor was going to x-ray her leg, but I haven't heard the results of that. Mrs Todd is popping over shortly to keep an eye on Cliff so I can return to the hospital. Are you coming?"

Dotty was relieved Aunt Beanie's injuries weren't life threatening, although she hoped that there wasn't too much damage to her leg.

Older bones didn't heal as quickly as younger ones, and Aunt Beanie would be frustrated if she couldn't get around with her usual vigour.

She would visit Aunt Beanie in hospital, but she'd better not crowd her, especially if she was still receiving treatment.

"Not this morning. I'll come later, after I've sorted something out."

Norman narrowed his eyes as he passed her a cup of tea. "You're not investigating the car which knocked Beanie down, are you?"

"Oh no," replied Dotty. "That is definitely a matter for the police." But weren't the lyrics and music score she'd been studying yesterday evening also a matter for the police? If she handed them over to Sergeant Unwin, would he agree that they were significant, or would he think her stupid and that she was jumping to conclusions?

And what if he did think they were important, and charged in and arrested Jay without discovering if there was a perfectly reasonable explanation?

It would be much better if she spoke to Jay first. After all, he was still a client, even though he'd told her not to buy any more furniture for the time being.

She made up her mind to drive to Windrush Hall even though a small voice in her head reasoned she was not handing the box over to Sergeant Unwin as she knew he would exclude her from the case, and she might never know what the lyrics and song sheet meant.

"Don't worry about Beanie," consoled Norman. "She was bright enough last night, although she did have a headache and couldn't remember why she'd been in the pub car park. I think it best we keep it that way."

"Yes," nodded Dotty in agreement. Norman had clearly taken her silent introspection to be concern for Aunt Beanie. It was best he didn't know that she was planning to confront a possible murder suspect. She gulped, realising that was exactly what she was about to do.

As Dotty drove down the sweeping drive towards the impressive Windrush Hall, she realised that, although the team triathlon had been less than two weeks ago, there was already an autumnal feeling in the air.

Most of the trees were still green, but she spotted an odd yellow leaf and she'd needed to wear a thicker cardigan over her long-sleeved top.

She'd fought against wearing tights beneath her below-the-knee orange and red gypsy style skirt and instead wore a pair of long brown boots.

Parking at the bottom of the stone steps which led up to the front door, she hesitated before climbing out. Should she knock on the front door or go round to the side and try the kitchen door?

She reached into the back of her car and removed the box she'd bought at the car boot sale. The corner of the dark record cover poked out of the top.

Noticing that the kitchen light was on, she carried the box round to the back door and, balancing it on a raised knee, knocked on the door.

She was about to put the box down and try again when Tracy opened the door wearing a black apron with 'King of the Kitchen' printed in large letters on the front, and a glum expression.

"What do you want?" he demanded.

"I'd like to see Jay," Dotty replied in as confident a voice as she could muster. Perhaps coming to the hall, on her own, without even letting Keya know, was a stupid idea.

"Is that Dotty?" Jay called.

"Yes, and she's on her own."

"OK, let her in."

Jay was sitting at the glass-topped table which had previously been in the dining room. A laptop was open in front of him and photographs of villas and large houses in exotic settings were scattered across the table.

"So you're definitely moving?" she asked.

"No," grunted Tracy.

Jay sat back on a high-backed black dining chair and rolled his eyes to the ceiling. "Why do you have to be so stubborn?" he implored.

"You like it here. You're not moving again because of me," stated Tracy as he opened the chrome oven door and, wearing a pair of black oven gloves, pulled out a baking tray.

There was a wonderful smell of roast chicken combined with sweet peppers and tomatoes. Dotty hadn't felt like breakfast, and now her stomach rumbled as she deposited her cardboard box on the table.

"What's that?" enquired Jay as he extended his head and neck and tried to peer over its top. "Is that one of my records?"

Dotty reached into the box, removed the record sleeve and handed it to Jay, who exclaimed, "Wow, this is one of the originals. And look, I've even signed it." Suddenly his face paled, and he dropped the record on the table. "Where did you find this?" he whispered.

Tracy must have noticed his change of tone as he stopped turning the contents of the baking tray and looked across at Jay, tilting his head to one side and drawing his eyebrows together.

There was silence in the kitchen.

Dotty coughed and explained, "I bought it at a car boot sale. I saw the record and thought Tracy might like it for his collection. It was only last night, when I was sorting through the box, that I realised there was something more to it."

"You did?" Jay responded mechanically.

Tracy made a noise which sounded menacing, like a growl.

Dotty looked across at his stony expression and then down at Jay before asking, "Did Rebecca Randall write the lyrics to that record?"

Jay nodded slowly and replied, "And the basic melody. Sure, we made some changes, but the original ideas were hers."

"And you bought the rights to the song, and sung and produced it. Was it successful?"

"Successful?" Jay's eyes opened wide. "Are you joking? This song made the Spinning Newts. Made me. We were number one for six weeks. It was everything we'd ever dreamed of. We performed live on Top of the Pops and were interviewed by newspapers, magazines and late-night TV shows. It was incredible."

Dotty sensed there was an edge to the excitement.

"But it was all a lie. I told myself it was OK," admitted Jay. "We were the ones who performed the song, who recorded it, and Becky was happily caught up in all the excitement. But then the money started to roll in and we were invited to tour America."

Jay and Tracy exchanged a knowing glance.

Jay continued, "Tracy said he'd take care of it. The real reason he started seeing Rebecca, or Becky as we knew her, was to find the original lyrics and manuscript. If we had those, there was nothing she could do. She'd just be seen as a smitten fan who was bitter she couldn't share in our new found fame."

"So you didn't pay Rebecca for the rights," remarked Dotty.

Jay shook his head.

"And did Tracy find what he was looking for?"

CHAPTER 35

Jay said, "Tracy had Becky's lyrics and music score in his bag the morning he was arrested, but the police didn't realise what it was, so they left it there. I picked it up later, with the rest of his possessions."

Tracy wandered across the black and white chequerboard tiled floor and stood beside Dotty, next to the glass-topped table. He peered into the cardboard box and said, "It wasn't your fault I was arrested."

Jay drew his lips together.

Tracy reached into the box and removed the stapled song lyrics and music score. "Here it is. This is what all the trouble has been for."

He flicked through the pages and then looked across at Dotty, his eyes narrowing as he asked, "You said you bought this at a car boot sale. When?"

"Sunday. Why?" replied Dotty, in a dubious tone.

Tracy and Jay looked at each other. "I swear it wasn't there. I looked everywhere, even inside the vents in the kitchen."

Who had talked about air vents being unscrewed in the kitchen? Keya.

Dotty's eyes widened. "You broke into Rebecca Randall's cottage."

She expected Tracy to deny her accusation, but instead a flush spread across his pale complexion.

"On my request," stated Jay.

Tracy slowly shook his head. "No. We both agreed it was the only course of action. But I'm sorry I left it in such a state. I heard someone approach and call out. I was worried they'd find me or call the police."

"A neighbour did call the police. You tipped them off by turning on a light," explained Dotty.

Tracy tapped his fingers on top of the table. "I had to. It was dark inside the living room as the curtains were drawn. I didn't think anyone would see a light through them."

"Keya, Sergeant Varma, arrived to investigate. Did you see her? Did you wait until she'd finished to break into the garage?"

Tracy froze.

"What garage?" asked Jay.

"Up a lane at the back of the house. Is that where you parked, Tracy?" Dotty's tone sounded bitter.

She remembered she'd come to see Jay and Tracy with an open mind. To discover if there was a compelling explanation behind the contents of the box, but all she'd heard so far was an attempt to cover up the past. To prevent a young woman, or girl as she was back then, receiving the recognition and money she deserved.

Tracy stopped drumming his fingers and his face was pale again. He whispered, "I didn't know about a garage."

In the silence that followed, Dotty replayed Keya's telephone conversation in her mind. The side door had been forced open and there were dust marks on a shelf where missing boxes had been stored.

She also remembered the confident young men on the stall at the car boot sale, the car parts and tools, and her earlier conclusion that these were stolen items.

"Somebody else broke into the garage," she surmised. "They grabbed this box but had no idea what was in it, and I bought it at the car boot sale."

Tracy smiled at Dotty, but it was a cold, reptilian look.

She really should have told Keya she was coming to Windrush Hall. Jay and Tracy could easily hide or bury her body on the Windrush Estate. As she stared back at Tracy, she had the impression he was thinking along similar lines.

"Enough, Tracy. Don't scare Dotty. She's done us a good turn bringing the manuscript here rather than turning it over to the police." He turned to look up at Dotty and asked, "Why did you do that?"

"I didn't want Sergeant Unwin jumping to any more conclusions." She bit her lip. "And I was afraid he'd dismiss my findings and think me stupid."

"Ah, he's not the most compassionate of policemen. But do you want to call him now? Perhaps it's finally time to own up about this song."

"No, you can't do that," blurted Tracy.

Dotty was surprised by his passionate tone.

Tracy continued, "The young Becky, I can understand you feeling guilty about. She was passionate, and at first trusting, but the Rebecca who's been demanding this and that from you. Who stole the song sheet from you. She was hard and cold."

"But don't you think she became that way because of the way I treated her? And why did she turn you into the police back then? Wasn't that also because of me?" insisted Jay.

"No, that was because she saw the attention you received when the song reached number one and she wanted some of that fame. And she got it as the victim of a crime. Don't you remember, she even wrote a book about her experiences with the band? Not that it sold many copies."

In a small voice, Dotty asked, "What was Rebecca demanding?" She remembered she'd seen Jay and Rebecca together outside the pool house and Rebecca had been shouting and accusing Jay of being boring.

"It started with her insisting we went out as a couple. I suppose she thought being seen with the latest celebrity to move into the Cotswolds would raise her standing in the community. And, of course, she wanted money and gifts."

"Like a new car?" asked Dotty, raising her eyebrows.

"That infernal car. But she loved showing it off. And there was jewellery, and events she insisted we attend."

"She was bleeding you dry," grunted Tracy. "You should have let me take care of her."

Tracy's tone was menacing and Dotty shivered. Had he taken care of her? But surely his methods wouldn't have been subtle.

Jay clasped his hands together on top of the table. "And then there was the party she insisted we throw, and the famous and influential people from London and Europe she wanted to invite. That's when I realised she was only using me to further her own career and become an international player in the antiques world. I'd had enough and I refused to go ahead with the party."

"How did she take that?" asked Dotty.

"Badly," muttered Jay. "At the time of her death, she was still trying to persuade me to hold it. I'm not sure what she would have done if I'd continued to refuse. Expose me with these, I expect." He indicated towards the box, and the music score and lyrics Tracy still held.

Dotty took a deep breath and asked, "Did you kill her?"

"What!" exclaimed Jay. "Of course I didn't."

"I felt like doing away with her," remarked Tracy. "I thought about hiding her body and her precious car in one of the lakes or ponds on the estate, but there'd probably be a drought next year and they'd be discovered. But I could have found somewhere to hide her body where nobody would find it," he mused.

"You didn't hurt her, did you?" blurted Jay. His eyes were wide and shining.

"No. I was still hatching a plan when she dropped down dead. Perfect, I thought. Problem solved."

"But it isn't, is it?" sighed Jay. He looked up at Dotty and asked, "What are you going to do with the lyrics and music score?"

"I'm not sure. If Sergeant Unwin does believe my theory, he's so desperate to prove there's a crime that he'll jump in with both feet and probably arrest you both. But I don't think that will help Rebecca or find out if someone deliberately set out to harm her. There again, it gives you both a motive, and I'm obliged to hand it over as evidence."

Jay leaned back in his chair. "I was thinking back to the day of the triathlon. I've seen Rebecca bothered by hay fever before, but the nasal spray she carries around always relieved it. So why didn't it work this time?"

"Because of the heat and the exertion of running?" suggested Dotty.

Jay shook his head. "She was fit, and she'd been practicing running around the estate in all types of weather. She was desperate to win. No, I keep coming back to the nasal spray."

Jay looked up at Tracy. Their eyes met, and Jay nodded.

Tracy left Dotty and Jay in silence and walked out of the kitchen. He returned a minute later carrying the white plastic nasal spray bottle.

Jay took the bottle, holding it up in front of him and said, "Can I ask you to delay handing over the manuscript, and instead give the police this, and somehow persuade them to test its contents? If it's just an antihistamine nasal spray, then I don't see there's a case to answer. But if it has been tampered with, the young sergeant will have the evidence he needs to continue investigating Rebecca's death. And if that happens, I promise to tell him how I stole Rebecca's song idea and cut her out of the royalties and recognition. How does that sound?"

It sounded a sensible approach. If Rebecca had died from natural causes, there was no need to rake up the past, even though Jay had acted badly taking the money and credit for the song. But it sounded as if Rebecca had made him pay. Tracy had certainly been punished for his crime.

If she gave Sergeant Unwin the nasal spray, she'd be helping him as Inspector Evans blamed him for losing it on the day of the triathlon. Perhaps he'd then treat her with more respect.

But if the nasal spray had been tampered with, and Rebecca had been murdered, they would all be under scrutiny, including herself.

She squared her shoulders, looked down at Jay and said, "I'll take the box home, with the record, lyrics and music score. And I'll hand the nasal spray over to Sergeant Unwin."

Jay nodded his head and replied, "Thank you."

CHAPTER 36

Dotty was deep in thought as she drove away from Windrush Hall. Had someone murdered Rebecca? And if so, why?

Jay and Tracy both had motives but having spent time with them and discussed Rebecca, she didn't believe they were guilty. But who was she to judge?

At a T-junction she braked to a stop. In front of her, a white metal sign stood tall on the verge, pointing towards Cheltenham to her right and Cirencester to her left. Which should she choose?

Cheltenham to visit Aunt Beanie in hospital or Cirencester to hand in the nasal spray. She hated carrying round secrets, and really wanted to know one way or the other if Rebecca's death was suspicious, but what about Aunt Beanie? She needed to be sure she was OK and that last night's escapade hadn't caused any long-term damage.

She turned right and drove to Cheltenham.

Parking at the front of the two-storey stone hospital building, she walked up the front steps between imposing double height stone columns.

Norman had told her Aunt Beanie was in the critical care unit, but she shouldn't panic as this was where all patients spent their first 24 to 48 hours after an accident or surgery so they could be closely monitored.

Following the large hospital signs, she turned left, walking along a wide corridor which opened out at several points into seating areas where people milled around or sat on blue plastic chairs, bolted to the floor.

As she passed one area, a blue clad nurse called out, "Mrs Robinson."

At the end of the corridor, she was directed to her right and walked up a slight incline as the corridor become narrower and more clinical.

The chatter of people was replaced by beeps and swishes broken by the occasional call for a doctor or nurse. This was the critical care unit. A pleasant lady smiled up at her from behind a blue plastic fronted counter and asked, "Can I help you?"

"Hi," replied Dotty timidly. "I've come to see Aunt Beanie, I mean Bernadette Devereaux."

"Your aunt," the reception replied, "let me see."

Dotty crossed her fingers behind her back, squeezing them tightly. She didn't like deceiving the receptionist, but she had the impression that if she told her she wasn't Aunt Beanie's real niece, she wouldn't be allowed to see her.

"Ward 4. Continue along this corridor and it's the third ward on your right," directed the receptionist.

The ward was small, and Dotty presumed there were three beds, although one was surrounded by a blue plastic curtain. A frail-looking woman lay in the bed on the left with a wire leading from her wrist to a monitor positioned on the wall behind her.

There were more monitors and machines surrounding the high-sided bed at the far end of the ward and the brown-haired patient had a mask strapped to his face and a large translucent ringed tube leading from it.

Dotty shivered. Nearly a year ago she'd woken up in this hospital with just such a mask covering her face.

The old woman in the bed to her left turned and smiled weakly. Dotty gasped. It was Aunt Beanie, but she looked so fragile with her long white hair loose and spread limply around her shoulders, rather than tied up in a brightly coloured headscarf.

As Dotty stepped closer, she noted Aunt Beanie's left leg was exposed and encased in a cast below the knee with only the tips of her purple bruised toes protruding.

"Hello," croaked Aunt Beanie.

"Hi," replied Dotty, hesitantly, as she tucked her hair behind her ear.

Aunt Beanie tried to say something, but only a rasping sound was audible.

"Would you like a cup of tea?" asked Dotty.

Aunt Beanie slowly shook her head and Dotty thought she whispered, "Water."

There were no water jugs in the Critical Care Ward, but Dotty found a water dispenser in the corridor and filled a white plastic cup.

Returning to Aunt Beanie, she held the cup to the older woman's lips and supported her head as she sipped the water. It was clearly an effort and, after consuming half a cup, Aunt Beanie laid her head back down and closed her eyes.

After a pause, she said in a clearer voice, "That's better. Thanks for the offer of tea, but the liquid they serve in here is like water, so I might as well have the real thing."

A nurse wearing a pale-blue trouser uniform bustled in, checked the monitor behind Aunt Beanie's head and suggested, "Shall we sit you up so you can talk to your daughter, and then you'll be ready for lunch?"

The nurse easily lifted Aunt Beanie's thin frame into a sitting position and supported her back with pillows. "That's better." She smiled at Dotty and moved on to the end bed, examining each monitor in turn.

Aunt Beanie stared at Dotty and, in a stronger voice, declared, "There's no need to look like that. I'm not about to keel over. I've had a nasty bump on the head and fractured my tibia and fibula, but nothing that a couple of screws, this cast and time won't heal, even in my aged body."

Dotty smiled weakly at Aunt Beanie's optimism. She wasn't sure it was as simple or as uncomplicated as the older woman insisted.

"I'm pleased you came. I was getting bored. Mrs Todd could only sit with Cliff for a short time as she was catching the bus into

Cirencester this morning. But she promised to be back on the three o'clock so Norman can visit this afternoon. And Gilly's told Norman not to worry, they'll manage without him for a few days. How are preparations for this month's auction?"

"I'm not sure," replied Dotty, glancing across to look at the patient in the end bed.

"Well, it's early days. The auction won't be for a few more weeks."

Dotty considered. Today was Thursday, and although it was only the first full week in September, the auction was only two weeks away.

"Two weeks. And I've sorted out over half the lots for this month's auction." But Dotty knew she still had a lot of work to do. She needed to get back to Akemans.

Aunt Beanie said, "Keya came this morning. It was so good of her to wait last night and drive Peter home. I think she feels guilty about what happened. But I'm sure it wasn't her fault. She wanted to complete her statement so she could submit it."

"Were you able to tell her anything more about last night?"

It was Aunt Beanie's turn to look towards the man in the end bed as she muttered, "No. I can't remember anything about last night."

Dotty furrowed her eyebrows. She had the impression Aunt Beanie knew more than she was letting on, so why was she hiding it? Maybe it was easier to feign loss of memory rather than admit to Norman she'd ignored his well-meaning and sensible advice.

Aunt Beanie turned back to Dotty and asked, "What about you? Have you made any progress tracing the car which hit me."

Dotty shook her head and replied solemnly, "I think I've done enough damage. I'll leave that investigation to the police."

"Quite right," announced a strong male voice, and she spun around to face Sergeant Unwin as he strode into the ward. "I hope you've learnt your lesson, and you'll stop meddling in police business."

Dotty touched her small black bag, which was secured across her body, and felt the cylindrical outline of Rebecca's nasal spray.

Sergeant Unwin appeared to take her silence as consent as he nodded his head briskly and declared, "Good. Now Mrs Devereux, I have Sergeant Varma's statement, but I wanted to run through a few details myself," he turned to Dotty and raised his eyebrows, "in private."

Sergeant Unwin crossed his arms and gave her a supercilious smile.

Dotty's shoulders drooped as she tucked her chin into her chest. She turned to Aunt Beanie and stuttered, "I better go."

Aunt Beanie gave her a lopsided smile and replied, "Don't worry. I'll be out of here soon."

CHAPTER 37

Dotty left Cheltenham Hospital and drove to Akemans in a dejected mood.

Not only did she still feel bad about Aunt Beanie and her accident, but she was burning with shame for not standing up to Sergeant Unwin at the hospital and giving him the nasal spray. She kept glancing across at her black bag, expecting the small plastic bottle to burn a hole through it.

At Akemans, she pushed open the heavy oak door into the antiques centre and was greeted by Gilly.

"Dotty, at last. George is on the warpath. The auction room is full of furniture and items which need photographing and itemising for this month's auction, and I've given Norman the rest of the week off to help Aunt Beanie and look after Uncle Cliff. But we do need to move some things through to the storeroom."

The front door opened behind them, and a stream of silver-haired women and bald-headed men entered the antiques centre, happily chatting to each other.

"And I can't help as we're really busy in here." She smiled at the first members of the new group and said cheerily, "Good afternoon."

Dotty bit her lip.

Gilly turned back, gave her a sympathetic smile, and squeezed her arm. "I'm sorry. You've had quite a twenty-four hours. How is Aunt Beanie?"

"She's putting on a brave face, but when I first saw her lying in that hospital bed, so frail and helpless, I just felt so bad." The guilt and anguish over Aunt Beanie's accident spilt forth and tears rolled down her cheeks.

Gilly stepped forward and wrapped her arms comfortingly around Dotty as more elderly visitors wandered past. She whispered, "Let's have a cup of tea," and led Dotty by the arm through the antiques centre, into the adjoining auction house office and reception area.

Dotty slumped down on the chair behind the antique mahogany reception desk while Gilly switched on the kettle.

As Gilly made tea, Dotty extracted the white plastic nasal spray bottle from her bag. Tracy had put it in a transparent plastic sandwich bag and picking it up, she absentmindedly considered the bag's red and blue flower decorations and grip seal.

Gilly pulled the spare chair across, placing it in front of the reception desk, and asked, "What's that?"

Dotty realised Gilly had put two cups of tea on the desk. As she lifted one, she replied, "It's Rebecca Randall's nasal spray."

"The one that went missing on the day she died?" Gilly's eyes widened. "Where did you find it?"

"I was at Windrush Hall this morning and Jay gave it to me. I think Tracy found it in the dining room."

"You should hand it over to the police, in case it had something to do with her death."

Dotty sipped her tea, but the fragrant liquid felt bitter in her mouth. "I know. And I was going to, but Sergeant Unwin arrived at the hospital and he was so full of self-importance, and I felt so worthless, especially with Aunt Beanie lying in that hospital bed, that I left without giving it to him."

"I'll tell you what. Why don't you get stuck into your work and take your mind off Aunt Beanie's accident, and Rebecca Randall's death? I'll call Peter and see what he suggests we do."

Dotty sighed with relief. "Thank you."

Dotty did feel better as the afternoon progressed, as she was doing something worthwhile, photographing items for the upcoming auction and writing brief descriptions of them.

She even ventured to add her own estimated values to some, although she was sure George or David would change them.

Towards the end of the day, Gilly appeared in the auction room. Her cheeks were flushed, and her eyes flashed excitedly. She gushed, "Rebecca's nasal spray which you found …."

"Tracy and Jay found," Dotty corrected as she positioned three angle-poise lamps on a white-clothed table, in front of a grey screen, so she could photograph them.

"Never mind that," Gilly rushed on. "Well, Peter picked it up on his way to visit Aunt Beanie in Cheltenham Hospital and while he was there, he asked the lab if they could run an urgent analysis on it, and …" Gilly paused.

Dotty was crouched down, about to take a photograph of the lamps, but she stopped and looked up at Gilly. "And what?"

"The bottle contained a saline solution."

Dotty stood up and asked, "So what does that mean?"

"Peter said some nasal sprays do only have a saline solution in them, as it clears the airways and helps against irritants like dust in the air, but this one was also supposed to contain axel elastic - no that's not right - but the point is it was supposed to contain an antihistamine, and various other components, but it didn't."

Dotty placed the camera on the white-clothed table as she thought through Peter's discovery. Out loud she said, "So the spray didn't relieve Rebecca's hay fever, and from what Keya told me, the summer heat and exercise would have made it worse. Poor woman. She was stuffing that bottle up her nose, believing it would help, but it didn't, and she would have felt worse. She must have really panicked at the end."

Dotty's whole body shivered. How helpless must Rebecca have felt?

"Peter thinks someone swapped the contents of that nasal spray bottle for those of a spray bottle containing only a saline solution."

Dotty started. "So someone deliberately tampered with it?"

CHAPTER 38

Dotty didn't arrive home until half-past six that evening. She'd continued to work through items for September's auction, photographing and writing brief descriptions, and as she did, she'd mulled over Gilly's news about the nasal spray.

She was still considering if it meant someone had deliberately set out to hurt Rebecca, and if so, if they only meant to scare her, or if their intention had been to kill her, when she walked into the kitchen at Meadowbank Farm and froze.

Aunt Beanie was leaning on a pair of tall aluminium crutches whose curved padded tops were nestled under her armpits.

She smiled warmly at Dotty and explained, "They let me out."

"Hardly," muttered Norman. "You made such a fuss, demanding to be freed, that you upset the other patients."

Grinning, Aunt Beanie added, "They couldn't wait to get rid of me."

"That's true enough," agreed Norman in a resigned voice, as he walked across to the Aga, lifted the lid on a round hot plate and placed the chrome kettle on it. "How was work?" he asked.

"Busy," replied Dotty. "The auction room is full of deliveries which I've been documenting today."

"I guess I should come in tomorrow."

"It would help," agreed Dotty. "We've a large delivery from a house clearance arriving late morning. But what about Uncle Cliff?" She looked across at Aunt Beanie. "He'll be too much for you."

The sparkle left Aunt Beanie's eyes and her voice was monotone as she replied, "I know, and I realised after you left that as there are only two weeks until the next auction, Norman will be needed at work. Mrs Todd will help, but it's not fair to rely on her. That's why I spoke to social services this afternoon. They're sending a nurse over twice a day and next week someone is coming to assess Cliff."

The lid of the kettle began to dance around and as Norman pulled the kettle off the hot plate, he said in a sympathetic tone, "We need to do what's best for Cliff. I know you want to keep him at home for as long as you can, but I don't think that will be practical for much longer."

Still leaning on her crutches, Aunt Beanie looked across at Uncle Cliff, happily sitting on a pine dining chair, watching the small television, and sighed, "I know."

As Norman made tea, Dotty helped Aunt Beanie lower herself onto another pine chair and then said, "I should think about making supper." She felt drained but also responsible for making sure everyone ate and kept their strength up.

"Don't worry," replied Norman, his back leaning against the front rail of the Aga. "We met Keya as we left the hospital. She was looking for you, and I think she has some news. Anyway, she offered to bring round supper for all of us, and she'll be here shortly."

Dotty found plates and set the table as Norman and Aunt Beanie sat at the kitchen table, sipping their tea.

Ten minutes later, the kitchen door opened and Keya appeared laden down with white plastic bags giving out a wonderful aroma of spices. Even Uncle Cliff looked round, wrinkled his nose and pronounced, "Supper."

"Yes, dear," agreed Aunt Beanie, leaning across the table and placing her hand reassuringly on his arm. "Just wait a few minutes while we sort out what Keya has brought." She turned to Keya and asked, "Did you cook all this?"

Keya laughed, "In the two hours since I saw you at Cheltenham Hospital. No way. But I've been dying to try the cooking of a lady who recently moved to the Cotswolds. She was a finalist on one of those TV amateur cooking shows, and now makes meals to order. They're all South Asian dishes, but I asked her not to make them too spicy."

"Sounds wonderful, my tummy's rumbling," announced Norman, and Dotty had to agree. She hadn't realised how hungry she was, having skipped lunch, until she smelled the food Keya had brought.

They were all sitting around the pine kitchen table, their plates filled with rice and noodles on top of which were dishes such as Thai green curry, satay chicken skewers, and a spicy black bean and eggplant curry.

"This Malaysian lamb curry is excellent," exclaimed Norman between mouthfuls.

Earl Grey must have been thinking the same thing as he jumped onto the table and sniffed at Norman's plate.

Norman growled and, looking put out, Earl Grey stalked along the table, his tail held high until he reached Dotty's place.

"I think this is too spicy for you," sympathised Dotty, but she cut a piece of satay chicken in half and put it on the table in front of him.

"You shouldn't encourage him," quipped Aunt Beanie as Earl Grey sniffed the chicken and then licked it. Clearly, he wasn't impressed as he jumped down and returned to Agatha, lying in her dog basket.

"I've been doing some follow-up investigations in Coln Akeman today," disclosed Keya.

"The landlord at The Axeman repeated what he told you, Dotty. Molly Vogt was in the pub earlier, drinking on her own, and the landlord presumed she was waiting for Didier, who didn't appear until later and rushed through the pub, from the back and left by the front door."

"After he left the packet and whatever was in it," added Aunt Beanie.

Dotty wrinkled her brow. Aunt Beanie did remember more about yesterday evening than she was letting on.

"I presume so," continued Keya. "It was the only time the landlord saw him. And nobody else in the village noticed him, or anyone else, acting suspiciously. The only complaint the owner of the post office had is his usual one, about traffic driving too fast through the village. He claimed a small cream, light blue or green car nearly knocked him over last night, and one of his customers reported a similar car, a Ford Fiesta, Mini or Renault Clio tried to run her off the road as she entered the village from Cirencester. But that was all I could find out."

"So that's all the news you have," stated Aunt Beanie, sounding disappointed.

Keya looked down at her plate.

"I have some, but it's nothing to do with last night," revealed Dotty.

"I thought you were working all afternoon," remarked Aunt Beanie.

"I was." Dotty paused and as she looked around the table at the expectant faces, her excitement grew. "But this morning I visited Windrush Hall." Keeping her promise to Jay, she skipped over the reason for her visit and continued, "And Jay or Tracy had found Rebecca Randall's nasal spray which went missing the day of her death."

"What does that mean?" asked Norman.

"Not much until Dr Peter had it analysed," replied Dotty.

"Did he tell you what he found? He called the police station with the results." In her enthusiasm, Keya grabbed her fork, flicking pieces of eggplant at Aunt Beanie, who casually wiped them away.

Dotty nodded. "Gilly told me. Or a least what the lab didn't find. There was no trace of antihistamine in the spray."

Keya grabbed the table with both hands and continued, "And Dr Peter and Sergeant Unwin think someone swapped the contents for a saline solution in a deliberate attempt to harm Rebecca, or at the very least, cause her distress."

"Could that have led to her death?" asked Norman in a level tone.

"As she was running, and it was very hot, yes, Dr Peter thinks it could," Keya confirmed.

"So, who are the suspects?" asked Aunt Beanie.

Dotty thought of Jay. She'd promised not to say anything about the lyrics or the song, but he'd promised to tell the police about them if the contents of the saline spray pointed towards foul play.

"Excuse me," said Dotty, pushing back her chair.

She entered her cottage through the communal door leading from the farmhouse and found her phone, still in her small black bag which was hanging from the handrail at the bottom of the staircase in the hall.

Jay answered her call in a hesitant tone. "Yes, Dotty."

"Sorry it's late, but I thought you'd want to know. The contents of the nasal spray have been analysed, and it does look as if someone deliberately tampered with them to cause Rebecca harm."

"So the young sergeant was right," Jay mused.

He was, and he'll probably be even more unbearable, thought Dotty.

"As we agreed," continued Jay, "I'll go to the police station in the morning and confess all. In a way, it'll be a relief."

CHAPTER 39

Dotty was at work by eight o'clock on Friday morning. She wanted to complete the inventory of items in the auction room before they were moved to the stone storeroom, across the gravel yard from the auction house and antiques centre. The space was needed for the delivery of house clearance items.

Norman arrived at half-past nine complaining, "I'm not sure what use a nurse is if she doesn't arrive until after breakfast. I helped Cliff get up and dressed, but Beanie was creating such a scene as she was still in bed. She'll have given the nurse such a tongue-lashing, I doubt we'll see her again. Still, it's Saturday tomorrow."

Which means, thought Dotty, Aunt Beanie might ask for her assistance getting dressed. She didn't mind. The older woman had helped her in so many ways, not least providing her and Earl Grey with a place to stay at a rent considerably lower than the market level.

Norman grasped his hands together and asked, "What do you need me to do?"

Dotty surveyed the auction room and replied, "We need to move as much of this as we can to the storeroom. I've finished my inventory, so I can help with the larger items?"

"Let's get started then," suggested Norman.

Dotty and Norman returned to the auction room, having moved an attractive but heavy oak sideboard to the storeroom when George Carey-Boyd appeared.

Dotty hadn't seen much of George since she'd returned from her holiday in Devon, and the children had returned to school, as she'd been travelling all over Gloucestershire and Oxfordshire valuing everything from an extensive collection of teacups and saucers to entire country houses, their gardens and outbuildings.

"I'm glad to see you're both busy," George quipped.

Dotty and Norman looked at each other and Dotty wondered what George wanted from them.

"Dotty, can you drive to Cirencester Auctioneers and collect some boxes of silverware and jewellery? They didn't reach their reserve in Cirencester's August sale and the client has asked us to try and sell them this month. I knew it was pointless holding an auction in the summer holidays. Everyone is too distracted by the good weather and holidays."

Dotty didn't think that was entirely true. Plenty of people had been at both Cirencester and the Fabulous Auction Boys' sales, but she was still grateful for the August break.

Smiling sympathetically at Norman, who was being given various instructions by George, Dotty left Akemans and drove fifteen miles through the Cotswolds and Cirencester town, to Cotswold Airport and the old hangar which housed Cirencester Auctioneers.

As she walked into the main auction room, she heard a woman's raised voice from the adjacent, smaller room where she had queued to speak to Molly Vogt through the hole in the wall. She hesitated, not sure what to do.

The door behind her opened and Molly walked in carrying a cardboard box. She said, "I presume George has sent you for these. There are several more boxes upstairs. Can you help me fetch them?"

The woman next door cried, "No."

"Oh, dear," groaned Molly. "Sergeant Unwin's upsetting Amanda."

Dotty turned to Molly, who looked down at her feet and muttered, "He's interviewing us all again, about Rebecca's death." She wrung her hands and wailed, "Why can't he leave it alone? Let her rest in peace." She pulled at a ringlet of her auburn hair.

From the next room Amanda laughed loudly and proclaimed,

"You've got it all wrong, sergeant. We weren't rivals for any man's attention. Not Jay Newton's, and certainly not Gilmore Chapman's. I'm happily married and if you want to confirm that, you can speak to my wife."

Molly was still twisting her hair as she said, "That'll put the sergeant back in his box. Mind you, Rebecca and Amanda may not have been rivals in love, but they were in work."

Dotty waited and Molly lowered her voice, as it was quiet in the next room, and continued, "Rebecca was ambitious and would do whatever it took to climb the greasy ladder of the antiques world. Her sights were set on London, or even New York."

Dotty considered this and asked, "Does Amanda own the auctioneers?"

"She's in partnership with Robert, who runs a niche showroom in Cheltenham specialising in rare books, coins and militaria."

Dotty's brow furrowed as she queried, "So couldn't Amanda just sack Rebecca? Why would she want to kill her?"

Molly shrugged her shoulders but then looked past Dotty and her eyes opened wide - in surprise or fear?

Sergeant Unwin declared, "Just the person I wanted to see."

Molly froze, and the colour drained from her face.

"I've a good mind to book you for withholding evidence, Dotty."

Molly fled from the auction room as Dotty turned to face the sergeant, the heat rising in her cheeks. Was the sergeant referring to the song lyrics, the nasal spray, or something else?

She tried to compose her face into an innocent expression as the sergeant continued, "And Amanda tells me Rebecca was furious you had the commission to buy furniture and antiques for Jay Newton at Windrush Hall. That's a big deal for you. Enough to kill for."

Dotty closed her eyes and shook her head in relief. What a ridiculous accusation. "Sergeant, Akemans has the commission to buy for Jay Newton, not me, and all the really expensive items and paintings are being sourced by David Rook."

Dotty heard the door open behind her and the soft tread of feet across the concrete floor.

She continued, "Besides, we've had to put the job on hold until Jay decides if he's staying or not."

Behind her, Molly gasped. "Oh no, why does he want to move? He's only just got here."

Dotty stared at Sergeant Unwin as she replied, "Police harassment."

CHAPTER 40

Dotty returned to Akeman's with five heavy boxes of items wrapped in newspaper. She parked at the side of the auction house and carried the first box through the double doors into the main auction room, where she stopped abruptly.

It was as if the room had the magical ability to refill itself the minute her back was turned. The space she and Norman had cleared earlier in the day was filled with sofas, mattresses, furniture and even a child's green plastic slide.

"Excellent," called George, striding towards her. "We'll keep those in the secure store over the weekend and photograph and itemise them next week. There's enough work in here for you to be getting on with this afternoon."

George wasn't joking. There was at least two days' work in the auction room.

Dotty made sure all the boxes from Cirencester Auctioneers were safely stored before returning to the auction office and switching on the kettle. She ate her sandwiches and sipped her tea while answering emails. When she'd finished, she wearily got to her feet and returned to the auction room.

The table, screen and camera were still in place, so she looked round for the first item to photograph. Two tall baluster shaped vases caught her eye.

The term baluster came from the shape of a stair rail, which the vases' elongated shape was supposed to resemble, and these ones were decorated in a Chinese style with panels of pink and blue birds.

As Dotty picked them up and placed them on the table, trying to find the best angle to take the photograph, a thick-set voice with a Gloucestershire burr declared, "I wouldn't spend too long with those. They'll only make £20 or £30."

Patrick, one half of the Fabulous Auction Boys, placed a box on the concrete floor. His brown curly hair was even more unruly than when she'd last seen him, standing at the stone pulpit in his converted church auction house.

"Now these," Patrick parted the packing material in a wooden box beside him and exposed the black porcelain top hats of a pair of Staffordshire Toby jugs, "could fetch £500."

He removed one and turned it in his hand. The jug was designed in the shape of an eighteenth-century man with a blue frock coat and red breeches sitting down, holding a jug of foaming beer.

Patrick placed the jug on the white-clothed table beside Dotty, and continued, "I'm afraid I've brought you more boxes of odds and ends. See if you can sell them and if not, give them away."

"And who shall I put down as the seller?"

"Nobody. The paperwork is more hassle than the money we'll make, so I've written them off."

Dotty had a sudden thought. "Would you mind if I went through the boxes and sold some of the items on my stall in the antiques centre? We've been really busy recently and my stocks are running low."

"Be my guest," replied Patrick, indicating to the box, "and I've six more in the car."

Dotty was going to be busy. Perhaps she'd need to work tomorrow morning.

Patrick reappeared carrying a second box, and as he placed it carefully beside the table he said, "I hear the police think someone did kill Rebecca Randall. I wonder which of her many men friends got rid of her?"

Dotty stared at him, and her mouth fell open.

Patrick laughed, a deep, hearty sound, but he stopped suddenly and said contritely, "Sorry, it's no laughing matter. But the look on your face. It's as if you thought she was the Virgin Mary."

"I wouldn't go that far," stammered Dotty, "and I knew she was going out with Jay Newton, and Sergeant Unwin thought she had designs on Gilmore Chapman."

"Gilmore, Didier and I suspect even your David was subjected to her wily charm."

"David is happily married," Dotty replied defensively, "and so is Didier."

Now it was Patrick's turn to look surprised. His eyes widened as he responded, "I don't know who told you that. Didier's had a wandering eye for years. I've no idea how Molly puts up with him."

Dotty thought back to the first time she'd met Molly, and seen Didier, at Cheltenham Lido. Didier had been talking to a woman, and she realised the way he was acting meant the woman was more than a just a friend. But who had she been?

Didier had attended Patrick's auction with Amanda, but today she'd found out Amanda was married, to a woman.

So what if the woman at the lido had been Rebecca? She'd been wearing a swim hat, but she'd had an athletic build and a tattoo on her back. And when she'd seen Rebecca berating Jay, outside the pool house at Windrush Hall, Keya had also mentioned a tattoo.

She looked up at Patrick, who was regarding her with a quizzical expression, and said, "I know this sounds strange, but did Rebecca have a tattoo on her back?"

Patrick gave a quick bark of laughter. "Her tattoo. Why on earth do you want to know about that?"

"Just humour me," replied Dotty.

Patrick shrugged his shoulders and said, "I joked with her about it and asked if it was the reason she was seeing Jay Newton. The tattoo was in the shape of a newt."

CHAPTER 41

On Saturday morning, Dotty woke in good time and showered and dressed before going through to the main farmhouse. Norman was in the kitchen, breaking eggs into a bowl, and Uncle Cliff was seated at the kitchen table, watching a breakfast TV show.

"Morning, Dotty," greeted Norman. "I took Beanie a cup of coffee at seven and she was awake, so she'll be ready for your help now. Would you like an omelette?"

Dotty shook her head and replied, "No, thanks. I should, but I don't feel up to it."

She climbed the stairs, with their worn, faded carpet, to the first floor. Aunt Beanie's bedroom was at the front of the house and the curtains covered a large window which Dotty knew looked out over the meadows to the River Coln.

Aunt Beanie was sitting up in bed, reading a magazine by the light of a table lamp with a plain cream shade.

"Good morning," said Aunt Beanie, brightly. "I'm so looking forward to today. It's going to be busy."

"It is?" queried Dotty, her voice rising in pitch.

"Of course. Tomorrow is Fairford Show. There's lots to do."

Dotty sighed and replied, "But I thought I would go into work today."

"Nonsense," chided the older woman. "It's Saturday, and you've enough to do here."

Despite her age and her broken leg, Aunt Beanie was surprisingly agile. Once Dotty had found her crutches, propped up behind the door, the older woman was able to use the bathroom without assistance.

As she reappeared, she commented, "Norman's going to work out a way for me to shower. He thinks some strong plastic bags and duct tape might do the job, but I might need your help tonight, if you're not squeamish about seeing my wrinkled old body."

Dotty blushed, and responded, "I'll help as best I can."

"Good girl, now find my brown cord skirt. It's hanging in the wardrobe somewhere."

Back in the kitchen at Meadowbank Farm, Dotty thought how odd and surprisingly feminine Aunt Beanie looked in a floral T-shirt top and a brown corduroy skirt, rather than her habitual tunic tops and leggings.

She still wore her trademark scarf, a bright blue one today, tied at a jaunty angle on top of her head.

Norman, Aunt Beanie, and Dotty joined Uncle Cliff at the kitchen table. As Norman tucked into his ham and cheese omelette, Aunt Beanie asked, "Is your frozen yogurt ready for judging tomorrow?"

Norman swallowed and replied, "No, I need to put it in a better container than the old ice cream one it's in."

"Which flavour did you decide on?" Aunt Beanie asked as she buttered a piece of multigrain toast.

"Bramble and apple. I thought it was unusual but seasonal. The bramble adds a tartness to the yogurt, but the apple pieces are sweet."

Dotty paused before sipping her tea and asked, "Is bramble the same as blackberry, and if so, aren't there lots of seeds?"

Before Norman could respond, Aunt Beanie explained, "The blackberry is the fruit of the bramble."

Norman added evenly, "And it does have lots of seeds. I had to sieve the pulp through a muslin bag before adding it to the yoghurt."

Aunt Beanie pointed to Mrs Todd's homemade raspberry jam. "Can you pass that, please?"

Dotty did as requested and, as Aunt Beanie unscrewed the lid, she said, "I need to re-bottle my damson gin. Can you write an attractive label for the show, Dotty?"

"I'll try," Dotty replied dubiously.

"And you have lots of cooking to do," continued Aunt Beanie. "Besides your Victoria sponge and tray bake for your classes, you need to cook something sweet and something savoury for the lunch."

"What lunch?"

They waited while Aunt Beanie chewed her toast. "The Women's Institute puts on a super spread for those attending the show. It's a great money raiser for the church and local groups, and we should all go."

"What about Cliff?" asked Norman.

Aunt Beanie looked lovingly across at her husband. "He'll enjoy looking around the entries, especially the fruit and vegetables, and it'll do him good to get out. Besides, this might be his last show."

Her shoulders sagged, and her gaze was forlorn.

On Sunday morning, Dotty woke from a heavy sleep. She recollected images of broken hearts, bunches of flowers and people driving too fast. Shaking her head, she padded to her bathroom.

"Dotty, are you ready?" called Norman from below. "Beanie's getting restless and wants to be up."

What time was it? She still needed to shower and get dressed.

"I'll be with you in twenty minutes," she called back.

Just over twenty minutes later, with her hair still damp, Dotty arrived in Aunt Beanie's bedroom.

"About time," declared Aunt Beanie with a pinched expression. "The exhibits have to be on display by 10 o'clock. Most of the judging takes place while we're in church, although the vicar always judges the children's classes after the service."

"Is Uncle Cliff coming to church?"

"No, we'll take Norman's frozen yogurt in a cool box, and he'll stay with Uncle Cliff and come along later for lunch. Now I'll wear the same skirt as yesterday and the yellow blouse you ironed for me, with the matching scarf."

Once again, Dotty helped Aunt Beanie dress. After assisting the older woman shower the previous evening, she had lost most of her inhibitions about the task.

After breakfast, Dotty sieved icing sugar over the top of her Victoria sponge, which was filled with Mrs Todd's homemade strawberry jam and freshly whipped cream from Buttercup.

She'd made two batches of flapjack, from rolled oats, butter, brown sugar and golden syrup, as she'd overcooked the first one, which was tasty but crunchy, whereas she wanted her show entry to be gooey in the middle. Her second batch was perfect and the remainder of the flapjack she'd boxed up for the WI's lunch. She'd also made a large leek and ham quiche.

Packing everything into an old, rectangular wicker basket, she added Aunt Beanie's bottle of damson gin, with the label she'd carefully written the previous day, copying a swirly script she'd found on the internet.

Norman entered the kitchen carrying a small green cool box, and asked, "Have you got everything?"

CHAPTER 42

Dotty and Aunt Beanie remained in their pew towards the back of St Mary's Church as the rest of the congregation filed out.

"A good turnout," declared Aunt Beanie, "but I doubt there'll be this many in church again until harvest festival."

Dotty collected Aunt Beanie's aluminium crutches, which were leaning against the back wall of the church, and the two of them slowly made their way outside into the bright, warm day.

"I don't think I can face the crush inside the town hall," admitted Aunt Beanie. "Why don't you have a look around and report back if we've won any prizes? I think I'll find a shady spot in the marquee and have a cup of tea."

All the items which were entered into the village show were being displayed inside the three-storey stone town hall, beside the church.

Although the rooms in the rear extension were large, with space to move around, those in the original building were small, with narrow passageways running between them. Dotty didn't know which would be the most hazardous, Aunt Beanie on crutches or the throng of people pushing between rooms.

She settled Aunt Beanie at a table in the corner of the open-sided marquee, erected at the rear of the town hall, in an unused section of the church's graveyard. "Will you be OK?" she asked.

"Perfectly. I've already spotted Mrs Todd, who can bring me a cup of tea. Now go and see how we've done," the older woman added impatiently.

Entering the rear extension of the town hall, Dotty was surprised to hear the rich, baritone voice of Inspector Evans. "That's crackin', that is," he proclaimed.

As Dotty pushed closer through the crowd of people, she saw he was standing beside a white-clothed table, on which sat an enormous onion with a bright red rosette next to it.

A man with wisps of grey hair patted the inspector on the back and said, "Well done, Dai." Inspector Evans beamed.

So the inspector's first name was Dai, and he grew onions. She knew he was interested in flower gardens, as he'd attended the Chelsea Flower Show with his mother during a previous case Dotty had found herself mixed up with, but she'd no idea he grew vegetables, and prize-winning ones at that.

Spotting Dotty, the inspector puffed out his chest and as she approached, he announced, "What do you think about this, Miss Busybody? I've won first prizes with my onion, my runner beans, and my potatoes. What do you think young Sergeant Onion would say about that?"

"That you should learn his correct name," Dotty retorted.

The inspector laughed heartily. "I have to keep him in his place. He's an ambitious lad, but prone to jumping to conclusions. I can't work out if he's on the right track with the death of that young auctioneer or if it's a complete wild goose chase."

His eyes narrowed as he regarded Dotty. "Either way, I'm pleased you're keeping your interfering hand out of it."

Dotty felt the blood rush to her cheeks, and she stammered, "Excuse me."

More people had entered the room and Dotty had to push her way to the other side where the flowers, jams, drinks and other items were displayed.

In the dairy section, a melted pool of dark purple liquid sat in a glass bowl next to a note which read Frozen Yogurt, and she was delighted to see a blue second rosette next to it.

Further down the table, the top of Aunt Beanie's bottle of damson gin was festooned with two large rosettes. One was a red first and the other a red white and blue one with the words 'Best in Show' printed on the centre circular panel.

"Bernadette always wins. I don't know why I bother entering," moaned a short lady with her black hair gathered tightly into a bun on top of her head.

"There you are," cried Keya, grabbing Dotty's arm. "Come with me. I'm too nervous to go on my own."

"Go where?" asked Dotty, her feet moving forward to maintain her balance as Keya pulled her towards the front of the room.

"To see how I've done. I entered a photo in the 'Watch the Birdie' class. It's one I took of a buzzard sitting on a fence post, early one morning, after I'd received a tipoff that a builder was dumping waste materials in a lay-by."

"And was he?"

"Was he what?" Keya frowned.

"Dumping building material?"

"Oh, yes. And I caught him red-handed. Come on." She tugged Dotty's arm, and they pushed their way against the tide of people into the older town hall building. In a front room, photographs were pinned to display boards.

"This is my class," observed Keya nervously. She scanned the photographs.

There were at least forty entries, and the winner was obvious, as it was a striking image of a diving kingfisher mounted on a cream background.

Keya jumped up and down, pointed towards the bottom of the display board and cried, "That's mine, and look, I've won third prize."

Dotty grinned, sharing her friend's infectious delight. Third was excellent considering the quantity and quality of entries.

Keya danced a little circle but stopped suddenly when she knocked into another display board. Dotty stepped forward, grabbed the falling board and stood it back in an upright position.

"What about you? Did you enter the cooking classes?" Keya asked.

"Two of the baking classes, but I doubt I've done very well. Not with competition from WI members."

Keya looked serious. "They probably practise all year."

Dotty and Keya found the baking class entries in two cooler rooms at the back of the original town hall building.

"Brilliant," exclaimed Keya, "a third for your traditional Victoria sponge. It looks yummy. Can we try it later?"

Dotty laughed. "I'm not sure. I think it has to remain on display until after the prize giving at three." She was pleased with her third place, and also a second in the tray bake class for her four matching pieces of flap jack.

As they returned to the considerably emptier room in the rear extension, Dotty said, "Did you know Inspector Evans grew prize-winning vegetables?"

"No," replied Keya, "Although I'm sure everyone in the station will be told tomorrow."

They grinned at each other.

They walked slowly along, beside the table displaying jams, dairy, and drinks, stopping every so often to comment on an entry.

Above the general murmur of chatter, Dotty heard a woman's haughty voice remark, "Molly Vogt has won four of the dahlia classes and her arrangement of garden flowers is most attractive. Personally, I can't grow dahlias as they give me hay fever." As if to emphasise her point, she sneezed.

Dotty froze and Keya, whose attention had been on the jars of lemon curd, bumped into her. She looked up at Dotty and said slowly, "What is it? You've a strange look on your face?"

Dotty glanced across at the flower arrangements and the tall, haughty lady standing beside them, who sneezed again.

"Come with me," she instructed Keya. "I think I know how Rebecca Randall was murdered, and by whom."

CHAPTER 43

Dotty led Keya into the marquee and across to the corner table where Aunt Beanie had been joined by Norman, Uncle Cliff, and, to her surprise, Inspector Evans.

"Ah, there you are!" cried Aunt Beanie, as Dotty and Keya sat down.

"The Inspector has been regaling us with his winning performances in the vegetable section."

The inspector cleared his throat. And was that a slight flush on his ruddy cheeks? "But I didn't win 'Best in Show', Bernadette."

It was Aunt Beanie's turn to colour.

"Never mind that," urged Keya, leaning across the table. "Dotty's worked something out."

"Worked what out?" Aunt Beanie asked, bright eyed.

By contrast, Inspector Evans narrowed his eyes at Dotty.

Dotty ignored him, the adrenaline pumping through her body, as she disclosed, "The riddle of Rebecca Randall's murder."

"You agree with my young sergeant, do you? That someone killed that lass?" asked Inspector Evans, in a dubious tone.

"I wasn't sure, not until Dr Peter tested the contents of her nasal spray. I saw how much she relied on her spray when she was changing before the triathlon, but it was ineffective when she used it before she started her run, and at the end, when she collapsed."

Dotty fished her car keys out of her small black bag, which was still strapped across her body. Holding them up she turned to Keya and asked, "Can you go to my car, in the car park by the entrance to Fairford Park, and bring back the water bottles that are sitting in the pouch behind the driver's seat?"

Keya clenched her jaw and looked round the table. "You won't go any further without me, will you?"

Dotty smiled. "Don't worry, we'll wait."

Keya scampered off and Dotty sat back in her seat, composing her thoughts.

Uncle Cliff raised his cup and Norman asked, "Would you like another cup of tea?"

Uncle Cliff nodded and whispered, "Scone."

"Just half," agreed Norman. "Lunch is being served, but I want to wait and hear what Dotty has to say before we eat."

Molly Vogt stepped out of the church hall extension accompanied by two smiling girls wearing matching pinafore dresses, their hair neatly arranged in long plaits.

A puffing Keya rejoined them, carrying two small, innocuous looking water bottles. "It smells funny in your car. Sweet but lemony."

"I haven't had time to clean it since Wednesday evening," replied Dotty, meeting Keya's gaze.

Keya's eyes widened in understanding and then she changed the subject, asking quickly, "Are these the bottles?" as she placed them on the table.

"Yes," replied Dotty. "I picked them up on the Tuesday after the triathlon. They were hidden under some lavender bushes in the formal garden at Windrush Hall, next to Molly Vogt's smashed, cut-glass vase. I also picked up the flowers she arranged in the vase for the ladies' changing tent."

"So," remarked the inspector, breaking into her introspection.

"So," repeated Dotty, tipping the empty bottle upside down before unscrewing the black plastic lid. Using her finger, she touched the inside of the lid and then the tip of her tongue. "This one contained a saline solution."

She passed the lid to Keya, who followed her example before wrinkling up her nose and passing the bottle top on to Inspector Evans.

Keya reached for the empty, capless bottle and read the label. "Fresh spring water. So who added salt to it?"

"Our murderer," replied Dotty. She lifted up the second bottle, which contained a cloudy liquid.

"We're not tasting that as well, are we?" asked the inspector suspiciously.

"No, but I would have the contents analysed. I think you'll find they match the ingredients of Rebecca Randall's nasal spray."

"Someone switched the contents," gasped Aunt Beanie.

"That's what I think happened." Still holding the second bottle, Dotty revealed, "I think someone tipped the contents of the nasal spray into this bottle, and filled it with saline solution from the other, now empty bottle."

Norman had been listening intently to the discussion, and he observed, "So when Rebecca inhaled the solution in the nasal spray, it didn't help her. There was no antihistamine in it."

"Which means whoever did this, planned it. Rebecca Randall's death was premeditated," announced the inspector, leaning back in his plastic chair.

People at the neighbouring table looked around with anxious expressions.

Aunt Beanie must have noticed as she leaned forward and whispered, "So who was it?"

"Her boyfriend, Jay Newton. He'd had enough of her threatening him," cried Keya enthusiastically.

This time, those at the adjacent table looked alarmed.

"Mr Newton visited the station yesterday and confessed to stealing Rebecca Randall's song," stated the inspector.

"So it was him." Keya bounced up and down in her chair.

"No," cut in Dotty. "Both Jay and Tracy had dealings with a young Becky Randall, when the Spinning Newts rose to fame, and Tracy came off the worst for it, but they had nothing to do with her death."

Keya looked dejected as she sagged in her chair. Then she raised her head and smiled. "I like Jay, and if Rebecca's death wasn't an accident, we might be able to run the triathlon again at Windrush Hall next year."

"So if not Jay or Tracy, who?" asked Norman.

"Someone who knew about her hay fever," summarised Aunt Beanie.

"Yes," agreed Dotty. "And which plants or flowers she reacted to. Hay fever is actually quite complex and sufferers react differently to types of flowers, grasses and even trees. I think dahlias really affected Rebecca."

"But they're so pretty, and they're not like lilies, with lots of visible pollen," remarked Aunt Beanie.

"This lass is right, though," added Inspector Evans. "Attractive as they are, dahlias really affect some hay fever sufferers."

"And whenever I saw Rebecca sneezing, she was near dahlias. The flowers in the ladies' changing room, in the pots by the transition area outside the pool house, and I believe I saw her standing next to some and sneezing at Cheltenham lido, when I finished training one day."

"So who else would have known?" asked Aunt Beanie.

"Her friends, colleagues and men friends, as Patrick of the Fabulous Auction Boys put it."

"The inspector's already ruled out Jay Newton, so who else was there?" Aunt Beanie asked.

"My astute young sergeant believes she was also involved with Gilmore Chapman ..."

Dotty felt Keya's eyes fall on her, and she was annoyed with herself for blushing.

"And Didier Vogt. And Sergeant Unwin thinks there were others in London. It appears she wasn't very picky as long as they had money, or influence in the antiques world."

Aunt Beanie's fingers drummed on the table. "Now listen here, I've known Gilmore for years and there's no way he'd kill anyone, not over a woman anyway."

Dotty wondered what Aunt Beanie thought Gilmore would kill for.

"But Didier Vogt is a married man," remarked Norman, staring into the lunch queue.

Dotty followed his gaze, which had fallen on Didier's wife and twin daughters.

"Stupid man," admonished Aunt Beanie.

Keya held up her hands. "So did he kill Rebecca?"

Dotty shook her head. "No, I don't think he has the aptitude to plan such a subtle death."

Keya threw up her arms and cried, "So who did?"

CHAPTER 44

Everyone in the marquee turned to look at the group sitting with Dotty after Keya's cry.

Keya ducked below the table, pretending to alter something on her shoe.

Aunt Beanie smiled at the other diners and called, "No need for alarm, just an excited competitor. She's delighted with her third prize."

From below the table, Keya asked in a subdued voice, "How did you know that?"

"Norman told me." replied Aunt Beanie. "You can come out now."

Gingerly, Keya raised her head and whispered, "So who do you think killed Rebecca?"

"Molly Vogt."

"No," said Norman defensively. His eyes found Molly, who was helping her daughters place food from the buffet onto their plates. "She's so petite and look how good she is with her girls."

"But if her husband was playing away," remarked the inspector.

"And she's juggling looking after them with working at Cirencester Auctioneers," added Aunt Beanie. "I heard Amanda say Didier was never at home and rarely helped with the girls, and he kept Molly short of money."

"Typical man," muttered Keya.

"Steady," growled Inspector Evans.

"I agree, Molly had a lot to put up with," said Dotty, "but I do think she killed Rebecca and knocked you down, Aunt Beanie."

"What?" Aunt Beanie shrieked and people in the lunch queue looked across nervously. She smiled sweetly back at them before hissing, "Now you are jumping to conclusions."

"No, she's not," reasoned Keya, speaking slowly, as if connecting the dots in her own mind.

"Molly was in The Axeman on Wednesday evening before your accident. The landlord thought she was waiting for her husband, but Didier didn't appear until later. And I saw her arrive this morning in a pale blue mini, which fits the description of the speeding vehicle spotted in Coln Akeman on Wednesday night. I was going to speak to her about her broken head light when I got the chance, but I forgot in all the excitement of the show."

Norman asked, "But why would Molly blackmail her husband?"

"To have enough money to leave him," replied Dotty.

Keya gasped. "There's a box and some bags on the front seat of Molly's car. I thought they must be something to do with today's show, but what if she is planning to leave? Today."

Everyone at the table turned in Molly's direction. She said something to one of her daughters and then looked up, her fork raised to her mouth. She stared back.

Then very calmly, she returned her fork to her plate, spoke to each of her daughters, who protested, and pushed back her seat.

"Sergeant Varma," growled Inspector Evans as he also moved his chair back.

Keya jumped up and ran across the church's graveyard in pursuit of Molly and her daughters.

Inspector Evans followed at a more sedate speed.

Dotty stood up but turned back to look at Aunt Beanie, Norman, and Uncle Cliff.

"Go on," urged Aunt Beanie. "I can hardly run after her with these." She tapped the aluminium crutches, which were leaning against the table.

At first, Dotty walked quickly past the seated diners, many of whom were watching the retreating figure of Inspector Evans, but she gave into her desire to know what was happening and she ran along the side of the town hall, onto the pavement.

Keya was standing bravely in front of Molly's Mini, and as Dotty approached, she heard Molly scream, "Get out of my way."

She thought she heard Molly's daughters crying in the back of the car.

Inspector Evans approached the driver's door and calmly opened it. "Please turn off the engine and apply your hand brake. Molly Vogt, you're under arrest for the murder of Rebecca Randall."

Dotty could definitely hear Molly's girls crying. She removed her phone from her bag and stepped away from the scene as Inspector Evans hauled a protesting Molly from the car while her daughters screamed, "Mummy".

"Hi, Dotty. How did you all get on at Fairford Show? I was hoping to come along for lunch but Peter was called away and time just disappeared and ..."

"Gilly," Dotty cut in.

Gilly was silent for a few seconds until she asked gravely, "What is it? What's happened to Aunt Beanie?"

"Aunt Beanie and Uncle Cliff are fine. We all are. But Inspector Evans has just arrested Molly Vogt."

"Molly, what for?" exclaimed Gilly.

"I'll explain later, but Molly's girls are with her and they're becoming hysterical. Can you come over and calm them down before Didier or social services arrive?"

"Social services," screeched Gilly. "I'll have to bring the kids. Where are you?"

"At Fairford Town Hall. If we're not out front, we'll be in the marquee at the back, and we'll wait for you before we start lunch."

Dotty's last words weren't quite true. When she returned to the marquee to update Aunt Beanie, Norman was carrying over two plates of food from the buffet, which he placed in front of Aunt Beanie and Uncle Cliff.

Oblivious to the drama unfolding around him, Uncle Cliff immediately tucked into his lunch. Aunt Beanie pushed her plate to one side and Norman returned to the buffet.

Aunt Beanie patted the seat beside her, and Dotty sat down looking around, aware for the first time that other diners were staring at her.

A few people stood in the graveyard watching the police proceedings and although the cries from Molly's daughters were less vocal, there was still the occasional heart-wrenching scream of 'Mummy'.

Dotty revealed, "I called Gilly, and she's coming over to look after Molly's girls until Didier arrives."

"If he's even in the country," complained Aunt Beanie. "So I take it Keya and the inspector were in time to stop Molly driving away."

Dotty nodded.

"A part of me can't help wishing she had escaped," sighed Aunt Beanie, "but she'd have been caught sooner or later. Poor woman must have been pushed to the edge by her philandering husband."

Norman returned with his plate piled high with pork pie, a scotch egg, slices of a variety of meats and a little salad. "Grab yourself some lunch before it all goes," he instructed Dotty.

"I promised to wait for Gilly. She's coming to mind Molly's girls."

Dotty looked beyond the town hall to the street, as blue flashing lights, but no siren appeared. Resisting the urge to see what was going on, she sat quietly, the excitement of her discovery giving way to guilt and remorse.

If she'd waited until tomorrow to voice her thoughts about Rebecca's death, she'd have given Molly a chance to escape. But where to? As Aunt Beanie had said, the police would have caught up with her somewhere. And better for her daughters not to be part of a countrywide manhunt.

She spotted Gilly walking along the path beside the town hall, her arms across the shoulders of Molly's pinafore-clad daughters.

Gilly's own children, Thomas and Olivia, trailed behind her. As they reached Dotty's table, Gilly pushed the girls onto two spare chairs and turned to her children, and said, "Go grab yourselves some lunch."

Happily, Thomas and Olivia ran off.

One of the girls said, in a tearful voice, "Mummy didn't let us finish our lunch. Please, can I get some pudding?"

"Of course you can. Go and join Thomas and Olivia."

The one who had spoken ran after Gilly's children while the second girl wandered slowly after her.

"Poor things," sympathised Gilly.

Keya joined them at the table and asked, "Where are Molly's daughters?"

"Getting pudding," replied Gilly as the four children marched back, but instead of all sitting at the table, they perched on a low stone wall, at the edge of the church graveyard.

"I'm starving," confessed Keya as her phone beeped. Picking it up, she tapped the screen and then gritted her teeth. "At last. Must dash."

CHAPTER 45

Keya had left the marquee behind Fairford Town hall without explanation. Dotty and Gilly helped themselves to lunch, although Dotty only picked at her slice of quiche and salad. The children ran around, playing tag in the graveyard.

Inspector Evans joined Dotty, Gilly, Aunt Beanie, Norman, and Uncle Cliff and said, "Uniform can transfer Molly Vogt to the station and deal with the preliminaries. I'm not missing the prize-giving." He tucked heartily into a mound of lunch.

Keya returned, taking a detour via the buffet table, and dumped a plate full of various salads and a blob of hummus on the table. Standing behind a chair, she beamed round the group and announced, "I got him!"

"Who, dear?" asked Aunt Beanie politely. "Didier Vogt?"

"Not yet. But I did arrest the fly-tipping wood craftsman before he dumped another load of ply board, offcut walnut veneer and antique mahogany in the entrance to your field, near Robin Wood."

"What's that? Robin Wood," croaked Uncle Cliff. "Has someone caught that crafty old fox?"

"No, dear," replied Aunt Beanie, squeezing his arm, "But Keya has caught a nasty man who was leaving rubbish there."

"Good girl," congratulated Uncle Cliff.

"Quite," agreed Aunt Beanie, turning back to Keya. "You emphasised walnut veneer and antique mahogany. I'm putting two and two together and coming out with four. Am I correct?"

"I'm lost," admitted Gilly.

Dotty thought she knew what Keya's discovery meant, but she sat quietly, allowing her friend to retain the limelight.

Keya sat down and addressed Gilly. "Fly-tipping's on the increase, so Chief Inspector Ringrose instructed me to tackle it. I've set up various online groups so people can report incidents. Earlier, someone in Poulton, who's an active member of the anti-fly-tipping movement, reported a van we've been looking out for, driving out of his village, heading north."

Gilly nodded.

Keya continued, "So I took the road out of Fairford, past Aunt Beanie's farm, and found the van parked up by Robin Wood. The driver had started unloading pieces of wood, so I caught him red-handed. And inside his van there were some large pieces of mahogany, and half an antique table, which made me think of Dotty."

"Me. But why?" queried Dotty.

"You told me how you had been duped into buying a modern, counterfeit table instead of the real thing. I questioned the man, and he confessed to building period pieces to order, but he'd had enough and thought the police were on to him, so he'd planned to do a runner. That's why he hadn't finished the table."

Keya looked around the group, before adding proudly, "And he admitted that the man who hired him was Didier Vogt."

"Did Didier use his own name?" asked Dotty in surprise.

"Pure arrogance," chipped in Aunt Beanie.

Inspector Evans put his knife and fork down on his plate. "So you've made another arrest, a man who was dumping bits of wood, but what has it to do with Molly Vogt's husband?"

Aunt Beanie explained, "Chief Inspector Ringrose has been investigating a gang which is breaking into large country houses when their owners are away ..."

That piece of information was new to Dotty, so she listened with keener interest.

"They are selling the pieces off, one by one at auctions, or to dealers or antique shops, but they also commissioned someone, an excellent craftsman, to copy some of the period furniture pieces they stole so the gang could increase its profit by selling them as originals. We suspected Didier was involved, and at least one member of the team at Cirencester Auctioneers."

"Amanda?" asked Dotty, remembering how Amanda and Didier had worked together to convince her to buy the Queen Anne style table.

"We believe so," agreed Aunt Beanie, "but we don't know if Rebecca was also involved. She was greedy, and used her charm to get where she wanted, but somehow, I don't think she'd have spoilt her shot at the top of the antiques game by becoming embroiled in a scam."

Dotty had to agree with Aunt Beanie, and she also doubted Molly Vogt would have been involved.

Keya chewed her lunch with a thoughtful expression on her face. She swallowed and said, "You thought on Wednesday evening that Didier was involved with the counterfeit furniture?"

Dotty admitted, "I did, but after Aunt Beanie was injured, I thought I'd jumped to conclusions and got it wrong, and that her accident was my fault."

Aunt Beanie placed her hand on Dotty's arm, and reassured her, "It wasn't your fault."

"No, it wasn't," repeated Norman irritably.

Aunt Beanie's face took on a pained expression, as Keya disclosed, "But I still don't understand why Molly blackmailed her husband, and how you knew she had."

"I didn't know. It just came to me. Whenever I met her, she was always sweetness and light but there was an underlying bitterness towards her husband. At my first auction, she suggested I look at a piece of furniture, which I subsequently bought, and Didier was the underbidder. I think I recognised in her the need to escape, and from there I deduced she'd need money, and she'd blackmailed Didier."

"Over the counterfeit furniture or his affair with Rebecca?" asked Norman sombrely.

"At first, I thought the furniture, but now I'm not sure. It could have been either I guess."

Dotty shrugged her shoulders.

Aunt Beanie sighed and pronounced, "What a tragedy."

CHAPTER 46

"Oh, they're all so cute. How do we choose just one?" asked Keya as she looked along a row of pens containing rescue cats.

Dotty had asked her friend to come with her to a rescue centre, south of Cheltenham, to find a cat for Windrush Hall, now the kitchen refurbishment had been completed.

She wandered along the pens observing different sizes and colours of cats.

Keya squatted down beside a pen containing a fluffy white cat, "Look at this one, it's so furry."

"I'm not sure Tracy would want such a hairy one, and it doesn't look much of a mouser."

She halted beside a compartment containing two tabby cats, cowering together in the far corner. Both of them were bald headed where someone had shaved off their fur. Why would someone do such a thing?

But they reminded her of shaven headed Jay and bald-headed Tracy. The pair had also been hiding from the world until the press coverage surrounding Molly Vogt's arrest for Rebecca Randall's murder had subsided.

Keya glanced into the cage without interest and cooed over the black and white cat next door. It certainly looked far healthier and friendlier than the pair Dotty was observing, but still, she couldn't drag herself away.

"You're not seriously considering those two, are you?" asked Keya. She sneezed, and added, "My antihistamine tablet is starting to wear off. Besides, I thought they wanted one cat. The label says these two are brothers and have to go together."

"Who else will want them?" sympathised Dotty. "They don't stand much of a chance next to all these other sweet, friendly cats. And with their bald heads, they remind me of Jay and Tracy."

Dotty and Keya carried the large rigid cat basket between them through the back door into the kitchen at Windrush Hall. Inside, the two tabby cats meowed pitifully.

The open-plan kitchen had been refurbished and comfortable armchairs were arranged around the wood-burning stove at the far end, beside the fireplace. In the middle was a large round pine table, which matched the dresser Dotty had bought at the Fabulous Auction Boys' sale.

Dotty had sold the large stainless-steel cooker in September's auction and replaced it with a British racing green Aga, and she'd found a bespoke kitchen cabinet maker who'd fitted hand-carved, oak-fronted kitchen units.

She was particularly proud of a large, round, white-faced clock, with a black wood surround, which completed the kitchen refurbishment. Akemans had been asked to help at what might have been Cirencester Auctioneer's final sale, and Dotty had spotted the large clock in a box of oddments.

Without anyone else's help, she'd researched its provenance and discovered it had originally hung at Kemble railway station and when the bidding stuck at £250, she had boldly stepped in and bought it.

Jay loved the clock, and David had subsequently valued it at £4,500. At last she had independently bought a quality item at a bargain price, like a real antiques expert.

"That's a very loud cat," called Jay above the meowing as he entered the kitchen.

"There are two of them. They're brothers and they've been mistreated and are very nervous. They were cowering in the back of their cage, and nobody wanted them."

Jay approached the cage and peered in as one of the cats hissed at him. "They're not very friendly."

"They're just nervous and frightened about being moved. You should keep them inside, in one room to start with, until they get used to their new home."

Dotty and Keya lowered the cat basket to the floor and Dotty lifted up the front flap. A shaved head poked out of the basket and then the cat scampered across to the fireplace, hiding behind an armchair. His brother raced after him.

"What's wrong with their heads?" asked Jay.

"Nothing, but someone shaved them," replied Dotty.

Jay touched his own head and murmured, "Poor things."

Dotty had also carried with her a bag of cat biscuits. "The rescue centre advised putting some of these in a bowl, and filling another with water. Why don't we put them at the far end, by the fireplace as that's where the cats are hiding?"

They found two plastic containers and one cat, with a white chin, lapped the water which Jay had placed beside the fireplace.

"I like them," announced Jay as the second cat gingerly stuck its head into the container of biscuits. "And they look like good mousers. Tea or coffee?" he asked.

When they were seated at the pine kitchen table with their drinks, Jay announced, "Now that the affair of Rebecca Randall has blown over, and Tracy's past has remained where it should …"

Keya looked at Dotty with a questioning expression, but Dotty shook her head.

"I'd like to organise a charity event. What about a Christmas ball, with Akemans running a charity auction?"

Keya jumped up, bumping the table, so coffee and tea splashed onto it. "Sorry, but that's a fantastic idea."

Dotty strode across to the stainless-steel sink and found a cloth to mop up the spilt drinks.

Jay continued, "We could erect a marquee on the front drive or on the grass beside the house."

The kitchen door opened and Tracy entered.

There was a flash of fur as one of the cats galloped across the kitchen and escaped through the back door. Its brother sat beside an armchair, watching it leave.

Tracy glanced out of the door before closing it and asked, "What was that?"

‘One of our new cats," replied Jay. "So much for keeping it in one room for a few days."

"Perhaps it's an outside cat, and prefers it out there," surmised Tracy, as he caught sight of the second cat. "And is that inside cat?"

"Inside cat and outside cat? We should come up with better names, but somehow, I think those ones will stick," mused Jay.

He turned back to Keya and Dotty. "So what about a date? I thought the first Saturday in December would work, before all the other Christmas parties."

"But that's less than two months away," replied Dotty dubiously.

Keya beamed, and announced, "Then we better get to work."

Will the Christmas charity ball be a success? Has Dotty given up on romance with either Gilmore or Sergeant Unwin? Find out in *Gavels, Tinsel and Murder*.

A charity ball. A dead guest. Can an amateur sleuth solve the case or will it ruin Christmas for ever?

Would you like to know how Dotty obtained her job at Akemans and solved a murder? Find out in the FREE prequel, *Hour is Come.*

A dead husband. A hidden body. Can an inexperienced amateur sleuth save herself and identify a killer in the stroke of time?

Download Hour is Come for FREE at
www.Bookfunnel.VictoriaTait.com/ep6qtlojl8

If you enjoyed this book, please tell someone you know. And for those people you don't know, leave a review to help them decide whether or not to read it.

Leave a review on
Amazon.com/review/create-review?&asin=B0B6Y4H13L

For more information visit VictoriaTait.com

Printed in Dunstable, United Kingdom

82135541R00127

Music at Hand

OXFORD STUDIES IN MUSIC THEORY

Series Editor Steven Rings

Studies in Music with Text, David Lewin

Music as Discourse: Semiotic Adventures in Romantic Music, Kofi Agawu

Metric Manipulations in Haydn and Mozart: Chamber Music for Strings, 1787–1791, Danuta Mirka

Songs in Motion: Rhythm and Meter in the German Lied, Yonatan Malin

A Geometry of Music: Harmony and Counterpoint in the Extended Common Practice, Dmitri Tymoczko

In the Process of Becoming: Analytic and Philosophical Perspectives on Form in Early Nineteenth-Century Music, Janet Schmalfeldt

Tonality and Transformation, Steven Rings

Audacious Euphony: Chromaticism and the Triad's Second Nature, Richard Cohn

Mahler's Symphonic Sonatas, Seth Monahan

Beating Time and Measuring Music in the Early Modern Era, Roger Mathew Grant

Pieces of Tradition: An Analysis of Contemporary Tonal Music, Daniel Harrison

Music at Hand

Instruments, Bodies, and Cognition

Jonathan De Souza

OXFORD
UNIVERSITY PRESS

OXFORD
UNIVERSITY PRESS

Oxford University Press is a department of the University of Oxford. It furthers the University's objective of excellence in research, scholarship, and education by publishing worldwide. Oxford is a registered trade mark of Oxford University Press in the UK and certain other countries.

Published in the United States of America by Oxford University Press
198 Madison Avenue, New York, NY 10016, United States of America.

Library of Congress Cataloging-in-Publication Data
Names: De Souza, Jonathan, 1982–
Title: Music at hand : instruments, bodies, and cognition / Jonathan De Souza.
Description: New York, NY : Oxford University Press, [2017] |
Series: Oxford studies in music theory | Includes bibliographical references and index.
Identifiers: LCCN 2016039254| ISBN 9780190271114 (hardcover) |
ISBN 9780190271145 (oxford scholarly online) | ISBN 9780190271138 (epub)
Subjects: LCSH: Music—Performance—Psychological aspects. |
Music—Psychological aspects.
Classification: LCC ML3838 .D32 2017 | DDC 784.1/1—dc23 LC record available
at https://lccn.loc.gov/2016039254

1 3 5 7 9 8 6 4 2

Printed by Sheridan Books, Inc., United States of America

This volume is published with the generous support of the AMS 75 PAYS Endowment of the American Musicological Society, funded in part by the National Endowment for the Humanities and the Andrew W. Mellon Foundation.

For Heather

CONTENTS

ACKNOWLEDGMENTS

While writing this book, I benefited from many conversations—some long and ongoing, others very brief. In particular, I wish to thank Emily Abrams Ansari, Shawn Allison, Andrea Bohlman, Seth Brodsky, Chelsea Burns, Mark Butler, Christine Carter, Eric Clarke, Nicholas Cook, Arnie Cox, Emily Dolan, Kimberly Dority, Helen Fielding, Michael Figueroa, Abigail Fine, Michael Gallope, Luis-Manuel Garcia, Robert Gjerdingen, Jessica Grahn, Shannon Heald, Mark Hopwood, Bryn Hughes, Sarah Iker, John Jenkinson, Ingrid Johnsrude, Alisha Lola Jones, Mariusz Kozak, Trent Leipert, Anabel Maler, Jairo Moreno, Roger Moseley, Katie Overy, Marcelle Pierson, Scott Richmond, Matt Schneider, Kris Shaffer, August Sheehy, Peter Shultz, Pete Smucker, Daniel Smyth, Martha Sprigge, Steve Van Hedger, Lee Veeraraghavan, Dan Wang, Kevin Watson, and Mark Yeary. I am also grateful to the Press's anonymous reviewers, to reading groups at the University of Chicago and the University of Western Ontario, and to audiences who responded to portions of this book at conferences and colloquia hosted by Cornell University, the University of Glasgow, Memorial University of Newfoundland, Northwestern University, the University of Toronto, and Rice University. These interlocutors' questions and comments have greatly enriched my thinking. Tips from Bob Kessler and John Kregor shaped Chapters 3 and 4, respectively. And I have learned much from my musical collaborators, including LeRoy Bach, David Brackley, Lance Brown, Mim Eichmann, Doug Lofstrom, Dan Lopata, Mark Kluemper, Dan Pearce, Ed Sullivan, Hans Vanderhill, and the late Ed Hall.

This project first emerged at the University of Chicago, and I would like to think that it bears the mark of that place. Faculty members and fellow students at Chicago both challenged and encouraged me; Thomas Christensen, Berthold Hoeckner, Steve Rings, and especially Larry Zbikowski served as perceptive, generous mentors. The book has taken its present form at the University of Western Ontario, where my students and colleagues form a stimulating artistic and academic community. At Chicago, my work was supported by fellowships from the Social Sciences and Humanities Research Council of Canada and the Mellon Foundation. At Western, Dean Betty Anne Younker and the chair of my department, David Myska, facilitated a term away from teaching that helped me complete the manuscript.

Suzanne Ryan has been a wonderfully enthusiastic, patient editor. Along with Steve Rings (in his role as series editor), she helped me develop and define the book.

At the Press, Adam Cohen, Jamie Kim, and Andrew Maillet promptly answered questions about various publication-related details, and project manager Damian Penfold guided the book through the production process. C. F. Peters Corporation and Breitkopf & Haertel gave permission to reproduce musical excerpts by John Cage and Helmut Lachenmann, respectively.

My brother-in-law Scott Brandon created the motion-capture images in his lab at Queen's University, and my father, Greg De Souza, produced the videos for the companion website. My parents, sisters, and in-laws also provided babysitting, birthday cake, and other much-needed diversions. Growing up in a home filled with instruments made me a musician, and this background still colors my interests as a music theorist: my father's father played harmonica (the focus of Chapter 3), while my mother's mother played organ (discussed in Chapters 2 and 5). Likewise, I am inspired by the musicality of my incredible daughters, Rilla and Audra. But most of all, I want to thank Heather, my partner in music and in life. She has both supported me personally and contributed to the book's content, offering critical insights on bowing patterns in Bach, brass performance, piano pedagogy, and countless other topics. I could not have written this book without her.

ABOUT THE COMPANION WEBSITE

www.oup.com/us/musicathand

Like many texts in music theory and analysis, *Music at Hand* invites readers to listen, watch, and play. The book's companion website presents audiovisual examples, comprising performances by the author, motion-capture videos, and music-analytical animations. These online examples are indicated in the text with the symbol ▶. To access the website, enter the username [Music5] and password [Book1745].

Much of the music discussed in the book, however, is not represented on the companion website. In such cases, recordings can generally be found in libraries and online. And readers of all levels of musical expertise are encouraged to try out examples at an instrument, as the website unfortunately cannot replicate the feeling of fingers on a keyboard or lips on a harmonica.

Music at Hand

Introduction

Music is fleeting. It disperses as it is heard. And though I sometimes feel its vibrations, I cannot touch, cannot see, and cannot hold them. Because of this, music has often been considered the most abstract, most metaphysical art. Yet at the same time, music is bound up with physical things: upright pianos and electric guitars, tambourines, turntables, violas, bagpipes, microphones, headphones, and iPhones, sitars, French or English horns, marimbas, flutes of metal, bone, or wood. And all of these, in turn, are bound to human bodies.

Music at Hand investigates music's corporeal grounding. This, in itself, is not especially original, for questions of embodiment are hardly new to music studies. In the 1990s, for example, some musicologists asked about music's role in the history of the body (e.g., Leppert 1993; McClary and Walser 1994). Attending to the embodiment of sexual and racial differences, their work recognized music as "one of the means by which people learn about their bodies—how to move, how to feel, how (finally) to *be*" (McClary 1998, 87). Contemporaneous theorists, drawing on psychology and philosophy, argued that embodied knowledge shapes musical concepts (more about this in Chapter 1). These perspectives, which are often combined, are complementary: where the first showed how music mediates bodies, the second clarified how bodies mediate music. A third, related approach considered aspects of musical organization and meaning that may be felt by performers but not always heard by listeners. Suzanne Cusick (1994, 18–20), for example, discussed a moment from one of J. S. Bach's organ preludes that creates a sense of physical imbalance for the player. For this style of "embodied music theory," musical sound and text are supplemented by performing bodies.[1]

Though inspired by these precedents, *Music at Hand* has a slightly different task: it emphasizes that performing bodies themselves are supplemented by instruments. That is to say, certain forms of musical embodiment are possible only with instrumental mediation.[2] As such, I am specifically interested in musicians'

1. Modes of analysis that focus on performers' bodies have been deployed by various scholars, including Fisher and Lochhead (2002), Le Guin (2006), Rockwell (2009), Montague (2012), Yearsley (2012), and Bungert (2015). This research participates in a broader musicological trend, theorized in Nicholas Cook's *Beyond the Score* (2014), that conceives of music as performance rather than text.
2. These kinds of musical embodiment are by no means universal, since there are musicians who do not play instruments and musical cultures that do not make them (Kartomi 1990, xvii–xviii). Nonetheless, humans have used musical instruments since prehistoric times (see De Souza 2014).

engagements with concrete objects, rather than musical gesture in general.[3] Insofar as players' actions take shape around keys, fingerboards, mouthpieces, and so on, it is necessary to examine how instruments are structured, how they make actions audible and sounds manipulable. Here the book can be understood as a music-theoretical counterpart to recent research, inspired by media theory and history of science, on instruments' epistemological significance (e.g., Dolan 2013, 10–13; Tresch and Dolan 2013; Moseley 2015). From this viewpoint, musical knowledge is grounded not in bodies alone, but in an interplay of techniques and technologies.

A theory of musical bodies, then, requires a theory of musical technics. This uncommon word "technics" refers to technical matters in general.[4] It corresponds to the German *Technik* or the French *la technique*, which, depending on context, can be translated as either "technique" or "technology." The ambiguity can productively bring these elements together, revealing their commonalities, their complementarity. Every technology, in this view, is associated with some technique. Technics, moreover, is an inclusive concept. It encompasses seemingly disparate objects and practices, from laptop computers to prehistoric hand axes, from the tools of industry and warfare to those of art and play. Accordingly, "music technology" would go beyond electronic devices and recording technology to include instruments and forms of musical writing. And "musical technique" would involve performing skills but also listening skills. Indeed, this book insists that such skills are closely connected, that the acquisition of instrumental technique—a process of bodily "technicization"—affects the ways that players perceive, understand, and imagine music.

To support these theoretical claims, the book marshals diverse musical examples—classical and popular, old and new. It also mixes several modes of performance analysis.[5] I examine specific recorded performances (many of which are improvised), while also reading scores in terms of their performative possibilities. I reflect on my own experiences as a multi-instrumentalist, while also exploring pieces and instruments that I cannot play, which I approach from the outside. And though I have not conducted formal fieldwork or interviews, I often consider statements by expert performers. Each of my case studies, of course, is historically and culturally specific. As such, I often have recourse to scholarship from music history and ethnomusicology. (In fact, though the examples reflect my own expertise in Western music, ethnomusicology offers some important antecedents to my approach.)[6] Yet my main goal is not to illuminate the musical cultures or social

3. Robert Hatten's approach to musical gesture, for example, is predicated on an expansive definition of the concept (2004, 93–95). By contrast, I tend to follow a distinction made by the psychologist David McNeill (1992, 78), who separates spontaneous communicative gestures from skilled forms of object manipulation. From this perspective, playing "air guitar" is gestural, but playing a real guitar is not.

4. Prominent writings on technics include Lewis Mumford's *Technics and Civilization* (1934) and Bernard Stiegler's *Technics and Time* series (1998, 2009, 2011). Gallope (2011) discusses technics and music.

5. For recent methodological reflections on performance and analysis, see Cook (2014, ch. 2) and the collection of essays titled "Performance and Analysis Today" in *Music Theory Online* 22/2, introduced by Barolsky and Klorman (2016).

6. Aspects of my work are anticipated in John Blacking's reflections on human musicality, which engaged both musical instruments and the anthropology of the body (1973, 17–21), in John Baily's (1977) study of body-instrument interaction in the performance of Afghan lutes, and in Bell Yung's (1984) work on kinesthetic and choreographic aspects of music for the *qin*, a seven-string Chinese zither.

contexts from which these examples are drawn. Instead, their juxtaposition allows generalizations about instrumental performance to emerge. Musical and analytical variety thus serves as a methodological feature. With this in mind, the book might be imagined as a kind of collage.

This collage of music and ideas mixes disciplines, too, relying most consistently on cognitive science and phenomenology. While I engage with experimental research from music psychology, I am equally interested in theoretical work related to embodied cognition. Embodied cognition—like "embodied music theory"—distinguishes itself from approaches that treat mind and body as independent entities. To be specific, embodied cognition principally reacts against a computational conception of mind, which emerged in the mid-twentieth century. According to this model, bodily input is converted into "nonperceptual" data, and the brain deals in abstract symbolic representations that are essentially independent of the senses. Proponents of embodied cognition, by contrast, argue for the integration of perception and cognition, body and mind.[7] Claiming that knowledge and experience are based in the body's sensorimotor capacities, they draw on behavioral studies, brain imaging, cognitive anthropology, and so forth. This discourse, then, provides a repository of theoretical concepts and empirical evidence about the relations among mind, body, and world.

Meanwhile, phenomenology—a philosophical tradition inaugurated by Edmund Husserl—offers a first-person standpoint that complements cognitive studies.[8] This, again, involves a blend of theory and observation. On one level, phenomenology is a descriptive method, a set of techniques for analyzing lived experience. Husserl examines things as they appear to consciousness, attending to the correlation of object and subject, to individual senses, to real or imaginary shifts in temporal and spatial perspective. His reflections on the sound of a violin provide a characteristic example:

> The tone of a violin with its objective identity is given through perspectives, it has its changing forms of appearance. They differ according as I approach the violin or recede from it, according as I am in the concert hall itself or listen through its closed doors, and so forth. No way of appearing claims to rank as giving its data absolutely, although a certain type, appearing as normal within the compass of my practical interests, has a certain advantage; in the concert hall, at the "right" spot, I hear the tone "itself" as it "really" sounds. (Husserl [1913] 2012, 83)

Briefly put, the phenomenologist develops *variations* on experience, much as a musician might compose variations to explore a familiar theme.[9] Such techniques

7. Embodied cognition does not necessarily invalidate findings of the symbolic-processing approach. Theoretical work in this relatively new area often aims to show how earlier results can be reinterpreted in terms of sensorimotor grounding, moving toward methodological synthesis (Barsalou 2010). Note also that these two streams of cognitive science have long inspired music theorists: for example, Fred Lerdahl and Ray Jackendoff's *A Generative Theory of Tonal Music* (1983) adapts hierarchical structures from Noam Chomsky's computationalist linguistics, whereas Lawrence Zbikowski's *Conceptualizing Music* (2002) adapts work on embodied metaphor from later cognitive linguistics.
8. For example, Varela, Thompson, and Rosch combine cognitive science with phenomenology in *The Embodied Mind* (1991). There is even a journal, *Phenomenology and the Cognitive Sciences*, devoted to this methodological pairing.
9. Here I am indebted to Don Ihde's use of phenomenological variations in his work on the phenomenology of sound (2007) and technology (2009, 16–19). For a practical introduction to the technique, see Ihde (1986).

can be separated from Husserl's transcendental philosophy. For example, David Sudnow's *Ways of the Hand* (1978)—a book that describes how the author learned to play jazz piano—employs these methods without explicitly discussing phenomenological theory. When analyzing my own experiences as a performer, I continue this style of applied phenomenology.

I also deal with phenomenology at a philosophical level, where experience is linked to ontology. Here my principal interlocutors are later figures: Martin Heidegger and Maurice Merleau-Ponty. Neither wrote much about music—Heidegger was more interested in poetry, Merleau-Ponty in painting—and some commentators have critiqued their treatment of sound (Dyson 2009, 85–95; Cimini 2012). But I am mainly concerned with other aspects of their thought, namely Heidegger's account of technology and Merleau-Ponty's philosophy of the body. For Merleau-Ponty, "the body is our general means of having a world" ([1945] 2012, 147). That is to say, my body—unlike external things that come and go—is always here for me. It is felt directly, imbued with affect and kinesthetic sensation. My body makes perception possible. Merleau-Ponty's *Phenomenology of Perception*, then, does more than celebrate somatic self-awareness. Its attention to bodily experience supports ontological claims that challenge computationalism's emphasis on disembodied informational patterns. In this view, we do not simply *have* bodies. We *are* bodies.

To some, these interdisciplinary commitments might seem to lead away from music theory proper. But I would argue, on the contrary, that this type of methodological synthesis is characteristic of the field. The history of theory is full of musician-scholars who took inspiration from contemporaneous science, philosophy, mathematics, linguistics, and so on. Furthermore, this particular triad—music theory, cognitive science, and phenomenology—is central to a well-known essay by the influential theorist David Lewin.[10] In "Music Theory, Phenomenology, and Modes of Perception," Lewin contends that theories of musical perception should consider production as well as listening. When we play the final movement of Beethoven's "Appassionata" Piano Sonata, he writes, "we are *not* matching the fingers and positions of our right hands to a preconceived 'perception' of the theme; rather we are *in the act of perceiving the theme* as we move the parts of our bodies to play it" (1986, 382, emphasis in original). As one way of responding to Lewin's phenomenology, the present book builds on his work in mathematical music theory, constructing transformational models of various instrumental interfaces.

Certain aspects of these models will interest mainly readers with a background in transformational theory. Yet this analytical apparatus also exemplifies something that music theory can bring to interdisciplinary conversations. While Lewinian formalism fixes aspects of musical performance, it also makes them legible for close analysis. It has helped me to listen more carefully and to think more rigorously about performative actions and instrumental spaces. In this regard, the associated musical excerpts and technical diagrams might be compared to the data and statistics presented in the

10. As Brian Kane (2011) has demonstrated, Lewin's phenomenology relies on a particular interpretation of Husserl (associated with West Coast phenomenology), even as he anticipates certain post-Husserlian developments. For an applied phenomenology of musical listening, see Clifton (1983).

results section of a psychology article. They test intuitions about particular pieces and performances. They reveal expected or unexpected patterns, confirming or denying musical hypotheses. That is to say, in the wealth of musical detail gathered by analysis, music theory seeks a kind of evidence. Such evidence might support claims about "intra-musical" principles (e.g., conventions of tonal harmony or form in classical music). But it might equally speak to broader humanistic and scientific concerns, involving cultural history, cognitive processes, representations of gender, race, and disability, or the co-constitution of bodies and technologies. Music-analytical results are admittedly partial, provisional, and susceptible to bias. Nonetheless, I cannot help but believe that music, if we listen to it truly, can teach us about the world. With this in mind, I have tried to keep the book's analytical discussions accessible to nonspecialist readers, who may find the audiovisual materials on the companion website particularly useful.

The book's opening chapters theorize connections among body, instrument, and sound. Chapter 1 takes performances by the deaf Beethoven as an instance of body-instrument interaction. It shows how instrumental practice gives rise to distinctive patterns of auditory-motor coactivation in players' brains, which may be reanimated in perception and imagination. Elaborating on this general framework, Chapters 2 and 3 examine particular instrumental interfaces. They focus, respectively, on sound production and instrumental space, on how instruments translate action into sound and how they distribute musical materials physically. Chapter 3 also introduces transformational tools that are used throughout the rest of the book. Its analyses—which compare various styles of harmonica playing—suggest that idioms emerge at the nexus of instrumental "sweet spots" and players' embodied habits.

Processes of instrumental alteration are explored in Chapter 4. When musicians alter their instruments, they open up new possibilities for sound and performance. But a series of analyses related to guitar improvisation indicate that this process, by disrupting established auditory-motor mappings, can also affect players' perception.

The final two chapters ask how composers and listeners relate to instruments. Chapter 5 focuses on the music of J. S. Bach, considering how instrumental idioms may function as a resource for composers. Ultimately it argues that composition is deeply intertwined with instrumentation. Turning to listeners who do not play instruments, Chapter 6 reflects on the interplay of sound and source in Haydn's use of valveless horns. If historically situated audiences recognize schematic textures referring to instruments—if, for example, they can hear virtual horns in a string quartet or piano piece—this implies that their perception also reflects multisensory associations centered on instruments. Like performance, then, listening would be both embodied and conditioned by technology.

CHAPTER One

Beethoven's Prosthesis

More than a decade after Ludwig van Beethoven's death, his secretary Anton Schindler remembered the composer at play:

> Beethoven was very fond, especially in the dusk of the evening, of seating himself at the piano to improvise, or he would frequently take up the violin or viola.... In the latter years of his life, his playing at such times was more painful than agreeable to those who heard it.... The most painful thing of all was to hear him improvise on stringed instruments, owing to his incapability of tuning them. The music which he thus produced was frightful, though in his mind it was pure and harmonious. (Schindler 1841, 174–76)

This intimate scene of musical pleasure is also, poignantly, a scene of breakdown. Deafness does not simply block Beethoven's hearing. It alters his music-making too.

Later accounts, unlike Schindler's, often romanticize this disability, claiming that it benefited Beethoven's music.[1] Hearing loss, in this view, distanced the composer from the perceptible materiality of sound and inducted him into an ideal, spiritual musicality. His late string quartets came to represent the belief, historicized by Carl Dahlhaus, that absolute music "'dissolves' itself from the sensual" (1989, 17). Understanding music as an unmediated expression of the Will, this discourse metaphysically opposes "pure musicality" and "mere technique." Beethoven's music, it argues, has nothing to do with instruments or manual skill.

Yet Beethoven enjoyed the physical practice of instrumental music despite his hearing loss. He continued to play privately and probably continued to write music at the keyboard (Ealy 1994, 273). Perhaps this is unsurprising, given his background as a composer-pianist and a renowned improviser. Still, what was it like for Beethoven to perform music that he could *feel* but not *hear*?

I want to use this scene not to demonstrate Beethoven's exceptionalism, but to explore cognitive processes that are common among hearing instrumentalists. The scene, on a certain level, suggests a kind of phenomenological reduction. In music scholarship, this Husserlian technique has been prominently associated with "reduced listening," a mode of purely aural perception in which sounds are freed

1. K. M. Knittel (1998) traces this view to Richard Wagner's 1870 Beethoven essay. For further discussion of Wagner's influence here, see Goehr (1998, 123) and Kane (2014, 114–16), and for a general discussion of Beethoven and disability, see Straus (2011).

Figure 1.1 Ludwig van Beethoven, Piano Sonata no. 8 in C minor, "Pathétique," op. 13, mvt. i, end of m. 10.

from their worldly sources.[2] By contrast, Beethoven's experience highlights everything that reduced listening excludes—kinesthetic, tactile, visual, and technological aspects of performance. Asking about Beethoven, then, is a way of asking a broader question: How do bodies and instruments condition musical experience?

Listening with the Body

Beethoven might have imagined music while resting in an armchair or strolling through the city. But in Schindler's anecdote, the composer moves his arms, wrists, and fingers, pressing keys, pulling a bow across strings. Insofar as the story connects Beethoven's bodily actions and his inner hearing, it resonates with arguments that present musical experience as essentially embodied.

Consider a brief excerpt from Beethoven's "Pathétique" Sonata, shown in Figure 1.1. The melody hovers, then descends through a chromatic scale, over the dominant harmony that closes the piece's slow introduction. It is a striking move, for several reasons. It falls more than two octaves, a distance that effectively covers the introduction's entire melodic range. At the same time it picks up speed, culminating in a series of one-hundred-twenty-eighth notes that are commonly performed in a free accelerando. This melody, then, gives a sense not only of musical movement, but of musical momentum. It does not simply descend. It plummets.

My description of the passage is obviously metaphorical, and it plays with an opposition of "high" and "low" pitches that pervades Western musical discourse.[3] Yet this spatial mapping, however familiar, is far from universal. For example, Sundanese musicians from West Java describe pitch relationships in terms of size and tension (van Zanten 1986, 85). High notes are "small" or "pulled"; low notes, "large" or "slack."[4] Many music theorists—drawing on work by the cognitive

2. The most influential proponent of this method is the French composer Pierre Schaeffer, to whom I return in Chapter 6.
3. As Lawrence Zbikowski notes, the high/low metaphor is not limited to theoretical language. It also supports "text painting," where composers use musical motion to represent ascent or descent (2002, 63–74).
4. These theoretical metaphors obviously relate to the construction of instruments. On pitch-related metaphors in other musical traditions, see Cox (1999), Zbikowski (2002, 67–68), and Eitan and Timmers (2010).

Figure 1.2 Diagram of the verticality schema (after Zbikowski 2002, 69).

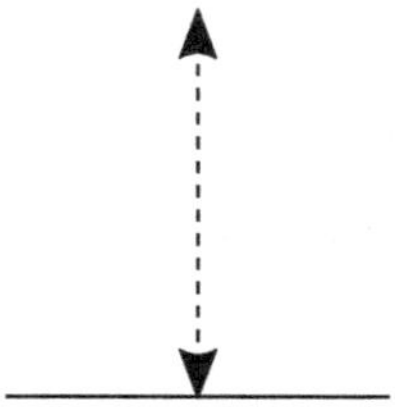

linguist George Lakoff and the philosopher Mark Johnson (1980)—argue that such linguistic metaphors are made possible by underlying conceptual metaphors. For Lakoff and Johnson, metaphoric processes of cross-domain mapping are basic to thought and action. And empirical research indeed shows that the conceptual mapping between pitch height and vertical position can affect perception and motor performance.[5] For example, in stimulus-response compatibility experiments, participants—with or without formal musical training—respond more quickly and accurately when higher pitches are paired with higher visual stimuli (Rusconi et al. 2006; Lidji et al. 2007). Conceptual metaphors are theoretically founded on "image schemas," gestalts abstracted from sensorimotor perception.[6] The orientational metaphor of pitch height would engage a verticality schema (illustrated in Figure 1.2), a pattern that remains invariant throughout countless experiences of up-and-down. For a Western listener, the passage from Beethoven's "Pathétique" might evoke such experiences: running down stairs, riding a roller coaster, dropping a stone, or watching an Olympic diver. For a Javanese listener, it might more readily suggest a process of expanding or loosening. In both cases, the conceptual metaphor for pitch is culturally specific, while also grounded in embodied experience.

Phenomenological terms can help clarify the meaning of "embodied experience" here. Edmund Husserl distinguishes between two German words for "body," *Körper* and *Leib* ([1909] 1973, 42–55). On one level, the human body is a material object. My hand and the piano are both concrete things, both physical bodies (*Körper*). This is, in fact, a precondition for their interaction: without this common substantiality, my fingers and the keys could not touch. Yet at the same time, my own body differs from external objects, because I experience it as a lived body

5. Eitan and Timmers review experimental research on pitch and space (2010, 405–6). Empirical research also suggests connections between the motor system and the perception of rhythm. Bodily movement seems to facilitate different metrical interpretations of an ambiguous rhythmic pattern (Phillips-Silver and Trainor 2005, 2007). And functional magnetic resonance imaging studies show that beat perception engages a network of motor-related areas in the brain, involving the basal ganglia, premotor cortex, and supplementary motor area (Grahn 2009).

6. Image schemas were introduced by Johnson (1987). Rohrer (2005) discusses neurobiological evidence consistent with the theory. Music-theoretical applications of the concept have been explored by Saslaw (1996), Brower (1997–98), Cox (1999), Mead (1999), Zbikowski (2002), Adlington (2003), Johnson and Larson (2003), Straus (2011, 107–12), and Larson (2012).

(*Leib*). It is always present for me, imbued with kinesthetic sensations, and I move it directly. Image schemas are based on this level of lived embodiment.

Husserl also extends the doubling to other people's bodies. I might see your hand as a material object or as a living hand like my own. Later phenomenologists, notably Maurice Merleau-Ponty, develop this theme further, conceiving of intersubjectivity as a kind of intercorporeality. We understand each other—and the world we inhabit together—via shared sensorimotor capacities. This resonates with recent investigations of a "mirror-neuron system," which is involved in both performing and perceiving actions.[7] Along these lines, Arnie Cox has proposed that metaphors of musical verticality (and musical meaning in general) involve "mimetic motor imagery": that is, imitation, either real or imagined, of performers' movements and sonic patterns (1999, 108).[8]

All of this suggests a preliminary interpretation of Beethoven's late improvisations. Building on the cognitive perspective that approaches metaphor as a basic structure of thought grounded in image-schematic structures, the composer's actions can be understood as *kinesthetic analogues* for the sounds in his mind, as embodied representations. If listeners perceive actual sound in terms of imagined movement, Beethoven would instead perceive actual movement in terms of imagined sound. The muscular exertions of his hands, arms, and feet would mirror the music's melodic, temporal, or textural outlines. Moving at the keyboard for Beethoven would be like dancing to a silent soundtrack, like a kind of musical mime that actualizes motor imagery already involved in musical listening.[9]

Though this interpretation accounts for some cultural influences it does not yet address the role of practiced techniques or musical technologies. It does not yet consider Beethoven as a pianist or violinist. In the earlier-cited experiments, musicians had more complex associations between pitch and space than participants without musical training (Rusconi et al. 2006; Lidji et al. 2007). Besides mapping pitch height to vertical position, they also connected higher pitches with the right and lower ones with the left—as on a piano keyboard.[10] Studying performers, then, may nuance theories of musical embodiment, by highlighting the effects of bodily skill.

Cognitive neuroscience can help reveal musician-specific connections between listening and playing. In one representative study, experimenters played familiar piano melodies for a group of student pianists (Haueisen and Knösche 2001). Though they listened while sitting still, the pianists exhibited significant

7. Rizzolatti and Sinigaglia (2008) examine the mirror-neuron system in general, while Overy and Molnar-Szakacs (2009) discuss its relation to music.

8. Mariusz Kozak argues that an overemphasis on musical mimesis is problematic. If listeners merely imitated performers, then their own bodies would be inessential to musical understanding, and listening would be only "quasi-embodied" (2015, 1.6). As an alternative, Kozak examines ways in which listeners' nonperformative movements organize musical experience, combining Merleau-Ponty's phenomenology with motion-capture analysis.

9. Cox's (2006) discussion of subvocalization also fits suggestively with Beethoven's habit of "growling" instead of singing (Schindler [1860] 1966, 125).

10. This mapping also affects action: for example, experienced pianists have great difficulty playing on a reversed keyboard (Laeng and Park 1999).

activation in the contralateral primary motor cortex (M1), as measured by magnetoencephalography (MEG). In another, amateur and professional violinists tapped left-hand fingerings for Mozart's Violin Concerto in G major, KV. 216 (Lotze et al. 2003). Though this performance was silent, functional magnetic resonance imaging (fMRI) showed activation in the right primary auditory cortex and left auditory association area. (Unsurprisingly, this activation was stronger for professionals.) But when the same violinists imagined playing the piece without also moving their fingers, the auditory-motor coactivation disappeared, leading the authors to conclude that "the motor and auditory systems are coactivated as a consequence of musical training but only if one system (motor or auditory) becomes activated by actual movement execution or live musical auditory stimuli" (1817). These studies showed distinctive patterns of *auditory-motor coactivation* in musicians' brains.[11] Note that this connection is bidirectional: sounding music elicits activity in motor areas, and action elicits activity in auditory areas. This auditory-motor coupling might be figuratively described as a *link between the ear and the hand.*[12]

Such results—and embodied listening more generally—can be explained via Lawrence Barsalou's theory of perceptual symbol systems (1999). As a proponent of "grounded cognition," Barsalou argues that cognition is based on sensory experience, not disembodied computational processing. In his account, perception activates sensorimotor areas in the brain: visual areas capture aspects like shape and color; auditory areas capture aspects like pitch and timbre; others involve proprioceptive states, bodily movement or action, emotion, and so forth. The brain, then, takes in distinct perceptual components, forming sense-specific representations. At the same time, different sensory modalities are coordinated through "convergence zones" that record patterns of coactivation (Damasio 1989). And such patterns may be reactivated through top-down processing to support mental simulations that, Barsalou claims, ground even the most abstract concepts and categories.

This empirical and theoretical work suggests another approach to Beethoven's improvisations. Early in his life as a pianist, Beethoven practiced common scales and melodic gestures, idiomatic textures and chordal patterns. He developed modally specific memories for their physical actions and sounding results, as any competent pianist does. These coordinated sensory representations supported

11. For further evidence of auditory-motor coupling in pianists, see Bangert, Haeusler, and Altenmüller (2001), Drost et al. (2005), Bangert et al. (2006), Lahav, Saltzman, and Schlaug (2007), and Chen, Rae, and Watkins (2011). Margulis et al. (2009) extend such research to violinists and flutists.

12. In general, instrumentalists' brains have a larger than average hand area in the motor cortex (Altenmüller and Gruhn 2002, 72). Yet there are also specific differences, depending on the instrument. Professional violinists, for example, have larger areas for left-hand fingers but not for the left thumb or right-hand digits (Elbert et al., 1995). And players who make music with other body parts—feet, mouth, and so forth—have corresponding differences in auditory-motor integration. For example, Schulz, Ross, and Pantev (2003) found that trumpet players develop strong connections between the auditory cortex and the lip area in the primary somatosensory cortex (but not the corresponding area for the index finger). Neural reorganization, finally, is more pronounced in players who began to study their instrument in childhood.

musical schemas and concepts that he could reactivate and creatively recombine. While improvising, for example, Beethoven could imagine a melody and realize it with his hands. Yet since auditory-motor coactivation goes both ways, moving his hands on the keyboard would activate auditory regions in his brain. This suggests that *Beethoven's actions would also enhance auditory simulations after his hearing loss.*[13] This conclusion is consistent with reports from musicians with significant hearing loss, who describe powerful experiences of auditory imagery during performance (Miller 2011). And it goes some way to explaining a statement by Beethoven himself: "when I am playing and composing, my affliction still hampers me least; it affects me most when I am in company" (quoted in Ealy 1994, 273).

The music Beethoven "heard" at the piano, then, would parallel the "phantasmal voices" sometimes experienced by people who become deaf after learning to speak—people who "hear" simulated speech while lip-reading.[14] Perceptual symbol systems theory would readily accommodate this auditory-*visual* integration. As a general theory of coordination between the brain's sensory systems, the model equally accounts for visual-motor coactivation in expert dancers watching dance and in musicians watching other instrumentalists (Calvo-Merino et al. 2005; Behmer and Jantzen 2011). However, even as this account of multisensory integration extends image-schematic and motor-mimetic perspectives from music theory, it prompts further questions. How are body-sound relations mediated? How is playing an instrument different from singing or dancing?

Instrumental Affordances

Embodied aspects of Beethoven's "inner hearing" challenge a spiritualism that often haunts Romantic visions of the deaf composer. Yet fixating on Beethoven's body can lead to other philosophical problems. First, to promote body over mind would court a materialism that is just as dualistic as the idealism it inverts. Both positions treat one term in the mind/body binary as essential and the other as accidental. Both positions, then, would inhabit the black-and-white world that Jacques Derrida calls "the metaphysics of presence."[15] This kind of metaphysics

13. Barsalou (1999, 586) emphasizes that such simulations must remain partial, and this is philosophically significant. Claiming that simulations can be complete would effectively reduce perception to the thought of perceiving, falling into an idealism that Merleau-Ponty critiques in *The Visible and the Invisible* (1968, 29–43).

14. Oliver Sacks discusses these phantasmal voices in his *Seeing Voices: A Journey into the World of the Deaf* (1989, 5–7).

15. As Derrida explains, this metaphysics involves "the enterprise of returning 'strategically,' ideally, to an origin ... held to be simple, intact, normal, pure, standard, self-identical, in order *then* to think in terms of derivation, complication, deterioration, accident, etc. All metaphysicians, from Plato to Rousseau, Descartes to Husserl, have proceeded in this way, conceiving good to be before evil, the positive before the negative, the pure before the impure, the simple before the complex, the essential before the accidental, the imitated before the imitation, etc." (1988, 93). Derridean deconstruction, in part, examines the inherent contradictions of such thinking, extending earlier critiques of metaphysical presence by Heidegger (2010, 21–25).

prioritizes one term in a pair (such as presence/absence, mind/body, nature/culture, or masculine/feminine).[16] The privileged term is thought to stand on its own, even though it is actually defined in relation to its partner, its supplement, its conceptual shadow. Second, the mind/body distinction cannot easily be dissolved. Arguments for radical integration risk reducing the body to the mind or vice versa. It seems more productive, then, to maintain the tension between mind and body, to accept that they intertwine without fully converging.

It can also be helpful to decenter the mind/body complex by situating it in an environment. In other words, cognition is not only embodied, but also ecological. The verticality schema, for example, is not simply a consequence of human anatomy. Rather, up and down are defined by gravity, by the earth under my feet and the sky over my head. For Merleau-Ponty, this means that a theory of the body must already be a theory of the body's integration with a world. I find myself always in the world, and each worldly perception is "synonymous" with some bodily perception (2012, 212).

Here phenomenology anticipates ecological psychology. Founded by James J. Gibson, ecological psychology argues for direct coupling between action and perception, between organism and environment.[17] Gibson describes this as a kind of "resonance" or "tuning" (1966, 271). Animals tune in to the world around them, as a radio tunes in to the airwaves, responding to both flux and regularity. This mix of variance and invariance can be illustrated with a visual example. When I walk toward a chair, it becomes larger in my field of vision. But because other aspects of the scene are constant and because the shift in perspective correlates with my movement, I do not think that the chair is growing. Invariants here provide information about the chair and the surrounding environment, while changes provide information about my own motion (Gibson 1979, 73).

Gibson would further claim that I see the chair primarily in terms of its *affordances*—for instance, my ability to sit in or stand on it. I perceive it not as a bundle of properties or qualities, but as a thing I can use (1979, 134). In Heideggerian language, I am oriented toward its "handiness" (*Zuhandenheit*). Affordances involve a specific complementarity of animal and environment. That is, they are possibilities for action *by a particular agent*. The chair affords sitting for me because of my abilities and because of its size and shape relative to my body. It would not afford sitting for a newborn baby or, to take an extreme

16. Such oppositions are often layered over each other. For example, Cusick argues that mind/body and masculine/feminine together color the music-specific opposition composer/performer. "The composer is masculine *not because so many individuals who live in the category are biologically male*," she writes, "but because the composer has come to be understood to be *mind*" (1994, 16, emphasis in original). Later in the essay, Cusick wonders whether the instrument/voice binary would be gendered in the same way, with singing as a feminized, bodily counterpart to instrumental performance (21). While this is plausible, the situation here is complex. Eighteenth-century Cartesian dualism, in fact, favored the opposite mapping: voice was thought to imbue music with rational expression, whereas instrumental music was merely a mechanical affair, a "body without a soul" (Chua 1999, 82–91).

17. I find ecological psychology to be a useful theoretical resource, whether or not one subscribes to Gibson's radical anti-representationalism.

example, for a humpback whale. Affordances and abilities, then, are essentially codefined (127).

While many ecological psychologists focus on invariant structures based in natural law (like the changes in vision just described), affordances may also be based in cultural regularities. For Gibson, the environment is both natural and cultural, so these aspects of affordances should not be opposed (1979, 130; 1982, 412).[18] Indeed, they are combined in musical instruments. A guitar's pitches, for example, become higher when the vibrating portion of the string is shortened, and each string affords harmonics at the octave, at the twelfth, and so on: these are physical invariants based in the acoustic properties of oscillating strings. Fret placement and tuning involve cultural invariants, the products of musical tradition. The fretboard is designed for hands, resonating with human physiology, but it also demands learned cultural techniques.

To capture some instrumental affordances in action, I return to the introduction from Beethoven's "Pathétique" (shown in Figure 1.3). The piece opens in a low register and slowly climbs, with voice exchanges expanding minor and then diminished-seventh chords. The opening dotted motif is recast in m. 5 as a lyrical melody, which continues to rise—before the aforementioned descent in m. 10.

Again, consider this massive chromatic descent. If the scale seems unremarkable, note that many instruments—even Western ones like harmonicas and valveless horns—do not afford this pitch collection or range. By using the smallest intervals available on the instrument, Beethoven enhances a sense of continuity in the sonic descent—and also makes audible one of the piano's defining invariants, its linear arrangement of twelve pitch classes within the span of each octave. The player's movement, like the sound, is conditioned by the instrument's affordances. When I play this measure, my right hand sweeps across the keys.[19] (Video 1.1 ▶ uses motion-capture imagery to trace this movement.) If I played the same notes on the clarinet, though, my hands would remain in place while my fingers and mouth did most of the work. And if I played them on a guitar or violin, I could think of two kinds of falling gestures: one that moves down *along* the fret- or fingerboard and one that moves down *across* the strings.

From this perspective, thematic elements in the sonata's introduction explore diverse pianistic affordances. Before the plummeting close, the quiet singing theme in octaves requires arm movement with a more or less fixed right-hand shape, while the left hand provides steady pulsing chords (mm. 5–8).[20] The melodic doubling exploits acoustic relationships between octave-related frequencies, but also

18. Along these lines, Eric Clarke extends the concept of affordance to music: "music affords dancing, worship, co-ordinated working, persuasion, emotional catharsis, marching, foot-tapping, and a myriad of other activities" (2005, 38).

19. This sweeping action returns in the descent that crashes into the recapitulation (mm. 186–93). Unlike the introduction's closing, this is not fully chromatic. But at the level of the hand, the movement from right to left, even larger than before, feels very much like an intensification of m. 9. The feeling, I think, is enhanced because both drops are followed by the same music, the allegro theme with thrumming left-hand octaves and rising right-hand dyads.

20. Beethoven sometimes specifies that parallel octaves be played in this manner, when they might be split between the hands. This creates a particular keyboardistic effect, discussed by Taub (2002, 27–28).

Figure 1.3 Ludwig van Beethoven, Piano Sonata no. 8 in C minor, "Pathétique," op. 13, mvt. i, mm. 1–10. Fingerings from an edition by Heinrich Schenker.

a keyboard that loosely coordinates this pitch distance with the average span of an adult hand. In Figure 1.3, the fingering for the octaves given by editor Heinrich Schenker alternates between thumb-pinky and thumb–ring finger pairings. This performance strategy is facilitated by differences in finger length—which make the distance from the tip of the thumb to the tip of the ring finger longer than the corresponding distance between thumb and pinky (Baber 2003, 71–72).

The sonata's opening involves two-handed chords with little lateral movement (mm. 1–4). The player's hands are rhythmically coordinated but move in contrary motion. This facilitates voice exchanges but also gives the player's actions a mirrored quality, reflecting the symmetry of the pianist's body.[21] Again, this reflects the instrument's affordances, the complementarity of piano and pianist. It is possible because pianists' hands develop more or less the same technique (as compared with the specialization of violinists' hands), because each finger can activate a note, and because both hands are free to roam around the instrument (as compared with saxophonists' hands). When Beethoven repeats this opening motif—before the development (mm. 132–35) and before the coda (mm. 294–97)—both sounding and kinesthetic patterns recur. This obviously reflects an invariant correlation between a pianist's action and the resulting sound. But more importantly, both sound and action are facilitated and constrained by the instrument's affordances.

Just as gravity grounds the verticality schema, *instruments provide the invariance that enables players' body-sound coordination.* Although instruments are not needed for gestural analogues to music, their consistent mediation is essential to instrumentalists' auditory-motor correspondences—that is, to specific mappings between actions and musical materials.

It is worth noting that perceptual symbol systems theory includes such external grounding: sensory representations map the world and may also be reactivated by affordances in it (Barsalou 1999, 587–88). Barsalou argues that situated simulations—like Beethoven's improvised auditory imagery—are organized around "the action-environment interface" (2003, 551–52). And this ecological emphasis distinguishes "grounded cognition" from "embodied cognition." The former assumes multiple forms of grounding, which might include bodily states but also aspects of the environment, situated action, cognitive simulations, and so forth (Barsalou 2008, 619).

A neuroimaging study by Marc Bangert and Eckart Altenmüller (2003) aligns suggestively with this theoretical account of instrumental affordances and embodied knowledge. The experimenters gave non-musicians a series of ten lessons during which they learned to play simple five-finger melodies on a keyboard (see Figure 1.4). The participants' brain activity was measured by electroencephalography (EEG) at the beginning, middle, and end of this five-week process. During the EEG recording, they listened to melodies like the ones they had played (but without actually playing), and they played the keyboard (but without hearing the output). In other words, their training always combined auditory and motor activity, but the testing kept them

21. Mirroring at the keyboard has been explored in various pieces, including Johannes Brahms's Intermezzi in E minor, op. 116, no. 5, and B♭ minor, op. 117, no. 2 (analyzed by Rings 2012, 41–43), and Béla Bartók's "Fourths" and "Reflection" (nos. 131 and 141 from *Mikrokosmos*).

Figure 1.4 Five-finger melody used by Bangert and Altenmüller (2003, fig. 8), representing the highest level of difficulty in the study. Pianists use numbers to label fingers, counting up from the thumb (1) to the pinky (5).

Figure 1.5 Carl Czerny, "The Five Fingers," op. 777, no. 1, mm. 1–8.

separate. There was one difference between the groups: one played on a regular keyboard; the other played on a keyboard where the mapping between pitch and key changed randomly after every piece. For the first group, then, the instrument's affordances were invariant; for the second, its affordances constantly changed. Bangert and Altenmüller found that the group with regular affordances developed a strong pattern of auditory-motor coactivation—the same kind of pattern seen in expert pianists. And these connections started to emerge after only twenty minutes of practice. The other group, despite weeks of practice, lacked this coactivation.[22] With a highly variable instrument, the usual links between hand and ear did not appear.

Though Bangert and Altenmüller use five-finger melodies as experimental stimuli, such tunes have been common in piano pedagogy since the early 1800s. Carl Czerny—a pianist-composer who studied with Beethoven—was a leading proponent of the method, and he exhorted fledgling pianists to practice five-finger melodies "daily, with untiring diligence and the greatest attention" (1851, 13). As is typical, Czerny's "twenty-four exercises on the five notes," entitled "The Five Fingers," start with the right-hand thumb on the tonic of C major (see Figure 1.5). Further exercises in the set transpose this basic position to other keys. Moving the hand during play, however, is deferred to a later stage, where it can be understood as a shift between familiar positions. This pedagogical approach, then, aims to establish a "home position," in which associations between finger and scale degree are fixed.[23]

22. Further experiments with this general design might tease out the effects of varied repertoire. With disjunct, dissonant melodies, it might take significantly longer to form a common representation of ear and hand. I would expect simple diatonic chord progressions, however, to give results closer to the five-finger melodies from the original study.

23. The first pieces in the Suzuki violin repertoire reflect a similar strategy, albeit adapted to the affordances of the violin: they are all in A major, using only the top two strings. The two semitones of

Such exercises do not simply strengthen the hands. They discipline students in a broader sense, through a process that Michel Foucault calls the "instrumental coding of the body" (1995, 153). As an example, Foucault cites instructions for handling a rifle, found in an eighteenth-century military treatise. Whether lifting, carrying, or lowering his weapon, a soldier must follow a series of precise steps. At each step, the instructions specify the position of hands, elbows, knees, fingers, and so on, as well as their contact with parts of the gun. Soldier and rifle are integrated like cogs in a machine, forming a body-tool complex that may, in turn, be incorporated into a larger military apparatus (164). Training in posture and movement helps turn recruits into soldiers. It empowers bodies in new ways, while also subjecting them to strict control.

In a similar way, Czerny's teaching restricts and reshapes the piano student's bodily comportment.[24] He explains how to sit at the piano and how to strike the keys through a set of detailed rules (Czerny 1851, 3–6), which recall the military's pursuit of correct posture and efficient movement. And his five-finger exercises coordinate parts of the body and parts of the instrument, combining and recombining basic action components. Limiting students' engagement with the keyboard, of course, limits musical possibilities. But these restrictions also guarantee a high level of invariance, a predictability that should help sensitize them to the instrument's tonal and physical affordances—or at least a basic subset thereof. Even if these exercises foster somewhat rigid correspondences, they may still effectively introduce beginners to instrumental links between action and sound.

Earlier I argued that Beethoven's piano playing would stimulate his inner hearing, but by now it is clear that this auditory-motor coupling depends on instruments. Beethoven's instruments provided invariant correlations that engendered patterns of neural coactivation. His instruments, then, did not just ground the sound of his improvisations or his physical technique. By systematically connecting the two, instruments made his embodied experience of phantasmal tones possible. Focusing on ecology thus leads to technology: the instrumentalist's musical capabilities emerge through interactions of body and world, technique and tool.

Habit, Concealing and Revealing

On this account, Beethoven's improvisations are thoroughly habitual. They rely on overlearned connections, developed through years of practice. Habitual playing,

A major are, in consequence, always located between the middle finger and ring finger, with the same fingering on each string. Other strings and then finger positions are gradually introduced throughout the method's first book.

24. This discipline, of course, is not unique to Czerny. Elisabeth Le Guin considers its role in instrumental method books and dance pedagogy from the eighteenth and early nineteenth centuries (2006, 148–53), while Ruth Solie (2004) shows how pianistic discipline contributed to the gendered experience of middle-class Victorian girls. Leslie Blasius (1996) relates this pedagogy, with its decomposition and reconstruction of action, to earlier epistemologies of sensation.

Figure 1.6 Basic keyboard chromatic-scale fingering. The pattern uses the thumb (1) on white notes and the middle finger (3) on black notes, adding in the index finger (2) when there are two white notes in a row.

of course, is often derided as mechanical, unthinking. But is this not another variation on the metaphysics of presence? A version that imagines self-directed subjectivity as the true origin of creative expression? This fantasy of pure self-awareness and self-control mixes easily with other dualisms—for example, setting the creative mind against the automatized body. Yet habit may be both motoric and mental. To be sure, because I am not fully aware of my habitual actions, they may at times work against my conscious intentions (as when I drive home "on auto-pilot," even though I had planned to go to the grocery store). Nonetheless, habit also enables human performance.

What do my fingers do when I play that descent from the "Pathétique"? They enact a series of interrelated moves, a chromatic-scale pattern. The most popular approach—known as the "French fingering"—alternates between the thumb and middle finger, interpolating the index finger whenever there are two white keys in a row (see Figure 1.6). Schenker's fingering in Figure 1.3 follows the same logic but exchanges the roles of the index and middle fingers.[25] In both versions, the thumb is kept on white notes, reflecting a general preference rule of keyboard fingerings: do not make this shorter digit reach for the black keys. (This principle is clearly set forth, for example, in Carl Philipp Emanuel Bach's *Essay on the True Art of Playing Keyboard Instruments* [(1753/1762) 1949].) If asked, most expert pianists could explain the rationale for this fingering. But they would rarely attend to this while playing the sonata. In performance, the fingering feels automatic. After all, how could they perform the piece fluently if they needed to consciously initiate every finger movement?

25. It locks into this pattern at the sixty-fourth-note septuplets. This fingering is associated with the Polish-Viennese pedagogue Theodor Leschetizky, a friend of Brahms (Verbalis 2012, app. 4).

Figure 1.7 Training melody and transfer melodies from Palmer and Meyer (2000, 64).

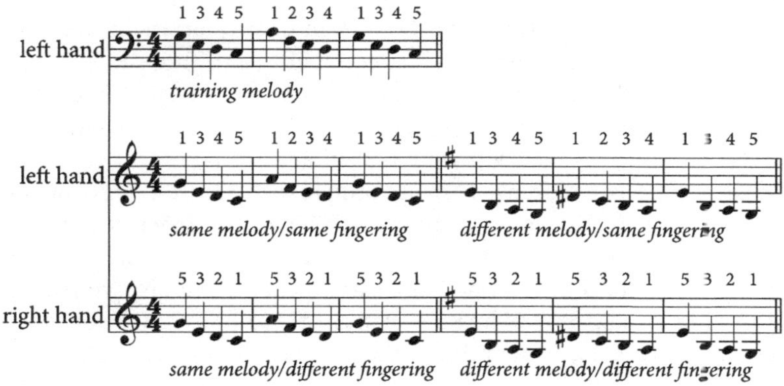

The action must become habitual, so playing the scale feels like a single flowing gesture.[26]

Such habitual actions are, again, both embodied and ecological. They integrate hand and tool, body and world. Strictly speaking, Figure 1.6 does not present a sequence of finger actions: it presents a sequence of *finger-key relationships*. Though pianists practice this fingering enough that it comes to feel relatively invariant, the chromatic scale's pattern of keys is actually more stable. Changing the fingering does not necessarily change the sound; changing the keys does.

An experiment by Caroline Palmer and Rosalee Meyer (2000) reflects this difference between bodily and instrumental elements. They presented experienced and novice pianists with a transfer-of-learning task. After practicing a particular sequence, they would play another one as quickly as possible. The new examples might share elements of the training melody: some had the same sequence of pitch classes but with different fingering; others preserved fingering patterns but had different pitch classes (see Figure 1.7). With novice children pianists, learning transfer involved both physical actions and pitch relationships. With skilled adult pianists, however, transfer occurred for pitch relationships, not motor relationships. Palmer and Meyer's results point to an important difference between experts with established performance habits, who may focus more on sound, and less experienced players, who must focus more on hand movements.

Yet the way these authors frame their results is, in some ways, at odds with my perspective, and examining these differences can help clarify the ecological importance of tools for perception. Palmer and Meyer write that "compared with novice performers, skilled performers demonstrate more dissociation between abstract sequence dimensions and movements, and a lower weighting of the movement dimension" (2000, 67). In my view, this formulation is slightly misleading. Palmer

26. Habitual actions generally involve less activation in the brain and greater reliance on subcortical regions than do novel actions. For a review of the neural underpinnings of habit, see Yin and Knowlton (2006).

and Meyer's description of pitch-class sequences as "abstract" or "conceptual" is, for example, somewhat problematic. The sound itself is immaterial, to be sure, but it is also perceptually immediate. Furthermore, the repeated pitch classes have a visible, tangible correlate in the pattern of keys on the instrument. The excerpts that Palmer and Meyer call "conceptually same" are simply transposed by an octave. In other words, this condition might just as accurately be described as "pitch-class same"—or even "keyboard same." This seems "abstract," then, only when the materiality of the instrument is overlooked.

Musical concepts, moreover, are not unique to the score or instrument: they are also present in the pianist's actions. After all, this experiment would not be possible if the musical notation could not represent both the notes and the fingering.[27] To interpret the notation, participants in the experiment needed pianistic finger categories (which differ from those of guitarists or violinists). Such categories are deeply ingrained: for example, pianists have difficulty sight-reading a notated melody that has incongruent fingering indications (Stewart et al. 2004).

Finally, the "dissociation" between pitch and movement might be better understood as a mobile, flexible *association* between action and instrument. While beginners often have one-to-one associations between fingers and keys (supported by the "home-position" pedagogy discussed earlier), skilled pianists can associate the same pitch-key pattern with any number of motoric patterns. Palmer and Meyer's experiment shows that this remapping is effectively effortless for experts, having no effect on their performance. Paradoxically, then, particular motor patterns seem less important for expert pianists—but only because they have developed their instrumental skills to a point where they require minimal attention.[28]

Phenomenologically, this situation is readily described in Martin Heidegger's *Being and Time* ([1927] 2010, 69). For Heidegger, tools are handy (*zuhanden*) because they "withdraw" from my awareness. This lets me focus not on the tools, but on the work. While I am fixing the porch railings with my father-in-law, I do not contemplate the hammer as an object. Instead I use it actively, as means to an end. Of course, this withdrawal is possible only when a tool can be trusted—in Gibsonian terms, when its affordances are invariant—and when its use is habitual.[29] In this sense, habit hides the hammer.

But as habit conceals, it also reveals. When the tool changes my abilities, it also changes the way I perceive the world. For example, objects beyond my normal reach appear closer when I plan to reach them with a tool (Witt and Riley 2014, 1356–57). As such, Merleau-Ponty argues that *motor habits are also perceptual habits*. To illustrate, he discusses navigation with a cane. Once the cane

27. For a philosophical discussion of keyboard fingering indications as a supplement to staff notation, see Szendy (2016, 47–68).

28. As Palmer and Meyer note, the expert performers might show greater motor learning if the task were more challenging (2000, 67).

29. If the hammer breaks or is missing, Heidegger adds, it demands conscious attention. Suddenly it is no longer handy but "present-to-hand" (*vorhanden*). When practicing a new piece of music, for example, I stop to work out fingerings only when a passage is especially difficult or unusual. This kind of breakdown will be explored in Chapter 4.

becomes familiar, it withdraws. The person using it feels things *through* the cane's tip. Merleau-Ponty emphasizes that this does not involve explicit reasoning about the pressure of the cane in the hand, the position of the tip, the position of things in the environment, and so forth. Instead, habit "relieves" the navigator of this work. As Merleau-Ponty writes, "The pressures on the hand and the cane are no longer given, the cane is no longer an object that the blind man would perceive, it has become an instrument *with* which he perceives" (2012, 154).[30]

My eyeglasses withdraw from my awareness in a similar way. I usually look *through* them rather than perceive them directly. Why is this, given that the glasses significantly modify my vision? According to the philosopher Don Ihde, they can withdraw because they are *transparent*. Though they modify perception, they isomorphically reflect invariants in the world. In this sense, the stick is "transparent" too. Yet the transformation of perceptual experience by the glasses or the stick is not neutral: "*for every revealing transformation there is a simultaneously concealing transformation of the world, which is given through a technological mediation*" (Ihde 1990, 49, emphasis in original). Ihde's studies of technoscience suggest that scientific instruments often create knowledge by modifying vision, making the invisible visible. With a telescope, I can see objects that are extremely distant; with a microscope, objects that are extremely small. Learning to focus a telescope or microscope again combines action and perception. As scientists learn to adjust these instruments, they also learn how to see through them. Ultrasound technicians, for example, view the images they produce in a different way than expectant parents, because they have acquired particular perceptual habits. As Hubert Dreyfus puts it, "What one has learned appears in the way the world shows up" (2002, 373).

Cultural or symbolic invariance can also facilitate a kind of transparency (Ihde 1990, 82). As you read this book, do you consciously identify each individual letter? Hopefully not. Instead, thanks to habits of literacy, familiar shapes on the page withdraw, revealing a world of discourse. (Of course, these same habits can easily conceal typographic errors!) Musical notation works in a similar manner. For literate musicians, the lines, clefs, note-heads, beams, flags, and dots on the page may coalesce into melodies and chords. In such moments, a score is less an object of perception than a medium for perception. And something similar can happen with musical instruments. As Merleau-Ponty writes, "Musical notation would not be a language and the organ would not be an instrument if the manner in which one writes and in which one plays a note did not comprise a systematic principle and did not as a consequence include the manner in which one writes and in which one plays the other notes" (1963, 121). The section on habit in his *Phenomenology of Perception* culminates in a discussion of the organ. It is a key passage, worth quoting at length:

30. The results of an experiment by Serino and colleagues (2007) are consistent with Merleau-Ponty's claims. Learning to navigate with a stick expanded participants' sense of personal space, and this effect was well established with blind participants who regularly used a cane in this manner. (I will return to this study in Chapter 2.) Incidentally, navigating with a stick is a classic philosopher's example, appearing as early as Descartes's *Optics* ([1637] 2001, 67–68).

> An experienced organist is capable of playing an unfamiliar organ, whose keyboards are more or less numerous, whose stops are differently arranged than those on his customary instrument. He needs but an hour of practice to be ready to perform his program.... He sits on the bench, engages the pedals, and pulls out the stops, he sizes up the instrument with his body, he incorporates its directions and dimensions, and he settles into the organ as one settles into a house. He does not learn positions in objective space for each stop and each pedal, nor does he entrust such positions to "memory." During the rehearsal—just as during the performance—the stops, the pedals, and the keyboards are only presented to him as powers of such and such an emotional or musical value, and their position as those places through which this value appears in the world. Between the musical essence of the piece such as it is indicated in the score and the music that actually resonates around the organ, such a direct relationship is established that the body of the organist and the instrument are nothing other than the place of passage of this relation. (2012, 146–47, translation altered)

During this brief rehearsal, the organist does not measure the distance between stops in centimeters or contemplate it in a disinterested manner. It is in this sense that the space of the organ is not an "objective space" but a lived space, an expressive space, a space in which the skilled body feels at home. Because of the organist's habits, the keys and stops show up as musical possibilities and, in a successful performance, the body and instrument seem to withdraw into the music. "From then on," Merleau-Ponty concludes, "the music exists for itself, and everything else exists through it" (2012, 147).

Likewise, for the expert pianists in Palmer and Meyer's study, the keyboard is less an object of perception than a medium for perception. They access melodies *in* or *through* the instrument. Beginning pianists gaze at their hands on the keys, working hard to find the right notes in this field of black and white. But for expert pianists, familiar patterns stand out at a glance. This allowed Beethoven to continue giving lessons, even after he had trouble hearing conversation. According to Carl Friedrich Hirsch, who studied with Beethoven from 1816 to 1817, the composer would catch students' mistakes by closely watching their hands on the keys (Thayer 1967, 664).[31] Like the Heideggerian handyman, Beethoven focused not on the piano, but on the music.

Later chapters will revise this initial account of habit, particularly Chapter 4. For now, I will note that withdrawal is never complete, and this is partly because habit is never complete. I am using two senses of the word "complete" here, meaning both "full" and "finalized." First, habits have limits. They apply only within a

31. Stories of Beethoven's teaching resonate with an fMRI study by Hasegawa et al. (2004). In it, pianists watched silent videos of hands pressing piano keys. Expert pianists were able to identify familiar pieces by sight. While watching the videos, they displayed increased activation in the left planum temporale, a part of the brain that is involved in lip-reading, which integrates auditory and visual information. In a similar study by Giacomo Novembre and Peter Keller (2011), pianists watched silent videos of a hand playing chord sequences and copied the sequences on a muted keyboard. They were slower to imitate chords that were harmonically unexpected. But even slower were responses to harmonically expected chords that were fingered in an unusual way. On visual expertise in guitarists, see Crump, Logan, and Kimbrough (2012).

certain genre of action. For example, chord shapes that are second nature to a jazz pianist may be foreign to a classical pianist. Second, habits, unlike innate reflexes, are acquired and more or less flexible. A habit can stagnate, of course. But since it has been learned in the first place, it can also be unlearned, relearned. Habit, in other words, is not fixed but dynamic, just like the patterns of brain activation discussed by Barsalou.

Note also that these examples of habit involve things—hammers, canes, eyeglasses, microscopes, books, organs, pianos. These objects are not neutral. They afford particular kinds of motor and perceptual habits; they reveal certain possibilities, while concealing others. Like the body, then, each of these things can be understood as a medium for having a world.

Prosthesis and Poiesis

If the keyboard enhanced Beethoven's auditory imagination, the piano might be described as a kind of hearing aid. Indeed, just as Beethoven used ear trumpets to help him in conversation, he sought modified instruments that might prolong his aural access to music. In 1817, for example, he wrote to Andreas Streicher, "Be so kind as to adjust one of your pianos for me to suit my impaired hearing. It should be as loud as possible." Years later, Conrad Graf, the pianoforte-maker for the imperial court, would build Beethoven an amplifying "resonance plate" that attached to his grand piano (Ealy 1994, 271). In this view, the piano, like eyeglasses or a blind person's cane, would be a prosthesis.

And yet there is a key difference between the piano and the ear trumpet. The ear trumpet transforms sounds in the world, amplifying them for a listener. But the piano is used to *make* sounds that do not already exist. A musical instrument, in other words, is poietic. "Poietic"—like *poiēsis*, the Greek noun from which it is derived—refers to the domain of production, to all kinds of making.

For many musicologists, these terms will recall the musical semiotics of Jean-Jacques Nattiez (1990), whose "poietic level" examines the perspectives of music-makers—principally composers and performers. But my use of the word draws on Heidegger's "Die Frage nach der Technik."[32] In this essay, the philosopher famously claims that the essence of technology is nothing technological. That is, technology is not just about modern machines or industrialization. Seeking an older concept of technology, Heidegger turns to another Greek term: *technē*. "*Technē*," he explains, "is the name not only for the activities and skills of the craftsman, but also for the arts of the mind and the fine arts. *Technē* belongs to bringing-forth, to *poiēsis*; it is something poietic" (1977, 12–13). At its core, technology is about making, about revealing a world.

Technē, though, does not refer to the *act* of making (Heidegger 2008, 184). Instead, *technē* is a mode of knowledge. Throughout antiquity, the term is

32. Heidegger's title is typically translated as "The Question Concerning Technology," though Samuel Weber (1989, 980–82) argues that a more accurate version would be "Questing after Technics."

persistently linked to music, even specifically with musical instruments. In dialogues by Plato and Xenophon, Socrates repeatedly says that *technē* is needed to play the flute and the lyre. A later Platonic work *The Sophist* similarly mentions a musician's *technē*, the art or craft of combining notes (Parry 2007). This active knowledge empowers a player to exploit an instrument's affordances, to bring forth a world of sonic relationships, to *make* music.[33]

At the etymological and conceptual root of "techno-logy," then, is poietic know-how, a way of understanding based in making. From this perspective, technique and technology complement each other. The instrument, together with my action, reveals a world. That phrasing—with the artifact first, as the subject of the verb—might evoke questions about technical agency, which I will defer until Chapter 3. At present, I want to suggest that poietic know-how may belong not only to the tool user, but also to the tool itself.

This suggestion invokes research on distributed cognition, such as Edwin Hutchins's *Cognition in the Wild* (1995). The book presents an ethnographic case study of a vessel in the US Navy, an amphibious helicopter transport that he calls the *Palau*. Besides analyzing the ship's social organization, Hutchins examines many of the *Palau*'s navigational instruments. He concludes that these tools do not simply amplify the cognitive capacities of their users. Instead, they typically, and sometimes radically, change the task at hand. For example, sailors must often calculate interrelated quantities of distance, rate, and time (147–55). A pencil and paper may be used to record the numbers, holding them in a kind of external memory while the navigator focuses on algebraic and arithmetic operations. Alternatively, the calculations can be done with a three-scale nomogram, a kind of nautical slide rule. Since the appropriate mathematical relations are encoded in the slide rule, the navigator's task then involves lining up indices with numbers on scales. Computational constraints are built into the physical structure of the tool (96). It embodies cultural knowledge and strategies, and precludes certain kinds of mistakes. In this sense, instruments may know things for their users.

The piano, for example, "knows" a certain pitch-class collection: the notes of the equal-tempered chromatic scale. But it does not present twelve undifferentiated steps. Instead, it materially highlights particular tonal structures endemic to Western music. Its physical opposition of a diatonic white-note scale with intervening black-note semitones corresponds to the notational culture of natural and chromatically inflected pitches, and the resulting pattern of twos and threes functions as a visual and tactile reference point for the player. This means, of course, that white-note modes like C major are easy to play. But the keyboard's topology highlights other patterns too. No less than Frédéric Chopin suggested that B major fits the hand better than C, because it matches black keys—*les touches hautes* (literally, "the high keys")—with long fingers (1993, 66). In certain

33. Turning briefly to a philosophical technicality, this does not involve fixed, unchanging presence, but a presence with temporality, presence that is revealed and concealed. In an essay on Rilke, Heidegger describes this kind of presence using a musical metaphor: "our being is song, and indeed a song whose singing does not resound just anywhere but is truly a singing, a song whose sound does not cling to something that is eventually attained, but which has already shattered itself even in the sounding" (2008, 184).

Figure 1.8 Frédéric Chopin, Étude in G♭ major, "Black Keys," op. 10, no. 5, mm. 1–4.

respects, the black-note pentatonic collection might be even easier to play. The concert pianist Lang Lang demonstrates this in a parody of Chopin's Étude in G♭, op. 10, no. 5. Like all of Chopin's études, this piece is a virtuoso tour de force. Its melody flutters up and down the keyboard, always on the black keys that give the composition its nickname (see Figure 1.8). Lang Lang brings out this "black-keyness" when he plays the piece backstage—with an orange![34] As he realizes the accompaniment figure with his left hand, he holds the fruit in his right and, following the melodic contour, drags it over the raised black keys. The result is not, of course, a precise rendering of Chopin's original—but it is remarkably close, instantly recognizable to listeners who are familiar with the piece. The trick is possible because the étude exploits some of the keyboard's distinctive tonal and physical affordances. It works because the piano "knows" the pentatonic scale and because it takes care of tuning.

Piano tuning, in fact, is an excellent example of distributed cognition. As Chopin himself observed, intonation is "the tuner's task," and consequently "the piano is free of one of the greatest difficulties encountered in the study of an instrument" (quoted in Eigeldinger 1986, 23). Pianists rely on specialist technicians to put their instruments in order. From there, tuning is a fact of the instrument. The player cannot change it in performance. With a poorly maintained piano, this can be a problem. Otherwise, it is quite useful. This is why Beethoven's late improvisations on violin or viola were "the most painful," while his piano playing might still be praised. For example, Clara Schumann's father, Friedrich Wieck, heard Beethoven improvise at the keyboard in 1826. "He played in a flowing, genial manner," Wieck reported, "... weaving in the clearest and most charming melodies" (quoted in Ealy 1994, 272). As Hutchins observed, the instrument fundamentally changes the task at hand. When I play a conventionally tuned piano, I might hit the wrong note—but I cannot produce a note between the steps of the chromatic scale, a note without a name. Even when played with an orange, the keyboard, as a space for action, brings forth a pitch world that is culturally and historically specific.

Given these ideas about poiesis and distributed cognition, it seems best to be careful about treating instruments as prostheses, as devices that extend the body's

34. This video can be accessed at http://youtu.be/oiziGLe1jBw.

"natural" sound-producing capacities.[35] Commonsense examples of prostheses, such as artificial limbs, may imply that prostheses replace some function that has been damaged. Marshall McLuhan takes this negative thinking to an extreme when he claims that extension involves a kind of "self-amputation" (1994, 45). I prefer a broader concept of prostheticity. According to the philosopher Bernard Stiegler, "A 'prosthesis' does not supplement something, does not replace what would have been there before it and would have been lost: it is added" (1998, 152). This definition goes back to an older, Greek sense of the word, which combines *thesis*—that is, putting or placing—with the prefix *pros-*, meaning in front of, in addition to, or close to. A pros-thesis is something placed in front. It is "what is outside" (193).

For Stiegler, the prosthesis can be outside in two ways. First, it is set in front of me *spatially*. The piano is an external thing, fairly solid and stable. Unlike my vocal cords, it is always located at a certain distance from my body. Second, the prosthesis might be set in advance of me *temporally*. The piano in my front room was built in the 1930s, which means that it is older than my parents. Yet even a new piano engages this temporal dimension, since the piano as an instrument preexists me. Here Stiegler's understanding of prosthesis is tied up in a phenomenological understanding of historicality. "Prostheticity," he writes, "is the being-already-there of the world, and also, consequently, the being-already-there of the past" (235). This draws on Heidegger's concept of "thrownness" (*Geworfenheit*), an essential part of human existence (2010, 127–28). I cannot choose when or where I am born. Instead I find myself "thrown" into a world, a history, and a culture that is already there, over which I have had no control. One of Stiegler's main tasks in *Technics and Time* is to show how technical objects contribute to this already-there, forming a kind of durable, external memory that makes human culture possible. The piano, as part of the already-there, offers a certain access to a past through which I have not lived. It makes it possible for me to play the "Pathétique," remaking music from long before my birth, long after Beethoven's death.

When Beethoven improvised, then, he was bringing forth a world made possible by instruments. That is not to deny the composer's agency or his musical innovations but to note how instrumentality is inevitably historical. To borrow an image from Theodor Adorno, the improviser is like a child at the piano, who feels around for a chord that has never been touched, never been heard. "This chord, however, was always already there," Adorno writes, "the possible combinations are limited, and actually everything is already stuck inside the keyboard" (2002, 32, translation modified). The interaction of body and instrument—with all its cognitive consequences—is an interaction of individual and culture, present and past. Instruments ground modes of music cognition that are embodied, technically conditioned, and historically situated.

35. Taking instruments as prostheses is common in writings on musical evolution—see, e.g., Cross (2007). (I discuss this trend more extensively in De Souza 2014.)

Conclusions

"The music which he thus produced was frightful, though in his mind it was pure and harmonious." In a sense, Schindler was right. When the deaf composer improvised, there was a gap between the sounds he made and the sounds he "heard." But to explain this situation, I have argued that Beethoven's mind was integrated with his hands, his tools, and a broader musical world. This means that Beethoven's imagination, which might have been understood as an instance of purest interiority, instead shows how interiority and exteriority are irreducibly entangled.

Interiority and exteriority, mind and body, self-control and habit… As the chapter wraps up, consider one more dichotomy: cognition and perception. For proponents of grounded cognition, there can be no clean break between the two (e.g., Goldstone and Barsalou 1998). On the one hand, higher-level cognition engages the brain's sensorimotor systems, and it is affected by bodily activity.[36] On the other, when an animal perceives a predator—even when a bacterium prefers one form of sugar to another—its behavior is already imbued with a kind of sense-making that, for some thinkers, represents a minimal form of cognition.[37] This is not to ignore useful distinctions between cognition and perception but to emphasize, once again, how they are entwined. It suggests that the essence of cognition is nothing "cognitive," meaning that thinking is just not about calculation or symbolic logic but is, more generally, about making sense of the world. Moreover, this implies that it is possible to think with one's body. In Heidegger's words, "All the work of the hand is rooted in thinking" (1968, 16).

Beethoven at the keyboard, then, would be thinking with his hands and thinking with his instrument. Instrumental practice would offer not only a way of making music, but also ways of perceiving, imagining, inventing, and reflecting on it. Of course, this argument is not specifically about Beethoven. His example evinces body-instrument interactions and cognitive processes that are widespread—forms of grounding that constitute instrumentalists as such. Still, some implications of this argument are more or less specific to expert instrumentalists. For amateur players, action-sound integration may develop to a lesser degree, and singers, dancers, and listeners who do not play musical instruments would exhibit different patterns of multisensory coactivation.[38] Yet this framework also predicts differences among skilled instrumentalists. Insofar as a keyboard differs from a fretboard, a pianist's habits will differ from a guitarist's habits. This should affect performative action, sound, and experience. To address these distinctions, though, the investigation must go beyond general principles to analyze the affordances of particular instruments.

36. Psychological studies of gesture offer evidence for bodily influences on thought (Goldin-Meadow and Beilock 2010). For example, problem-solving strategies change when participants' hand movement is restricted (Alibali et al. 2011).

37. The biologists Humberto Maturana and Francisco Varela advance this view in *Autopoiesis and Cognition*. For them, "*living systems are cognitive systems, and living as a process is a process of cognition*" (1980, 13, emphasis in original).

38. For example, extensive vocal practice leads to structural changes in the brain, which differentiate expert singers from instrumentalists (Halwani et al. 2010).

CHAPTER TWO

Sounding Actions

According to Leonard Meyer, listening to music is like riding a bike (1973, 15–16). An experienced listener may safely ignore music theory and history, just as a cyclist may ignore the bicycle's engineering or physics. Riding a bicycle, of course, is a standard example of *know-how*.[1] That is to say, knowing how the bike works is not the same as knowing how to work it, and I cannot acquire this skill merely by reading a book or watching others ride. Instead I learn how to do it by doing it. I become a competent cyclist by pedaling and breaking, balancing or falling, again and again. Meyer's analogy usefully frames musical listening as habit and skill, as procedural rather than declarative knowledge. Yet there is also a significant difference between these activities: cycling is a form of human-machine interaction. And on this level, riding a bicycle seems less like listening than like playing a musical instrument.

A phenomenological description of cycling can help flesh out the comparison, and such a description might begin with the rider's body. On the bicycle my feet alternate, much as they do while I walk. Right and left, up and down, forward and backward. But cycling feet, unlike walking feet, never strike the ground. Instead they stay in contact with the pedals and move with them, while my hands do the same with the handlebars. As the handlebars swivel to the left or right, as I turn them with my hands, the bike tilts; my whole body leans. Steering, like riding in general, thus involves a play of balance and instability. In all of this, my body is integrated with the bicycle. Together we form a system. After all, the bike cannot ride itself without me.

In a sense, I am the bicycle's engine. My legs power the wheels, and when I pedal harder, they go faster. Still, there is a gap between my action and the bicycle's movement. It continues to roll after I have stopped pedaling. The bicycle, then, does not simply absorb my energy; it amplifies it. Of course, this process is mediated by the terrain, which is why cycling can reveal subtle declines and inclines in an otherwise familiar path. While coasting downhill with the wind in my face, riding faster than I can run, I need not pedal—even if I do, the pedals may spin freely. But while I am climbing uphill, those pedals feel stiff, and I become aware of my own heaviness and that of the bicycle. In both cases, I may shift gears, trying to maintain a satisfying resistance in the pedals, a sense of grip. Here I feel the bicycle but also the ground *through* the bicycle. I can feel, for example, when the path

1. This example is famously discussed by the scientist and philosopher Michael Polanyi (1958, 50), who is cited later in Meyer's essay.

changes from asphalt to gravel. Riding a bicycle, in the end, can be understood as a way of being in the world. As it alters my capacity for movement, the bicycle transforms my experience of space, of speed, and of my own body.

Both riding and playing instruments involve a complementarity of technology and technique. Both involve habit and withdrawal. But where the bicycle converts action into momentum, musical instruments convert action into sound. This chapter's first task is to theorize that conversion. How do various instruments transmit a player's actions? How do they transform a player's energy? Which sonic parameters reflect bodily action? Which reflect instrumental affordances? Though it starts by investigating sound production, this line of thinking ultimately reveals how a musical instrument, like a bicycle, can mediate experiences of the body itself.

Sounding Objects

Strike a cowbell with a stick, and it rings. A momentary touch has initiated vibrations that stretch out in time and space. Of course, just as terrain affects the bicycle's momentum, performance environment can modify the bell's sound. For example, its ringing lasts longer in a reverberant concert hall. Nonetheless, the sound emanates from the cowbell itself, from this quivering piece of metal. And its sonic texture reflects that origin.

This relation between sound and source is central to ecological acoustics, a branch of Gibsonian psychology that considers how animals tune in to sonic aspects of their environments. People can *hear* the size of an object dropped into water and the hardness of a mallet hitting a pan; they can *hear* the difference between running upstairs and downstairs, between clapping with cupped or flat hands (Gaver 1988; Freed 1990; Repp 1987). For ecological acoustics, sounds are rich in information about the material forces that create them. Of course, such information does not determine perception. Attending to sources represents only one possible mode of listening, and the source of a given sound may be ambiguous, unfamiliar, or misidentified.[2] Still, this seems more likely with listeners who are distanced from a sound source than with players who can hear, touch, and see their instruments. Here different senses interact without fully converging. Insofar as sound indexes objects, hearing communicates with other sensory modalities. "I hear the hardness and the unevenness of the cobblestones in the sound of a car," writes Merleau-Ponty, "and we are right to speak of a 'soft,' 'dull,' or 'dry' sound" (2012, 239).

Or, with the cowbell, a metallic sound. In other words, the instrument's timbre can reveal aspects of its material. As William Gaver explains, "The damping of

2. Such misidentification may be fostered, though, by instruments that imitate other instruments—for example, the lute clavier (which I discuss in Chapter 5) or synthesizers (see De Souza, forthcoming). Chapter 6 examines modes of listening in greater detail. For a critique of deterministic applications of ecological acoustics (in discourse on electronic music), see Demers (2010, 36–37).

Figure 2.1 A standard cowbell pattern from salsa music (used with a 3:2 clave pattern). The bottom line corresponds to the mouth of the bell, the higher line to the body.

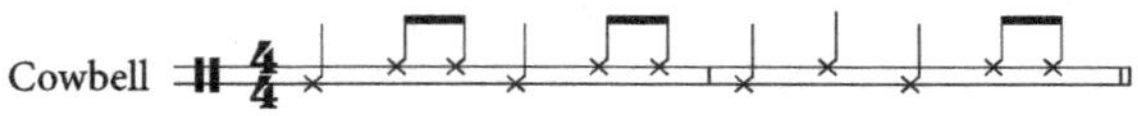

wood tends to be much greater than that of metal, which is why wood 'thunks' and metal 'rings'" (1993, 11).[3] Meanwhile, the bell's frequency reflects its size and shape—aspects of the instrument's configuration. Bigger bells, obviously, are pitched lower. And parts of a single cowbell afford distinct tones: the mouth sounds lower and fuller; the body, higher. This contrast is central to cowbell playing, for example, in salsa music (see Figure 2.1). In all of this, the sound of the instrument is predicated on its physical structure.

Yet ecological acoustics also considers the physical interactions that give rise to sound—in this case, how the cowbell is struck. Gaver specifically distinguishes between the sonic effects of interaction, material, and configuration (see Table 2.1) and describes how interaction principally affects dynamic and temporal features of the sound.[4] Tapped gently, the bell is quiet; whacked, it yelps. The loudness communicates the force of my attack. Note, too, the temporal difference between striking the bell and scraping it. And the timing of the attacks corresponds exactly to the sounding rhythm. From this perspective, sounds express ecological relationships. Recall the example of looking at a chair as I walk toward it (in Chapter 1), where visual invariants give information about the chair and changes give information about my movement. Likewise, in the cowbell pattern in Figure 2.1, sonic invariants reflect the instrument, while changes reveal the player's movement. This doubling—this intertwining of action and effect—underlies instrumentalists' auditory-motor coupling. Like a bicycle wheel, the instrument converts and amplifies an aspect of my action. As I make the bell speak, it makes my energy audible.

So hitting a cowbell may not be as simple as it seems. But how well does this percussive model generalize to other instruments? Consider an instrumental continuum proposed by Arnie Cox, which starts from a similar understanding of sound production.[5] Cox's continuum ranges from instruments with "no mediating device between the hands or mouth," to instruments played via implements (like mallets, bows, or keys), to electronic instruments, to mixers and computers (2011, 16).[6] By this point, musicians no longer provide the

3. Damping reduces the amplitude of oscillations (for example, through resistance, friction, or absorption of energy).
4. The stick's material again affects timbre: obviously, the attack of a wooden drumstick differs from that of a soft-tipped mallet.
5. For Cox, the relation between embodied action and sonic patterns fits into broader ideas about listening and mimetic motor imagery, already mentioned in Chapter 1.
6. Cox's continuum also extends to "music not performed primarily or solely by performers," such as birdsong or the "music" of a noisy factory (2011, 16). Since this category involves neither instruments nor players, I will set it aside here.

Table 2.1 Acoustic effects of source attributes (Gaver 1993, 11)

Source	Effects on the sound wave
Interaction	
Type	Amplitude function, spectrum
Force	Amplitude, bandwidth
Material	
Restoring force	Frequency
Density	Frequency
Damping	Amplitude functions; also frequency
Homogeneity	Complex effects on amplitude; also frequency
Configuration	
Shape	Frequency, spectral pattern
Size	Frequency, bandwidth
Resonating cavities	Spectral pattern
Support	Amplitude functions, frequency, spectrum

energy that produces sound. This is a continuum of increasing mediation, then, in which the player gradually loses touch with the site of sound production. On one side, action and sound correlate; on the other, they dissociate. This difference, however, cannot be reduced to an opposition between analog and digital instruments. Though digital technologies sometimes obscure a performer's movement, they may also amplify it. For example, the sensors in Tod Machover's "hyperbow" modify sonic output through gestural control.[7] Insofar as they afford continuous sonification of my movements, such technologies arguably give *more* information about the body than the pointed sound of a cowbell. And this is to say that the coupling of action and sound is not just natural but often engineered. On an electronic piano with touch-sensitive keys, the dynamics reflect the force with which I press the keys. A seventeenth-century harpsichord, by contrast, does not convey this aspect of my action. Whether it is played roughly or softly, the harpsichord's volume stays the same. Action and sound, then, do not necessarily diverge as instruments become more complex or as the number of mediators between my body and the vibrating medium increases.

Besides ranking different *degrees* of mediation, then, it is important to identify different *kinds* of mediation. The challenge is to tease apart various aspects of the sound, various functions of the instrument, to make sense of the diverse ways that musical instruments transform energy into sound. To that end, I turn to a distinctive scholar in the field of organology—whose work has surprising affinities with contemporary music theory.

7. For more on Machover's "hyperinstruments" see http://opera.media.mit.edu/projects/hyperinstruments.html.

Instrumental Systems

Organology, the study of musical instruments, is inherently interdisciplinary, covering the science and engineering of instruments as well as their historical and cultural aspects. Modern organology typically classifies instruments in terms of the physics of sound production. For example, the widely used system of Erich von Hornbostel and Curt Sachs divides instruments into four categories: idiophones ("self-sounding" instruments, such as bells and woodblocks); membranophones (instruments with a stretched, vibrating membrane, such as drums and kazoos); chordophones (instruments with vibrating strings, such as guitars and pianos); and aerophones (instruments with vibrating air columns, such as flutes and pipe organs). This scheme aims to include "the whole range of ancient and modern, European and extra-European instruments"—and even instruments that have yet to be invented (Hornbostel and Sachs 1961, 7).[8] Its claims to universality are founded on the science of acoustics. Yet somewhat paradoxically, this foundation also reveals modern organology's historical origins in nineteenth-century Europe, where acoustical research enjoyed great prestige and influence.[9] By contrast, Herbert Heyde's *Grundlagen des natürlichen Systems der Musikinstrumente* (1975) develops an organology that is grounded in a scientific trend of the mid-twentieth century: cybernetics.[10]

Cybernetics is popularly associated with virtual reality (as in the terms "cyberspace," "cyberattack," and "cybersex") and human-technology hybrids (as in the "cyborg" or "cybernetic organism"). But the field of cybernetics, as developed in the 1940s and 1950s, investigates systems in general, whether technological, biological, psychological, or social. Cybernetics is concerned not with a system's material properties but with its abstract structure and behavior. As Ross Ashby puts it, "Cybernetics stands to the real machine—electronic, mechanical, neural, or economic—much as geometry stands to a real object" (1956, 2). For example, consider Claude Shannon's model of a general communication system, first published in 1948 (see Figure 2.2).[11] In this system, a message from some information source is fed into a transmitter. The transmitter encodes this message and passes it

8. In practice, electrical and electronic instruments pose problems for Hornbostel and Sachs's scheme (Kartomi 1990, 172–74). Also, some scholars have criticized organology for prioritizing a kind of scientism over social context (e.g., Bates 2012), in an argument that parallels attacks on music-theoretical formalism.
9. More broadly, nineteenth-century organology emerged at the intersections of acoustics, industrialized instrument-making, museum culture, and colonial encounters with non-Western music (see De Souza 2013, 7–14).
10. My discussion here responds only to the central section of Heyde's 1975 treatise, titled "Systemklasse" (Kartomi gives a brief overview of the book [1990, 189–90]). Moreover, cybernetic thinking does not characterize Heyde's later scholarship, which explores diverse topics in the history and science of musical instruments and organological methodology (e.g., Heyde 2001). He has also had a distinguished curatorial career, at the Metropolitan Museum of Art and other institutions, and received the Curt Sachs Award from the American Musical Instrument Society in 1991.
11. Incidentally, Shannon—one of the founders of information theory—collected musical instruments (Gallager 2001, 2683).

Figure 2.2 Claude Shannon's general communication system (after Shannon 1964, 34).

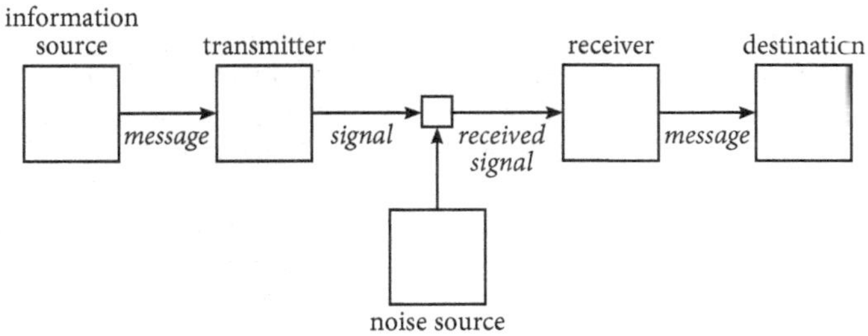

to a receiver, though not without interference from an external noise source. The receiver then decodes the signal, hopefully reproducing the original message. For Shannon's purposes, it does not matter whether the signal is sent via telephone wires, radio waves, or light beams. For a mathematical theory of communication, each element in the system may be treated as a "black box," reduced to a particular function. This generalizing move—a strategy of dematerialization—has provoked philosophical critiques of cybernetics (and the computationalist cognitive science that still bears its influence), though it also facilitates the application of cybernetic ideas in diverse domains.[12]

To approach musical instruments as cybernetic systems, Heyde starts by black-boxing instrumental components (1975, 22). The difference between Heyde's and Hornbostel and Sach's approach is striking. For Heyde, a string, a reed, and a drumhead belong to the same basic category (27). Each is a *transducer*, which takes energy from some *activator*—for example, a percussionist's hand or an organ's windchest—and changes it to sound. Every instrument couples an activator with a transducer. Instruments may optionally include further functional components, which are listed in Table 2.2, with Heyde's abbreviations and original German terms. The signal may pass through a *mediator* (like a violin bow) on its way to the transducer or through a *channel* at any stage. *Controllers, resonators,* and *couplers* may modify the signal. The remaining categories—*intermediate transducer, modulator,* and *amplifier*—are specific to electric and electronic instruments. After describing these categories (and subcategories within them), Heyde combines them in a general musical instrument system (*Ganzsystem der Musikinstrument*) (62). Any musical instrument, he claims, can be constructed as a subset of elements from the *Ganzsystem.* Like Shannon's communication system, a musical instrument system is a system of inputs and outputs, which transmits and transforms a signal.

For music theorists, Heyde's functional categories—arranged in a particular order, with some essential and some optional elements—may resemble a common

12. Hayles (1999) and Pickering (2009) offer critical histories of cybernetics, while Meyer (1967) combines music theory with information theory.

Table 2.2 Instrumental elements from Heyde (1975)

Label	German term	English term	Examples
A	*Anreger*	Activator	Muscles, lungs, bellows
V	*Vermittler*	Mediator	Violin bow, guitar pick, piano keys
W	*Wandler*	Transducer	Strings, membranes, reeds
ZW	*Zwischenwandler*	Intermediate transducer	Electric guitar pickup
M	*Modulator*	Modulator	Distortion pedal, electronic organ tone filter
Ampl	*Amplifikator*	Amplifier	Electric guitar amp, loudspeaker
R	*Resonator*	Resonator	Violin body, piano soundboard
K	*Kopulator*	Coupler	Flute tube
[circle]	*Kanal*	Channel	Violin bridge, flutist's throat
St	*Steuerelement*	Controller	Fingers, keys, switches

model of harmonic functions.[13] Just as a tonal phrase starts with tonic function (*T*) and leads to dominant function (*D*), instrumental sound production must start with some activating energy (*A*) and lead to a transducer (*W*, for *Wandler*); and just as predominant function (*P*) may intervene between *T* and *D*, a mediator (*V*, for *Vermittler*) may intervene between *A* and *W*. Of course, Heyde's ten instrumental functions are more numerous than the three harmonic functions, and they do not return to their starting point. Still, the comparison is useful. The interesting thing about a particular tonal phrase is not *that* it uses harmonic functions, but *how* it deploys them. Likewise, what is distinctive about an instrumental system is not just the functional components involved, but the structure of connections between components, what Heyde calls their "energetic, material, and informational couplings" (22).[14]

To analyze such structures in particular instruments, Heyde draws schematic circuit diagrams, diagrams of signal flow. For convenience, I will call these "Heyde diagrams." This graphic technique again recalls music-theoretical methods, since these schematics—like Schenkerian voice-leading graphs—are more than mere illustrations. Instead they supplement the written text, as a form of visual, symbolic argumentation. Heyde often presents the diagrams with minimal commentary, leaving it to his readers to investigate them independently. As a preliminary example, I offer a simple Heyde diagram for the cowbell in Figure 2.3. In this case, my body is the activator (*A*) and the bell itself is the transducer (*W*). These two functions, which appear in every Heyde diagram, have distinctive shapes: a "cone" for *A* and a trapezoid for *W*. Other components are represented as labeled rectangles. So one initial strategy for interpreting a Heyde diagram is to find the cone and follow the arrows to the trapezoid. In Figure 2.3, they are not immediately

13. For a critical interpretation of harmonic function, see Hyer (2011).
14. All translations from Heyde are mine.

Figure 2.3 Heyde diagram for cowbell sound production.

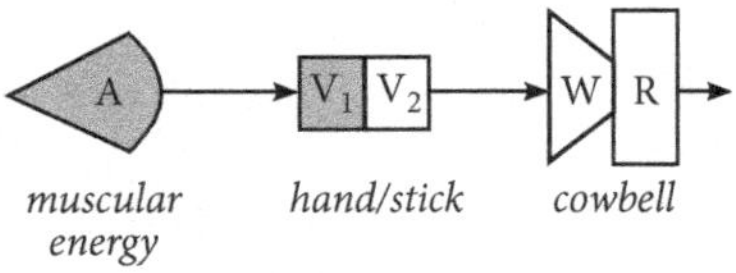

connected. Instead, mediators—the stick (V_2) in my hand (V_1)—direct energy to the bell. Note also that the bell itself performs a double function: it is a transducer but also a resonator. The distinction in shading is also meaningful here. In Heyde diagrams, human elements are shaded, while nonhuman elements have a blank background. Therefore, another strategy involves looking for boundaries between shaded and nonshaded zones. With the cowbell, that boundary comes between my hand and the stick. "Reading" such diagrams involves comparing interrelated levels, tracing various pathways through them—a practice that is not unfamiliar to music theorists. This type of analysis simply looks at the organization of an instrument rather than a piece of music.

Of course, most of Heyde's analyses are far more intricate than this preliminary example. Figure 2.4 reproduces and annotates his schematic for a Boehm flute. Boxes on the right side of the diagram represent parts of the instrument: sixteen keys (k_1–k_{16}) and a mouthpiece (*W*), joined to the cylinder that constitutes the flute's body (coupler, *K*). Fingers of both hands are connected to the keys, though the diagram indicates differences between the hands. Each right-hand finger operates multiple keys, while the right thumb is connected with none. Meanwhile, each finger of the left hand is associated with a single key, and the left thumb operates two. The activating energy here originates in the player's respiratory system. Air passes from the lungs (*A*), through the windpipe (a small circle, representing a channel), to the mouth (a switch symbol). Lips and mouthpiece together form the transducer (*W*)—and this symbol combines human (shaded) and nonhuman (nonshaded) elements. On the whole, then, this diagram shows the integration of flute and flutist. To paraphrase Heyde, the flute itself is only a subsystem (26).

Heyde diagrams present systems of linked nodes. In mathematical terms, these are a kind of graph.[15] A mathematical graph is a collection of points connected by lines. Formally a graph is defined by two sets: a set of vertices *V* (the points) and a set of edges *E* that pair vertices from *V*. For example, imagine a graph where $V = \{A, B, C\}$ and $E = \{\{A, B\}, \{B, C\}\}$. This simple graph would have three points and two lines. It might be drawn in various ways (as demonstrated in Figure 2.5), but such visual representations are, strictly speaking, not a constitutive feature of the graph.

15. Heyde's main source on cybernetics—a book by the neo-Marxist economist Oskar Lange (1965)—is effectively a mathematical treatise on transformations, networks, and graph theory.

Figure 2.4 Circuit diagram for a Boehm flute (adapted from Heyde 1975, 63).

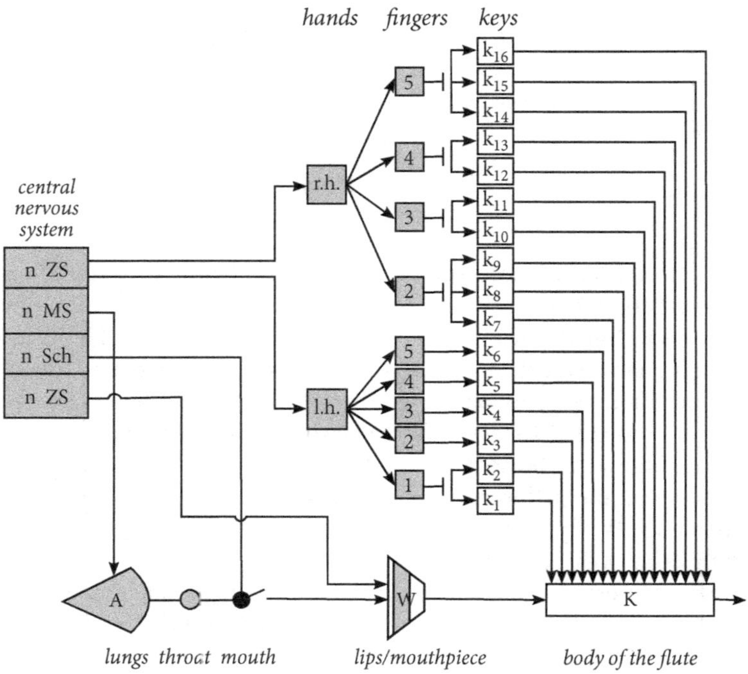

Figure 2.5 Four ways of drawing the same mathematical graph.

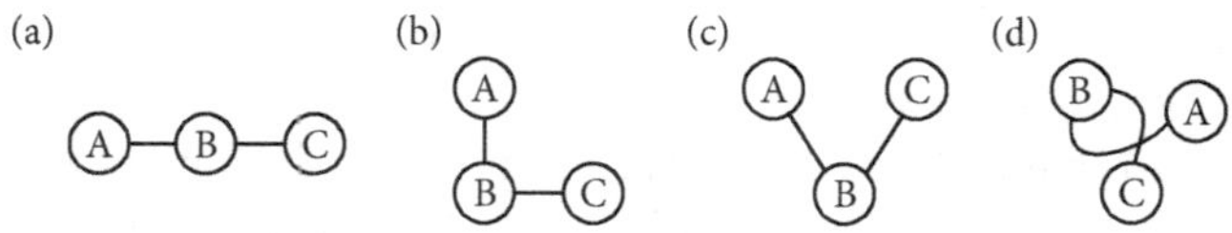

Graphs and networks are used in many diverse fields.[16] In music theory, they are central to transformational theory. Pioneered by David Lewin (1987), transformational theory uses mathematical group theory to model musical spaces, which may include but are not limited to pitch.[17] (For example, later chapters of this book will use transformational graphs and networks to explore various instrumental spaces.) The similarities go beyond the underlying mathematics to include conceptual attitudes: cybernetics is interested in systemic behavior, just as Lewin

16. Sporns (2010), for example, examines the importance of graph theory for neuroscience.
17. Rings discusses graph theory as part of a broader introduction to transformational theory (2011, 110–16). Readers who are familiar with transformational theory might note that whereas the "contents" of a transformation network are discrete elements from a mathematical group, Heyde's schematics model a more or less continuous flow of energy. However, cybernetics often models continuous variables in terms of a "discrete machine," using the framework of transformations, graphs, and networks as a more general conceptual resource (Ashby 1956, 28).

is interested in "musical behavior" (1986, 377). For example, Ashby's statement that cybernetics "does not ask 'what *is* this thing?' but '*what does it do*?'" (1956, 1, emphasis in original) resembles Lewin's "transformational attitude," which prioritizes subjective musical actions over objectified intervallic measurements.[18] More practically, this means that aspects of graph-theoretical thinking exercised in transformational theory—for example, ways of thinking about a graph's connectivity or directedness—can reveal interesting properties of particular Heyde diagrams.

From four source nodes representing the energy source, the graph in Figure 2.4 proceeds through a greater number of intermediate nodes before the arrows converge on a single "root" node, what Lewin calls an "output node" (1987, 207–8). Beyond that, its structure meets the conditions for an oriented digraph, employed in the study of tonal music by Steven Rings (2011, 111). Shared aspects of graphic structure suggest a surprising analogy here: just as independent voices in a tonal composition may start and finish in harmony, independent functional chains in flute playing unite in the final sound. Except for their final convergence at *K*, the two pathways in Figure 2.4 are indeed separate: there is an *activation pathway* involving the player's respiratory system and the mouthpiece, and a *control pathway* involving hands, fingers, and keys.

The energy that passes through this system originates in the performer's nervous system (*n*), represented by the four stacked, shaded rectangles on the left side of the diagram. Yet this energy is not undifferentiated. Heyde distinguishes between "energy-state control" (*Energiezustandssteuerung*, labeled *ZS*) and "energy-volume control" (*Energiemengensteuerung*, labeled *MS*). The former involves qualitative distinctions (for example, on or off), while the latter is quantitative (58).[19] This roughly corresponds to Shannon's distinction between discrete and continuous signals (1964, 34–35). Flute playing involves both forms of energy: the fingers set the keys' state (open or closed), corresponding to discrete pitch changes, while the breath involves variable amounts of energy (more or less), which create continuous fluctuations in volume.

In a way, Heyde's diagram shows relatively little about the flute's sound. Figure 2.4 does not specify what notes are produced by the various holes or key combinations on the flute. It represents a generalized Boehm flute rather than any particular flute or type of flute. For the moment, this abstraction, by usefully bracketing out pitch and rhythmic patterns, can focus attention on the process of sound production.

By bracketing off materiality, Heyde's organology, like cybernetics in general, posits a continuity between the mechanical and the organic. This theme is developed in Gregory Bateson's *Steps to an Ecology of Mind*:

> Some of these pathways happen to be located outside the physical individual, others inside; but the characteristics of the system are in no way dependent upon any

18. Here it seems worth mentioning that David Lewin, like Shannon, worked at Bell Laboratories, and Lewin is cited as a contributor to Jasia Reichardt's computer art exhibition *Cybernetic Serendipity* (1968, 7).
19. The opening and closing of the mouth corresponds to a third kind of control, what Heyde calls switch control (*Schaltsteuerung*, labeled *Sch*).

> boundary lines which we may superpose upon the communicational map. It is not communicationally meaningful to ask whether the blind man's stick or the scientist's microscope are "parts" of the man who uses them. Both stick and microscope are important pathways of communication and, as such, are parts of the network in which we are interested; but no boundary line—e.g., halfway up the stick—can be relevant in a description of the topology of this net. (1972, 251)[20]

If player and instrument are integrated in a "control circuit" (Heyde 1975, 25), aspects of technique can be distributed to the technology, and ultimately the player can be replaced by a nonhuman substitute.[21] For example, the human flutist can be replaced by a mechanical one, as in a celebrated eighteenth-century automaton created by Jacques de Vaucanson. One of Heyde's diagrams for the machine appears in Figure 2.6. Vaucanson's automaton plays the flute with mechanical fingers and a mechanical mouth, powered by a system of nine bellows. This translation from the human to the technical already implies an analysis of the human as part of a mechanical system, and indeed Vaucanson had studied the mechanics of human flute playing while designing his android (Riskin 2003, 613–16).[22] This means that not only the flute but also the flutist is a subsystem. The flutist who can be replaced by an android is already a cyborg.

Activation versus Control

And yet cybernetics misses something important. The flute-playing automaton might reproduce certain musical behaviors, but it cannot re-create the flutist's lived experience.[23] Heyde's distinctions, then, demand phenomenological interpretation. I am particularly interested in the distinction between activation and control, as represented in the two converging pathways in the flute system. Returning to my bicycle analogy, this resembles the gap between feet that pedal and hands that steer. In fact, the German word that Heyde uses, *Steuerung*, can be translated as either "control" or "steering."[24]

When I strike the cowbell, I use the stick to relay my energy to the instrument. But at the same time, I aim the stick at a particular part of the bell. Something

20. Focusing on the topology of the net is part of Bateson's cybernetic refusal of Cartesian dualism, which denies the distinction between the internal and external.
21. More generally, Bruno Latour theorizes both *associations* among human (H) and nonhuman (NH) actors and their mutual *substitutions*. "Of course, an H-H-H assembly looks like social relations," he writes, "while a NH-NH-NH portion looks like a mechanism or a machine, but the point is that they are always integrated into longer chains" (1991, 110).
22. For reflections on the historical and philosophical significance of musical automata, with their mechanical doubling of human performers, see Abbate (1999) and Yearsley (2002, ch. 5).
23. Here I echo Merleau-Ponty's ambivalence about cybernetics, which he discussed in lectures during the 1950s (2003, 165–66).
24. Note also that Norbert Wiener (1948) derived the term "cybernetics" from the Greek *kybernao*, meaning "to steer."

Figure 2.6 Circuit diagram for Vaucanson's flute-playing android (adapted from Heyde 1975, 61). In this diagram, the box labeled *T* represents a "junction" (*Verteiler*).

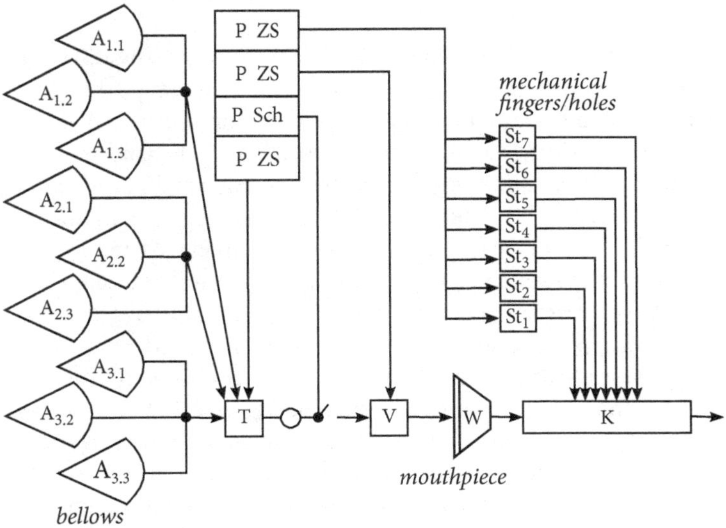

similar happens with the piano: my fingers make the strings sound (via the key-and-hammer mechanism), but they also select the keys. With such instruments, activation and control functions are mixed. These doubled actions might be compared to vector quantities in physics, which combine magnitude and direction. In this analogy, magnitude might correspond to the strength of the attack (communicated in dynamics), and direction to its placement (communicated in pitch). Even with these percussive instruments, though, the functions may diverge to some degree. Cowbell players often use a finger on the nonsticking hand to damp the bell, adding some control over timbre and duration. And though pianists' feet do not typically produce tones, they can control aspects of duration or dynamics through the pedals.[25] Thus, activation and control—though they can be combined and must be coordinated—are mutually irreducible.

These functions are distributed throughout the body in various ways. With the piano accordion, for example, my fingers control the keys, but pushing and pulling arms supply the energy—and thereby control the volume—via the bellows. Because of this single power source, all simultaneous notes on the accordion share the same dynamic, and it is not possible for the accordionist to bring out a line in a polyphonic texture by playing it more loudly. Whereas playing a note on the piano

25. With certain kinds of piano, the player's feet do produce sound: "pedal pianos" include a keyboard for the feet, and pianos with Janissary stops, popular in late-eighteenth- and early-nineteenth-century Vienna, have pedals that activate percussive effects inspired by Turkish military bands. Such pianos, however, are rare today.

is a percussive act, on the accordion I can hold a chord with my fingers and work the bellows to sustain it, "breathing" in and out with my arms. In this situation, I would be focused on activation and not control. As with other wind instruments, I may seem to be maintaining and manipulating a stream of energy rather than percussing an object.

With the violin, my right hand typically activates the sound, either through the bow or through plucking fingers, while my left hand stops the strings.[26] That is to say, my left hand cannot make the notes louder or longer. Usually both hands collaborate to produce pitches and rhythms, since the bow hand selects the string or strings to be played, and the left-hand fingers may rhythmically change notes during a sustained bow.[27] When I combine active bowing with an unchanging left hand, the violin has the feel of a percussion instrument. When long, sustained bows support rapid finger changes, I am more likely to feel as though I am manipulating a flow of energy. Either way, violin hands are more highly differentiated than piano hands or accordion hands, but also less independent.

The opposition of activation and control becomes clearer as functions are distributed between the player and the instrument. Figure 2.7 plots these possibilities on a semiotic square.[28] Each combination of terms creates a category, illustrated with musical instruments in Figure 2.7a and with vehicles in Figure 2.7b.

If the piano is like a bicycle, the pipe organ seems closer to a Harley-Davidson. When I play the organ, I guide the instrument without providing its energy. Slamming or caressing the keys does not affect the organ's volume, which is set by an expression pedal. The gentlest touch can create a thunderous tone. Though I have surely initiated this sound, the instrument's response may seem disproportionate. And the breath filling the pipes is not like my breath. This wind instrument has an endless air supply, sustaining tone indefinitely. The organ, then, combines two kinds of superhuman power—in its endurance and in its strength—and puts them at my disposal. These possibilities are, of course, central to the idiomatic technique of the pedal point. For example, consider the fourteen-measure pedal near the opening of J. S. Bach's Prelude and Fugue in A minor, BWV 543, an unstoppable sonic force grounding the passage work above (see Figure 2.8). The excess of instrumental energy in such gestures engineers a sense of transcendence, as powerful as any hidden orchestra or choir.[29]

The organ's nonhuman breath is thematized even more clearly in György Ligeti's *Volumina* (1962), a piece that explores overwhelming sustained clusters, shifting in color. At the end of the piece, Ligeti instructs the organist to switch off the organ blower. The organist continues to hold down the keys, and the sound

26. An exception to this is left-hand pizzicato, a technique found, for example, in the ninth variation from Niccolò Paganini's Caprice in A minor, op. 1, no. 24.

27. Note that the bow offers continuous control over rhythm and dynamics, but discrete control over pitch. And though the left hand can produce continuous pitch variation (in vibrato or glissandi), its fingers often seek to reproduce a discrete system of pitches.

28. The semiotic square is a tool for exploring structural oppositions, introduced by Greimas and Rastier (1968).

29. On the transcendental effects of concealed orchestras (a technique particularly associated with Richard Wagner), see Dolan (2013, 258–64) and Kane (2014, ch. 4).

Figure 2.7 Semiotic squares exploring activation and control (a) with musical instruments and (b) with vehicles. (Note that the handcar is a crank-powered railway vehicle, popularly associated with Wile E. Coyote.)

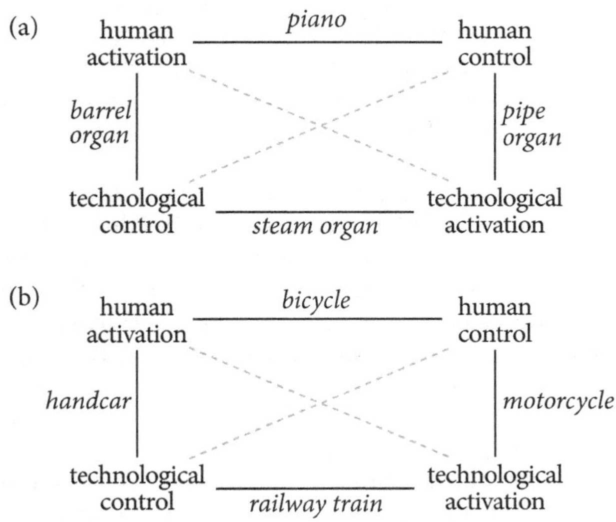

Figure 2.8 Johann Sebastian Bach, Prelude and Fugue in A minor, BWV 543, mm. 10–15. The pedal tone in the bass continues to m. 24.

gradually falters as the instrument runs out of air. Here Ligeti reveals the limit of a seemingly limitless energy source, highlighting an aspect of the organ that can easily be taken for granted.

So far, I have focused on human-controlled instruments. Yet as the square in Figure 2.7a shows, other possibilities are latent in the opposition of activation and control. Whereas the pipe organ combines mechanical energy with human control, the barrel organ inverts this pattern, combining human energy with mechanical control. With this inversion, however, some may question whether it is truly a musical instrument at all.

In the eighteenth and nineteenth centuries, the barrel organ was commonly used as a street instrument and in churches alongside "finger organs."[30] To play the instrument, an organ grinder turns a crank. This crank performs two functions, both hidden inside the instrument: it pumps the bellows, filling an air reservoir; and at the same time, it rotates a cylindrical barrel that is covered with a pattern of pins and staples. Each pin and staple opens a pipe to pressurized air from the reservoir, releasing a note in a programmed sequence. (Most barrels have multiple settings, to play multiple tunes.) Despite their popularity, barrel organs were widely denigrated (Hicks 2014). This is perhaps not only because of their contributions to urban noise or their populist repertoire, but also because of the organ grinder's ambiguous status as a musician. Some might view organ grinding as a purely mechanical activity, in which the player is automatized or instrumentalized. But playing the barrel organ does involve some skill. At the very least, the crank must be turned in the correct direction, since reversing it can damage the instrument. The organ grinder also controls the tempo, keeping it steady or varying it for expressive effect. And barrel organs, like pipe organs, often have multiple stops. Finally, many organ grinders obviously treat their work as a kind of performance. They often wear distinctive costumes, and gesture, dance, or sing along with the music. In this regard, they resemble the DJs studied by Mark Butler (2014, 95–105). Because their music-making obviously involves technological mediation, both organ grinders and DJs "perform performance." They work to convey personality and agency, to engage audiences, to emphasize "liveness." Despite the barrel organ's commonalties with musical automata and later recording technologies, then, it is still actively played.

Devices on the bottom edge of Figure 2.7a, in which both components are nonhuman, might seem even more liminal as instruments. Again, these are not necessarily digital or mechanical. A prime example here might be the aeolian harp, whose strings are activated by wind (an instrument that was discussed by Athanasius Kircher in the seventeenth century). But what of instruments that have to be *started* by a human? For example, a steam organ, which matches the pipe organ's mechanical power source with the barrel organ's programming? Is pressing an on/off button the minimal form of instrumental technique?

30. As a sample performance, I recommend the following YouTube video: https://youtu.be/ZClrDGnqd1Y. The earliest description of a barrel organ, however, appears in a ninth-century treatise by the Banū Mūsā brothers of Baghdad (Langwill and Ord-Hume 2001).

Of course, such questions are not uniquely related to musical instruments. Instead they engage broader issues in the history of technology, which are discussed in Jean Baudrillard's *The System of Objects*. For Baudrillard, older objects rely on human energy and ability, and are therefore shaped for the body. A hammer's handle—or a piano's keyboard—presupposes a strong, skilled hand. Yet, he continues, as technical objects have become more intricate, the related gestures have grown simpler, ultimately creating technologies that are more complex than the techniques required to operate them: "Buttons, levers, handles, pedals (even nothing at all—as when one passes in front of a photo-electric cell) have … replaced pressure, percussion, impact or balance achieved by means of the body, the intensity and distribution of force, and the abilities of the hand" (1996, 51). Buttons, in this account, demand neither effort nor dexterity. They reflect an increasingly abstract—but also increasingly free—connection between body and object.

The Monome 64, developed by Brian Crabtree and Kelli Cain, presents an 8 × 8 grid of identical square buttons.[31] The buttons can light up, but they are not pressure-sensitive and have no predetermined function. In Crabtree's words, "The wonderful thing about this device is that it doesn't do anything really" (quoted in Emsley 2011, 43). A button takes on an effect—triggering a sound, an audiovisual clip, or an action in a video game—only when the Monome is coupled with some software. The Monome, then, combines strict constraints with endless customizability. On this level, its buttons seem to embody the kind of abstraction theorized by Baudrillard.

But although the Monome could easily be set up as a kind of jukebox (where the press of a button would play a complete prerecorded track), it is more commonly used to realize various musical spaces and processes. For example, Crabtree's "flin" app (released under his performance name, "tehn") creates an instrument with repeating notes.[32] Figure 2.9 models this arrangement. Each column of buttons corresponds to a single pitch, with lower pitches on the left and higher ones on the right. Similarly, the rows map onto duration, with higher rows producing shorter notes. Pushing a button, then, produces a looping note with a unique pitch and length. Each note is visually represented by a line of lights descending along the column like slow-motion raindrops. It is possible to press a few buttons and let the app run indefinitely, to watch and listen as the notes go in and out of phase. Here the Monome, like an automaton or aeolian harp, seems to play out a nonhuman musical process. Activation and control both come from the instrument itself. Yet it is also possible to intervene, to thicken or thin the texture, to change the notes or durations, to reintroduce human control.

Butler describes this mode of performance as "playing with something that runs" (2014, 106–8). His description draws on his performing experience with both classical music and electronic dance music (EDM). While playing piano, he must remain constantly involved in sound production. But while DJing, he can

31. The Monome grid is available in larger sizes too. Butler examines these controllers in the context of various technologies used in electronic dance music (2014, 87–89). As he notes, the Monome is not associated with any particular software. Instead, it works with a variety of programs, including open-source software developed by a community of users (88).

32. For a demonstration, see https://vimeo.com/418349.

Figure 2.9 Diagram showing pitch and duration layout for "flin" on a Monome 64.

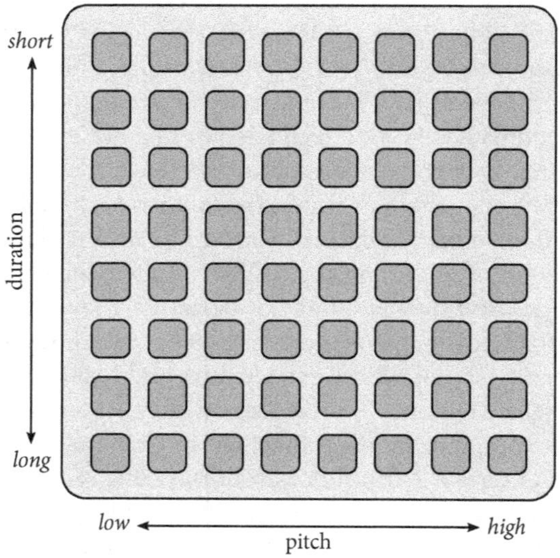

step back and listen to a process unfold, taking time to plan his next move. "By shifting some of the responsibility for sound production from the performer to the machine," Butler concludes, "EDM technologies cultivate the emergence of a distinctively interpretive role *during performance*" (108, emphasis in original). A related difference between pianists and DJs might involve the habits of auditory-motor integration discussed in the preceding chapter. Though DJs might develop similar multisensory connections, they would likely be more flexible than those found in classical pianists. (Again, the abstraction of the Monome may engender a certain kind of freedom.)

In terms of the semiotic square in Figure 2.7a, "playing with something that runs" might involve an alternation between human and technical control. It is also possible to combine human and technical energy sources. With the electric guitar, for example, I directly activate the vibrating string—but the unplugged guitar responds in a whisper. When I connect it to an amplifier and hit the on switch, it feels like a different instrument. Simply tapping the string now produces a bold tone, especially if I have added a distortion pedal to this musical circuit. The force with which I pluck the string is still reflected in the guitar's volume, but magnified, supercharged. Here, again, technical and phenomenological aspects of instrumental sound production mingle with cultural values. For better or worse, the way that the electric guitar "empowers" its player is bound up with the ways that the instrument has been gendered in popular culture.[33] Instead of being pinned in a single place on the square, then, this

33. Robert Walser (1993) and Steve Waksman (1999) have both examined such aspects of electric guitar culture.

instrument offers experiences of sound production that are defined by dynamic tensions among the square's elements.

From Feedback to Incorporation

Sound production—conceived as the transmission and transformation of energy—might seem like a one-way process. After all, the arrows in the Heyde diagrams presented earlier always point forward. Yet for a performer, sound also provides a kind of *feedback*. Indeed, Heyde's first circuit diagram includes a feedback loop—an arrow that wraps around, going back to the nervous system through the ear (1975, 24). Such a loop, in a sense, is implicit in all later diagrams.[34] (That said, certain self-powering instruments let the player experiment with auditory feedback. Here I am particularly thinking of an electric guitar technique known as "volume swells," in which the guitarist activates the string with the volume off, then fades in with the volume knob or a volume pedal.)[35] Auditory feedback helps guide specific aspects of performance, particularly with continuous parameters. For example, auditory feedback is essential for intonation on bowed string instruments. When experienced cellists shift along the fingerboard but do not bow the string, their left hand drifts away from the correct position (Chen et al. 2013). In this case, the control pathway cannot properly function without the activation pathway. Despite years of practice, the cellist's motor performance depends on auditory feedback.[36]

Instrumental performance involves other forms of sensory feedback too. Many performers can *see* their hands on the instrument, and this visual information can be useful when they are executing certain actions (such as large leaps). Visual feedback is often important for beginners as well: for example, an experiment with beginning piano students indicated that "covering the hands of the learners so that they could not see the keyboard was to some extent detrimental to learning" (Brown 1934, 527). Still, not all instruments offer an equal amount of visual feedback. A flute can be seen only peripherally, and a diatonic harmonica is completely hidden in the player's hands.

Tactile feedback is also essential, particularly for timing.[37] Aschersleben, Gehrke, and Prinz (2001) found that anesthetizing participants' hands did not affect their ability to tap as rapidly as possible or to air-tap along with a beat. But their ability to synchronize key taps with a beat was significantly compromised.

34. Feedback is a central concept for cybernetics, because of its role in a system's self-regulation.
35. Eddie Van Halen's solo electric guitar track "Cathedral" from the 1982 album *Diver Down* uses volume swells to imitate an organ. For an analysis of "Cathedral," see De Souza (2016b).
36. Similarly, Hafke-Dys, Preis, and Trojan (2016) investigated the effects of altered pitch feedback on violinists' motor performance. In this experiment, violinists accurately compensated for the pitch shift, even when they could not consciously perceive the alteration.
37. Tactile feedback can be distinguished from kinesthetic or proprioceptive feedback, which involves bodily movement but not touch.

From this perspective, the hand is not just an output device. Rather, information flows in both directions. The hand touches and is touched.[38] Unlike its auditory or visual counterparts, tactile feedback allows for experiences of resistance. I feel my finger make contact with the piano key, and I feel it when the key hits bottom. This feedback, again, is important for temporal regulation. As the tempo becomes faster, pianists lift their fingers higher and strike the keys more forcefully, and increasing tactile information in this way improves temporal accuracy (Palmer and Dalla Bella 2004; Goebl and Palmer 2008). Clarinetists do the same, even though their fingers do not affect note onset or volume (Palmer et al. 2009). Tactile feedback can also pass through a mediating implement. For example, I feel the cowbell at the tip of the drumstick, not at the position of my hand.[39]

The key point here is that playing an instrument mixes multiple streams of feedback, involving what Merleau-Ponty calls "exchanges" between the visible, audible, and tangible (1968, 143). This multisensory integration underlies the action-effect binding discussed in Chapter 1, shaping players' perception and production of sound. Beyond that, though, such feedback may modulate the experience of one's own body.

Here, while recalling the Husserlian distinction between *Körper* and *Leib*, it is useful to invoke a related distinction *within* the category of the lived body—a distinction between body image and body schema.[40] The body image involves a conscious awareness of my body, the lived body as intentional object.[41] The body schema, on the other hand, is preconscious and supports automatic movements. Though the body schema involves reflexes and so on, note that this does *not* correspond to a distinction between a natural and a cultural body. Learned skills and habits register at both levels.

Though these two aspects of the body are typically mixed in lived experience, they may come apart. The classic example of a gap between body image and body schema is the phantom limb. Since the patient is aware that the limb

38. Both Husserl ([1929] 1960, 97) and Merleau-Ponty (2012, 94–95; 1968, 147–48) discuss this doubling in terms of one hand touching the other. For Merleau-Ponty, touching and being touched intertwine without fully coinciding. "When I press my two hands together," he writes, "it is not a question of two sensations that I could feel together, as when we perceive two objects juxtaposed, but rather of an ambiguous organization where the two hands can alternate between the functions of 'touching' and 'touched'" (2012, 95). This non-coincidence, to use a harmonic analogy, might be compared to a pivot chord: it functions in two keys, but I can hear it only in one key at a time. Wiskus (2013) approaches Merleau-Ponty's philosophy of non-coincidence via music, painting, and literature.

39. Yamamoto and Kitazawa (2001) use a temporal discrimination task with crossed hands to show that stimuli are not located at the position of the hand, but sensed at the drumstick's *tip*.

40. Merleau-Ponty discusses the body schema (*schema corporel*) in *The Phenomenology of Perception*, drawing on earlier work in neurology by Henry Head (1920). For terminological issues here, see Gallagher (1986) and Sheets-Johnstone (2005). In a review of neurophysiological and psychological research on the body schema, Graziano and Botvinick (2002) emphasize its reliance on interconnected sensory and motor areas in the parietal lobe and premotor cortex.

41. In phenomenology, intentionality refers to the "aboutness" or "directedness" of experience. That is, every experience is an experience of *something* (and that something is an "intentional object").

has been amputated, it is no longer part of the patient's body image. Yet it persists in the body schema.[42] As Merleau-Ponty writes, "To have a phantom limb is to remain open to all of the actions of which the arm alone is capable and to stay within the practical field that one had prior to the mutilation" (2012, 84).

More rarely, the body schema itself may be impaired, resulting in a loss of the sense of bodily position and movement (Cole and Paillard 1995). One patient suffering from this unusual neuropathy can verbally explain where her body has been touched or locate it on a diagram but, without visual information, cannot point to the place on her body. She knows the touch in terms of body image but not body schema (254). Such patients are able to move their bodies but must consciously regulate every move. Sitting on a chair, holding an egg without crushing it, gesturing while talking—these usually automatic actions, for them, require effort and attention. As another patient puts it, he cannot walk and daydream at the same time (262). Besides revealing the everyday reliance on automatic bodily habits, such cases demonstrate the nonidentity of body image and body schema.

Exploiting this gap can produce fascinating phenomena, such as the "rubber hand illusion" (Botvinick and Cohen 1998). While a participant is seated at a table, one of the participant's hands is hidden by a screen, and a rubber hand is put in its place. An experimenter uses paintbrushes to stroke the hidden real hand and the visible rubber hand at the same time. Through this coordination of visual and tactile feedback, participants come to feel that the rubber hand is part of their own body.[43] Surprisingly, such an illusion can take place in the absence of the artificial hand: if the experimenter systematically strokes an empty space while stroking the unseen hand, the participants may come to feel that they possess an invisible hand (Guterstam, Gentile, and Ehrsson 2013). And if the experimenter then "stabs" the invisible hand with a kitchen knife, this evokes increased skin conductance (a common physiological measure of arousal). The body schema, then, can incorporate even empty space, inducing a kind of phantom-limb experience.[44]

In a similar study, the experimenter gently taps a participant's hand with a small hammer (Senna et al. 2014). The participant wears headphones, in which the sound of the hammer against the participant's skin is gradually replaced by the sound of a hammer tapping marble. If the marble sounds are temporally coordinated with the felt taps, uncanny effects appear after five minutes: the hand begins to feel numb, stiff, heavy, and hard. It feels like a marble hand. In the rubber hand illusion, I come to feel what I see; in the marble hand

42. Phantom limbs are consistent with the phantasmal voices and other simulations discussed in perceptual symbol systems theory (see Chapter 1). Indeed, some commentators argue that phantom limbs provide strong evidence consistent with Barsalou's theory (Edelman and Breen 1999).

43. Neuroimaging research suggests that the premotor cortex is involved in the multisensory integration that produces a sense of bodily ownership (Ehrsson, Spence, and Passingham 2004).

44. It is, however, considerably more difficult to induce the sense of ownership with an object that does not resemble a hand, such as a wooden stick (Tsakiris and Haggard 2005). This suggests that such illusions require a mix of bottom-up and top-down processes.

illusion, what I hear. Multisensory feedback reconstructs the sense of one's own body.

These experiments indicate conditions under which the body may incorporate tools or other objects. Navigating with a stick alters the body schema because it provides multisensory feedback. When blind people regularly use a cane, their sense of personal space expands. Tactile and auditory awareness focuses on the area at the tip of the cane. For experts, the perceptual changes are more or less permanent, but they can be temporarily induced in sighted people who have been trained to use a cane (Serino et al. 2007). Like riding a bicycle, navigating with a stick involves practical know-how, which, despite its conscious aspects, must be grounded at the level of the body schema. "If I want to become habituated to a cane," writes Merleau-Ponty, "I try it out, I touch some objects and, after some time, I have it 'in hand'" (2012, 144).[45]

All of this, finally, can help explain why musicians sometimes claim that an instrument feels like part of the body. I would hypothesize that such experiences are more common when multisensory feedback is maximized—that is, when an instrument's sound reflects multiple aspects of the player's action and when tactile and visual feedback match the auditory image. In other words, the illusion of instrumental incorporation seems more likely with human activation and control than with a self-propelling instrument like the Monome. Mediators like bows or drumsticks (which, like the cane, can be felt *through*) might also enhance the illusion. Gibson's distinction between "detached objects" (which I can pick up and move) and "attached objects" (which are fixed) seems relevant too (1979, 133). But this might simply be because detached instruments like the violin or flute stay in continuous contact with the body.

Some players actively seek a sense of bodily extension. The trumpet virtuoso Jens Lindemann, for example, tries to foster it in his students. "It's a lifelong pursuit trying to get to that point of comfort," he says, "but when you do arrive there you realize that you're just taking a piece of metal and you're blowing through it. It's that simple and that complicated at the same time."[46] Of course, the feeling of incorporation, like any form of withdrawal, will be fleeting. The experience, surely, differs in notable ways from the experience of having a rubber hand, and musicians may not intend that their statements about such experiences be taken literally. Still, these psychological and philosophical perspectives suggest that playing an instrument can change the experience of one's own body, that in music as in other domains the boundaries of the lived body can be reshaped by technics.

45. Another study by colleagues of Serino showed that tool use can alter perceptions of one's own body. After participants used a mechanical grabbing arm, their reaching behavior changed, and their estimates of their own arm length slightly increased. Briefly put, they acted as though they had longer arms (Cardinali et al. 2009).

46. See http://www.artistshousemusic.org/videos/your+instrument+as+an+extension+of+your+body.

Conclusions

Instrumental sound production, generally speaking, involves a certain reciprocity: actions are converted into sounds, and sounds give feedback about actions. As such, player and instrument together can be understood as a system that generates and transforms musical energy. Yet because this coupling is realized in countless ways, analyses of particular instruments must untangle the contributions of bodily technique and instrumental technology, considering their phenomenological and sonic effects.

Physical traces, of course, are also audible in voices. This is central to Roland Barthes's reflections on the "grain of the voice." The "grain" refers not just to vocal timbre but to contributions of "the tongue, the glottis, the teeth, the mucous membranes, the nose" (1977, 183). "The 'grain,'" Barthes explains, "is the body in the voice as it sings, the hand as it writes, the limb as it performs" (188).[47] Additionally, the sense of vocal ownership, like bodily ownership in general, can be influenced by multisensory feedback. In one notable experiment, the participants spoke words while simultaneously hearing a voice in headphones say the same words (Zheng et al. 2011). With this congruence between auditory information and vocal motor activity, the participants came to feel that the other voice was their own.[48] This "rubber voice" illusion is possible because vocal production is both felt and heard.

As my voice resounds outside of me, it may sometimes be experienced as a kind of object. Whereas instrumental incorporation brings a tool into the body schema, this objectification exteriorizes voice, projecting corporeal activity outward. But a voice is a slippery thing.[49] After all, my voice originates *inside* my body. I can neither grasp nor see it, and I hear it "from within" (Merleau-Ponty 1968, 144; Vitale 2008). In the end, then, this chapter differentiates instrumental and vocal sound production. Singing is like running rather than cycling. Though running and singing are undeniably technical, they do not require a prosthesis—something set before me—that transforms my energy and grounds my actions.[50] Variations in vocal tension, for example, are not tethered to tangible spots in the world. I can point to a middle C on the piano or violin but not in my voice. Voices, that is, do not spatialize pitch in the same way that many instruments do.

47. Barthes explicitly extends the grain to instrumental music, with a brief discussion of keyboard performance (1977, 188–89).

48. I would hypothesize that the voice can incorporate other sounds as well. This could be tested by modifying the procedure of Zheng et al. (2011), replacing spoken words with sung notes and the stranger's voice with instrumental tones.

49. For a discussion of the ambiguities surrounding voice—and a concise overview of the extensive scholarly literature on voice—see Feldman (2015). I discuss voice-instrument relations in De Souza 2014.

50. Of course, this presumes a "naked" voice. Various musical technologies—from kazoos to vocoders to microphones—*do* transform vocal energy. These instruments, it might be said, are "played" with the voice.

The question of instrumental space, however, goes beyond sound production. Heyde diagrams may outline an interface's topology, but they do not show how it affords specific sets of pitches. Yet this will be crucial for understanding how instrumental organization relates to tonal organization and how an instrumental space, with its boundaries and privileged zones, might affect players' creative actions.

CHAPTER Three

Idiomaticity; or, Three Ways to Play Harmonica

In an experiment at the Max Planck Institute for Human Cognitive and Brain Sciences, guitarists were asked to finger a chord in response to an on-screen cue (Drost, Rieger, and Prinz 2007). The chords were not difficult, either A major or A minor. But as each visual prompt appeared, the participants heard a chord that might—or might not—match the one they were supposed to play. That is, sometimes they heard A major when they had to play A minor (and vice versa). The mismatched chords slowed reaction time *but only when they had the timbre of a guitar*. If the distractor sounded like a piano, an organ, flutes, or voices, it had no significant effect on the guitarists' performance. When pianists did this same task, though, they were influenced by piano sounds *and* organ sounds. The researchers explained this result in terms of affordances: because piano and organ are both keyboard instruments, they afford similar actions and musical textures. Despite differences in action-sound coupling, expert pianists may hear organ music kinesthetically, sensing movement on the keys.

A subtle difference between the guitarists' and pianists' tasks raises further questions. Guitarists played A major and minor, but pianists played C major and minor. Why would the designers of the experiment choose one key for the piano, another for the guitar? The answer, for a guitarist, is obvious. The chord voicings used in the experiment involve open strings, and they are particularly easy to play. The corresponding hand shapes for C major and minor, though, are barre chords—that is, chords where the index finger stops multiple strings at the same fret. Similarly, C has a special relationship to the piano, since the key of C major entails only white notes. Such contrasts have less to do with the instruments' modes of sound production than with the way they organize pitch materials. With other instruments, the experimental task would have to be further modified. The diatonic harmonica, for example, cannot play a major and minor triad over the same root. How, then, do particular instruments realize pitch spaces in physical space? How are instrumental interfaces structured? And how might they structure players' actions?

These questions evoke broader debates about technology and agency, which are often framed around two theoretical poles.[1] On one side, voluntarism and social reductionism suggest that tools are merely vehicles for human intentions. The most common expression of this view might be the National Rifle

1. For further discussion of such debates, see Ihde (1990, 4–5) and, in a musical context, Taylor (2001, 25–31).

Association's slogan, "Guns don't kill people. People do." On the other, technological determinism claims that tools shape or control their users. This is conveyed by Marshall McLuhan's famous claim that "the medium is the message" (1994, 7). Both extremes are problematic. Clearly we make choices when using instruments, and yet it sometimes feels as though they have a hold on us.

Ecological perceptual theory avoids deterministic oppositions here. As emphasized in Chapter 1, affordances and abilities are always codefined. But Gibson also insists that a thing's affordances exist independently of an agent's needs or skills. As he puts it, "The object offers what it does because it is what it is" (1979, 139). This realism distinguishes Gibson's "affordance" from Gestalt psychology's earlier term, "valence" (*Aufforderungscharakter*). Though both concepts suggest that objects invite particular actions, the Gestalt theorist Kurt Koffka argues that valences belong to a perceived "phenomenal object," not the physical object itself. Gibson rejects this dualism. Noticing or ignoring affordances does not change them. They are "always there." Note how this invariance unsettles voluntarism and social reductionism. Affordances are not produced by agents' intentions, nor are they merely projected onto an object. That is why my attempt to use an object might fail, why the object might resist certain uses, why it might do things that I do not want it to do.

Given those real constraints, though, an object's affordances are potentially endless. A chair never forces me to sit in it. I could stand on the chair instead. I could hide behind it. I could use it as a doorstop, an end table, a clothes horse, or a music stand. It is impossible to list all of the chair's uses or features. This openness subverts technological determinism. A tool can always be put to some unexpected use.

This nondeterministic reciprocity between agent and thing challenges both sides of the dialectic. But it also raises new problems. If affordances are theoretically innumerable, why are certain uses of an object preferred over others? Why does it seem that a tool should be used in a certain way? Extending ecological psychology here requires an account of artifact-based skills that are learned, culturally and technically situated, and directed toward goals. To this end, David Kirsh offers the idea of the "enactive landscape," a set of affordances that are activated for an agent. In other words, an enactive landscape is a space of possibilities, in which technology and technique coevolve. As Kirsh puts it, "Music teaches us that these … landscapes multiply furiously" (2013, §2.6). Musical instruments, specifically, "provide musicians the physical landscape necessary to change their possibilities—to create a perfect niche for making music" (§2.6).

This chapter investigates enactive landscapes associated with a specific instrument: the diatonic harmonica, colloquially known as the "blues harp." Though the harmonica's origins are poorly documented, it was likely invented in Germany around the 1820s as part of a vogue for free-reed instruments that also produced the accordion, the concertina, and various forgotten cousins (like Christian Buschmann's "aura" and Charles Wheatstone's "symphonium").[2] In the second half

2. These free-reed instruments were directly or indirectly inspired by traditional Asian mouth organs such as the Chinese *sheng*, which had been known in Europe since the seventeenth century (for example, Marin Mersenne described such an instrument in his 1636 *Harmonie universelle*). On the origins of the diatonic harmonica, see Missin (n.d.) and Field (2000, 23–24).

Figure 3.1 A ten-hole diatonic harmonica, or "blues harp."

of the nineteenth century, the diatonic harmonica would be industrially mass-produced and exported globally (Wenzel and Häffner 2006). It was portable, fairly durable, and inexpensive—and these features contributed to its widespread popularity. The harmonica's use in folk music, blues, and jazz shows how this seemingly simple instrument supports multiple enactive landscapes. Such landscapes call for a mode of analysis that investigates performers' moves through instrumental space, an approach that may be informed by statements from expert players and by Lewinian transformational models. At the same time, this analysis motivates theoretical reflections on instrumental spaces and idioms—and ultimately an argument about technical agency.

Instrumental Spaces

The harmonica fits in my palm, but my hands cannot make it sound. The harmonica, after all, is a particular sort of wind instrument, a "mouth organ."[3] It has ten square holes, lined up on a comb (Figure 3.1). Breathing through these holes activates tuned reeds hidden beneath the instrument's metal cover plates. Here air and sound are immediately joined, in their timing and their strength. The instrument is louder when I blow harder; it stops resonating when I stop moving air through it. Briefly put, the harmonica converts my breath into music.

This action-sound coupling differentiates the harmonica from free-reed instruments that have bellows. With the accordion, squeezing and pulling arms activate sound while fingers control pitch. With the harmonica, breathing provides both power and steering. Breath strength controls dynamics, while breath placement and breath direction control pitch. Because of its two sets of reeds inhaling and exhaling through the same hole give different notes. Moreover, the "draw" notes (produced by inhaling) and the "blow" notes (produced by exhaling) form two tonally distinct collections. Each of the harmonica styles analyzed here somehow

3. This is reflected in its original German name, *Mundharmonika* (mouth harmonica). Note, however, that it affords breathing-through for other animals too: for example, the Smithsonian's National Zoo has a harmonica-playing elephant that holds the instrument in her trunk (Fazeli Fard 2012).

Figure 3.2 Two instrumental "arrays" (after Baily 2006, 116): (a) with the *dutār*'s linear array, the player moves *along* a single string (for example, the pitch "Ma" is five "steps" to the right of "Sa"); (b) with the *rubāb*'s tiered array, the player can also move *across* strings (finding "Ma" at the same fret as "Sa," on the adjacent string).

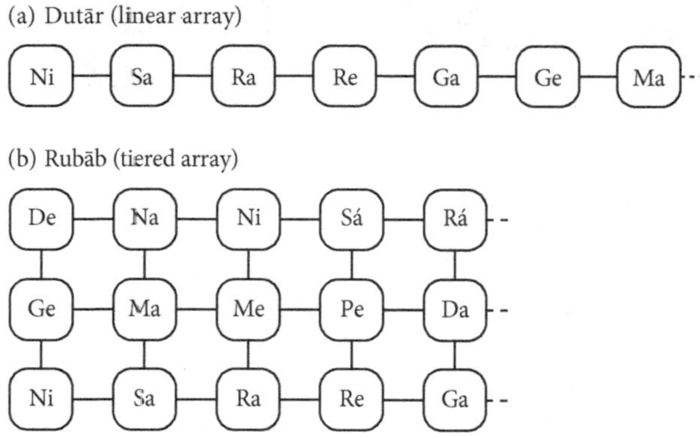

responds to this complementarity between the instrument's pitch affordances and human physiology. In a sense, the harmonica musicalizes respiration.

At the same time, the ten holes on the comb set out a pitch continuum much like a keyboard. Low notes are on one end (typically held on the left); high notes, on the other. Such linearity is common among instruments, though not universal. (Instruments that set out pitch space in a nonlinear way include mbira, steel drums, and bandoneon.) As I play, I coordinate my lips and the holes, moving the harmonica left or right with my hands and sliding my mouth along the comb. Since I can also change pitch by reversing the direction of my breath, harmonica space offers two basic ways of moving—side to side and in and out. It has two "dimensions."

The ethnomusicologist John Baily explores this multidimensional aspect of instrumental interfaces in his study of two Afghan lutes, the *dutār* and the *rubāb* (1977, 2006). Though their repertoires overlap, their instrumental spaces are quite different.[4] With the *dutār*, melodies are usually played on one string, shifting along a single dimension. With the *rubāb*, melodies are usually played across three strings. Baily calls the former a "linear array" and the latter a "tiered array."[5] He illustrates their difference with a diagram resembling Figure 3.2.

Thinking in terms of "arrays" highlights different kinds of *proximity* in instrumental space. I imagine their dimensions in terms of intersecting instrumental "scales" (using Dmitri Tymoczko's [2011, 116] expansive definition of "scale" as "a kind of musical ruler"). If I am blowing through the harmonica's third hole, I can move "one step" along the comb to the fourth-hole blow *or* I can move "one step"

4. In fact, musicians in the city of Herat devised the fourteen-stringed *dutār* in the 1960s so they could play classical music associated with the *rubāb*.

5. Baily and Driver (1992) extend this thinking to folk-blues guitar playing.

with my breath, changing to the third-hole draw. In both cases, I sense a kind of adjacency, although neither move would sound a diatonic "step."[6] Before investigating the harmonica's pitch affordances, however, I want to formalize this idea of instrumental spaces with particular dimensions.

Instrumental arrays—instruments with dimensions that are divided into steps—can be represented via Lewinian transformational theory. As mentioned in the preceding chapter, this approach uses mathematical groups to model various kinds of musical spaces and actions, involving pitch, rhythm, texture, or other domains. Joti Rockwell (2009), for example, has used transformational techniques to analyze picking patterns on the five-string banjo. Since transformational theory deals with grouplike structures involving discrete quantities, it may not apply to instrumental spaces that lack countable steps (such as the timbral space of a drumhead). Nonetheless, it offers a productive way to model many kinds of instrumental patterns.

Tiered-array instruments like *rubābs* and guitars involve two dimensions—across and along the strings. In other words, any spot on the fingerboard can be modeled as a combination of fret position and string position. I write this as an ordered pair of the form (f, s), with both variables represented by integers.[7] Elements can then be transposed in either dimension: across-string operations would take the form $(0, +x)$ or $(0, -x)$, where x is any nonzero integer; along-string operations, $(+x, 0)$ or $(-x, 0)$. Note that the numbers in my operation labels are marked with a plus or minus sign. This emphasizes that they indicate movement and also differentiates them from the notation for elements. That is, $(+1, +1)$ represents an action (going up one string and up one fret), whereas $(1, 1)$ represents a place (the first fret on the first string). Such transformations can be applied either to individual elements in the space (that is, notes) or to sets (melodies or chords). The network in Figure 3.3, for example, models such moves in a passage from the Kinks' 1964 song, "All Day and All of the Night." This sequence moves a single fretboard shape around the fretboard. There is, however, more than one way to realize this: moving along and across the strings or staying on the lowest three strings throughout (see Video 3.1▶).[8] As with Heyde diagrams, transformational graphs and networks can be read in various ways. It is generally useful, however, to trace the pathways formed by the arrows.[9]

By comparison, elements in harmonica space can be modeled as ordered pairs of the form (h, σ), where h is the hole (represented by an integer) and σ is a sign (+ or −) that corresponds to blow or draw. For example, (3, +) is the third-hole blow. (This labeling method resembles common forms of harmonica tablature.) In

6. The first move, from third-hole blow to fourth-hole blow, creates a perfect fourth the second, from third-hole blow to third-hole draw, produces a major third.

7. For a more technical treatment of fretboard transformations, see De Souza (2016b).

8. Timothy Koozin analyzes this passage in a network that combines "fret-interval types" with neo-Riemannian operations and pitch-class transposition (2011, ex. 2). I analyze more complex along-string transformations in Chapter 4 and more complex cross-string transformations in Chapter 5.

9. The layout of Lewin's graphs and networks was partially inspired by Jeanne Bamberger's use of Montessori bells in cognitive research (see Lewin 1993, 45–53). These bells can be arranged in diverse ways, effectively enabling children and adults to design their own instrumental spaces.

Figure 3.3 Introduction/verse riff from the Kinks, "All Day and All of the Night" (1964): (a) notation; (b) transformation network, showing two ways of realizing the riff in fretboard space. The riff uses a single fretboard shape. The upper route in the network includes cross-string transformations, whereas the lower route includes only along-string transformations. Note that guitar strings are conventionally labeled 1–6, with 1 as the string with the smallest diameter (typically the highest string) and 6 as the string with the largest diameter.

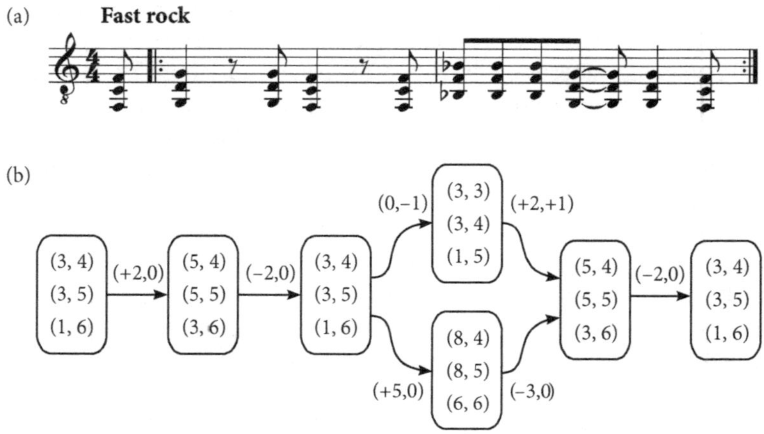

the ordered pairs that label harmonica transformations, though, the signs + and – represent preservation or change in blowing direction.[10] This is illustrated by the spatial network in Figure 3.4. In the nodes, the signs refer to breath direction; on the arrows, they refer to preservation or change. To get from the third-hole blow (3, +) to the fourth-hole draw (4, –), for example, I move one step up the comb and reverse my breath (+1, –). Again, this works for individual elements or sets.

Readers who are familiar with transformational theory may note that the group structures underlying these two models reflect different kinds of dimensionality. The tiered array is based on a group that is isomorphic with $\mathbb{Z} \times \mathbb{Z}$, while harmonica space is based on a group that is isomorphic to $\mathbb{Z} \times \mathbb{Z}_2$. Neither is modular like pitch-class space—that is, the top never flips around to the bottom. This also means that they must be theoretically infinite, that an actual instrument partakes of only a selected range of the abstract space.[11]

10. Julian Hook's uniform triadic transformations use these same signs for modes and modal changes. As Hook explains, "The set {–, –} forms a multiplicative group isomorphic to the additive group $\mathbb{Z}_2$ of integers mod 2" (2002, 62). Multiplying a sign by itself gives +; multiplying the two signs together gives –. This group can model other instrumental features too: for example, bowing or picking direction readily maps onto $\mathbb{Z}_2$, and trumpet valve positions can be represented as ordered triples of the form (σ, σ, σ).

11. Imposing boundaries here would cause formal problems, since it would no longer be possible to define intervals or transformations that hold for any element in the space (see Lewin 1987, §2.3.1; Rings 2011, 19). This is why the models of Rockwell (2009) and Koozin (2011), which specify finite sets of strings, cannot define cross-string transformations (see De Souza 2016b).

Figure 3.4 Spatial network for three adjacent harmonica holes. Reversing breath on the same hole is represented by the operation (0, –); moving along the comb, by operations of the form (+*x*, +) or (–*x*, +). These are combined in (+1, –), which moves up one hole and changes breath. Note that many operations in this space are not shown on this network. These include inverses—for example, (–1, +) is the opposite of (+1, +)—and compound moves, such as the (+2, –) action that would take (3, +) to (5, –).

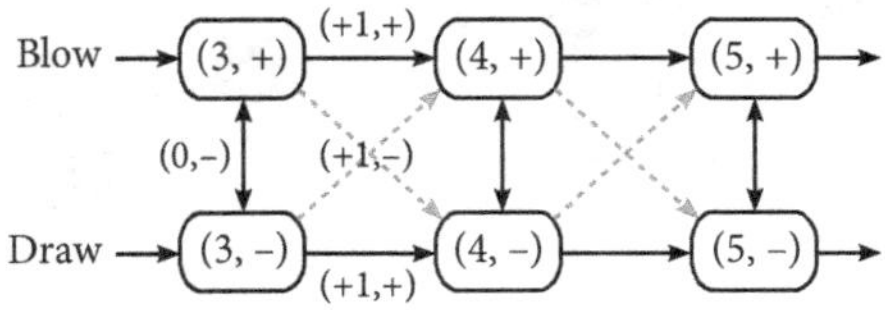

Figure 3.5 Stevie Wonder, electric-piano introduction from "I Wish" (1976). The head of this riff starts on E♭ and moves up through black-key space. Its tail starts on C and moves up chromatically to E♭. Though each measure repeats the same sequence of key and pitch classes, they have distinct pitch contours.

Some instruments, though, can be modeled as modular spaces. For example, it is possible to imagine the twelve "key classes" on a piano in terms of the integers mod 12 ($\mathbb{Z}_{12}$)—that is, the mathematical group that corresponds to the numbers on a clock face. This keyboard space, unlike fretboard or harmonica space, has a single dimension. Yet it, too, involves more than one kind of adjacency. I can move chromatically to the next key, or I can move to the next key *of the same color*, as in various "white-note" or "black-note" pieces (like the Chopin étude in Figure 1.8).[12] Mark Spicer (2011) cites the electric-piano riff from Stevie Wonder's 1976 hit "I Wish" as an example of a black-note figure (see Figure 3.5).[13] In fact, this riff involves *both* types of adjacency in keyboard space. Though it initially climbs through a black-note pentatonic scale, the riff later drops to C and ascends chromatically to its starting note. While chromatic movement would be represented

12. In a presentation at the Society for Music Theory's mathematics interest group, Hook (2014) discussed key-color invariance and pitch-class transformations, an issue with interesting consequences for fingering choices. James Bungert (2015) also considers key color in his analysis of performance gestures in a Bach corrente, though his approach eschews mathematical formalism.
13. Noting that Wonder's keyboard riffs often highlight black keys, Spicer (2011) speculates that the blind musician might use these raised keys to orient himself at the instrument. Will Fulton confirms the tactile significance of the black keys, showing a distinctive hand position in which "Wonder keeps the thumb of his right hand at or below the ridge of the keys' surface, allowing him to gauge his position, with his remaining digits on the black keys" (2015, 275).

Figure 3.6 (a) "Key-class" space and (b) a transformation network that shows the mapping for an operation Key. Key takes each key class "up" to the adjacent key class while preserving key color, creating a white-key cycle and a black-key cycle.

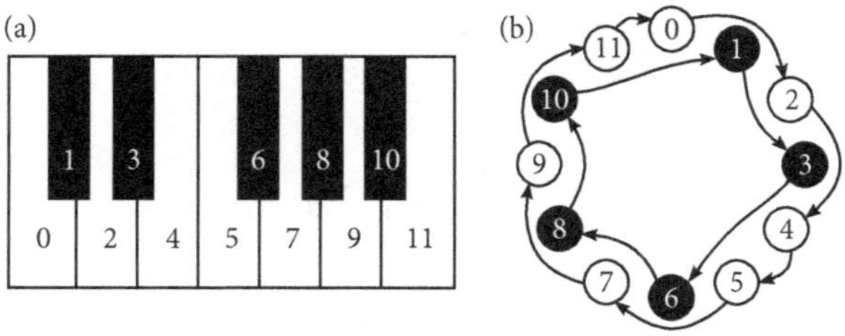

Figure 3.7 Transformation network for Wonder, "I Wish" riff. Node shading indicates key color.

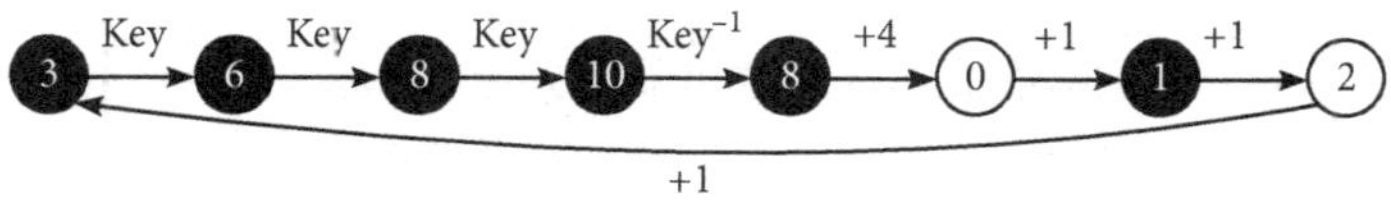

via mod-12 addition, same-color movement can be modeled by an operation that I will call Key. As shown in Figure 3.6, this function neatly partitions the key classes into discrete white-note and black-note families. Note also that it can be compounded and inverted: for example, Key^2 moves up two same-color key classes, and Key^{-2} reverses that. With this new theoretical tool, it is easy to create a transformation network for the "I Wish" riff, which highlights these two kinds of movement at the keyboard (see Figure 3.7).

This model of key-class space conveniently replicates numerical note labels from pitch-class set theory. However, my networks represent locations on the instrument, not notes themselves.[14] In other words, *the topography of an instrumental interface is theoretically independent of any particular tuning*. Before particular melodies or harmonies can be derived from these networks, the space must be connected with some set of notes. I call this an instrument's *place-to-pitch mapping*.

The piano has a *one-to-one* mapping: each pitch has a single location on the keyboard. Yet other instrumental spaces—such as the guitar's tiered array or the organ's multiple manuals—have a *many-to-one* mapping, in which the same pitch might be found in more than one place.[15] This kind of many-to-one place-to-pitch mapping is also common to woodwinds like the clarinet, whose side keys permit a range of alternative fingerings. Still others have a *one-to-many* mapping. On the

14. In this regard, my approach aligns with Joti Rockwell's transformational model of five-string banjo music. Rockwell defines a function called PITCH that maps fret/string locations on the banjo to pitches (2007, 205).

15. In mathematical terms, such mappings are "onto" or "surjective" (see Rockwell 2009, 140).

Figure 3.8 Pitch layout for a ten-hole diatonic harmonica in C: (a) chart of pitch layout for a harmonica in C, opposing blow and draw notes on each hole; (b) pitches of a harmonica in C in notation (with tablature). Note that pitch references follow the nomenclature established by the Acoustical Society of America, where C4 is middle C.

(a)

Blow	C4	E4	G4	C5	E5	G5	C6	E6	G6	C7
Hole	1	2	3	4	5	6	7	8	9	10
Draw	D4	G4	B4	D5	F5	A5	B5	D6	F6	A6

(b)

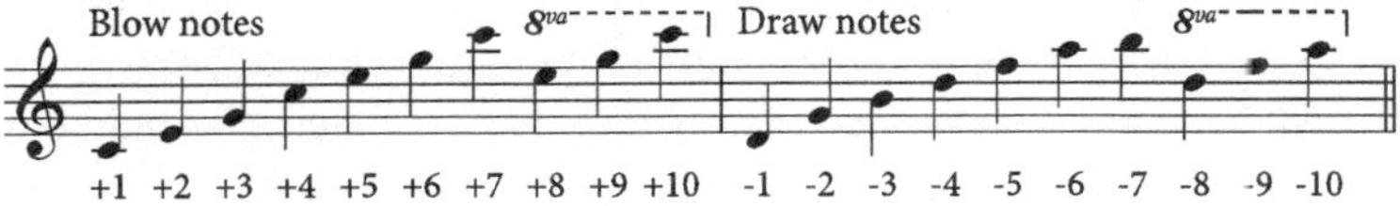

trumpet or tuba, for example, a particular set of valve positions affords not one note but a series of harmonics. The harmonica's mapping is, in a sense, both many-to-one and one-to-many. One pitch appears in two distinct places, and certain hole–breath direction combinations offer multiple notes.

Blowing through a standard ten-hole harmonica gives a major triad spanning three octaves; inhaling gives the remaining notes of a diatonic scale (see Figure 3.8 and Video 3.2▶). This tuning pattern—known as "Richter tuning"—has several idiosyncrasies.[16] It repeats $\hat{5}$ among the drawn notes (in an isolated many-to-one mapping), so the in-breath and out-breath give tonic and dominant chords. The bottom octave (holes 1–4) opposes these triads, skipping $\hat{4}$ and $\hat{6}$. The other end of the instrument omits the leading tone. That is, the harmonica does not just lack nondiatonic "chromatic" notes: depending on register, certain diatonic scale steps are absent too. (In its middle register, for example, the harmonica affords "Oh! Susanna" but not "Amazing Grace.") This might be understood in terms of a distinction, made by Tymoczko (2011, 11), between "scale" (again, a musical ruler) and "macroharmony" (the total collection of pitches actually appearing). The notes on the harmonica can be reckoned in terms of a diatonic scale, but its macroharmony is a pattern of nineteen pitches where no two octaves are identical.

Register also affects the relation between blow and draw notes. On holes 1–6, draw notes are higher than blow notes; this is reversed for holes 7–10. In the words of one player, above the sixth hole "is where the harmonica flip flops" (Holmes 2002). This spot stands out when one is learning to play a major scale on the instrument. As the network in Figure 3.9 shows, movement along the comb is consistent throughout the scale: after every second note, I move up one hole. (Note the regular alternation of 0 and +1 in the first part of the ordered-pair labels on the network's arrows.) But I must change my breathing pattern above hole 6: when

16. As Pat Missin (n.d.) shows, we do not know exactly who "Richter" was or when he developed this tuning.

Figure 3.9 Network for a harmonica's central major scale. The asterisk between scale degrees 6 and 7 marks a deviation in breathing pattern: this is the only place where the player preserves breath direction, inhaling twice in a row.

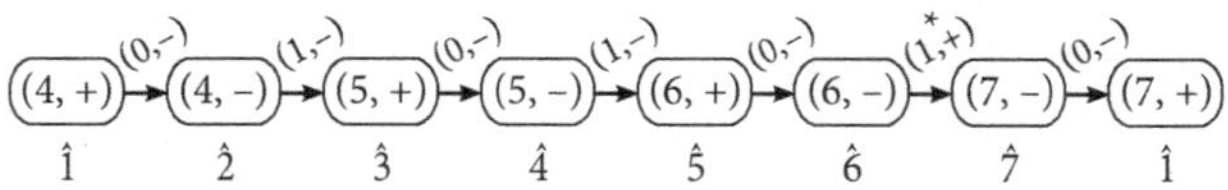

I move to the seventh hole, I keep my breath direction the same and inhale for two notes in a row. This (+1, +) transformation, marked with an asterisk, is the only one in Figure 3.9 that involves a + sign for breathing direction. More generally, this "flip-flop" means that any tune that combines blowing and drawing will have a different breathing pattern for each octave. Note, in fact, that only one pair of holes has the same pitch-class affordances. (Holes 1 and 4 both offer $\hat{1}$ on the blow and $\hat{2}$ on the draw.)

Many harmonica players explore the instrument's two dimensions without explicitly thinking about individual notes from Figure 3.8. Picking up the instrument as a child, I simply felt the consonant stability of the blown major triad. Draw notes, from this perspective, could fill in the gaps in this triad. This shows how an instrument's place-to-pitch mapping may involve hierarchical levels, somewhat like the nested pitch spaces theorized by Fred Lerdahl (2001, 49–50). Here the harmonica's major triad—the piano's white keys, the five-string banjo's open G chord, perhaps even the diatonic notes of the saxophone's finger keys—functions as a *referential pitch framework*, whose steps can be subdivided. In the cases just mentioned, the referential structure is essentially diatonic, which adds a certain asymmetry to the interposition of intermediate notes.

Because of its characteristic gaps, the harmonica's place-to-pitch mapping exhibits a certain *irregularity*. That is to say, consistent moves in harmonica space produce variable pitch intervals. The (+1, +) transformation, as highlighted in Figure 3.9, produces a major second when it starts from (6, –). But this move—going one step up the comb while maintaining breath direction—more commonly sounds a minor third, major third, or perfect fourth. There is a mismatch here between instrumental scale and pitch scale. By contrast, chromatic button accordions like the Russian *bayan* have a *uniform* place-to-pitch mapping. The evenness of its equal-tempered pitch collection is matched by its physical topography. The *bayan*'s regularly spaced melody buttons set out three maximally even interval cycles: as Figure 3.10 shows, the vertical axis moves by minor thirds, creating a diminished-seventh space; the major seconds of the northwest/southeast diagonal offer whole-tone scale segments; the minor seconds of the northeast/southwest diagonal, chromatic-scale segments.[17] This means that each pitch interval or melodic pattern has a consistent shape, which may theoretically start on any button. Furthermore, keyboard shapes transpose and invert just like pitch collections.

17. On symmetrical divisions of the octave in the English concertina, see Gawboy (2009). On the theory of maximally even sets more generally, see Clough and Douthett (1991).

Figure 3.10 Partial map of a *bayan*'s tuning pattern. Unlike the piano, the *bayan* offers the same pitches in multiple places. This network shows the octave between C4 (middle C) and C5. (Lower pitches are at the top of the network, reflecting the way that the instrument is held.) Each button, represented by a node, can be understood as the intersection of three consistent dimensions. Descending arrows move +3 semitones in pitch space; rightward arrows, +2 semitones; leftward arrows, +1 semitone.

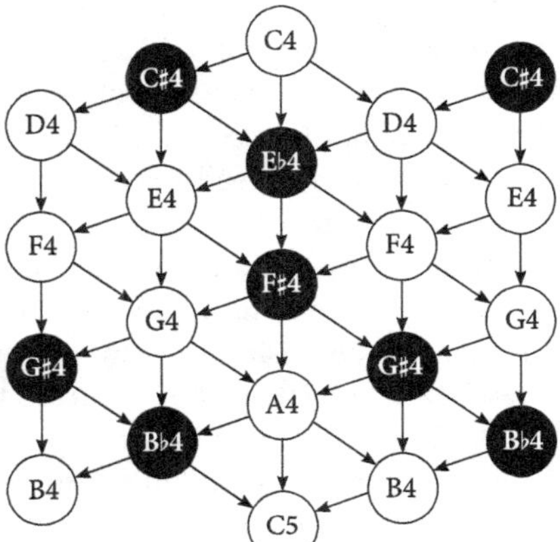

Because of the *bayan*'s many-to-one place-to-pitch mapping, there are also many opportunities for alternative fingerings. These features, of course, differ in significant ways from the nonrepeating breathing patterns of the harmonica and the one-to-one mapping of the piano.

For emphasis, let me briefly present another variation on irregularity/uniformity with strings instead of free-reed instruments. The standard tunings for violin and double bass involve consistent intervals between adjacent strings, moving by perfect fifths or perfect fourths, respectively. This means that a fingering pattern generally creates the same sounding intervals, starting on any string.[18] The five-string banjo, though, is tuned to a G-major chord. Its place-to-pitch mapping is irregular, much like the harmonica's. Because each pair of adjacent banjo strings forms a different pitch interval, melodic fingerings change depending on their position in cross-string space.

If uniform mappings facilitate transposition, irregular ones may foster the sense of a privileged "home key." Players of instruments with irregular mappings, then, often change their instrument when they want to change keys. I put a capo on the banjo to create open strings that fit a new key, or I get another harmonica from the case.[19] Such adjustments can help preserve connections between locations in

18. To be precise, this works only for fingering patterns that do not involve the open strings—a boundary of the instrumental space.
19. A capo is a small device that clamps onto the neck of a guitar or banjo, stopping all the strings at the same fret. By transposing the open strings, it allows a player to use familiar chord voicings in any key. For example, I might use a capo to play in A♭ major: playing in "G major" with a capo on the first fret, in "E major" with a capo on the fourth fret, and so on.

an instrumental space and particular tonal qualia. It is easy to switch from one harmonica to the next because their physical interface is identical and their instrumental scales are related by exact pitch transposition.[20] (A similar situation applies to the various members of the saxophone family—and is reflected in their transposing notation, which specifies the note on the instrument, not the concert pitch.) That said, there are subtle differences in the feel and timbre of harmonicas that are tuned in different keys. In terms of ecological acoustics, these distinctions between high and low harmonicas are related to differences in material, specifically the reeds' restoring force (see Gaver 1993, 10). Lower-pitched harmonicas—for example, in A or G—speak easily and have a more mellow sound. Their reeds are more flexible. Higher-pitched harmonicas, like E, require stronger, supported breathing and have a brighter tone. The reeds' flexibility also affords one of the harmonica's most characteristic gestures: bending.

Once again, my breath not only initiates but also sustains the harmonica's sound. I can use breath, then, to add accents or vibrato. By changing breath pressure, along with mouth and tongue position, I can temporarily shift the pitch. This adds a degree of *mobility*, a term that I borrow from the Renaissance theorist Gioseffo Zarlino (1588, 218–20). The concept emerges from Zarlino's disputes with Vincenzo Galilei about tuning.[21] "Mobile" instruments can bend notes. This means that, like voices, they can make music in just intonation (which Zarlino believed to be numerically perfect). By contrast, "stable" instruments have fixed pitches and, therefore, require tempering. Violin, trombone, and theremin are mobile instruments, while piano and xylophone are stable ones. The former group can slide through the pitch continuum, whereas the latter divides it discretely. Since the intonation for mobile instruments is not strictly governed by holes or keys, playing them in tune relies on physical and auditory feedback. Players of these instruments, in other words, have to worry about tuning in a way that pianists do not. That said, they also have greater flexibility in the pitch discriminations they can employ, which makes it possible to more precisely match their pitch to that of other players. Zarlino includes a subcategory for stable instruments with some measure of mobility, since performers of certain instruments can alter pitches through blowing or fingering. The harmonica belongs here, combining stability and mobility.

The harmonica affords bending only in particular places (see Figure 3.11). This depends on the physics of the paired reeds.[22] Only the higher note on a hole can be

20. This suggests that canonic music-theoretical relations may be relevant to instrumental pitch mapping. Open strings on the violin and mandolin share the same pitches, while those of the viola and cello share pitch *classes*. Viola and violin have the same pitch intervals between strings, but with different pitches. Ukulele strings share unordered pitch-class intervals with the highest four strings of a guitar (but neither pitch classes nor pitch intervals). This is far from abstract for a guitarist picking up the ukulele for the first time: recognizing it allows a guitarist to use familiar fretboard shapes on the unfamiliar instrument.

21. For a discussion of Zarlino and Galilei's relationship and its historical context, see Palisca (1961). Note that Zarlino's distinction—in terms of Heyde's organology—would roughly correspond to a distinction between "continuous volume control" and "discrete state control" for pitch.

22. For an experimental investigation of harmonica pitch bending, see Johnston (1987).

Figure 3.11 Bending chart for a diatonic harmonica in C.

										B♭6
Blow bend								E♭6	G♭6	B6
Blow	C4	E4	G4	C5	E5	G5	C6	E6	G6	C7
Hole	1	2	3	4	5	6	7	8	9	10
Draw	D4	G4	B4	D5	F5	A5	B5	D6	F6	A6
Draw bend	D♭4	G♭4	B♭4	D♭5		A♭5				
		F4	A4							
			A♭4							

bent, meaning that the breathing direction for bends again "flip-flops" around hole 6. The bent note is always pulled down, and notes can be bent only into the space between the blow and draw. That is why there are the most possibilities on hole 3, where the blow and draw are a major third apart, and why bending is impractical on holes 5 and 7, where they are only a semitone apart. In general, the draw bends on the bottom half of the instrument are the easiest to play, because the reeds are lower-pitched and therefore more flexible. And this difference is important for various styles of harmonica performance.

Idiomatic Multistability: Folk, Blues, and Jazz Harmonica

Mapping an instrumental space only begins to reveal how players inhabit it, for the enactive landscapes that an instrument supports appear most fully in performance. Here the investigation proceeds on two levels. It examines individual performances, using transcription and close analysis. Yet these details also inform broader comparison. Like a set of phenomenological variations, interlinked analytical vignettes bring out broader patterns of variance and invariance. They show how an instrument's affordances ground its styles without fixing them. Analyzing harmonica performance thus drives a music-theoretical argument against technological determinism. It demonstrates how instrumental idioms are negotiated, emerging from the interaction of player and instrument.

Bob Dylan, "Queen Jane Approximately"

Such negotiation is particularly clear when a melody needs one of the harmonica's "missing notes." My grandfather played this way at family sing-alongs, either substituting a nearby pitch for the missing note or breaking away from the melody

Table 3.1 Harmonica tablature symbols used in transcriptions (numbers refer to holes on the instrument)

+	Blow
–	Draw
′	Semitone bend
″	Whole-tone bend
″′	Minor-third bend
o	Overblow
s.	Tongue slap
vib.	Throat (not hand) vibrato

to add an accompanying line. This is required less frequently, though, when one is playing major-key folk tunes that emphasize the tonic triad. Figure 3.12a, for example, presents basic harmonica tablature for Bob Dylan's "Queen Jane Approximately" from his 1965 album *Highway 61 Revisited*. In this notation, numbers correspond to the holes of the instrument: a number on its own represents a blown note; one with a minus symbol represents a drawn note. Figure 3.12b presents the tune in notation. (For an explanation of symbols used in this and following transcriptions, see Table 3.1.) The melody is quite easy to play, despite its demand for nearly constant exhalation. Only seven of its forty-eight notes are drawn. (It is also easy because it mostly involves staying on the same hole or moving to an adjacent one.)

Since the basic tablature of Figure 3.12a gives single numbers, it might seem that only one hole is played at a time. But the harmonica readily affords chords—within specific limits. It is easy to play I and V triads, and V^7, ii, and $vii^{ø7}$ chords are also possible in particular spots. (Other chords, of course, are not available.) Harmonica players often use chords as a kind of melodic thickening, with the player's mouth taking in more of the comb.

This approach is central to a folk-harmonica style that is particularly associated with Dylan. His solo on the studio recording of "Queen Jane Approximately" begins in the middle register: a two-note pickup leads to a held single tone (at 3:13 on the original track), which Dylan gets by pursing his lips (see Figure 3.13). As he repeats the pickup gesture, however, Dylan takes in more notes (m. 5). He starts the third phrase with a similar pickup but shoots to the top of the instrument, repeating the held G/C dyad on holes 9 and 10. Dylan then ends the phrase by jumping down to a tonic chord (end of m. 10). The final phrase—the eight-bar group where the song repeats "Won't you come see me, Queen Jane?"—stays with this open-mouth chord, rhythmically huffing and puffing, gradually returning to hole 6 (3:41–3:58). This short solo shows off several of the harmonica's affordances, exploring its possibilities for single notes and full chords, the tonal opposition of blow and draw, and all three octaves. Dylan explores the instrument's side-to-side dimension in m. 9, while the end of the solo privileges its in-and-out dimension.

Figure 3.12 Bob Dylan, melody from "Queen Jane Approximately" (1965).

```
 8    8        8    8    8    8   8    -8  7  6  5
When your mother sends back all your invitations

 8   8     8  8  8    8     8  8  8 -8 7 -6 6 5 -4
And your father to your sister he-- ex---plains

 8     8     8  8  8   7   8     -8 -8  7   7   -6  6  5
That you're tired of yourself and all of your creations

  7    7   7    7   7    7    7
Won't you come see me, Queen Jane?

  7    7   7    7   7    7    7
Won't you come see me, Queen Jane?
```

(a) Tablature from harptabs.com, posted by "chibluesteve"

(b) Notation (annotated with harmonica tablature)

The transformational networks set out in Figure 3.14 reveal a correspondence between the solo's beginning and its end, which is demonstrated in Video 3.3▶. The repeated "pickup gesture" and the cadential "huffing and puffing" are rhythmically and melodically distinct. Yet they involve the *same operations in harmonica space*. (Recall that I model elements in this space as the combination of hole and breath direction, written as an ordered pair of the form (*h*, σ [sign]).) Dylan's pickup melody, represented as a single line in Figure 3.14a, reverses breath on the same hole (0, –) and then reverses breath again while moving up one hole (+1, –). The closing realizes these actions on lower holes (first in mm. 15–17, then in mm. 17–19; see Figure 3.14b). Here Dylan realizes the gesture with full chords throughout, cycling the initial (0, –) before the final (+1, –).

Figure 3.13 Bob Dylan, harmonica solo from "Queen Jane Approximately" (1965).

This ((0, –), (+1, –)) motion is characteristic of the major-scale pattern presented earlier in Figure 3.9. Yet the opening of Dylan's solo places this gesture on holes 6 and 7, the spot where the harmonica switches between drawing-to-move-up and drawing-to-move-down. (Recall that this is where the scale in Figure 3.9 deviated from this characteristic pattern.) This strategy produces the pentatonic-tinged G–A–C that is prominent throughout the solo: Dylan moves directly between (6, –) and (7, +) seven times, adding the intervening (7, –) only once. The instrumental placement of $\hat{6}$, then, shapes the sound of this solo and, more generally, Dylan's style of playing harmonica.

Figure 3.14 Transformational networks for Dylan's solo on "Queen Jane Approximately": (a) network for melodic pickup from mm. 1–2 and mm. 4–6 of Dylan's solo on "Queen Jane Approximately"; (b) network for end of Dylan's solo on "Queen Jane Approximately" (mm. 15–17, then repeated immediately in mm. 17–19).

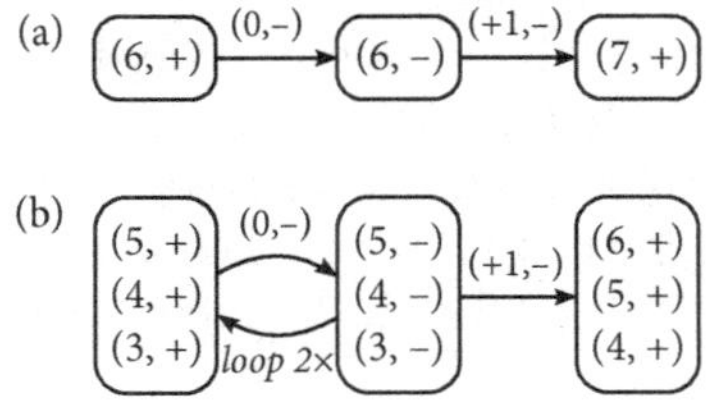

It bears mention that this style has often been criticized. One player describes it as follows: "Almost no bends, lots of chords, lots of go-forth-and-back-notes. No harp teacher I know will teach his students to play like that" (Shikida 2007). In this view, Dylan's harmonica playing lacks skill; it reflects the technology's raw affordances. Dylan himself acknowledges that this technique is not considered to be "proper," but says it defines his "harmonica and guitar sound." "Most of the time, I would blow out of the harmonica," he explains, "because everybody sucks in. The proper way to play is like Little Walter or Sonny Boy Williamson would play—which would be to cross it—and I found myself blowing out more because nobody was doing it in that area" (quoted in Appleby 1992, 20).

Sonny Boy Williamson II, "Born Blind"

Dylan's reference here is to the "cross-harp" or "second-position" style of playing associated with blues harmonica.[23] Cross-harp playing interprets the instrument's tonal affordances in a way that its nineteenth-century designers never expected. Where first position takes the blow chord as the tonic triad of a major scale, second position takes the *draw chord as the tonic* of a Mixolydian mode. A C harmonica, for example, can be used to play blues in G, affording both bending and a flat seventh scale degree. While folk-harmonica players, like most other wind players, inhale between phrases, blues players usually use such moments to expel air.[24] (This works well for blues-harmonica players who are also vocalists: they can breathe out while singing and breathe back in during short harmonica breaks between phrases.) This reflects the phenomenon that Don Ihde calls "multistability," which

23. Dylan also plays this style, though it is less closely associated with him. His cross-harp playing often ends up in a high register that blues players typically avoid (for example, see "Pledging My Time" from *Blonde on Blonde* [1966]).

24. Blues-harmonica tablature reverses the marked/unmarked categories represented by Figure 3.12. In blues-harmonica tablature, that is, an unsigned number denotes drawing, and blowing requires a plus symbol.

he finds in both visual illusions and technological variation (1986, 67–79). Like a figure/ground reversal, cross-harp playing flips the hierarchical relation between the harmonica's two chords, remapping the link between breath and tonal qualia while preserving the inhalation/exhalation pair.

Demonstrating G blues with a C harp, the noted harmonica player John Sebastian discusses one tonal consequence of this position: "What you don't have really is what they call the dominant or the D chord. All you have is your D note [on the first- and fourth-hole draw]." Sebastian, however, thinks of that challenge as an *opportunity*. "And so that's where your creativity is really going to come into play here because it's during that V chord, dominant chord, whatever you want to call it, the D-seventh or D chord that the harmonica has to play around to get the sound" (1992, 3:08).

Cross-harp playing also exploits the relatively easy draw bends on the bottom half of the instrument. This adds bluesy inflections and the chromatic notes that define the blues scale ($\flat\hat{3}$, $\sharp\hat{4}$, and $\flat\hat{7}$). Referring to a chart that resembles Figure 3.11, David Barrett (1995, 32) explains that the draw notes include twice as many bendable notes and three times as many "blue notes" as their blown counterparts. The draw bends, then, complement the flat Mixolydian seventh, and in this sense, the style is overdetermined.

Cross-harp position defines the dominant blues-harmonica idiom.[25] For example, consider Sonny Boy Williamson II's "Born Blind" (1957).[26] "Born Blind" is a blues in F played on a B♭ harmonica (see Figure 3.15). His solo features a repeated gesture that, in many ways, resembles Dylan's opening on "Queen Jane Approximately": a short pickup, a sustained note, then falling off (1:07 on the track). Williamson, however, mainly inhales, going between non-bent and bent notes. It is possible to hear the reeds' resistance in bent-down notes that rise up to their straight counterparts: for example, note the bending on hole 4 in m. 2 or the slow release of G up to A in m. 9.[27] (The latter also shows one way to "play around" the dominant in Sebastian's sense.)

While most of the solo is inhaled, in mm. 5–6 Williamson combines blowing and drawing in a characteristic triplet riff over the subdominant (1:16). This riff—which appears on other tracks by Williamson, such as "Help Me" (1963)—is demonstrated in Video 3.4▶. His tongue-slapping articulation thickens the texture here, subtly bringing out the I and IV chords that underlie cross-harp.[28]

25. The relatively rare examples of straight-harp blues—by Jimmy Reed or the Harmonicats—stick to the top register to exploit blow bends. Their sound is marked by the major-sounding sixth and seventh scale degrees.
26. "Born Blind" was a new version of 1951's "Sight to the Blind," which Williamson had recorded in Mississippi.
27. This bending can be understood in terms of ecological acoustics: here it is possible to hear deformation and return, as discussed by Gaver (1993, 10).
28. Barrett explains tongue slapping as follows: "When in the tongue blocking embouchure your lips are over three holes and two of those holes are blocked by your tongue. If you breathe in first and then quickly slap your tongue into position, all the air that it took to vibrate three holes is then punched through the one hole left over. The effect is a thicker sound because of the initial vibration of the three holes, and a wicked attack on the hole left over" (1995, 92).

Figure 3.15 Sonny Boy Williamson II, harmonica solo from "Born Blind" (1957). (A slightly different transcription appears in Weiser 2001, 55–56.)

Figure 3.16a presents a schematic version of the riff and labels its three distinct segments α, β, and γ. Locating them on a spatial network derived from Figure 3.4 shows how each segment involves a kind of "neighboring" motion in harmonica space: γ moves along the comb, while α and β alternate breathing on the same hole (see Figure 3.16b). Figure 3.16c frames each of these as a loop. This clarifies some relationships between α and β. First, they grow out of the same basic (0, –) transformation. Moreover, α actually becomes β when it is transposed down one hole with inverted breathing (–1, –). The flipped breath pattern that takes α to β is physically immediate when one is learning this riff, as is their dimensional difference from γ.[29] One player visualizes this as a kind of "knot" in harmonica space (Graham, n.d.).

The emphasis on drawing repeats with the return of tonic harmony in m. 8, when Williamson returns to a variation on his opening gesture. The remainder of the solo stays with the bottom three holes of the harmonica. With the final return of tonic harmony (m. 11), though, a moment sticks out: at the bottom of a falling

29. In *Mel Bay's Complete Classic Chicago Blues Harp*, Barrett (1995, 59) presents an exercise that systematically takes the γ triplets from one end of the harmonica to the other, both blowing and drawing.

Figure 3.16 Williamson's triplet riff from "Born Blind," mm. 5–6: (a) notation with tablature; (b) spatial network, placing riff segments in harmonica space; (c) network showing (−1, –) relationship between segments α and β.

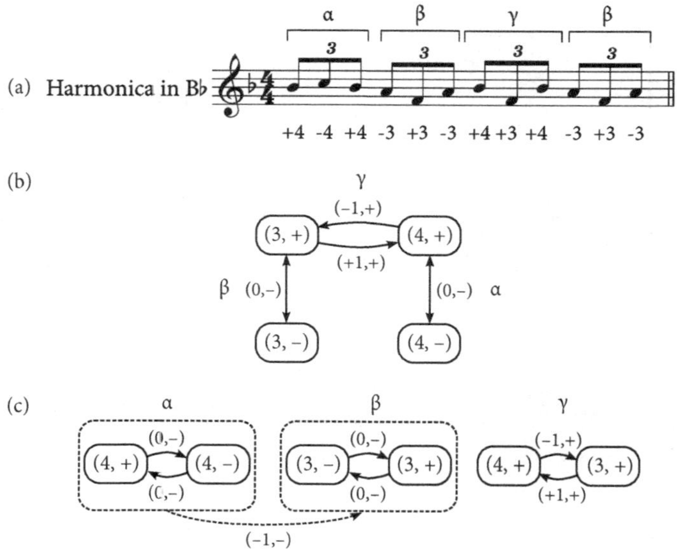

line, Williamson briefly blows the first hole, sounding a B♭ ($\hat{4}$), which is the bottom boundary of the instrument but which does not fit the chord. For a knowledgeable listener, this example of what David Temperley (2007) calls "melodic-harmonic divorce" briefly reveals the instrument's underlying pitch collection.

Where Dylan effectively uses the harmonica's full range on "Queen Jane Approximately," Williamson's solo stays on the bottom four holes. In other words, his high point is around Dylan's midregister home base. This registral preference responds principally to the possibilities for drawn bending in holes 1–4. This is not to say that Williamson never exceeds this range, only that it is less common in blues-harmonica playing. It does not seem coincidental that a solo in which he ventures into a higher register—during an extended jam on "Take Your Hand Out of My Pocket" (1958)—was not released until fifteen years after Williamson's death. When he uses the pentatonic subset around holes 6 and 7 and slides to the top holes—gestures central to Dylan's solo—the unbent notes, particularly the unadorned major IV triad, sound very unusual (2:12–2:29 on the recording). They go to the edge of the instrument and the edge of the blues-harmonica idiom.

Howard Levy, "Blues in Six Keys" and "Sweet Georgia Brown"

Just as second-position playing involves a Mixolydian interpretation of the harmonica's diatonic affordances, higher positions may exploit other modes. Third

Figure 3.17 Overbending chart for a diatonic harmonica in C.

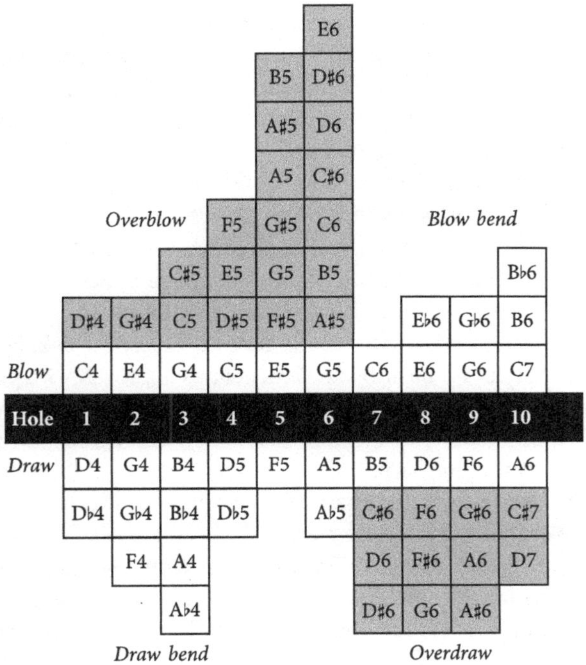

position (or "double-cross-harp") is Dorian, the fourth is Aeolian and so on, moving through a diatonic cycle of fifths.[30] Dylan, for example, uses such positions on minor-key songs like "All Along the Watchtower." Yet this technique has been explored most thoroughly by the Grammy-winning jazz-harmonica player Howard Levy, who has developed the ability to play any diatonic harmonica in any key.

Of course, extended modal positions do not, by themselves, step outside of the instrument's diatonicism. Levy also uses a technique of "overbending" that provides a full chromatic scale. "I realized that there were some missing notes on the ten-hole diatonic harp that just weren't there," he explains. "Being a pianist, I thought that this was impossible. They had to be there somewhere. So by stubborn experimentation, I found the missing six notes that allowed me to get a three-octave chromatic scale" (Musicians Professional Resource, n.d.). Without going into the physics of the phenomenon, overbending is effectively the opposite of bending: overblown notes are on the bottom half of the instrument, opposite to the draw bends; overdrawn notes are on the top, opposite to the blow bends; and where bending gave lower notes, overblowing gives higher ones (Holmes 2002; see Figure 3.17).

30. For a detailed introduction to harmonica positions, see Holman (2000).

Levy says that he visualizes a piano keyboard when he improvises on the harmonica (Paulson 2009). His extended technique, then, overcomes the harmonica's conceptual constraints by simulating another instrumental space.[31] By his account, he always thinks in C major, mapping the harmonica's open notes onto the keyboard's white notes and the bends and overbends onto the black notes (Levy 1992). This natural/chromatic opposition reveals a similarity between the conventional piano keyboard and Levy's overbending harmonica.

Levy demonstrates this approach in "Blues in Six Keys," the introductory performance from his instructional video *New Directions for Harmonica* (1992). With each twelve-bar chorus the tune moves up a semitone, starting in F major and ending in B♭. With the Dylan and Williamson examples, tonal patterns make it clear—to a harmonica player, at least—which key the instrument is in. Here this is less obvious. Overbending, after all, lends itself to single-note melodies, which Levy plays in a fully chromatic bebop style. Yet he also supplements this approach with gestures that are particularly idiomatic to the harmonica. These characteristic gestures reveal that Levy is playing a B♭ harmonica, which means that he begins the track in cross-harp position and finishes in straight-harp.

Several aspects of Levy's cross-harp section echo the blues style I illustrated with "Born Blind." Near the beginning, for example, he alternates between the $\hat{3}$ and the lowered $\flat\hat{3}$ that are both available on the third hole (mm. 5–6 in Figure 3.18). At the end of the first line (m. 8), Levy slides down to $\flat\hat{7}$ with a whole-step bend on the second hole—a gesture that Williamson explores in the corresponding measure of his solo from "Born Blind" (see Figure 3.15, m. 4).

The instrumental space may be even clearer when Levy plays on more than one hole at the same time. As Figure 3.19 shows, he repeats an A/C dyad in the fifth chorus, a blues in A (mm. 57–58). This gesture adapts part of the B♭ harp's drawn F dominant chord to the key of A major.[32] The start of the final chorus (in B♭) brings another trick typical of the harmonica: the shake. Shaking involves the sustained, rapid alternation between two adjacent holes; it is particularly characteristic of blues harmonica. Levy holds sustained shakes throughout mm. 65–66, gradually moving up the comb. Unlike most of "Blues in Six Keys," these measures reflect simple movement in harmonica space: the network of Figure 3.20 illustrates this repeated (+1, +) shift up the comb. (The D♭/F♭ blow bends on holes 8 and 9 maintain the exhalation from m. 65, even though they require different breath pressure.) After the sophisticated tonal twisting of several intervening keys, Levy has returned to the harmonica's stylistic and tonal home, to one of its easiest and most characteristic tricks.

In a complementary demonstration, Levy plays the jazz standard "Sweet Georgia Brown" in F, using several harmonicas (see transcriptions in Figures 3.21–3.23). He describes the tune's opening progression (D^7–G^7–C^7–F) as a series of modal positions and then uses the four harmonicas that place one of those chords in cross-harp (that is, harmonicas in F, B♭, C, and G).[33] The different positions

31. Levy, in fact, sometimes plays both instruments at once—holding the harmonica in one hand, using the other to comp or play piano melodies in unison with the harmonica.
32. This chorus, in other words, is a rare instance of the Locrian sixth position.
33. Since Levy does not play the main tune on the G harmonica, I have omitted it here.

Figure 3.18 Howard Levy, “Blues in Six Keys,” mm. 5–17. The performance opens with a blues in F, played in cross-harp position.

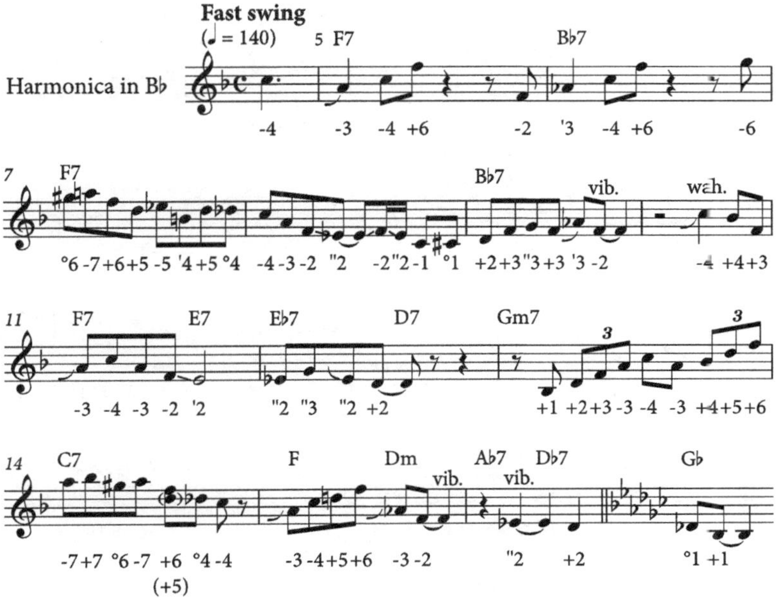

are audible here in contrasts between bent and straight, drawn and blown notes. Straight-harp and cross-harp are also the positions where he uses chords and more arpeggios. These differences are perhaps clearest in Figure 3.23. Its second phrase, in cross-harp position, involves nearly constant inhalation and bluesy bending (mm. 6–9). In the following straight-harp phrase (mm. 10–13), by contrast, there are no bent notes. Here Levy moves up and down the comb, outlining a C-major triad (m. 12). When he reaches the more unusual “first flat position” in m. 14, though, Levy abandons the composed melody and improvises a flowing bebop-style line.

In Levy’s own words, his improvisations respond to the instrument’s “sweet spots.”

> Every time you play a different mode on the harmonica the bends and the sweet spots on the harmonica change. For example the first note of the scale when you play in the Lydian mode is a bend in this [low] octave. It’s a straight note when you play in this [middle] octave. And you get all sorts of juicy bends like around the sixth and the third over here.... So when you play in these positions, there’s all sorts of expressive possibilities that start happening on the instrument that are totally different from when you’re playing in cross-harp. (Levy 1992, ch. 9)

In ecological terms, a “sweet spot” would be a place where the object’s affordances converge with the agent’s abilities in a particularly strong way. The sweet

Figure 3.19 Howard Levy, "Blues in Six Keys," mm. 53–73. Blues in A and then B♭ close the piece.

Figure 3.20 Transformational network for Levy, "Blues in Six Keys," mm. 65–66.

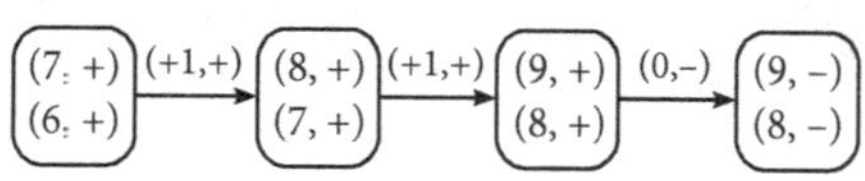

Figure 3.21 Howard Levy, "Sweet Georgia Brown" (straight-harp).

Figure 3.22 Howard, Levy, "Sweet Georgia Brown" (cross-harp).

spot offers less resistance, more possibilities. Unlike the difficult and unstable overblown notes, for example, draw bends are fairly easy to play and can be colored with throat vibrato. They are unique—unique in the sense that they appear only at certain places on the instrument and also in the sense that they are particularly characteristic of that instrument. Levy's "new directions for harmonica," then, build on the same sweet spots—the same privileged affordances—that drive

Figure 3.23 Howard Levy, "Sweet Georgia Brown" (first flat position).

folk and blues harmonica. His innovation is not to leave them behind but to add to them, systematically multiplying the modal thinking of cross-harp, putting the sweet spots into new musical contexts.[34]

Idiomaticity

Instrumental "idioms" typically engage such "sweet spots." When Dylan goes back and forth between tonic and dominant-plus-$\hat{6}$ or when Williamson bends under $\hat{1}$, $\hat{3}$, and $\hat{5}$ (but never $\hat{7}$), their music seems to be organized around the harmonica's characteristic affordances, its physical and sonic possibilities. In other words, idiomatic playing makes it possible to hear aspects of action-sound coupling and instrumental space. In moments of instrumental idiomaticity—from the harmonica's bending to the horn's hunting calls, from the fiddle's string crossing to the

34. These technical variations, of course, are not comprehensive. The openness of affordance theory, mentioned earlier, means that they could not be. Rapper Doug E. Fresh, for instance, plays harmonica while beat-boxing. Since he is using his lips to articulate the beat, he cannot always have his mouth on the instrument. Instead, he holds the harmonica in front of his microphone and sends percussive blasts of air through it. With this technique, it is not possible to isolate single melody pitches. Instead, Fresh capitalizes on the *harmonic* affordances of the harmonica: he gets his audience to sing a melody while he accompanies them with harmonica chords and mouth percussion. The resulting tonic/dominant alternation—similar to the end of Dylan's solo on "Queen Jane Approximately"—demonstrates the pitch affordances of the ten-hole harmonica in a particularly clear way.

harp's glissandi—in these moments, instruments do not seem neutral or transparent. Their individuality, their materiality, their presence as mediators is sounded.

Idiomatic music reflects what an instrument can and cannot do, what it does willingly and what it does reluctantly. Yet as David Huron and Jonathon Berec emphasize, "What makes something idiomatic is not that it is easy to play, but that it is easier to play given the specific prescribed circumstances compared with other possible performance circumstances" (2009, 119). Huron and Berec develop a computational model that shows how idiomatic compositions for trumpet become more difficult when they are transposed up or down and when the tempo is changed. In my terms, their "transposition idiomaticism" has to do with instrumental space and place-to-pitch mapping. Their "tempo idiomaticism," on the other hand, involves action-sound coupling: if a trumpet piece's tempo becomes too slow, the player may run out of breath; if it speeds up too much, tonguing may become impossible. With both, idiomatic trumpet music plays to the instrument's sweet spots—not too slow, not too fast, in a key that fits just right.

Instrumental idiomaticity seems distinct from tonal idiomaticity. Though they obviously overlap, an instrument may win out in moments of melodic-harmonic divorce. But like the linguistic and tonal idioms discussed by Robert Gjerdingen (2007b, 121–24), instrumental idioms involve characteristic patterns that cannot be predicted by grammatical rules alone. When speaking a foreign language or composing for an instrument I do not play, I may easily construct utterances that are grammatically correct but stylistically nonsensical, and such mistakes may be identified only with reference to standard practice. (A francophone learning English, for example, might say, "Let's call a cat a cat." This literal translation of a French idiom contains no syntactic errors. Nonetheless, anglophones call a spade a spade.) Corpus analysis suggests that about half of spoken and written language involves conventional word combinations (Erman and Warren 2000). To address this, teachers of English as a second language often use special dictionaries of collocations, whose closest musical equivalents would come from improvisational pedagogy—books of jazz licks, eighteenth-century *partimenti*, or the Persian *Radif*.[35] In idiomatic performance, then, speakers or players do not select every word or note individually; they also draw on larger, ready-made sequences.

Gjerdingen brings up this aspect of idiomaticity in a brief response to Huron and Berec, arguing that difficulty depends not only on "particular fingering or registers" but also on a performer's "musical upbringing" (2009, 124). Indeed, from an ecological standpoint, idiom must involve *both* instrumental affordances and players' habits. Overemphasizing one or the other risks a return to technological or social determinism. As the multistable opposition of straight- and cross-harp demonstrates, the instrument itself does not give rise to an idiom. The idiom is realized in players' overlearned actions, in the ways they typically move through an instrumental space, revealing some affordances and concealing others.

35. *Partimenti* are figured or unfigured basses to be completed in keyboard performance (see Gjerdingen 2007a). The *Radif* is a collection of melodies in each of the Persian modes (*dastgāhs*), whose motifs are used in improvisation (see Nettl 1992).

Beyond that, the linguistic analogy can help clarify how musical idioms reflect *social habits*. Idioms are produced, maintained, and negotiated in communities. My individual case studies, then, also stand in for particular traditions. Dylan's harmonica playing, however idiosyncratic, is linked to Woody Guthrie's folk style, Jimmy Reed's straight-harp blues, and so on.

Here it seems productive to consider the ecological understanding of sociality offered by the anthropologist Tim Ingold. "Sociality," he writes, "does not depend upon the organization of sensory data, initially private to each perceiver, in terms of an objective system of collective representations. Rather, sociality is given from the start ... in the direct, perceptual involvement of fellow participants in a shared environment" (2000, 167). Sociality, from this perspective, is about shared perception and action, shared abilities and affordances, about inhabiting an enactive landscape together. For Ingold, an object becomes a tool only when it is joined to a technique (319). In other words, to see something as a musical instrument is already to have an idea, however rough, of how it might be played.

The communal perception of affordances is important to Bernard Stiegler too. Recall Stiegler's general argument (outlined in Chapter 1): tools reveal traces of their users' actions, forming a kind of external memory that makes human culture possible. Idiomaticity, for Stiegler, coordinates individuals, communities, and technical objects (2009, 67). While individuals develop distinctive personal styles, idioms are rooted in social groups (157). And this localization creates a certain untranslatability, even as idioms inevitably overlap (84). Stiegler illustrates his argument with the common Latin origins of French, Italian, and Spanish, yet the musical elements shared by different instruments also facilitate idiomatic crossover. Levy's harmonica playing, for example, shares something with his piano playing; Williamson's playing, with his singing. Ultimately, Stiegler thinks that idioms show how the relation between humanity and technology—between speakers and their languages or musicians and their instruments—is socially conditioned, though not socially determined. With a characteristic ontological twist, he even claims that this kind of idiomaticity marks all human existence (157).

Technical Agency and Motor Agency

A theory of idiomaticity helps explain how instruments shape players' actions, how coordinated affordances and habits give rise to distinctive musical dialects made of seemingly prefabricated patterns. Yet this can also shed light on ambiguities related to technology and agency. Why might I sometimes feel that my body is improvising on its own? Or that I am being played *by* the instrument? As with questions about instrumental incorporation, the answers here are related to the prereflective body schema, for the body schema supports both the perception of affordances and the sense of agency.

A series of experiments by Mike Tucker and Rob Ellis shows that objects prime the actions they afford (1998, 2001, 2004). Seeing a graspable object—or even reading its name—elicits unconscious simulations of hand action.[36] These simulations are particular to the thing's affordances: for example, grapes and hammers evoke different kinds of gripping. Merleau-Ponty seems to anticipate these results in *The Phenomenology of Perception*: "The gesture of reaching one's hand out toward an object contains a reference to the object, not as a representation, but as this highly determinate thing toward which we are thrown, next to which we are through anticipation, and which we haunt" (2012, 140). He refers to this as a mode of "being-toward-the-thing," in which the body is aimed at objects and responds to their call. Embodied responses to affordances go beyond simulation for people with anarchic hand syndrome (Marcel 2003, 76–81). Such patients, who typically have brain damage involving the supplementary motor area, respond involuntarily to objects in their environment. They might pick up a pen and start writing, without any conscious intention to do so.

These responses instead involve what Merleau-Ponty calls "motor intentionality" (2012, 113). Motor intentions drive automatic movements. They are phenomenologically recessive, difficult to describe in words. Elisabeth Pacherie (2008) gathers evidence to show that motor intentions have a separate neural substrate from conscious intentions and a different timescale. For example, when skilled drivers encounter an unexpected obstacle in the road, they may avoid it a split second before consciously recognizing it. Quick responses like this can outpace conscious thought, creating a momentary dissociation between action and subjective awareness (Jeannerod 2006, 46–49). Note, also, that motor intentions or automatic movements are not limited to biological reflexes; they equally involve learned, technical skills (like driving a car). All of this complicates common notions of agency, demonstrating that actions are not always "caused" by self-conscious decision-making.

Psychologists and philosophers, then, distinguish between action, a *sense of ownership* (the experience of my body being mine), and a *sense of agency* (the experience of causing or controlling action). These elements, though usually integrated, can come apart in delusions of control, whether pathological or experimentally induced. Patients with schizophrenia typically have no problem with motor control or the sense of ownership. They can complete physical tasks following an experimenter's instructions, and they feel their moving bodies as their own. But for some of these patients the sense of agency is severely impaired. Their bodies seem to be controlled by alien forces. Neurologically this is related to problems with bodily representation and self-monitoring, to a breakdown in the unconscious correspondences among predicted action and visual, proprioceptive, and kinesthetic feedback (C. Frith 2005, 754–56; Graham et al. 2014). Disruptions to perceived agency and disruptions to the body schema often go together.[37]

36. Simulation is key to many theories of grounded cognition (Barsalou 1999, 2008). For a review of other relevant experiments, see Kirsh (2013, §2).

37. For a discussion of the distinction between ownership and agency, see Gallagher (2012). In general, problems with the sense of ownership relate to disorders of the body image, whereas problems with

So it is perhaps unsurprising that instrumentalists' sense of agency can be reduced by altered auditory feedback (Couchman, Beasley, and Pfordresher 2012). They feel less control when pitch or timing changes unexpectedly, upsetting the multisensory integration that subtends experiences of instrumental withdrawal and incorporation.

But I would further argue that idiomatic fluency, paradoxically, might either enhance or reduce a player's sense of agency. Both effects are likely most common with music that is idiomatic and also difficult. At fast tempos, I sometimes react musically before I know exactly what I am doing, like the driver dodging an unexpected obstacle. On the one hand, this mix of skill and challenge is characteristic of "flow," a psychological state that combines an increased feeling of control with decreased self-consciousness (Csikszentmihalyi 1990, 52–66). On the other hand, because objects prime motor intentions for actions they afford, the overlearned patterns of idiomatic performance may seem to be inevitable responses to some external imperative.[38] For a fleeting moment, it may feel as though my body or the instrument or the music itself is in charge. Examining this paradox, the philosopher Eddy Nahmias argues that musicians and athletes do not make detailed, self-conscious decisions in the course of play. This kind of overthinking, in fact, would hinder performance. Instead, Nahmias suggests, the player has "a general intention or plan to play well" and then lets the details unfold (2005, 774).[39] I monitor my playing as if from a distance, watching in wonder my own fingers move.

Let me elaborate by describing a performance at a late-night gig in a Chicagoland café. During an up-tempo blues, I switch from mandolin comping to a harmonica solo. I step up to the microphone, but there is no time to plan, no time to select a particular starting note. So I start by drawing air through the bottom half of the instrument, orienting myself as I play. I glance at the guitarist, the bass player, the small audience. In this moment, I do not explicitly think of chord changes, breathing patterns, or licks I have learned. Instead, I feel that I am listening to the harmonica's suggestions, following pathways that seem both familiar and new. I respond to possibilities as they present themselves: here I can bend and here I can shake; here I reach a boundary and must turn around. I manage a flow of energy that passes through the harmonica—leaving space at first, then building to a climax. As my solo finishes, I hardly know what I have played. But I know that it would have been very different had I chosen to solo with the mandolin or another instrumental partner. My sense of technical agency here relies on motor agency, on my schematic responses to the harmonica's affordances. The instrument might not be an autonomous agent—but, in a

the sense of agency relate to disorders of the body schema (Gallagher and Vaever 2004, 121). As a side note, patients with schizophrenia tend to be especially susceptible to the rubber hand illusion discussed in Chapter 2 (Peled et al. 2003; Thakkar et al. 2011).

38. For the phenomenologist Alphonso Lingis, things themselves are experienced as imperatives that "order the diagrams and variations of our postural schema and exploratory manipulations" (1998, 64).

39. In such cases, Nahmias claims that general intentions may support a sense of authorship (an experience of being the source of action), even without a robust sense of agency.

sense, neither am I. My own embodied agency is distributed; my actions respond to the instrument's call.

Conclusions

Movement around an instrument—like all movement—involves a certain spatiality. In fact, instrumental interfaces coordinate different varieties of space.[40] Place-to-pitch mapping links technological and tonal spaces, each with particular dimensions and scales of measurement, and this doubled space is inhabited by a performing body.[41] As Merleau-Ponty put it in his description of the organ rehearsal, the player may settle into the instrument "as one settles into a house" (2012, 146). Instrumental space, then, is not simply a homogeneous geometric field, but the correlate of a lived body, an affordance space, an enactive landscape. Here the player is both constrained and free, since the interface conditions performance without determining it. The idioms that emerge from this negotiation show people and instruments truly making music together. These idioms make the fit between space and action audible, in music that sounds like it feels good to play.

By focusing on variations of technique, this chapter has more or less treated the instrument—in this case, the diatonic harmonica—as a given. Yet expert players are highly aware of differences among harmonica models. Levy favors Hohner Golden Melody harmonicas, which have plastic combs and equal-tempered tuning, whereas many blues players prefer Marine Band harmonicas, with wooden combs and a tuning that is closer to just intonation. On this level, there is no such thing as "the" ten-hole diatonic harmonica. The instrument does not correspond to a single technological object.[42] Moreover, though some durability is essential for instrumental prostheticity, instrumental technology is not immutable. Its stabilization requires active maintenance, and though the social actors that reproduce musical instruments and idioms often act in predictable ways, they do not always do so.[43] In other words, instrument and idiom may be transformed as well as preserved.

A more complete study of harmonica playing would also have to consider variations in technology. While Levy uses overblowing to get the equivalent of "black notes," for example, others have done so by using redesigned instruments. Chromatic harmonicas are typically equipped with a button that raises the note being played by a semitone. While their form is less standardized than a ten-hole blues harp, one common model is a sixteen-hole instrument developed for the

40. In the context of painting and dance, Merleau-Ponty argues that aesthetic experience opens up new forms of spatiality (1964, 159–90; 2008, 39–42; 2012, 546n86). A painting, for example, can be experienced as having depth, despite the canvas's flatness.

41. Of course, instrumental performance may involve other kinds of space as well, such as the visual space of notation or the architectural space in which the music is played.

42. Timothy Taylor (2001, 7) elaborates this idea with reference to clarinets; De Souza (2016a, 148–58), with reference to guitars.

43. For a theoretical discussion of stabilization in technology and society, see Latour (1991, 123).

classical harmonica player Larry Adler. This essentially offers a C-major harmonica and a C♯-major harmonica, played through a single comb.[44] To play it in various keys requires the kind of pervasive natural/accidental (or white-note/black-note) thinking reflected in Levy's pianistic visualizations. (Indeed, Stevie Wonder, whose sensitivity to keyboard topography was mentioned earlier, is a master of the chromatic harmonica.) This shows how Levy's technique and Adler's technology end up in the same place conceptually, loosening the consistent association between instrumental space and tonal qualia.

Other harmonicas, however, specifically avoid this kind of reconceptualization. Some preserve straight-harp relationships between hole and scale degree but afford the minor mode. Harmonic-minor harps flatten the thirds in the blown triad, while keeping the same dominant-function draw notes; natural-minor harmonicas also have a minor draw chord (to permit minor cross-harp playing). "Melody-maker" or "country-tuning" models similarly shift to a Lydian mode, so that cross-harp position offers a major scale. This allows blues players to play their habitual licks—but with a leading tone in place of the Mixolydian subtonic. Other ten-hole models like Brendan Power's "PowerBender" maximize bends: placing every drawn note above its blown counterpart permits draw bends on every hole.

These alternative harmonica tunings already show how *modifications of the technology presuppose certain techniques*. Melody-makers or PowerBenders are of little value to first-position players; harmonic-minor models are similarly ineffective for dedicated cross-harp players. This suggests that instrumental alteration can provide insights about how players' habits can be adapted or disrupted. And this can help refine my account of auditory-motor integration, complicating the connections between instrument, action, intention, and sound.

44. The sixteen-hole chromatic harmonica also regularizes pitch and breathing patterns, repeating the complete major-scale pattern from the blues harp's middle register in all octaves.

CHAPTER Four

Voluntary Self-Sabotage

My wife and I are playing violin-piano duets at a wedding reception. And as soon as I start the accompaniment to Jules Massenet's "Meditation" (see Figure 4.1), the rickety baby grand starts to give me trouble. The F♯ below middle C sticks. It refuses to bounce back into position. I reset the key without stopping the piece, but the problem persists. Every time I hit the note, it has to be manually fixed, and for the rest of the gig I remain acutely aware of this single, previously unremarkable black key.

This experience recalls Martin Heidegger's discussion of handiness (*Zuhandenheit*) in the "tool analysis" of *Being and Time* (2010, 72–74). While I am busy hammering, Heidegger says, I hardly notice the tool. I am more focused on the work, on whatever I am doing with the hammer. Likewise, while playing piano, I rarely think about the keys; usually I am more focused on the music. But sometimes my hammer breaks. I stop. I look at the tool. Suddenly this *thing* demands my attention. Instead of being handy (*zuhanden*), the broken hammer is "present-to-hand" (*vorhanden*).

Musicians are familiar with such moments of "presence-to-hand" (*Vorhandenheit*), moments when an instrument's affordances change unexpectedly. A sticky key, a broken string, or a tuning problem can disrupt my integration with an instrument. Here I am made aware of its materiality, distracted by its "thingness." I become conscious of my equipment and my body, improvising around the problem, adjusting the instrument or my fingering in the course of play.

Some musicians create a similar kind of breakdown on purpose by altering their instruments. Like Heidegger's broken hammer, an instrument that has been retuned, prepared, or redesigned can "get in the way." It may surprise, resist, or provoke its player.

The guitar offers a rich set of case studies here. Like most stringed instruments, the guitar is easily retuned or prepared. But tinkering is also an essential part of guitar culture, especially with electric guitars. Players often customize instruments, pickups, effects pedals, or amplifiers. They personalize mass-produced gear. Historically this interplay appears alongside the development of jazz guitar, which depended on amplification technologies that were often homemade (Waksman 1999, 20).[1] Jazz and rock guitarists' practices of alteration show how

1. Of course, certain adaptations, like Les Paul's solid-body design, initiated lasting changes. Here instrumental alteration intersects with the history of instruments: individual experimentation may become stabilized in communal practice (see Pinch and Trocco 2002; Bijsterveld and Schulp 2004).

Figure 4.1 Jules Massenet, "Meditation" from *Thaïs*, mm. 1–4.

changes to an instrument relate to sonic organization and bodily technique. Yet statements by the players themselves—along with insights from psychology and philosophy—suggest that these changes also affect perceptual experience.

Auditory-Motor Disalignment

Instrumental modifications can interrupt learned connections between hand and ear. Does this disruption contradict my earlier emphasis on auditory-motor integration? Not exactly. As discussed in Chapter 1, sensorimotor integration in perception and memory relies on repeatable patterns of coactivation. Yet such associations are dynamic, not rigid. Since sensory modalities have distinct neural substrates, *they are always potentially separable*. Brain injuries can make this tragically clear. The possibility of dissociation, then, is built into the theory of grounded cognition. At the neural level, even a "single" sense is not holistic. Seeing, for instance, involves multiple neural pathways (Jeannerod 1997). An object's visual properties activate various groups of neurons, cuing perceptual schemas related to shape, color, and so on. Because these schemas are independent at the neural level, they can be transformed and combined in novel ways (Barsalou 1999, 593–94). Schemas may form a framework that is "filled in" with new content; other times, the structure of a schema itself may be altered. Such changes, additionally, might involve bottom-up or top-down processes.

Experiments with altered auditory feedback provide some insights into dynamic remapping in musical performance. Steven Finney (1997), for example, asked expert keyboard players to play two-part inventions by J. S. Bach—but manipulated the instrument's MIDI output to produce unexpected sonic results. The keyboard might be silent, or participants might hear their playing delayed by 250 milliseconds. During some trials, single notes would occasionally sound a tone or semitone off (producing a note outside of the current key). In others, key-to-pitch mapping was randomized. Another condition produced a wholly different piece, with each key press activating the next note in the *giga* from Bach's D-minor Sonata for Solo Violin.

These alterations affected participants in distinct ways. The silent keyboard did not impair performance. Like the deaf Beethoven's improvisations, this represents a situation where motor action and auditory simulation work together.[2] With delayed auditory feedback, however, participants played more wrong notes, their performances took longer (meaning that the tempo decreased), and their hands were less coordinated. The delay introduces a mismatch between production and perception.[3] It violates the binding of action and effect, which is not specific to music but basic to ecological acoustics.

Perhaps surprisingly, Finney's pitch alterations had no significant effect on performance. Why is that? Certainly, an instrument's pitch organization is arbitrary in a way that action-effect coupling is not.[4] Yet it also turns out that Finney's remappings—to random scales or even another piece by Bach—are so radical that players quickly learn to ignore the unpredictable pitches. As with a silent keyboard, they let their hands lead. Later experiments indicate that altered pitch feedback impairs performance only when the perceived music is structurally similar to the planned music (Pfordresher 2005).[5] Wrong notes from earlier or later in the melody I am trying to play are more confusing than wrong notes from outside of the key (Pfordresher and Palmer 2006). A kind of auditory-motor "disalignment," then, is generally more disruptive than dissociation. In disalignment, sound and action are connected but not identical. There is a gap or divergence between them.

Though the following analyses examine disalignment with altered instruments, it bears mention that a sense of disalignment may also arise with unaltered instruments. For example, the ethnomusicologist Steven Friedson discusses "a dialectic between what is heard and how it is played" in the *vimbuza* drumming of northern Malawian healing rites (1996, 132–58). This stems from the gap between a polymetric rhythmic surface and bimanual playing technique. The music within these rites seems to switch between twos and threes, creating multistable acoustic illusions like the optical illusions discussed by Ihde (1986, 67–79). Nonetheless, players' motor patterns *feel* fundamentally duple because *vimbuza* drumming technique maintains strict alternation between hands. Something comparable occurs in the music of the Shona mbira, whose sound is enhanced by the rich buzzing and overtones created by bottle-top vibrators and a gourd resonator. As Paul Berliner writes, "The music reflected back to [the mbira player] by his resonator as he plays

2. This matches the results of Repp (1999). Unsurprisingly, the absence of auditory feedback is a greater problem for ensemble performance (Goebl and Palmer 2009).
3. For a review and theoretical discussion, see Pfordresher (2006). Delayed auditory feedback is less disruptive if the delay can be perceived in terms of subdivisions of the beat (Pfordresher and Palmer 2002). This is because the player is able to synchronize action with sound via a larger metric structure.
4. This also differentiates instruments from voices. As discussed by Pfordresher and Mantell, musical instruments have a certain "susceptibility to disruption" (2012, 168; see also Howell, Powell, and Khan 1983, 773).
5. Playing a reversed keyboard—where high and low pitches are systematically inverted—is also more difficult than playing a keyboard that generates random pitches (Laeng and Park 1999).

seems to be more complex than that which his fingers alone produce" (1993, 130). Here the effect emerges both from rhythmic complexity and from the way that the mbira, as an instrumental system, amplifies and modifies a player's musical input.

"Extended techniques" in contemporary music can give rise to similar experiences. For example, Helmut Lachenmann's "Dal niente" for solo clarinet decomposes the clarinetist's usual technique. It unyokes action schemas—of fingering, breathing, and tonguing—that are usually integrated. Certain sections involve fingering or blowing alone; sometimes notes fade in and out, playing with the boundary between breath and tone (see Figure 4.2a). This demonstrates the separability of different motor schemas. But Lachenmann also plays with the clarinetist's habits. The rapid key clicking that opens the work often involves stepwise motion. (This means that it often involves sequences of individual finger movements.) Surprisingly, Lachenmann sometimes mixes this technique with familiar motor schemas. Line 28, for instance, has a descending D-major scale (see Figure 4.2b)! Such diatonic patterns might not be audible to the audience, but they can jump out at the player, since overlearned patterns like scales engage strong auditory-motor habits. Like the violinists tapping Mozart in the fMRI machine (discussed in Chapter 1), the clarinetist here may experience sonic simulations driven by physical action.

"Dal niente" belongs to a series of compositions from the late 1960s and 1970s that Lachenmann calls *musique concrète instrumentale*. He defines this as "a music in which the sound events are chosen and organized so that the manner of their production takes at least as much importance as the resulting acoustic properties" (Lachenmann 1996, 381). These pieces, then, try to sustain a kind of breakdown, to prevent the player's bodily exertions and the instrument itself from withdrawing into the music.

Another piece in the series, "Guero," treats "the piano as a six-manualed variant ... of that Latin American instrument" which gives the piece its name (Lachenmann 1996, 384). The graphic notation, shown in Figure 4.3a, sets out the space of the keyboard and measures time in seconds. Then it specifies different

Figure 4.2 Helmut Lachenmann, excerpts from "Dal niente" for solo clarinet (1970): (a) opening, annotated with playing techniques; (b) line 28, highlighting an unexpected, silent D-major scale. © 1974 by Musikverlage Hans Gerig, Köln, 1980 assigned to Breitkopf & Härtel, Wiesbaden. Used with kind permission.

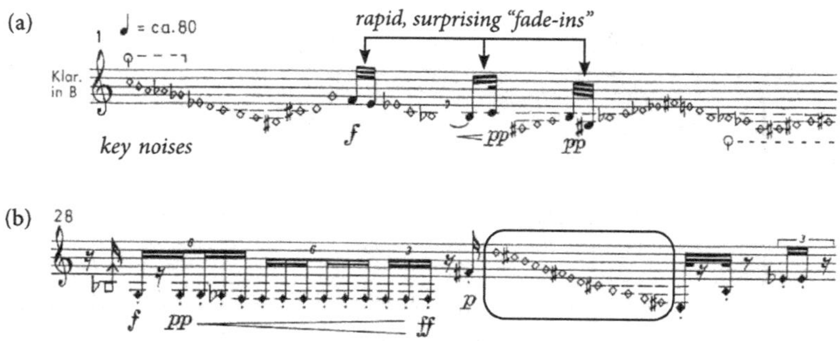

Figure 4.3 Helmut Lachenmann, excerpts from "Guero" for piano (1969): (a) opening, showing Lachenmann's "instrumental clef" (with translation); (b) lines 12–13, with annotations explaining graphic notation and scraping technique. © 1972 by Musikverlage Hans Gerig, Köln, 1980 assigned to Breitkopf & Härtel, Wiesbaden. Used with kind permission.

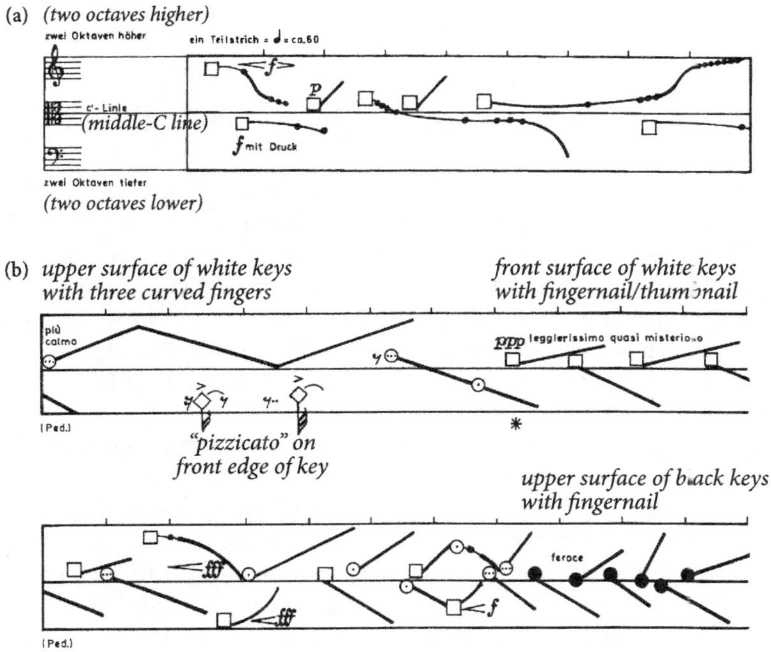

surfaces to be scraped or struck—the upper surface of the white keys, their front edge, their top, and so on (see Figure 4.3b). It might seem that such pieces do not require preexisting instrumental techniques, that Czerny's finger exercises or Chopin's études will not prepare you to play "Guero." In this view, anyone could learn these pieces, since they make everyone a beginner. Yet this would miss out on part of Lachenmann's aesthetic goals. He is interested in subverting musical habits, in pushing against established auditory-motor associations. Hence the composer describes "Guero" as "a manual and also a psychological study for the pianist" (384). It aims to develop new performative and perceptual skills by disrupting a pianist's technique. Lachenmann's musical experiments with disalignment and dissociation thus parallel Finney's and Pfordresher's psychological experiments, using disalignment and dissociation for artistic rather than scientific ends.

All of this relates to the composer's distinctive modernist understanding of "beauty." Beauty, for Lachenmann (1980, 22), is found in moments of human potential—the potential to know oneself and the world, to change one's actions, to change one's mind. "By allowing oneself to experience this 'non-music,'" says Lachenmann (1995, 101), "... listening becomes genuine perception. It is only now that one begins to listen differently, that one is reminded of the changeability of listening and of aesthetic behavior, reminded, in other words, of one's own structure, one's own structural changeability." Lachenmann's music, then, can be understood as a kind of phenomenology, "deliberately incorporating, provoking and revealing perception."

The rest of the chapter shows how this can be achieved through altered instruments. With an altered instrument, realizing the simplest tune may become confusing: I no longer know what notes I am playing.

Retuned Instruments: Kurt Rosenwinkel, "Zhivago"

The jazz guitarist Kurt Rosenwinkel (b. 1970) describes creative development as a cycle of stability and instability, learning and unlearning. "You start off not knowing what you're doing," he says, "then you organize things so they become ordered. When that order becomes static, you have to break it up to create another state of instability, which, in turn, throws you back into chaos. That's what continuing on to the next step is all about" (Rosenwinkel 2007). On his 2001 album, *The Next Step*, this dynamic process is driven largely by instrumental modification: he uses alternate tunings for four of the record's eight tracks.[6]

Rosenwinkel had found success in the mid-1990s with a Composer's Award from the National Endowment for the Arts and a recording contract with the prominent jazz label Verve. But at the point when he started work on *The Next Step*, Rosenwinkel was dissatisfied with his playing. "My knowledge of the guitar was hindering my relationship to the music," he explains. "I felt like I knew too much about what I was doing and not hearing the music directly." This is not simply about practiced hands falling into predictable patterns. Rather, Rosenwinkel frames this as an inability to *hear* the music properly. It involves *perceptual or conceptual habits* as much as performative ones. In cognitive terms, Rosenwinkel is describing particularly tight auditory-motor connections. If he already knows what his actions will sound like, he may come to hear his playing as unsurprising, overly schematic. A description by Rosenwinkel's colleague Christian Rover (2006) evokes the instrumentalized simulations discussed in Chapter 1: "To have a certain collection of voicings for every harmony, and a sound you already internally hear before you actually play it, would eventually make it redundant to still play it."

Rosenwinkel's solution was to retune his guitar in a form of "voluntary self-sabotage." "Anyone who has ever tried this," Rover comments, "knows that one twist of a tuning peg can turn you into a beginner in an instant. Just like the first time you touched a guitar all you have is your ears to rely on—and that's exactly what Kurt's intention was." There is some sense to this metaphor. Beginners rely more on visual feedback and pay more attention to motor patterns than do expert performers (see Palmer and Meyer 2000, discussed in Chapter 1). Since their

6. While alternate tunings are uncommon in jazz, they are often used in other guitar traditions, from the widespread drop-D tuning (that lowers the lowest string a whole step) to various open tunings of folk and slide blues guitar.

mapping between hand and ear is still being formed, they lack the perceptual habits that Rosenwinkel found frustrating.

In other ways, though, this professional musician was quite different from a beginner. Rosenwinkel was able to adapt various motor skills to the altered instrument. His right-hand picking, for example, would be unaffected. This reflects a general principle: *retuned instruments change place-to-pitch mapping, while preserving the instrumental interface*. The experiments by Pfordresher and colleagues, cited in the preceding section, imply that new mappings might be most challenging when they preserve aspects of a familiar tuning too.

I analyze relationships between standard and altered tunings through transformational voice leading theory, an application suggested by a speculative "scordatura fantasy" by David Lewin (1998, 38–41). Figure 4.4 represents alternate tunings as mappings between two pitch sets. This shows each string's movement in pitch space and sums up the mapping as a whole with two metrics of transformational voice leading, "consistency" and "displacement." "Consistency" measures the mapping's uniformity: it counts the number of voices that move by the same pitch interval (Straus 2003, 315). Higher consistency values mean that the mapping is closer to transposition—and that it preserves more inter-string intervals from standard tuning. Rosenwinkel's favored retuning takes three strings down a semitone; it is semiconsistent. By comparison, the scordatura for Toru Takemitsu's "Equinox" keeps four strings consistent. "Displacement"—the total number of semitones traversed (Straus 2003, 320)—further quantifies distance from standard tuning. Where Takemitsu's tuning moves only two semitones overall, Rosenwinkel's tuning moves twelve.

Rosenwinkel's scordatura is further from standard tuning than Takemitsu's. Every string moves, and the tuning does not repeat pitch intervals between adjacent strings. Yet Rosenwinkel also maintains some familiar features. Because three strings transpose together, he can play standard fretboard patterns involving those strings. This is particularly notable with the perfect fourth between the highest

Figure 4.4 Tuning transformations for guitar scordatura by Kurt Rosenwinkel and Toru Takemitsu. "Consistency" counts the number of voices that move the same distance; "displacement," the total number of semitones shifted.

	Kurt Rosenwinkel "Zhivago" (2001)	Toru Takemitsu "Equinox" (1993)
	E4 —(−1)→ E♭4	E4 —(0)→ E4
	B4 —(−1)→ B♭4	B4 —(−1)→ B♭4
	G3 —(+1)→ A♭3	G3 —(0)→ G3
	D3 —(−1)→ D♭3	D3 —(0)→ D3
	A2 —(−2)→ G2	A2 —(0)→ A2
	E2 —(−6)→ B♭1	E2 —(−1)→ E♭2
Consistency:	3	4
Displacement:	12	2

Figure 4.5 Kurt Rosenwinkel, "Zhivago," mm. 1–9. (This follows an improvised solo-guitar introduction.)

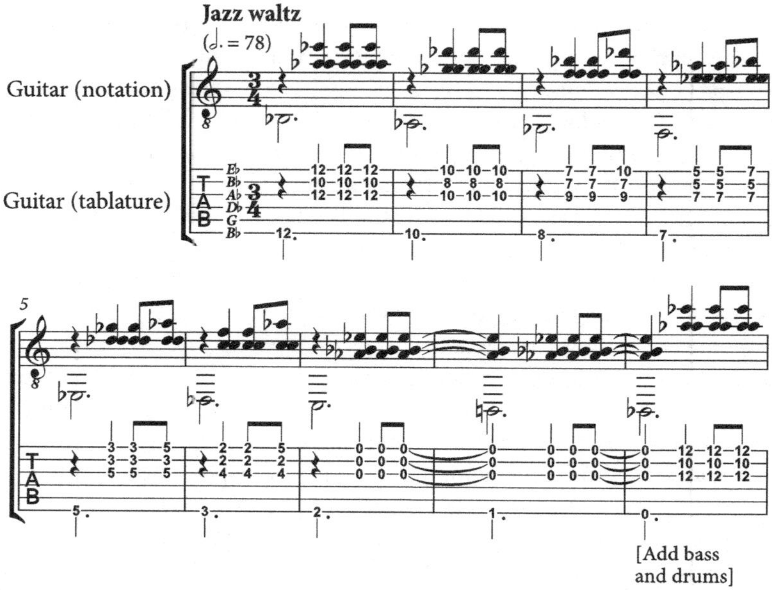

two strings. Such zones engage established performance habits. They allow the player to forget temporarily about the retuning, making other areas on the instrument more surprising by comparison. All of this involves cross-string intervals, of course; relative pitch relations along the strings, which are determined by acoustics, remain constant. It is perhaps unsurprising, then, that Rosenwinkel privileges motion along the strings in the opening track from *The Next Step*, "Zhivago."

"Zhivago" is a contemporary jazz waltz. After a free solo lead-in, Rosenwinkel establishes the driving triple-time feel of the composition proper. The guitar descends for eight measures, then repeats the progression with bass and drums (see transcription in Figure 4.5). Together they develop a new vamp, shown in Figure 4.6. At m. 33, the saxophone joins the guitar with a skipping theme that will return throughout the eighty-six-measure composition (see Figure 4.7).

The following analytical notes consider these opening sections, using the transformational model of guitar space introduced in the preceding chapter. As illustrated in my network for a riff by the Kinks in Figure 3.3, I represent fret/string positions as ordered pairs of the form (*f*, *s*). (Transformations in this space are represented by ordered pairs that show movement in these dimensions with integers marked by + or –.) This model makes it possible to show how "Zhivago" thematizes certain kinds of movement on the fretboard, even more than specific hand shapes or harmonic objects.[7]

7. For a similar approach, see Montague (2012) and Bungert (2015), who analyze thematic keyboard gestures in Chopin and Bach.

Figure 4.6 Kurt Rosenwinkel, "Zhivago," mm. 17–24.

In the first section's descent, the bass note begins at the twelfth fret of the bottom string (12, 6) and steadily works its way to the open string (0, 6). Here Rosenwinkel alternates between two basic hand positions, labeled α and β in Figure 4.8. I add subscript numbers to distinguish different instances of these chord shapes: the number refers to the position of the sixth-string fret (that is, the bass note). The move from α_{12} to α_{10} is a straightforward along-the-string transposition, (–2, 0). The shift between α and β, however, is also an along-the-string move. The two shapes hold frets on the same strings, and my fingers slide along the fretboard as I shift from one to the other.

Defining two contextual transformations will help us conceptualize the relationship between the two shapes. J formalizes a "pivoting" gesture. J holds the fret on the lowest string of the shape constant and moves the others up by one. A complementary perspective is provided by another transformation, K. K moves the lowest-string fret down one, while holding the others. This will prove to be a kind of "thematic move" throughout the piece. Figure 4.9 and Video 4.1 ▶ demonstrate these operations, applying each to α_{10}. These transformations, however, might apply to any fretboard shape and may appear in standard tuning. For example, K and J^{-1} can be used to toggle between two voicings in a common descending "ii–V" progression (see Figure 4.10 and Video 4.2 ▶).

Readers versed in transformational theory will note that J and K are operations (not simply transformations), since they are invertible. Their inverses—J^{-1} and K^{-1}—undo the move, taking β back to α. More specifically, I am describing groups of operations isomorphic to the integers under addition.[8] This means that

8. This means that the model incorporates negative fret numbers, which must be included for formal reasons (Rings 2011, 25–27; De Souza 2016b).

Figure 4.7 Kurt Rosenwinkel, "Zhivago," mm. 33–46.

Figure 4.8 Kurt Rosenwinkel, "Zhivago," mm. 1–6, labeling basic hand positions. Subscript numbers refer to the fret on the lowest string. For these hand positions, I include only the lower anchor note on the highest string (excluding the added melodic neighbor note). This underlying schematic shape for α—with the highest two strings sharing a fret—emerges clearly in mm. 4–5. Here the higher note on the first string is added at the end of the bar, whereas throughout mm. 1–2 this highest note covers the basic shape.

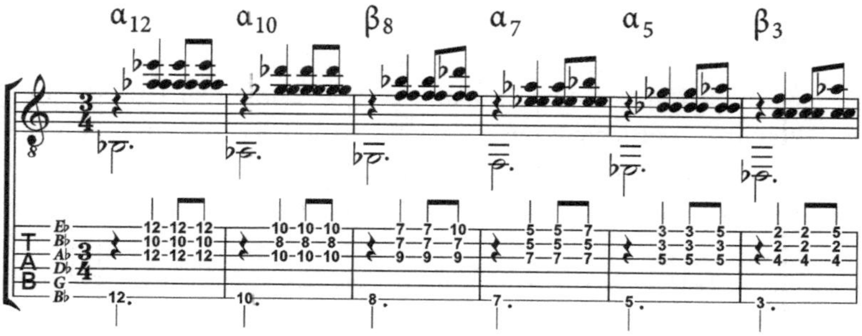

Figure 4.9 Two contextual operations for fretboard shapes in Rosenwinkel, "Zhivago." Both connect α and β. J holds the bottom-string fret and moves the others up one; K moves the bottom-string fret down one, holding the others. The inverses of these operations (J^{-1} and K^{-1}) take β back to α.

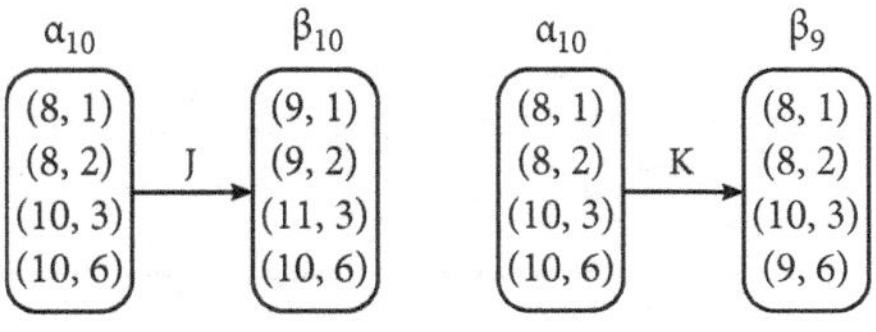

Figure 4.10 Contextual fretboard operations with a chromatically descending ii–V progression, which appears in many jazz standards (including Duke Ellington's "Satin Doll," Miles Davis's "Four," and John Coltrane's "Lazy Bird"): (a) an idiomatic voicing for this progression, using only the highest four strings on a guitar in standard tuning; (b) transformation network modeling these voicings via K and J^{-1} (the inverse of J).

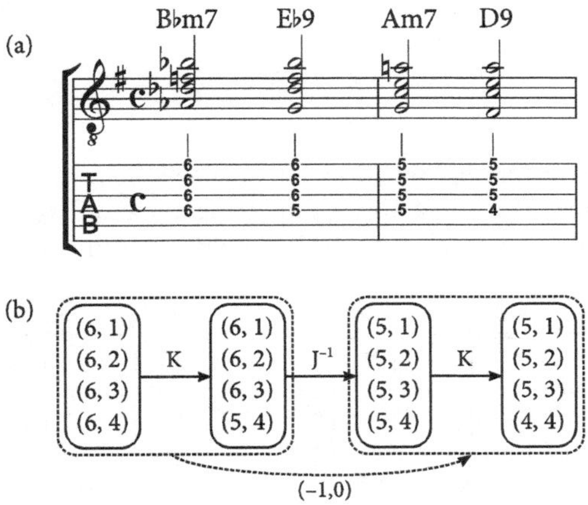

the operations can also combine with themselves: for example, performing K twice in a row (K^2) moves the lowest-string position down two frets. Furthermore, these contextual operations commute with transpositions in fretboard space The order in which these transformations are combined does not change their product: for example, $(-2, 0)J = J(-2, 0)$. Figure 4.11 demonstrates the combination of pivoting and shifting along the fretboard with the middle section of the Beatles' "Blackbird" (see Video 4.3▶).

Figure 4.12 represents the opening section of "Zhivago" in networks that combine J and K with transpositions along the string. (This section is performed in Video 4.4▶.) The first two networks show that Rosenwinkel repeats a sequence of hand shapes as he moves down. The interpretation that uses J highlights the bass line, showing that it always drops two frets after α forms. Thinking in terms of K obscures this somewhat. Yet as Figure 4.12c shows, K also accounts for the descending motion in mm. 7–9 and 15–16. Though these measures introduce new

Figure 4.11 John Lennon and Paul McCartney, "Blackbird" (1968), mm. 13–14: (a) notation; (b) a network that combines the pivoting gestures J and K with along-the-string transpositions on a guitar in standard tuning. (The interested reader can pursue such gestures throughout the rest of "Blackbird," starting with the characteristic (+8, 0)J leap in the song's first two measures.)

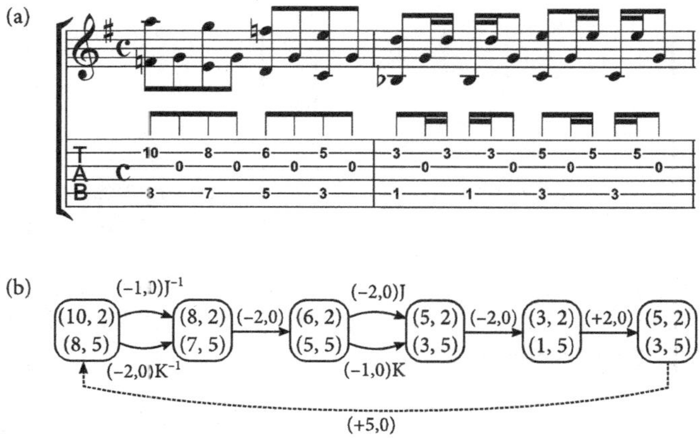

Figure 4.12 Transformation networks for Rosenwinkel, "Zhivago," mm. 1–16: (a) network for mm. 1–6, 9–14, using J to connect α and β; (b) network for mm. 1–6, 9–14, using K to connect α and β; (c) network for mm. 7–9, 15–16.

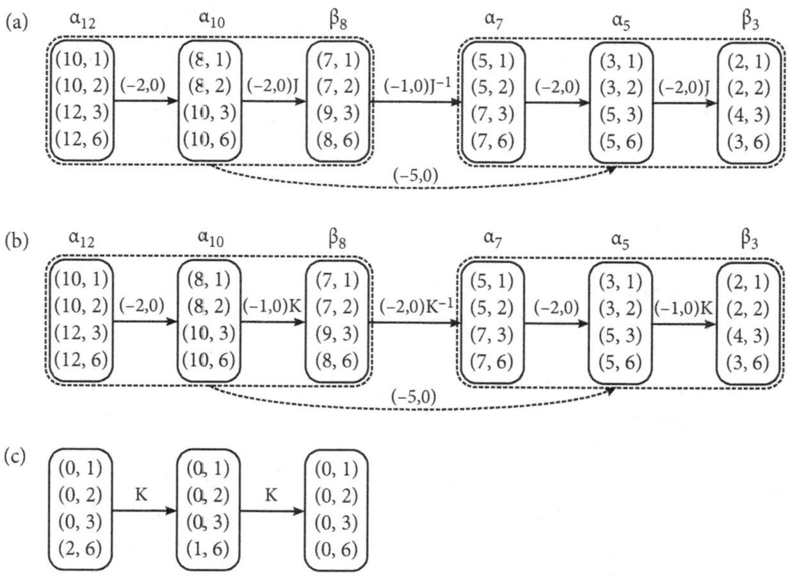

Figure 4.13 Transformation networks for looping schema from Rosenwinkel, "Zhivago," mm. 17–32: (a) network with fretboard transpositions; (b) network with variant of K.

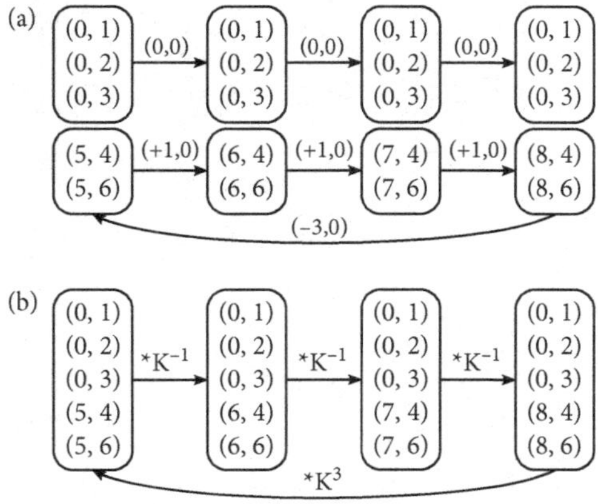

hand shapes—that is, new chord voicings—*they involve comparable movement along the fretboard.*

The second section reverses and extends the K motion from mm. 7–9. It takes a parallel shape up the neck, against stable higher strings (see Figure 4.13 and Video 4.5▶). Rosenwinkel loops the process four times, adding to the higher strings with each repetition. The step-by-step action on the lower strings can be modeled as the inverse of a K variant—call it *K—which would move the frets from a shape's lowest *two* strings (instead of just the lowest).[9]

The new theme at m. 33 also involves cycling between hand positions (mm. 33–39, 47–52, 63–68). The chords that support it can again be modeled by J or K, alternately straightening the shape and offsetting the lowest-string note (see Figure 4.14a and Video 4.6▶). The melody itself, though, introduces the first cross-string movement as it explores the instrument's many-to-one place-to-pitch mapping. The "same" melodic figure is alternately realized on different strings, related by the first transformations involving string crossing, (+2, +1) and its inverse (−2, −1). As shown in Figure 4.14b, this figure is also shifted along the fretboard by (−2, 0), outlining part of a whole-tone scale. In later sections (which are not shown here), this action loop forms an antecedent that is answered differently each time.

These analytical sketches highlight some characteristic physical positions and movements in "Zhivago." Rosenwinkel privileges along-the-string movement and bass-pivoting or bass-displacing gestures (modeled by J and K). These sections can be further understood as a series of action cycles: an eight-measure loop, repeated

9. With the second pass through the cycle, Rosenwinkel adds the top string; with the third, a held note on the top string's seventh fret. In the last place in the loop, the eighth fret is fingered on the fourth string—but this fret is *sounded* only after the final repetition of the cycle, shifted onto the *third* string (in m. 32).

Figure 4.14 Transformation networks for Rosenwinkel, “Zhivago,” mm. 33–46: (a) chord pattern from mm. 33–39; (b) melodic transformations for mm. 33–46. In (b), “Ret” stands for retrograde.

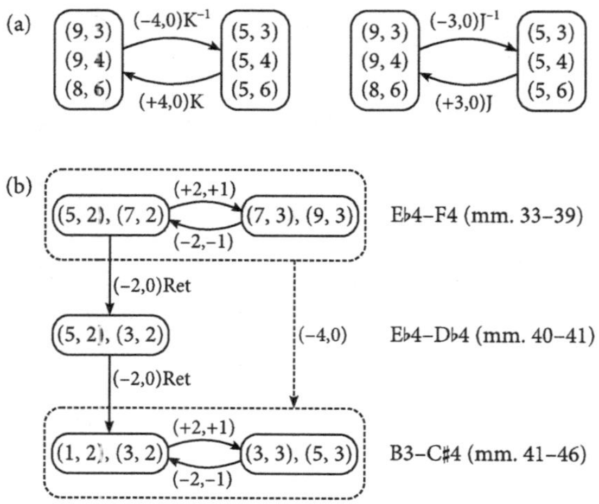

twice (mm. 1–16); a four-measure loop, repeated four times (mm. 17–32); a two-measure loop, also repeated four times (mm. 33–39). Each loop is shorter, more focused, than the one that precedes it.

The way Rosenwinkel lingers in these grooves, which make up most of the composition, foregrounds a kind of haptic engagement with the music. By this I mean that physical shapes on the instrument take precedence over usual harmonic labels. Rosenwinkel discussed this in a 2010 master class:

> What was cool about it was that I didn't really know what this chord was. [Plays a chord.] What is that? I don't know. It seems like a major seventh. I wasn't sure, you know, and I didn't know what the notes were. So I had to take a tuner, to plug into a chromatic tuner to tell me what that note was, you know, so I could write it down. And then I kind of started to figure out what the harmony was. Slowly, very slowly. But it was really cool because no longer did I have this intellectual relationship with it. It was just pure sound and discovery.[10]

This suggests that Rosenwinkel's motor habits and auditory expectations readjust more quickly than his theoretical awareness. Even as his hands and ears become familiar with the altered fretboard used in “Zhivago,” his “intellectual” perception of the music lags behind. Rosenwinkel's retuning temporarily disrupts his

10. A brief video from the event can be viewed at http://www.youtube.com/watch?v=QVSNccMNtJU. Of course, this master class is a performative and pedagogical situation, in which Rosenwinkel consciously models a certain type of musicianship. Still, his comments fit with my own experience of “Zhivago” and its unusual guitar tuning. I find it difficult to name the notes or chords as I play it, even though I have transcribed and analyzed the piece.

symbolic experience of the music and instead foregrounds its sensory, "aesthetic" qualities.

Prepared Instruments: Fred Frith, "Hello Music"

The English multi-instrumentalist Fred Frith (b. 1949) has more than four hundred items in his discography. He has played with experimental rock, folk, and jazz groups, written film scores and orchestral pieces, and taught composition at Mills College. One of his most acclaimed recordings, though, is a forty-minute set of unaccompanied improvisations, simply titled *Guitar Solos*. For this 1974 album, Frith modifies a 1936 Gibson K-11 archtop by adding a second pickup at the nut (that is, the end of the strings farthest from the bridge). He then taps the strings with his hands or with found objects, recording the results. This explores, Frith says, "the difference between the touch of stone, the touch of glass, the touch of wood, the touch of paper—those kinds of basic elements that you're using against the surface of the strings which produce different sounds" (Milkowski 1983, 24).[11] Clearly, like Rosenwinkel, Frith seeks to defamiliarize the guitar. But instead of retuning, his approach involves *instrumental preparation*.

Where retuning changes an instrument's pitch mapping, preparation incorporates foreign objects *at the site of sound production*, and this often transforms pitches into complex inharmonic sounds. Preparation, in a sense, turns any instrument into a percussion instrument. It disrupts habitual associations by crossing categories. That is, a prepared instrument may not simply produce unexpected notes. It may instead produce unexpected *noises*—metallic or wooden, thudding, rattling, or ringing.

Preparing an instrument, then, suggests a certain openness to noise that Frith first encountered in John Cage. "Reading [Cage's] *Silence* when I was about eighteen changed my attitude completely, far more profoundly than listening to any music ever would have," says Frith. "That book brought very sharply into focus the idea that sound, in and of itself, can be as important as … melody and harmony and rhythm. The sound itself is just as important. And from that notion I started viewing the guitar itself from a different point of view altogether, just to see what I could get out of it" (quoted in Milkowski 1983, 23). Frith's exploration of the guitar, of course, parallels Cage's approach to the piano. The composer "invented" the prepared piano in the late 1930s, adding screws and bolts to the instrument's strings to make it sound like a percussion ensemble. Cage (1979, 8) describes this as a process of "continual discovery," full of delight and surprise.

That sense of surprise is central to Cage's concept of *experimental action*, "an act the outcome of which is unknown" (1961, 13). Experimental music for Cage disrupts the "straight line between anticipation of what should happen and what actually happens" (167–68). When the composer formulated this idea in the

11. For more details of Frith's performance techniques, see Dawe (2010, 78). They are also documented in the film *Step Across the Border* (Humbert and Penzel 1990).

Figure 4.15 John Cage, *Our Spring Will Come* (1943) for prepared piano, mm. 1–4. All the strings in this excerpt are prepared, so the apparent harmonic progression indicated by Roman numerals does not sound. © 1977 by Henmar Press, Inc. Used by permission of C. F. Peters Corporation. All rights reserved.

1950s, he explained "experimental action" in terms of chance composition and music with indeterminate performance (69). Yet Cage's work with the prepared piano—principally between 1938 and 1951—precedes these techniques: *here the altered instrument itself renders an action's result unpredictable*, transforming the habitual into the experimental.

In cognitive terms, this reshapes expected action-effect coupling, learned associations between hand and ear.[12] Playing prepared instruments might feel less disorienting than playing retuned ones, since their remapping is closer to the random auditory feedback that induced auditory-motor dissociation in Finney's studies. But a prepared instrument, like a silent or random keyboard, may suspend auditory expectations *while preserving motor schemas*. Cage's notation for prepared piano—which indicates the keys to be pressed, not the resulting sounds—presumes "normal" pianistic habits. (In this respect, it resembles notation for string music in scordatura.) *Our Spring Will Come* (1943), for example, even uses familiar tonal patterns (see Figure 4.15). On the page and under the hand, it projects a sense of F minor. An apparent V^4_2 chord even seems to "resolve" to a kind of i^6, more or less as it would in a tonal context (mm. 2 and 6). But since all of these strings are prepared with bamboo strips or screws, the resulting sounds are percussive, lacking clear pitches. Tonal schemas and motor schemas are pulled apart; the action's result becomes unpredictable.

The continuity of technique reflected in this example correlates with a continuity of technology: *preparation changes an instrument's sound production, not its interface*. The piano and the prepared piano both have keyboards, just as the guitar and prepared guitar both have fretboards. In other words, preparation does not obscure the basic instrumental space.

I will illustrate with some analytical comments on "Hello Music" from Frith's *Guitar Solos* (1974). "Hello Music" brims with jaunty energy. Frith starts with a jazzy, syncopated motive that recurs throughout the first third of the piece. After

12. For Cage this helps deconstruct the traditional separation of matter and spirit, life and art, action and sound—which results partially from the way that tones are rationalized, possessed, or made repeatable by music theory.

Table 4.1 Formal outline for Fred Frith, "Hello Music" (1974)

Letter	*Time*	*Gesture/texture*
A1	0:00	Chord/cross-string gesture (4×)
	0:05	Answer (cross-string)
A2	0:10	Opening chord/cross-string gesture (4×)
	0:14	Answer (along-string steps; vibrato at 0:16)
	0:21	Strumming (vibrato at 0:24)
A3	0:25	Opening chord/cross-string gesture (4×)
B1	0:31	Chords up and down along string
	0:38	Contrary motion
C1	0:46	Bimanual tapping triplets (parallel)
D	0:51	Slide/hammer-on counterpoint
E	1:00	Free transition
C2	1:06	Tapping triplets (wedge)
A4	1:15	Opening chord/cross-string gesture (3×)
B2	1:21	Chords along string
F	1:27	Ascending scale

contrasting middle sections, he comes back to this opening gesture for an upward-spinning codetta (for an overview, see Table 4.1).[13]

In the context of the album, "Hello Music" represents a balance between more atmospheric tracks (like "Glass C/W Steel") and more tonal ones (like "Not Forgotten" and "Hollow Music"). The pitches throughout this track are mostly indistinct, hovering around a threshold of inharmonicity. But its gestural qualities still reflect the space of the guitar's tiered array.

The additional pickup at the nut defines the overall sonority of "Hello Music." Like more common forms of preparation, this alters the way the instrument produces sound. It makes it possible to hear two sides of a stopped string—both the side between the finger stopping the string and the bridge, and the usually inaudible side between the finger and the nut. One tap of the string, in other words, produces two interlinked notes. Despite the pitches' fuzziness, there is a systematic inversional relationship here. Dividing a string at its midpoint would create a point of balance: the pitches for both sides would meet an octave above the open string. Away from this midpoint, though, whenever one side of the string is shortened, the other is lengthened.

Frith exploits these affordances through finger tapping, a technique that would become a standard part of the solo rock guitar vocabulary, particularly associated with the virtuoso Eddie Van Halen.[14] With tapping, both hands articulate notes through hammer-ons and pull-offs.[15] In other words, the guitarist strikes a string

13. This method of charting free improvisation parallels a mode of "phenomenological analysis" by Borgo (2005, 77–78).

14. For a discussion of Van Halen's use of the technique, see Waksman (2001).

15. "Hammer-ons" and "pull-offs" are guitar techniques whereby notes are attacked by the fretting hand alone. With a hammer-on a finger is percussively placed on the fret; with a pull-off it is percussively removed.

instead of fingering-and-plucking it. Tapping thus introduces a disjunction within the kinesthetic domain: besides freeing up associations between hand and ear, it undoes the guitarist's usual coordination between hands. Like Lachenmann's "Dal niente" for clarinet, it breaks playing technique into schematic components.

"Hello Music" thematizes several patterns of body-instrument interaction. The A motive, which opens and pervades the piece, engages the guitar's cross-string dimension. It features a loud chord repeated twice, followed by quieter, quicker plinks. The chord, obviously, stops multiple strings at once, and Frith maintains its placement as he repeats the motive. He does not move it up or down the neck. The motive's plinking tail descends across the strings in clean, disjunct leaps. (Near the beginning of the track, these downward skips involve successive perfect fourths, a characteristic interval from standard guitar tuning.) The self-doubling created by the guitar's preparation further clarifies this movement: with the plinking, the two "parts" have the same contour. (As just noted, moving along one string would create contrary motion between parts.)

Frith's A motive, then, juxtaposes two common ways to articulate a guitar chord, activating the strings simultaneously and activating them in succession. Despite the unusual timbre, the motive's basic gestural or textural profile can be found in much music for non-prepared guitar.

After establishing the string-crossing motive, Frith gradually introduces motion along the guitar's neck. While this strategy briefly appears in his "answer" to A2 (0:14), it becomes prominent in the middle sections of "Hello Music." In the section I have labeled B1 (0:31), Frith moves a chord up and down the neck, an action that brings out the inversional relationship between doubled pitches. This is especially clear at 0:38, when the two parts move fret by fret in contrary motion. Sections C and D also highlight movement along the neck. The bimanual tapping of C creates rapid triplets on a single string, involving the open string and then two higher notes (one played with the left hand, the other with the right). In C1, the two tapped notes move up and down in parallel; later (C2), they diverge in a "wedge" shape. The independence of hands is also particularly audible in the D section that intervenes between C1 and C2: here Frith develops a kind of counterpoint between a sustaining part that slowly slides up a string and another that taps in place. These prolonged glissandi, near the piece's midpoint, are the most expansive along-string gestures in the piece.

From this perspective, the central "themes" of "Hello Music" are distinctive modes of exploring the prepared guitar's fretboard. Its "form" emerges from the contrast between these strategies. In Table 4.1, I separate these large-scale sections with horizontal lines. From A1 to A3 Frith focuses on the chords and string crossing of the opening motive. The middle section (from B1 to C2) is more varied, exploring several ways of moving along the strings. The final section (from A4 to F), perhaps surprisingly, resembles a conventional recapitulation, juxtaposing his earlier themes. Frith returns to the opening motive, then a gesture from the middle section (B2), and closes with a kind of codetta (the quickly ascending scale of F). As mentioned earlier, the pitches throughout "Hello Music" are fuzzy. But Frith's gestural strategies are clearly differentiated and audibly related to the guitar's space. That is why this prepared guitar—a thumping, plinking guitar—still sounds *like a guitar*. On this level, "Hello Music" is experimental and, at the same time, highly idiomatic.

Note that "Hello Music" explores one particular setup, just as other tracks on *Guitar Solos* take shape around other preparations—playing with objects, placing a capo in the middle of the fretboard, and so on. Each preparation offers distinctive materials for a player to explore. Similarly, the same preparation on individual instruments may produce different results.[16]

In the words of Frith's collaborator, the guitarist Derek Bailey, "The instrument is not a tool but an ally. It is not only a means to an end, it is a source of material, and technique for the improviser is often an exploitation of the natural resources of the instrument" (1992, 99). From this perspective, the instrument can be understood as a creative partner. The linear motion developed in the middle sections of "Hello Music," then, responds to the inversional relations created by the nut pickup. Imagining body-instrument interaction as collaboration recalls Frith's writing about improvisation with human partners: "Improvising is … a place where we can meet on equal terms and discover things we never knew, or hear what we thought we knew in a new light. It's a conversation, an exchange. There are no rules, other than to listen well and act accordingly" (Frith 2005). Improvising with other musicians—or instruments—demands listening, respectfully attending to their difference from me. In this sense, instrumental alteration reveals instrumental alterity.

Redesigned Instruments: Pat Metheny, "Into the Dream"

As instrumental preparation modifies the body of the instrument, it overlaps with instrumental redesign. Whether or not Frith's extra pickup creates a "new" instrument, his later work moved in that direction. From the 1980s, much of his solo improvisation involved homemade instruments: pieces of wood with strings, a pickup, and a bridge. Imposing too crisp a distinction between preparation and redesign would be unhelpful, but let me propose a working definition. Retuning and preparation change an instrument's sonic affordances but not its basic interface. Redesign, by contrast, alters an instrument's basic shape or space and, correspondingly, possibilities for interacting with it.

The Grammy Award–winning jazz guitarist Pat Metheny has long been involved in processes of instrument design, and his work here illustrates a range of possibilities. His collaborations with the Ibanez guitar company, for example, produced the PM-100 and PM-120 models, promoted as "the first radically new body shape in a major commercially released jazz guitar since the late seventies" (Metheny 2000, 11). These archtop guitars feature a double cutaway that is more commonly associated with rock guitars like the Gibson SG. This cutaway is not

16. Cage, for example, said that his experiences with prepared piano "showed [him] how different two pianos are from one another [even though] music (so-called) makes us think two pianos are the same" (1961, 182).

merely cosmetic: it lets Metheny curl his thumb over the top of the neck at higher fret positions. Still, this represents a relatively subtle change.

With Metheny's "Orchestrion" project, he uses a guitar, equipped with MIDI technology, to control an array of mechanical acoustic instruments, including pianos, basses, tuned and untuned percussion, and "guitarbots."[17] These may play preprogrammed parts or improvised loops. This redesign affects action-sound coupling, much like the self-activating instruments discussed in Chapter 2. When the Orchestrion functions as "something that runs," the guitar acts as an input device, the means by which Metheny intervenes in a technologically sustained process. This innovation changes the overall instrumental system but has minimal effects on the interface. The Orchestrion's varied robotic parts are all played through a standard fretboard.

For present purposes, I am most interested in the kind of redesign that alters the instrument's interface. This is realized in one of Metheny's collaborations with the Canadian luthier Linda Manzer. Manzer has created many instruments for Metheny, including a baritone guitar, an acoustic soprano guitar, an acoustic sitar-guitar, and a fretless classical guitar. Arguably their most unusual creation, however, is the forty-two-string Pikasso II guitar (see Figure 4.16).[18] "In 1984," remembers Manzer, "Pat Metheny asked me to design and build a guitar with 'as many strings as possible.'"[19] To achieve this goal, however, they did not expand the fretboard: the Pikasso's main neck, like a standard guitar's, has only six strings. Instead they added three new sets of twelve strings, which are always open. This means that the Pikasso participates in a tradition of "harp guitars," dating from the nineteenth century, that include additional, unstopped strings.[20]

To describe the Pikasso, Metheny has offered an instrumental analogy. "It's really the closest thing I've come to something like a piano that's also a guitar," he says. "You can really have a lot of notes ringing and sustaining over other notes without using any kind of electronics."[21] With its capacity for sustained notes and its extended range, the Pikasso may certainly recall the piano. Beyond any sonic similarities, though, the Pikasso may resemble the piano in terms of interface and playing technique. Though the baritone neck replicates a standard tiered-array

17. Metheny names this system after various historical "orchestra machines," which are discussed by Dolan (2013, 187). The main distinction between the Orchestrion and MIDI guitar controllers—which Metheny has used since the 1980s—is that its sounds are not synthesized or sampled but produced live.
18. The first Pikasso guitar is an electric version, played, for example, on Metheny's collaboration with Ornette Coleman, *Song X* (1986). Here I will simply refer to the acoustic Pikasso II as the "Pikasso," since it has featured more prominently in Metheny's work. I have discussed the Pikasso and "Into the Dream" in a chapter on the Pat Metheny Group's 2001 concert video *Imaginary Day Live* (De Souza 2016a). Though certain analytical details overlap, the focus there is on visual aspects of performance rather than instrumental alteration.
19. See http://www.manzer.com/guitars/index.php?option=com_content&view=article&id=25&Itemid=24. Manzer would later increase this maximum by ten for the fifty-two-string Medusa guitar made for Henrik Andersen.
20. On the history and organology of harp guitars, see Miner (2015).
21. For Metheny's comments on the Pikasso, see "About the instrumentation," http://www.patmetheny.com/features/imaginary/inst.htm.

Figure 4.16 Pat Metheny playing the Pikasso II guitar (Rodby 2008).

fretboard, the other set of strings offer spaces that are linear, like a keyboard. Moreover, when Metheny plays the instrument, his hands are independent, and they combine activation and control. The right hand typically realizes the principal melody, while accompanied by the left. He keeps his left hand on the baritone-guitar neck, using hammer-ons and pull-offs exclusively. Meanwhile, the right hand explores the other areas, plucking or strumming the strings with fingers or a pick. This separation of hands, like Frith's bimanual tapping, pulls apart guitaristic action schemas that are usually coordinated. That said, pianistic or tapping hands are independent but develop effectively the same technique. With the Pikasso guitar, by contrast, the hands serve different functional purposes. This instrumental redesign, then, heightens the distinction between fretting and picking hands. The disalignment of existing motor schemas, responding to the instrument's affordances, is the basis of what is claimed to be a "totally new guitar technique" (Metheny 2000, 10).

Metheny's preferred tuning for the Pikasso both differentiates and unites the different sets of strings. The six strings on the fretboard are tuned as a baritone guitar. That is, they transpose standard E tuning down a major third, producing the notes C2, F2, B♭2, E♭3, G3, C4. The strings that are connected to the headstock above the neck, which nearly parallel the fretboard, are tuned to a G-minor pentatonic collection (G, B♭, C, D, F); the zitherlike strings that cross the instrument's body, to an incomplete C natural-minor or C Dorian scale (C, D, E♭, F, G, B♭). The almost vertical strings connected to the top headstock are tuned to a G-minor triad (G, B♭, D). Since these pass beneath two other sets of strings, they function mainly as sympathetic strings. Though each set of strings maps to a distinct set of pitch classes, their collections overlap substantially. In fact, the forty-two open strings instantiate only six pitch classes, which form a segment from the cycle of fifths.[22] This tuning strategy minimizes dissonances among the Pikasso's open strings. Metheny refers to the result as a "big C-minor kind of sound" (Adelson 2002). With the Pikasso, as with the harmonica, there is a gap between scale and macroharmony, and irregularity fosters the sense of a home key. Each set of open strings offers a fixed tuning that can variously be understood as a chord or a scale.[23] Each involves its own subset of a C-minor scale that is never presented in full.

Metheny most often plays the Pikasso on tracks titled "Into the Dream," and I have consulted fifteen performances of the piece, ranging from 1997 to 2010.[24] Melodic and rhythmic details vary widely across these versions. Nonetheless, "Into the Dream" has a clear four-part form:

> Section A: During a slow introduction, Metheny develops a rhythmically free fingerstyle dialogue between the two right-hand areas. This starts with the zither-like strings and is accompanied by hammer-on trills in the left hand. This section typically lasts around a minute and a half, although … it may vary from 44 seconds (New York, 1998) to over two minutes (2006). The original 1997 version from the CD involves this section only and does not follow the form established by Metheny's later live performances.
>
> Section B1: Next, while maintaining active right-hand plucking, Metheny establishes the meter with sustained bass notes. Though the baritone-guitar neck can play all twelve pitch classes, the bass part only uses a C natural-minor mode; Metheny plays most of these notes with his left index finger, tending to move stepwise. (On occasion, Metheny also taps on the body as part of this section.)
>
> Section C: For a climactic third section, Metheny switches to a pick, alternately strumming the two right-hand sets of strings over a more active bass line. While this section usually runs longer than a minute, Metheny keeps it to 30 seconds in a 2000 live recording and omits it in a 2009 performance.
>
> Section B2: Finally, he returns to the calmer fingerpicking texture of the second section, using the bass to set up a final cadence. (This cadence is where he most often strums the G-minor sympathetic strings.) In the performances I have examined, this recapitulation is never the longest section and its variation is least pronounced, ranging from 44 seconds (New York, 1998) to 1 minute 23 seconds (2010). (De Souza 2016a, 164–65)

Overall, "Into the Dream" explores two oppositions: one between the C-minor and G-pentatonic collections and another between fingerpicking and strumming

22. In set-theoretic terms, this hexachord is a member of set class 6-32 [024579]. Uniquely among hexachord classes, it includes no instances of interval class 6 and only one instance of interval class 1.
23. This conceptual crossover, like my discussion of instrumental "scales" in Chapter 3, resonates with Tymoczko's idea that "a scale is a large chord, and a chord is just a small scale" (2011, 153).
24. For many years, the exceptions here were duets: "The Sound of Water" with the pianist Brad Mehldau (on their 1996 album, *Quartet*) and "*Cichy Zapada Zmrok* (Here Comes the Silent Dusk)" with the Polish singer Anna Maria Jopek (on their 2002 album, *Upojenie*). More recently, though, Metheny used the Pikasso on *What's It All About* (2011) to cover Paul Simon's "The Sound of Silence."

with a pick. The first has to do with the Pikasso as musical technology; the second, with Metheny's playing technique. From this perspective, "Into the Dream" is not a precomposed sequence of notes and harmonies. It is a series of idiomatic performance strategies, a kind of improvisational template to be realized anew in each performance.

Of course, while the Pikasso offers new sounds, it also constrains Metheny's improvisation. The fixed pitch collections cannot be changed in performance, the pitches in the supplementary collections cannot be bent, and so on. Most of Metheny's compositions are not easily played on the Pikasso, since they involve chromatic shifts that exceed its tonal affordances. (While they could be played on the baritone-guitar neck, the sympathetic resonance from the overlapping strings and the bulk of the instrument make this less than feasible.) This particular instrumental redesign, then, becomes so specialized that in the end it feels less flexible than a regular guitar. For all its complexity, it almost seems that Metheny's Pikasso II, like a purpose-built music box, can play just one piece.

This kind of constraint, however, points to the Pikasso's influence on its players' perception. Where Rosenwinkel's retuned guitar skewed expected associations between action and sound and where Frith's prepared guitar reduced auditory expectations by rendering pitches doubled and indistinct, Metheny's redesigned guitar refocuses his musical imagination by splitting apart performance techniques and fixing—or radically reducing—tonal possibilities. This instrument does not afford the performative or conceptual habits associated with the performance of jazz compositions with wide-ranging chromaticism. As Metheny puts it, "You have to learn to think like the instrument you're playing" (Webb 1985). Since most of the Pikasso's strings are fixed and its macroharmony (overall pitch collection) is consonant, it is possible to stop thinking about particular notes and focus on gesture, density, and so on. As the instrument neutralizes harmonic movement—or achieves a kind of tonal stasis—it redirects attention to the instrument's timbre and the player's physical actions; it engenders particular modes of performance and perception. In terms of sound, technique, and visual spectacle, the Pikasso II guitar creates a piece that stands apart from Metheny's other playing, a kind of musical breakdown.

Conclusions

This chapter's analyses show three ways that alteration can change an instrument's affordances. Retuned instruments produce unexpected pitches; prepared instruments produce unexpected sounds; redesigned instruments reconfigure a familiar interface. Instrument, technique, and sound coevolve, as elements of each are preserved or adjusted. There are, of course, countless other idiosyncratic extensions of instrumental resources—from J. S. Bach's five-string violoncello piccolo to Tod Machover's "hypercello" (Ledbetter 2009, 43–45; Rothstein 1991). Still, the music of Rosenwinkel, Frith, and Metheny has highlighted some broad connections between altered instruments, performance, and perception. Whether retuned, prepared, or redesigned, altered instruments offer new possibilities in terms of harmony, timbre, texture, and so on. But at the same time, they play with habitual connections between action and sound, between performers' auditory and motor perception. They create new opportunities to relearn my instrument, moments when I become conscious of my bodily engagement with it, when I begin to listen to and think about and feel the sound differently. Changing the instrument, then, changes the player. Alteration illuminates everyday experiences of instruments, even as it disrupts them.

By way of conclusion, I wish to briefly relate these musical examples to some problems in phenomenological theory, problems around the opposition of *Zuhandenheit* and *Vorhandenheit*. "When we discover its unusability," says Heidegger (2010, 72), "the thing becomes conspicuous." But this conspicuous presence, he suggests, is temporary: "Mere objective presence makes itself known in the useful thing only to withdraw again into … handiness." On one level, this fits with my dynamic account of perception and action (for example, I get used to my guitar's alternate tuning). Yet this dismissal of "mere" presence has been critiqued even by Heidegger's supporters (e.g., Stiegler 1998, 245; Harman 2002, 3–4). And the philosopher himself abandoned the dialectic of *Zuhandenheit* and *Vorhandenheit* after *Being and Time*. The post-Heideggerian phenomenology of Emmanuel Levinas shows that handiness and presence are not simply opposed—rather, they coexist (see Harman 2009). This refines the philosophical framework underpinning the book's earlier chapters and interacts suggestively with the cases of instrumental alteration discussed here.

Recall how Rosenwinkel plays a chord on his radically retuned guitar but claims not to know what it is. In the moment, he cannot name it or place it in a theoretical system. He cannot reduce its sensual qualities—its felt shape, its sonic color, even its specific pitches—to an internal idea. Levinas associates this sort of "deconceptualization" with music (1989, 133). But more generally, this irreducibility is also crucial to his phenomenology of enjoyment, a mode of intentionality that supplements handiness. Levinas argues that tools' materiality produces a kind of sensory contact that goes beyond their usefulness (1969, 133).[25] From this perspective, my relationship to the guitar is not simply "instrumental" (that is, directed toward some purpose); it is also aesthetic. The instrument never fully disappears in its practical functioning: it is also savored like wine, caressed like a lover. Here the grooves of "Zhivago" or Metheny's interaction with the Pikasso can be understood in terms of the pleasures of repetition or the sensual interplay of the erotic.

Where earlier chapters explored instrumental extension, then, this one highlights instrumental exteriority. For Levinas, touch always encounters something exterior, something outside of myself: "In contact itself the touching and the

25. Likewise, where Merleau-Ponty focuses on bodies' competence, Levinas highlights bodies' sensible or sensual exposure to things.

touched separate, as though the touched moved off, was always already other, did not have anything in common with me" (1981, 86). Touch, both literal and figurative, depends on separation, otherness.[26] This alterity is central to Levinas's ethics—and also his aesthetics. I never totally know another person, just as I never totally know a favorite piece.[27] Earlier I broached this topic through Frith's discussion of improvisation as conversation, a responsible practice of listening and responding to another musician. In this regard Simon Critchley's summary of Levinasian ethics seems to echo Frith: "In speaking or calling or listening to the other, I am not reflecting upon the other, but I am actively and existentially engaged in a non-subsumptive relation, where I focus on the particular individual in front of me. I am not contemplating; I am conversing" (2002, 12). Frith's conversational attitude, extended to instruments, again goes beyond the transparency of *Zuhandenheit*. Playing an altered instrument, like being with the Other, is a practice of co-presence where two touch without fusing, without losing their mutual strangeness.

"Hello Music" and "Into the Dream" show how such practices unfold in time. I have suggested that they might be understood as gestures or strategies for interaction, as object-centered processes rather than musical work-objects themselves. A template for improvisation, Levinas might say, is a *how*, not a *what*. In fact, when the philosopher wishes to emphasize temporal aspects of presence he turns to musical instruments:

> Music, for example in Xenakis' "Nomos Alpha for Unaccompanied Cello," bends the quality of the notes emitted into adverbs. Every quiddity becomes a modality, the strings and wood turn into sonority.... The cello *is* a cello in the sonority that vibrates in its strings and its wood, even if it is already reverting into notes, into identities that settle into their natural places in gamuts from the acute to the grave, according to the different pitches. Thus the essence of the cello, a modality of *essence*, is temporalized in the work. (1981, 41, emphasis in original)

The sound of the instrument may "revert" to notes. It may return to the *zuhanden*, withdrawing into melody or harmony. But this never exhausts its sonority, its sensible presence. Here Levinas's work points toward a phenomenology of listening, to experiences of music's materialization, a line of thought that will be developed more fully in Chapter 6.

Though this chapter highlights the flexibility of technology and technique, it nonetheless focuses on individual, isolated instruments. In truth, however, instrumental alteration takes place within social networks that include players, instrument builders, listeners, and so on, as well as with other instruments, other

26. This underlies the paradoxes of self-touch explored by Merleau-Ponty (1968, 133). When I touch my left hand with my right, I find myself both inside and outside of my body, both touching and touched.

27. Against claims that art expresses something "more real than reality," Levinas asks, "Does not the function of art lie in *not* understanding? ... Will we then say that the artist knows and expresses the very obscurity of the real?" (1989, 131, emphasis added). On the relation between ethics and aesthetics in Levinas, see Harman (2007).

machines, other technologies. Note, for example, how Metheny describes the Pikasso II in terms of the piano, how Frith's idea of prepared guitar responds to Cage's prepared piano, or how Cage and Lachenmann describe their new approaches to the piano in terms of percussion instruments. The following chapter explores relations among instruments in the music of Johann Sebastian Bach. Yet in theorizing such connections, it cannot avoid practices of musical writing—which is to say, it must consider the relation between instruments and composition.

CHAPTER Five

Compositional Instruments

When Johann Sebastian Bach died, he owned *eight* harpsichords. And this was only part of a larger collection. The composer also had two violins plus a piccolo violin, three violas, two cellos, a lute, a viola da gamba, and a five-string viola pomposa (*NBR*, 251–52).[1] Bach rented and sold instruments. He was an expert in organ building and, of course, a renowned keyboard virtuoso. The man, by any standard, was deeply involved with instrumental technology.

Nonetheless, Bach's counterpoint is sometimes envisioned as a kind of composition without instrumentation. *The Art of Fugue*, for example, is transcribed for countless instrumental combinations but belongs exclusively to none. Related to this is the notion that *The Art of Fugue* was intended purely for contemplation, that it need not be played or heard. Though such idealist views are rare among musicologists today, they linger in popular discourse. This interpretive tradition—to quote Bach's first biographer, Johann Nikolaus Forkel—imagines the composer as "a true disembodied spirit, who soars above everything mortal" (*NBR*, 438). It understands his counterpoint as abstract rather than concrete, music of the mind and soul, not the body.

This is, again, a metaphysics of presence related to the nineteenth-century aesthetics of absolute music. Yet it would be a mistake to dismiss it too quickly, for it uncovers interesting tensions between performance and composition, between instrumental technics and a technics of musical writing.[2] A composition is realized only through some musical medium, where seemingly self-sufficient tonal patterns may be supplemented by layers of corporeal or instrumental organization. But at the same time, the composition cannot be reduced to the means of its realization. How, then, might composers respond to instruments? And how do instruments relate to each other? This chapter pursues such questions by analyzing varied instrumental resources in Bach's music, from clavier to violin to lute.

1. Throughout this chapter, I use the abbreviation *NBR* for *The New Bach Reader*, edited by David, Mendel, and Wolff (1998).

2. In a way, such tensions define the modern conception of composer and composition, which emerged in the late fifteenth century as part of a shift from improvised counterpoint toward written counterpoint (Wegman 1996). That said, impressive feats of oral counterpoint continued throughout the Renaissance (Canguilhem 2011).

Figure 5.1 Johann Sebastian Bach, excerpts from the Canon at the Twelfth from *The Art of Fugue*, BWV 1080: (a) mm. 1–11 (note the fleeting imitation in m. 9); (b) mm. 34–45 (note return to the opening in the left hand, m. 42).

Figure 5.2 Two networks for invertible counterpoint at the twelfth, which use numbers to represent generic intervals: (a) a mod-12 mapping indicates that unisons become twelfths (and vice versa), thirds become tenths (and vice versa), and so forth; (b) a mod-7 mapping gives the same practical results but asserts octave equivalence (e.g., octaves are reduced to unisons, ninths to seconds, tenths to thirds, and so on).

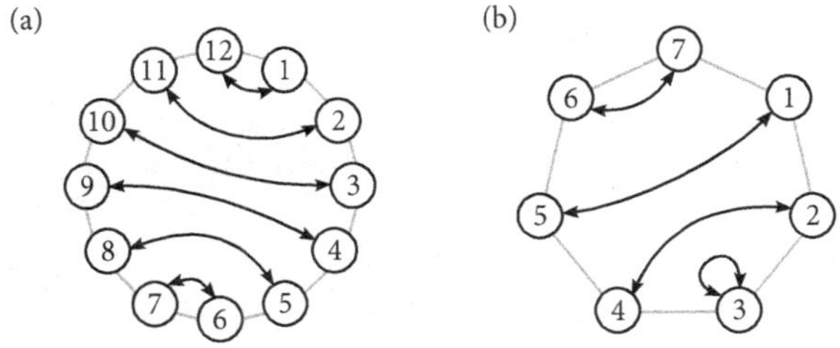

Contrapuntal Hands

A canon is a kind of self-referential music. For the *comes* (or follower) is not an independent line, but a reflection, an echo of the *dux* (leader). With the canons from *The Art of Fugue*, such reflections proliferate as in a hall of mirrors. In the Canon at the Twelfth, for example, the *comes* enters after eight measures (see Figure 5.1a). But Bach introduces additional, fleeting resemblances at a half-measure distance (m. 9, mm. 34–35, mm. 66–71). In this contrapuntal funhouse, it is sometimes hard to tell the copy from the original. When the opening subject returns in m. 42, it is no longer the leader in a canon at the twelfth but the follower in a canon at the octave (see Figure 5.1b). Bach, it turns out, has written two canons in one. Just as *comes* follows *dux*, the second canon derives systematically from the first: the lower line moves to the top, with the intervals between parts transformed according to the well-known formula for invertible counterpoint at the twelfth, a form of "double counterpoint."[3] Though the composer and his contemporaries represented these intervallic exchanges in numerical tables, they can equally be understood via modular arithmetic, as a self-mapping of the cyclic groups $\mathbb{Z}_{12}$ or $\mathbb{Z}_7$ (see Figure 5.2).

Other exchanges are possible with triple invertible counterpoint. Bach's Sinfonia in D major (BWV 789), for example, has a main subject (A) and two countersubjects—one with slower syncopations (B) and one with running sixteenth notes (C). Each of these lines can serve as top, middle, or bass part (see Figure 5.3). Following Daniel Harrison (1988), I use ordered letters to represent arrangements of these melodies. The arrangement ABC would have theme A in the highest part, B in the middle, and C in the bass. Harrison's group-theoretic analysis shows how the D-major Sinfonia explores these arrangements (31–37).[4]

3. Invertible counterpoint is a technique whereby parts in a polyphonic texture exchange registral positions (for example, the bass becomes the melody, while the melody becomes the bass). For a more detailed analysis of the *Art of Fugue*'s Canon at the Twelfth, see Yearsley (2002, 190–201).

4. The simplified analysis presented here departs from Harrison's in two ways. First, it uses Edward Gollin's revised labeling of parts, which names the opening subject A (2000, 328–34). Second,

Figure 5.3 Johann Sebastian Bach, Sinfonia in D major, BWV 789.

Figure 5.3 Continued

Figure 5.4 Transformation network for registral arrangements in Bach's D-major Sinfonia. The operation R and its inverse R^{-1} rotate the parts, whereas F flips the position of the middle and bass parts.

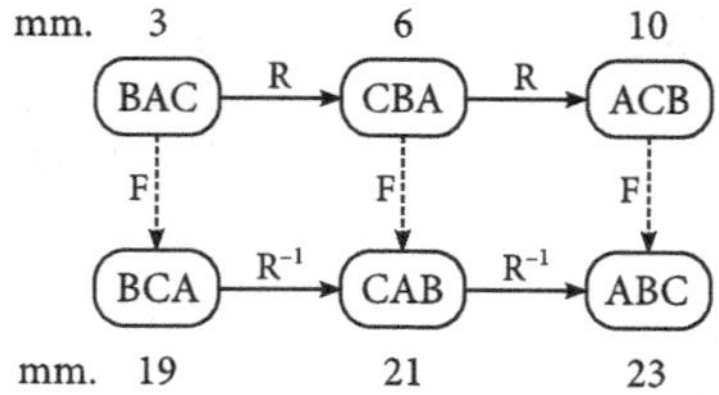

In the piece's exposition, Bach repeatedly rotates the melodies through the three registral positions: BAC becomes CBA, then ACB (see Figure 5.4 and Video 5.1). The slower countersubject, which first appears in the highest part, ultimately ends up in the bass. In the recapitulation, the rotations reverse: the bass's material goes to the middle voice, the middle part's to the top, and the top's to the bass. This second set of rotations is flipped relative to the first set—that is, the first element stays in place while the others swap positions. With its final rotation, the piece exhausts all the possible arrangements of these three melodic elements in a process that combines musical and mathematical constraints.

And physical constraints too. These pieces are both performable (meaning that they fit a keyboardist's hands) and also performative (meaning that they are showy, full of rhetorical flourishes).[5] As David Yearsley argues, "Canonic artifice and virtuosic display [in *The Art of Fugue*] are equally audible, and indeed are inseparable" (2002, 189). The contrapuntal exchanges in the Canon at the Twelfth, then, are also manual exchanges, a kind of choreography. If the hands, in this metaphor, form a dancing couple, then the left hand plays Ginger to the right hand's Fred.[6] It does all the same things, only backward. Much keyboard music—even the layout of the keyboard itself, with the higher notes on the right—is designed for a right-handed player. But Bach's keyboard canons balance the parts, challenging the player to overcome the nondominant hand's resistance. They demand not just dexterity but ambidexterity.[7]

whereas Harrison and Gollin approach triple counterpoint via the symmetric group S_3 (the group of permutations on a set with three elements), I approach it through the dihedral group D_6 (the group of symmetries of an equilateral triangle). The groups S_3 and D_6 are isomorphic. Note, however, that Harrison's permutation transformations act on thematic elements—for example, the permutation (ABC) takes A to B, B to C, and C to A, regardless of the starting arrangement—whereas my approach, based on the rotations and flips of an equilateral triangle, highlights registral positions—for example, R always takes the first position to the second, the second to the third, and the third to the first. For further discussion, see Harrison (1988, 48n12).

5. Here I am thinking of Richard Schechner's definition of performance as "showing doing" (2013, 28).
6. According to an often quoted line by the cartoonist Bob Thaves, "Ginger Rogers did everything [Fred Astaire] did ... backwards and in high heels."
7. With claviers with multiple manuals, the hands may even play on separate keyboards. Certain moments in Bach's Goldberg Variations, for example, are composed for two manuals. Their difficulty

Matthew Hall notes this correspondence between double counterpoint and ambidexterity. But he further argues that the effects of two-handedness are clearer in triple counterpoint, where one hand must realize two lines at the same time (2015, 96). For Hall, then, the arrangement ABC is either [AB]C, with two higher parts in the right hand and a lower one in the left, or A[BC], with one in the right and two in the left. Drawing on historical thoroughbass pedagogy (and, certainly, his own expertise as a keyboardist), Hall links triple counterpoint with three keyboard techniques (103):

(1) With a "contrapuntal inversion," the hands exchange material ([AB]C becomes C[AB]).
(2) With a "thoroughbass inversion," the two parts in the same hand trade places, and the other hand is unaffected ([AB]C becomes [BA]C).
(3) With a "voice transfer," the middle part switches hands ([AB]C becomes A[BC]).

Hall is dissatisfied with descriptions of triple counterpoint that emphasize "abstract permutational structure" and "disembodied, purely conceptual operations" (88), and he critiques Harrison's essay at length (92–95). Yet Hall's keyboard gestures are easily formalized and integrated into a transformational model of triple invertible counterpoint.

To do so, I use ordered pairs that combine letter arrangements discussed earlier with the +/– system used for harmonica breathing in Chapter 3.[8] Pairs with a + sign have two parts in the right hand, and pairs with a – sign have two in the left. That is, (ABC, +) is the same as [AB]C, and (ABC, –) the same as A[BC]. As such, I will continue to use this more compact notation. Note that this doubles the number of arrangements, giving twelve possibilities instead of six. Ordered pairs can also serve as transformations. The operation (R, +), for example, would rotate the parts while maintaining their distribution between the hands. This, in fact, models the first move in the D-major Sinfonia, taking [BA]C to [CB]A.

Hall's keyboard operations can fit into the model too. For convenience, I label each one with a letter: X for contrapuntal inversion between hands, Y for the thoroughbass inversion within one hand, and Z for the voice transfer involving the middle part. The operations X and Z change the sign, while Y preserves it. In the ordered-pair notation, Z is equivalent to (*e*, –), where *e* is the identity element. Technically speaking, each of these actions is an involution—an operation that is its own inversion. Like flicking a light switch, repeating an involution undoes it. Figure 5.5 maps these routes between the twelve elements in the system, giving three isographic visualizations of the same structure. Alternating between any two of the three operations produces a cycle. For present purposes,

is compounded when both hands share the same keyboard. For a reflection on the challenges of ambidexterity in Bach, see Kramer (1995, 232–42).

8. In other words, this has the structure of a direct product group, $D_6 \times \mathbb{Z}_2$.

Figure 5.5 Three isographic maps of the space created by Hall's keyboard operations, emphasizing (a) XY cycles, (b) XZ cycles, and (c) the YZ cycle. Note that there are three XY cycles (with four elements each), two XZ cycles (with six elements each), and a single twelve-element YZ cycle.

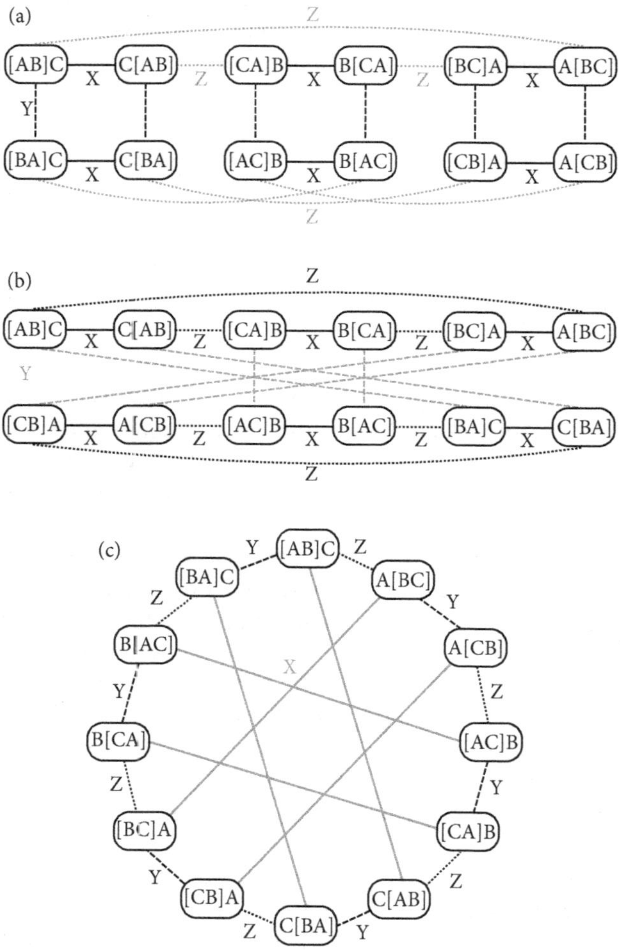

I am most interested in XZ cycles, produced by the combination of contrapuntal inversions and voice transfers. There are two such cycles. Each has six elements, and they are analogous to the hexatonic cycles used to study triadic transformations.[9]

9. Each of these XZ cycles corresponds to one of Harrison's "conjugations" (1988, 31). For an introduction to hexatonic cycles, see Cohn (2012, ch. 2). A simple exercise can give a sense of these cycles. Play any triad at the keyboard, with a single note in one hand and two in the other. Performing one of Hall's keyboard operations will give a new voicing of the chord, and repeatedly alternating between any two of them will eventually bring you back to your starting arrangement.

Figure 5.6 Transformation networks for contrapuntal-manual arrangements in Bach's D-major Sinfonia: (a) an interpretation using ordered-pair transformations; (b) an interpretation using Hall's keyboard operations. (The versions in mm. 19 and 21 can be linked by either XZX or ZXZ.)

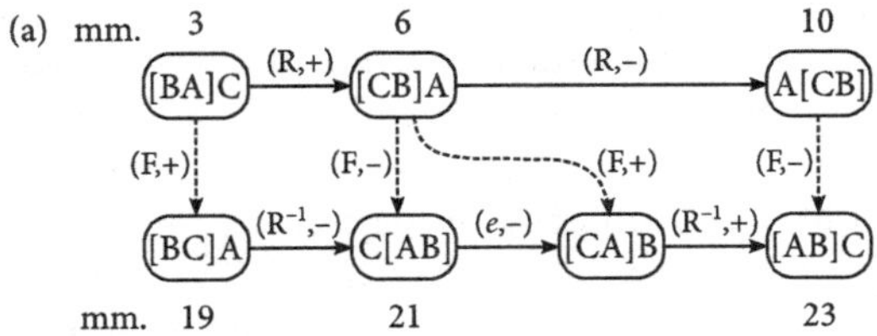

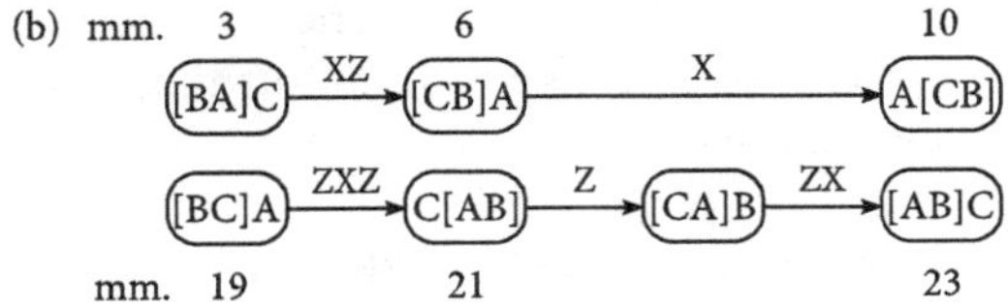

These operations and cycles offer new perspectives on the D-major Sinfonia. The two transformation networks in Figure 5.6 analyze the piece using ordered-pair operations and Hall's keyboard operations. (The contents of the networks' nodes are identical. Video 5.2 animates the analysis based on XZ cycles.) Its first arrangement, [BA]C, has two parts in the right hand. The "rotation" into the second arrangement [CB]A can be understood as (R, +), or the compound transformation XZ.[10] In the third arrangement, A[CB], the left hand takes two parts. It might be approached as a rotation with change of sign (R, –) or as a single contrapuntal inversion X. Either way, this keeps the subject A in a hand by itself and maintains the relative position of the countermelodies. Note that, from Hall's perspective, the second and third arrangements are "closer" to each other than the first and second are.[11]

The recapitulation begins with [BC]A, again keeping A on its own.[12] Thus far, each presentation of the themes has corresponded to a single element within the system. But the version in mm. 21–23 splits in two: the subject's head and tail are separated by a voice transfer, which takes C[AB] to [CA]B. And these brief parallel thirds are the only time in the piece that A and C—the more active lines—are grouped in the same hand. The concluding arrangement, [AB]C, can be understood as the thoroughbass inversion (Y) of the first.

10. Note that these operations do not commute: XZ does not give the same result as ZX (in fact, XZ is the inverse of ZX).

11. The first and third arrangements, [BA]C and A[CB], are as far away from each other as two elements in the cycle can be. In other words, they resemble hexatonic poles. Though Hall does not examine these cycles, he notes this distance between two configurations in the A♭-major Fugue from *The Well-Tempered Clavier*, Book I (2015, 104).

12. In m. 19, Bach adjusts the parts to avoid a voice crossing in the right hand (Hall 2015, 104–5). Hall suggests that the arrangement here derives from m. 6, via thoroughbass inversion (Y).

But it is also interesting to note that the ordered-pair transformations combine both R and R^{-1} with + and – exactly once. Both contrapuntal and manual operations repeat, but their repetitions do not align, increasing transformational variety.

This interpretation addresses aspects of the sinfonia's physical organization that may be felt by performers but not necessarily heard by listeners.[13] Yet this in no way invalidates the earlier, sonic analysis. The two analyses simply address different *levels*, and the relation between these levels can begin to explain how instrumentation participates in composition. To illustrate the concept of levels, Merleau-Ponty uses a linguistic analogy (1963, 91–92). A word has a motoric level, a sonic level, and a semiotic level. It can be approached as bodily action, sound, or meaning. Concentrating on a certain level may cause the others to withdraw temporarily. (If I say a word again and again and again, it seems to lose its meaning, turning weirdly into a sound my mouth makes.) Yet these levels are not opposed. Instead, they fit together. They harmonize.

It is likely that the semiotic level itself includes a similar kind of harmonization. Bidirectional influences between the motor system and language comprehension have been demonstrated in both behavioral and neuroscientific experiments, even with abstract language (Aravena et al. 2010; Guan et al., 2013). Arthur Glenberg, a psychologist who has made important contributions in this area, describes this interplay in terms of "mesh." In human cognition, he proposes, affordances in the environment are meshed with invisible properties, known through prior experience. Through this process, "the path becomes the path *home* and the cup becomes *my* cup" (Glenberg 1997, 4).[14] The perceived object is meshed with concepts, memories, or goals.

A similar integration is involved in composition, for music, too, has motoric, sonic, and semiotic features. In this view, composition is not just about putting together notes. It is also about putting together these different levels. In the D-major Sinfonia, Bach negotiates contrapuntal, corporeal, and instrumental constraints. He avoids combinations that would be tonally but not physically viable (for example, keeping A and C in separate hands). The relation between these levels is not fixed or deterministic. Composers often use notation to work through ideas, and there are always possibilities for alternate fingerings and so forth. Still, a piece can be performed only if it has been adequately "instrumented." From this perspective, instrumentation is not a mere adjunct to composition. Instrumentation is, instead, a fundamental part of composition, for just as counterpoint coordinates melody and harmony, instrumentation coordinates tonal and performative patterns.

13. Where my interpretation focuses on the disposition of *hands*, Bungert (2015) focuses on *fingering* in the Corrente from Bach's Keyboard Partita in E minor.
14. Here Glenberg emphasizes different modes of experience: I may attend to patterns in the environment, or I may also consciously suppress them (1997, 3).

Transcription and Instrumental Ensembles

But what about transcription? Here the composer and the arranger are often different people. In such cases, it seems that composition precedes instrumentation, that the instrumental level changes without affecting a piece's identity. This kind of faithful transcription, however, requires particular technical conditions. It is possible because instruments are not isolated, but joined in a larger technological ecosystem.

For Heidegger, such coordination characterizes "useful things" in general. "Strictly speaking," he writes, "there 'is' no such thing as *a* useful thing" (2010, 68). A utensil is encountered not on its own, but in some context. This is a context of use—since by definition I take up a useful thing *in order to* do something with it—and it is also a context of other utensils. "Useful things," the philosopher continues, "always are *in terms of* their belonging to other useful things: writing utensils, pen, ink, paper, desk blotter, table, lamp, furniture, windows, doors, room" (68). Heidegger figures this "in order to" and this "in terms of" as a kind of reference. Pen and paper "refer" to each other, to their own materials, and to the activity of writing. All of this is readily translated into musical terms. My violin, bow, shoulder rest, rosin, mute, case—they belong or refer to each other, as do various parts of the violin itself (tuning pegs, strings, nut, bridge, tailpiece, fine tuners). I use the violin in order to play fiddle tunes while my daughters dance, to sight-read a string quartet with friends, to perform in an orchestra or a band.

Among other things, then, the violin alludes to other violins, to violas and cellos. It refers to other instruments that it plays with, to a greater ensemble. At the beginning of an orchestra concert, it is possible to hear varied instruments being calibrated to the same standard. Players adjust their instruments to the oboe's A440, while also checking characteristic notes or patterns (such as open strings). Here it is worth noting that mutual tuning of instruments precedes the standardization of pitch and that tuning to a unison is just one way of "sounding together." For example, consider the ocarina duets played by the Venda people of southern Africa, analyzed by John Blacking (1959). The *tshipotoliyo* ocarina, made from fruit shells, is used to produce four tones, but the exact notes are unpredictable. A single ocarina's pitches change over time and are easily adjusted by the embouchure, and multiple ocarinas generally produce different notes. In fact for players of these duets, ocarinas with the same pitches do not "sound well together" (17). They find this musically uninteresting (19). Keeping that in mind, standard tuning should not be naturalized. This kind of tuning is, rather, a musical technology that affords unison playing and the transfer of pitch patterns from one instrument to another.

Notation plays a role here too. Many keyboard instruments even have built-in music stands, which refer clearly to scores. For Bach and his contemporaries, the keyboard correlated with various kinds of notation, both German keyboard tablature and "Italian tablature" (that is, staff notation). German tablature involves a one-to-one relation between symbols and keys on the instrument, since it differentiates among octaves but not enharmonically equivalent pitches. C♯4 and D♭4, for example, are represented by the same sign, since both are played on the black key between C4 and D4. While staff notation distinguishes between C♯s and D♭s, it involves an opposition of natural and accidental notes that generally maps onto the instrumental opposition of white and black keys. With few exceptions, notes bearing flats and sharps fall on black keys, and the resulting key signatures frame different tonal keys as inflected deviations from a white-note mode. Bach often used German tablature for compositional sketches, including parts for non-keyboard instruments (Marshall 1972, 141). And staff notation, of course, was used for diverse vocal and instrumental parts. Both forms of notation, then, were situated in a broader technical context, referring to notes and to instruments. In this view, notation achieves a quasi-abstract representation of tones not by eliminating instrumental references but by multiplying them. A shared notational system, like a shared tuning, makes it easier for multi-instrumentalists like Bach to realize violin or vocal parts on the keyboard, to translate among performance media.

Yet such translations are rarely exact. They require shared pitch affordances, involving scale, range, and texture. It would be difficult to transcribe Bach's D-major Sinfonia for a solo violin, though it works well for a string trio. (Zoltán Kodály boldly transcribed Bach's BWV 903 Chromatic Fantasy for a solo viola, but that piece does not combine independent contrapuntal lines.) Even closely related instruments, though, may diverge in significant ways.

Compare the organ, harpsichord, and clavichord.[15] Their keyboards support very similar actions in performance. Still, their ranges vary, from the smallest spinet to the largest pipe organ. And this involves not only the length of the keyboard but also the number of keyboards. Organs and pedal harpsichords include keyboards for the feet, and pieces like the Goldberg Variations exploit multiple manuals (without them, the hands run over each other).[16] Variations in timbre and loudness relate to the instruments' social affordances or musical environments: the organ's sonic power makes it arguably the most public of keyboards (except perhaps the carillon); the harpsichord's cutting tone suits its continuo role in large ensembles; and the clavichord's softness fits more intimate settings. Further differences involve action-to-sound conversion. With organ or harpsichord, the force of the player's fingers is not reflected in the dynamics. On these instruments, in contrast to clavichord, the player does not require an even or expressive touch. Thus C. P. E. Bach states, "A good clavichordist makes an accomplished harpsichordist, but not the reverse" (1949, 37–38). The clavichord also affords modification of the tone during play: the player can raise the pitch to create a kind of vibrato, or

15. Though I consider the clavichord here, there were no references during Bach's lifetime to his playing clavichord. As David Ledbetter explains, the first such reference was made by Johann Friedrich Agricola in 1775 (2002, 18–19). In 1802, Bach's biographer J. N. Forkel claimed that the clavichord was the composer's favorite clavier—but this statement is tied up with anti-French nationalism, since he considered the clavichord more expressive and, therefore, more "German."

16. Of course, temperament was also not standardized in Bach's day, meaning that not all instruments were suited to the keys the composer explored in his *Well-Tempered Clavier*.

Figure 5.7 Comparison of Bach's transcriptions of Concerto in C by Johann Ernst, Prince of Saxe-Weimar, for clavier (BWV 984) and for organ (BWV 595), mm. 1–6.

Bebung.[17] Finally, the organ's unlimited sustaining capacities contrast with the others' rapidly decaying percussive sound.

Such differences are evident in J. S. Bach's two transcriptions of a concerto by Johann Ernst, Prince of Saxe-Weimar—one for organ (BWV 595) and one for clavier (BWV 984). The piece begins with a two-measure subject that moves from tonic to dominant, which alternates with episodic sequences. To be sure, the differences between the two versions go beyond instrumentation. The organ version, for example, is longer, having more iterations of the subject. Yet the instruments' distinct affordances are also immediately apparent. From the start, the organ pedals add a bass part that constitutes its own rhythmic-metric layer in a tiered polyphonic texture (see Figure 5.7).[18] In the first sequential episode, the hands move

17. For a discussion of this idiomatic clavichord technique, see Brauchli (1998, 267–74).

18. Auerbach (2008) theorizes different kinds of tiered polyphony, with analytical applications to Brahms's piano music.

Figure 5.8 Sequential episode from BWV 984, mm. 14–17, and BWV 595, mm. 20–23. Note the organ's alternation between *Oberwerk* and *Rückpositiv*.

in parallel, alternating at the half-measure between more widely and more closely spaced consonances (mm. 3–6). On the clavier, this division is based on the opposition of tenths and sixths. On the organ, however, Bach also switches between manuals, setting the *Oberwerk* (the main manual or "great organ") against the secondary *Rückpositiv* (the department at the player's back, typically used for soloistic or coloristic effects). The organ thus offers a timbral, spatial, and kinesthetic juxtaposition that the composer exploits throughout BWV 595.

In the second sequential episode, Bach interpolates solo moments on the *Rückpositiv* (see Figure 5.8). As his beaming shows, this instrumental shift suggests an antiphonal texture that is not necessarily apparent in the clavier version.[19] A later variant of this sequence introduces a canon at the fifth below over a new bass line (see Figure 5.9). On the clavier, the left hand takes the bass while the right

19. For a discussion of instrumentation and perceived textural organization, see De Souza (2015). Bach's repetition of the bass figure here also clarifies the similarity between this descending fifths sequence and the first.

Figure 5.9 Variation on the previous figure's sequence from BWV 984, mm. 43–46, and BWV 595, mm. 58–61, with a canon in the organ manuals.

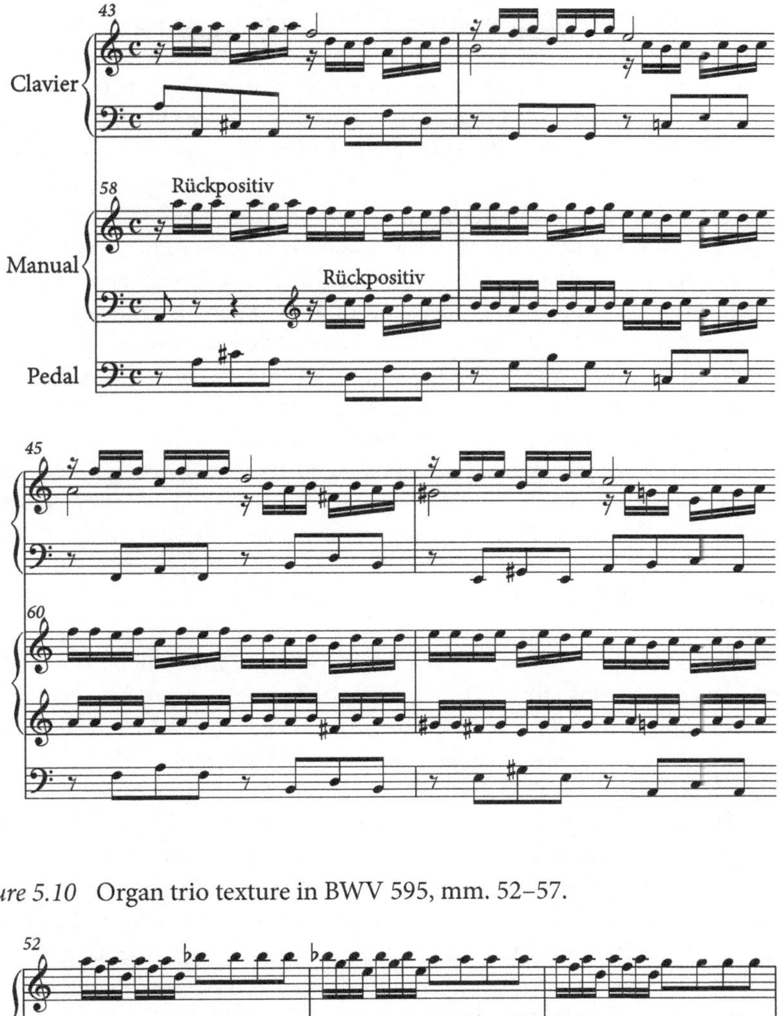

Figure 5.10 Organ trio texture in BWV 595, mm. 52–57.

has both parts of the canon; on the organ, the feet cover the bass, and each upper part is given to a single hand in a busier *Rückpositiv* passage. While both versions offer a three-part texture here, the performative realization is distinct.

The independence of the organist's hands and feet is perhaps even clearer in the preceding section (mm. 52–57), which has no counterpart in the clavier version (see Figure 5.10). Such passages recall a Germanic "organ trio" tradition, in which three lines are mapped onto three keyboards, realized by the organist's two hands and feet. "It is as if each part of the body must have a mind of its own," says Yearsley (2012, 50). "Anyone who has played a trio at the organ ... knows what thinking this way feels like in the body."

This is not to say that Bach's clavier version is a lesser imitation of the organ work. The clavier's unique passages often highlight the linear dimension of the keyboard instead of the contrast between multiple manuals. The sweeping contrary motion of mm. 26–29 indexes both the spatiality of the instrument and the symmetry of the player's body (see Figure 5.11). While the melodic material of the organ version partially overlaps with this passage, its texture is wholly different (continuing the interplay of *Oberwerk* and *Rückpositiv*).

Obviously these pieces are closely related, just as the instruments are closely related. Yet subtle differences between the versions also show the *limits* of translation, which are often more immediate for performers. Parallel passages in Figure 5.9 may sound similar but feel different. This kinesthetic element of the music, which is ultimately grounded in particular instrumental spaces, is often "lost in translation."

Bach's transcriptions, then, show him attending to instrumental affordances. Thanks to connections among instruments, he is able to reproduce the piece in another medium. Yet adjustments at the instrumental level affect tonal organization too. In this sense, the instruments might be understood as tools for investigating a piece. As Christoph Wolff puts it, "organ and clavier [served] as indispensable pieces of equipment in Bach's experimental musical laboratory" (2000, 8). The analogy is worth pursuing, since scientific instruments, like musical ones, are found in ensembles. For a laboratory's results to be directly comparable, its scientific instruments must be calibrated to each other; for its experiments to be repeated consistently in other labs, the instruments must also be standardized. Likewise ensembles of musical instruments are tuned to each other and standardized, so that they can consistently reproduce particular compositions. For the historian of science Peter Galison (2005), material culture thus supports theoretical culture; instrumental conditions facilitate generalization. Yet he argues that generalization does not simply involve "translation" of preexisting meanings. Generalization, for Galison, is fundamentally a form of delocalization. It involves negotiations, changing contexts, communication through pidgins (that is, "exchange languages" that are both hybrid and simplified). In brief, transcription both preserves and transforms. And this suggests, again, that composition and instrumentation are not opposed but entwined.

Figure 5.11 Comparison of BWV 984, mm. 25–30, and BWV 595, mm. 38–43. Note contrary motion in the clavier.

The Violin as Compositional Instrument

Two passages from Carl Philipp Emanuel Bach reveal his father's engagement with possibilities on both contrapuntal and instrumental levels:

> When he listened to a rich and many-voiced fugue, he could soon say, after the first entries of the subjects, what contrapuntal devices it would be possible to apply, and which of them the composer by rights ought to apply, and on such occasions, when I was standing next to him, and he had voiced his surmises to me, he would joyfully nudge me when his expectations were fulfilled. (*NBR*, 397)

In a fugal exposition, the elder Bach heard possibilities, or almost obligations. He sensed immediately whether a subject could (or should) be combined with itself in stretto, whether a subject-countersubject pair could (or should) be inverted at the octave or twelfth. Bach, in other words, was attuned to *contrapuntal affordances*. Here, again, expertise "appears in the way the world shows up" (Dreyfus 2002, 373). To write the rest of the fugue, then, the contrapuntist pursues tendencies that seem latent in the material. The subject constrains a composer, just as the instrument constrains an improviser—shaping but never determining the music.

Yet C. P. E. Bach also suggests that his father's ability to play various instruments informed his compositional practice:

> In his youth, and until the approach of old age, he played the violin cleanly and penetratingly, and thus kept the orchestra in better order than he could have done with the harpsichord. He understood to perfection the possibilities of all stringed instruments. This is evidenced by his solos for the violin and for the violoncello without bass. (*NBR*, 397)

These solos are difficult but highly idiomatic. Through open strings, multiple stops, and string crossing, Bach creates rich polyphonic textures with a single violin. This is particularly notable in fugues and in movements where a continuous bass line supports an upper melody (such as the Andante from the Second Sonata or the Adagio from the Third Sonata). If the pieces are transposed into other keys, many of these instrumental features are obscured, and certain passages become impracticable. Figure 5.12, for example, presents two versions of an excerpt from the Second Sonata's Fugue. In the original key of A minor, my left hand stays in first position throughout. The three contrapuntal voices map onto the three strings in play (the only exception is the brief G-sharp neighbor note in m. 6).[20] Transposing the passage down to F minor introduces uncomfortable leaps: since it is impossible to simultaneously play E♭4 and G4 on the D string, I must jump to third position for the second half of m. 5, then back again; to

20. Throughout this fugue, the descending chromatic figure introduced in mm. 5–7 never crosses strings. Its semitones always move along the string. This is also true of the figure's inversion, which first appears at m. 239. In terms of the transformational model of fretboard space developed earlier in the book, this figure's falling semitones are always of the form (0, –1), not (–1, +6).

Figure 5.12 Johann Sebastian Bach, Fugue from Sonata no. 2 in A minor for Unaccompanied Violin, BWV 1003, mm. 5–9. The original key stays in first position, with each contrapuntal voice effectively staying on a single string. Transposed to F minor, however, the passage demands frequent position changes and difficult triple stops. (The use of arrows to indicate position changes follows Argent [2000, 19].)

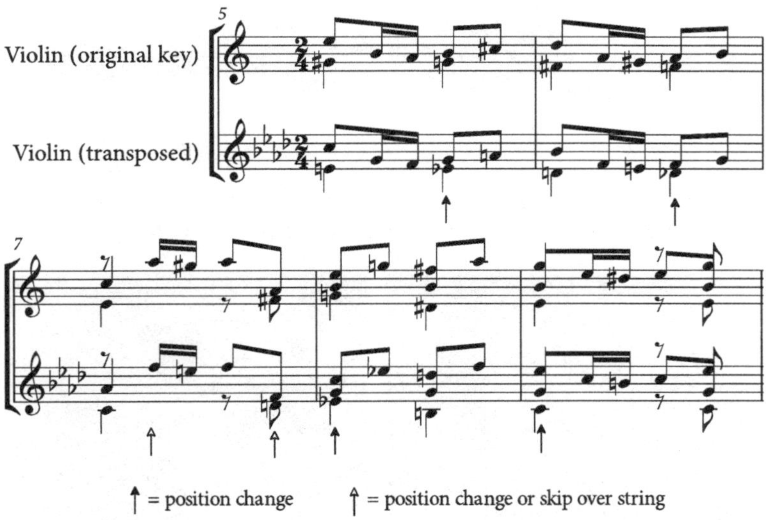

catch the high entry of the subject in m. 7, I must either shift positions again or skip the bow over the A string. Using open strings does not make the passage easier. While not impossible, the F-minor version is significantly less idiomatic, less satisfying in my hands.

Bach's solo string music, then, goes beyond competent instrumentation. In these compositions, Bach responds to instrumental affordances as much as contrapuntal ones. He investigates musical possibilities that are specific to the interactions between four strings, four fingers, and a bow. The instrument, then, seems not to express preexisting ideas but to reveal new ones. It shapes both the invention of musical material and its disposition throughout a piece.[21]

Consider the Prelude from the Third Partita in E major for Unaccompanied Violin (BWV 1006). After a two-measure introductory gesture, the piece launches into the running sixteenth notes that will continue until the dominant of the final cadence (mm. 134–35; see Video 5.3▶). Bach then juxtaposes two figures that form the *inventio* of the movement: a figure with a repeated pedal note in mm. 3 and 5 and a scalar figure in mm. 4 and 6 (see Figure 5.13). In the pedaling figure, by contrast, the left hand is anchored: my index finger stops two strings at the same location, forming a perfect-fifth frame. This creates the repeated B4 on the A string,

21. I borrow this distinction between invention and disposition from Laurence Dreyfus's *Bach and the Patterns of Invention* (1996).

Figure 5.13 Johann Sebastian Bach, Prelude from Partita no. 3 in E major for Unaccompanied Violin, BWV 1006, mm. 1–6. The opposition of string crossing and scalar motion in mm. 3–6 forms the basic material for the movement.

Figure 5.14 Motion-capture images tracing bow-hand movement in the Prelude from BWV 1006: (a) string crossing in m. 3; (b) scalar figure in m. 4.

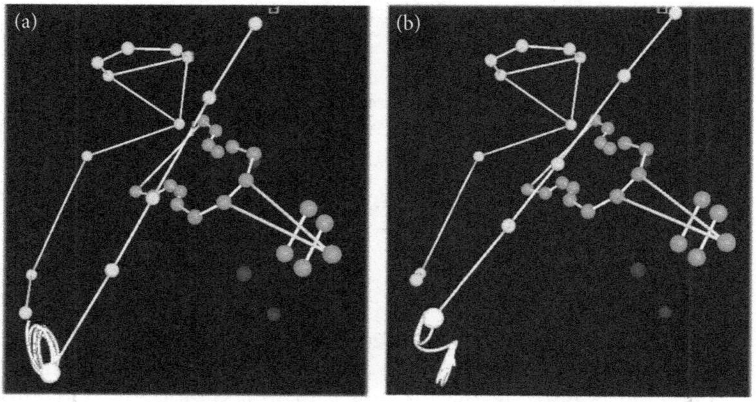

as the second through fourth fingers walk up and down the D string.[22] Meanwhile my bow moves in a simple string-crossing routine, pulling down on the D string and pushing up on the A string. As the motion capture in Video 5.4 shows, my bow hand moves in a circle (traced in white; see Figure 5.14a). In the scales, mobile fingers form a single melody, descending along the string with linear fingering (4–3–2–1).[23] Here the bowing, traced in red on the video, involves more of a back-and-forth motion, shifting down with the change of string (Figure 5.14b).

Bach focuses on string crossing in mm. 13–28 (see Figure 5.15).[24] The technical term for such bowing patterns, which combine open and stopped strings,

22. This movement resembles the contextual operation K in the analysis of Rosenwinkel's "Zhivago" in Chapter 4, in which notes in a higher position were held constant while other fingers moved along a lower string.
23. Here I use violinists' numbering of fingers (which, of course, differs from pianists'): the index finger is 1; the middle finger, 2; the ring finger, 3; the little finger, 4.
24. Uniquely, the higher variation on this figure in mm. 9–12 does not necessarily involve string crossing: if it is played exclusively on the E string, though, it introduces an open-string pedal that will be important in the following section.

Figure 5.15 Johann Sebastian Bach, Prelude from Partita no. 3 in E major for Unaccompanied Violin, BWV 1006, mm. 13–28.

is "bariolage" (from the French, meaning "odd mixture of colors"). First, in mm. 13–16, he explores the instrumental gesture established in m. 3: crossing back and forth between two strings with movement along the lower string (see Videos 5.5–5.6▶). Bach is careful to indicate the string crossing, notating two melodic strands with opposed beaming. Note, however, that most of the pitches on the lower A string sound *higher* than the open E-string pedal! Basic bowing and fingerboard schemas repeat; the pitch relationship between melodic strands does not. Throughout this passage, I play the "same" E5 in two different places, a clear instance of the violin's many-to-one place-to-pitch mapping.

In m. 17, Bach adds a third string to the pattern (see Video 5.7▶). Down bows stay on the A string, but up bows alternate between the E and D strings. In accordance with the method of numbering strings introduced in Chapter 3 (which labels the highest string as 1), this pattern of strings is represented as 2–1–2–3.[25] The transformational graphs in Figure 5.16 isolate moves in cross-string space: they show how Bach expands the bariolage by taking the original two-string pattern (−1, +1) and adding on its inversion (+1, −1). The central

25. To be clear, the E string = 1, the A string = 2, the D string = 3, and the G string = 4. These numbers are conventionally used by violinists, though they typically write string numbers in Roman numerals.

Figure 5.16 Transformational graphs for cross-string moves in the Prelude from BWV 1006. The first graph (a) represents the crossing introduced in m. 3 on the D and A strings (and repeated in mm. 13–16 on the A and E strings): it moves up one string (−1), then back down (+1). A second graph (b) expands this to the three-string bariolage from mm. 17–28. The bowing pattern starts in the middle node of the graph (on the A string): the first loop (−1, +1), on the right, doubles the smaller graph (moving up to the E string and back), while the second (+1, −1), on the left, inverts it (moving down to the D string and back).

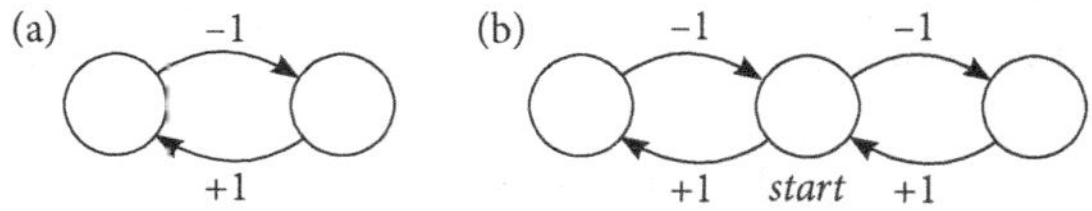

Figure 5.17 Motion-capture image tracing bow-hand movement in the three-string bariolage pattern from the BWV 1006 Prelude, mm. 17–28.

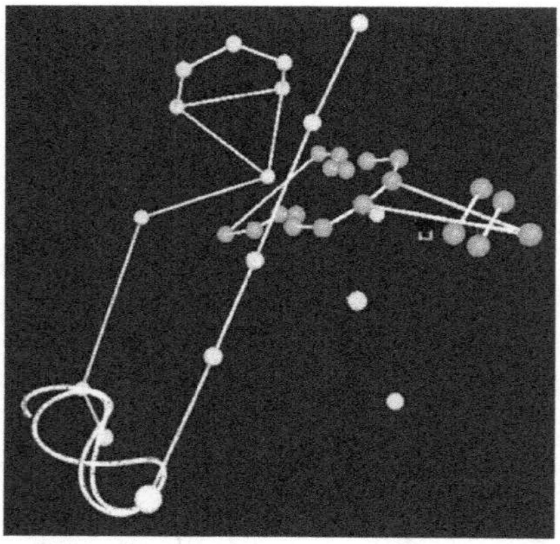

string in the pattern—here the A string—forms a balance point, from which I reach up and down. This means that that the bow hand moves in a figure eight (see Video 5.8 and Figure 5.17), doubling the loops shown Videos 5.4 and 5.6.

At first the three-string bariolage sounds a repeated third—the pitch E5 is alternately presented on the open E string and high on the D string. Then, continuing the established instrumental strategy, the position on the lowest string moves while those on the upper strings remain constant (mm. 17–19). This downward motion spreads to the A string in the following chain of 7–6 suspensions (mm. 20–28). Two-measure-long "links" in this chain repeat fingerboard movement exactly—the A-string note moves down, then the D-string note—but because the open-string pedal never moves, they are not pitch transpositions of each other

Figure 5.18 Transformational network for the Prelude from BWV 1006, mm. 21–28, showing movement in fingerboard space. Lines without arrowheads correspond to the identity element (0, 0). The lower two strings alternately descend one step while the top string remains open.

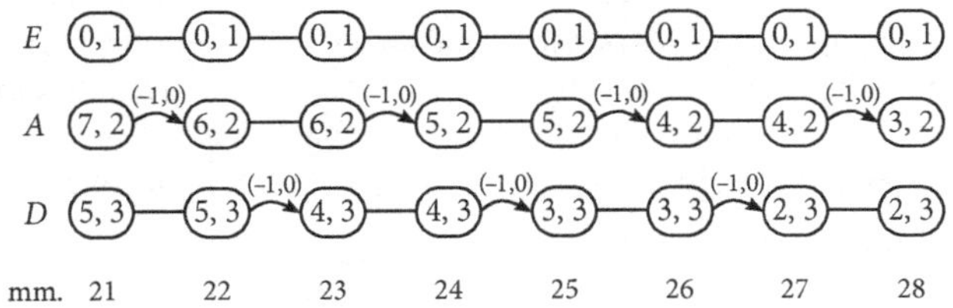

Figure 5.19 Johann Sebastian Bach, Prelude from Partita no. 3 in E major for Unaccompanied Violin, BWV 1006, mm. 43–50.

(see Figure 5.18).[26] Here the piece comes closest to chordal figuration preludes like the Prelude in C major from the first book of *The Well-Tempered Clavier*. The passage from mm. 13–28 will reappear, transposed down a fifth—that is, down one string (0, +1)—in mm. 63–78. Here the pedal note is an open A string.[27]

Before that, though, Bach turns the bariolage patterns inside out (mm. 43–50; see Figure 5.19). Mobile and fixed strings are flipped: the lowest string, not the highest, holds the pedal note; the note on the D string generally moves each bar;

26. The transformational model of fingerboard space underlying this network is isomorphic to the fretboard-space model discussed in Chapters 3 and 4. However, unlike the fully chromatic steps of guitar frets, here I represent steps on the violin's fingerboard in terms of diatonic "positions." For example, "second position" (2, *x*) is found two letter names above the open string, regardless of accidentals. (Second position on the A string, then, would involve either C♮ or C♯.) While this approach involves some ambiguity (which could be problematic in highly chromatic situations), it has the benefit of following an important way that violinists conceptualize space on their instrument. Bow direction could easily be added to this model, through the +/– system used for harmonica breathing.
27. As Joel Lester discusses, this cross-string transposition strategy appears elsewhere in Bach's oeuvre for solo violin, as in opening movements from the G-minor and A-minor Sonatas (1999, 52).

Figure 5.20 Transformational networks for three-string bariolage patterns in the Prelude from BWV 1006. Numbers in the nodes refer to strings (1 = E string, 2 = A string, 3 = D string, 4 = G string), and labels on arrows represent cross-string transformations. In (a), the formation on the right (for mm. 43–50) reverses the ordering from the left (for mm. 17–28). The spatial network in (b) shows "prime forms" of three-string bariolage patterns with four elements and adjacent string motion. Bach uses the patterns on the left side of the network, which have similar contours in string space. Both move to higher strings, then lower ones. (Ret stands for retrograde, and I for inversion.)

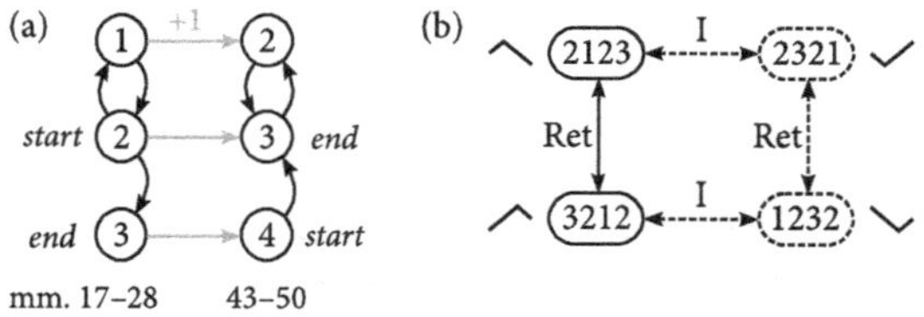

the A string, each beat. Each measure's initial four-note group reverses the three-string bowing pattern, while the remaining groups reverse the two-string pattern.

The transformation networks in Figure 5.20 help clarify this reversal in cross-string space. The string sequence 4–3–2–3 is a backward, one-string-down version of 2–1–2–3 (see Figure 5.20a). Again the pattern orbits a central string. But with down bows on the outer strings, it feels as though I am *reaching in* to the repeated string, instead of *reaching out* from it.[28] Now I move across three strings at the beginning of the pattern rather than the end. Yet as the spatial network of Figure 5.20b shows, this reversed string sequence (unlike its unused inversions) preserves the string-space contour of the original: both cross to higher strings, then come back down. Video 5.9▶ shows how my bow hand again moves through a figure eight—but with the direction reversed, relative to the pattern in Video 5.8—then cycles between the two higher strings (see Figure 5.21).

Throughout, these extended string-crossing passages are interposed with more linear sections based on the scalar figure that first appeared in m. 4. Without going into more detail, I will note that bariolage recurs near the end of the piece—for example, between mm. 109–12 and leading up to the chords of the final cadence (mm. 130–33). Here again the notes on the A string ascend above the open E5.

In this prelude, Bach treats string-crossing patterns the way that he often treats melodic or contrapuntal themes: repeating, extending, inverting them. This persistent development of an instrumental gesture, though, involves constantly varied pitch material. As abstract sequences of notes, these passages seem to have little in common; as I play them on the violin, they feel wonderfully connected.

Of course, it is impossible to know how Bach used the instrument in composing this piece. He might have generated ideas by improvising, then worked them out on paper. He might have composed on paper but tested out finished passages

28. While some editions add slurs to this pattern, these are not present in the autograph manuscript (unlike, say, the slurs in the string crossing that leads to the final cadence).

Figure 5.21 Motion-capture image tracing bow-hand movement in the three-string bariolage pattern from the BWV 1006 Prelude, mm. 43–50.

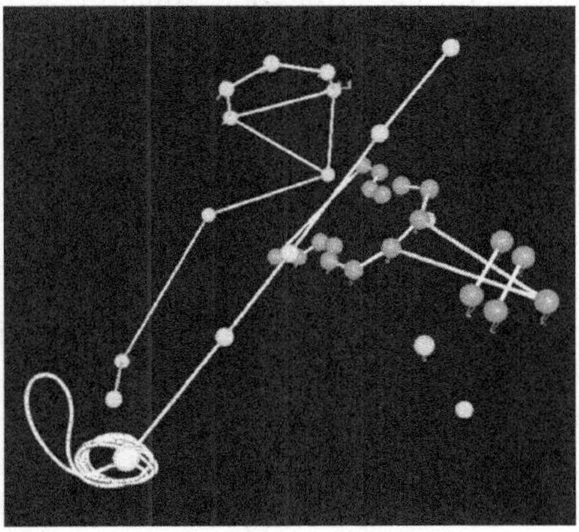

on the instrument. C. P. E. Bach remembered his father using both strategies (*NBR*, 399). On another level, though, such details are unimportant: either way, Bach certainly drew on his embodied know-how as a violinist. Just as instrumental practice may drive improvisation, such know-how becomes a resource for composition.[29] The composer's instrument-specific habits and auditory-motor connections reveal certain possibilities, shaping the way that musical affordances show up. This goes beyond *instrumental composition*—that is, writing music that is playable or idiomatic. The violin here functions as a conceptual tool and a source of material; it becomes a *compositional instrument.*

Idiomatic Translations

Bach's student Johann Friedrich Agricola reported that the composer often played his solo violin pieces on the keyboard, filling out the harmony as needed (David and Mendel 1945, 447). An autograph manuscript from the 1730s presents a suggestive record of this practice: here Bach recasts the E-major Partita, transposing it down an octave and adding a bass line. The range and texture of this arrangement—which is cataloged as BWV 1006a—suggest the lute, and it is often played on this instrument. The composer also arranged the Partita's Prelude for organ and orchestra as part of his civic cantata *Wir danken dir, Gott, wir danken dir* (BWV 29). With the two versions of the C-major Concerto, Bach translates between instruments with similar interfaces, much as one might translate a text from French to Spanish, drawing frequently on cognates. With his arrangements of the violin piece, though, the instruments involved are less similar. The bariolage

29. This aligns with the computational model created by Huron and Berec (2009), which suggested that composers who can play the trumpet write more idiomatically for the instrument.

passages from the original, in particular, serve to illustrate sonic and physical translations.

Playing the prelude on the lute brings out similarities to the violin. With both, a tiered array allows for the juxtaposition of strings, the elaboration of held, shifting chordal shapes. The left-hand fingers stop the strings, while the right hand activates the sound. Yet there is an important difference in this action-to-sound conversion: the difference between the violinist's bow and the lutenist's fingertips. The bow is a tense line of horsehair drawn down or pushed up, sustaining sound as it rubs against the string. As a single surface, this allows for the activation of multiple strings—but they must be adjacent. This unity of the bow contributes to a concept of string crossing that seems less important with the lute, where each right-hand finger can independently activate a string. These plucking fingers, unlike the scraping bow, make momentary, percussive contact with the string. They can also move up or down—as in strumming—but lutenists' fingers (like classical guitarists'), typically pluck upward. The difference between the violinist's bow hand and the lutenist's plucking hand can be summed up by a distinction, articulated by the philosopher Raymond Tallis (2003), between the brachiochiral hand—the hand at the end of the arm, which reaches and gestures—and the chirodigital hand—the hand with fingers that can tie knots, that can count, that can play the flute.

This flexibility in plucking correlates with two other differences. The first is the addition of bass notes, played with the thumb. These may add to the original melody (see Figure 5.22a) or be pulled out from the original in an idiomatic fingerpicking routine (mm. 43–50, see Figure 5.22b).

A second, subtler difference involves the instruments' contrasting sizes. Given the lute's longer neck (and string length), the span of my hand covers fewer semitones. On the violin, I can easily reach an octave from my index finger to my little finger on the string above. On the lute, this is not possible: for example, I cannot set up the chain of 7–6 suspensions in mm. 20–28 on adjacent strings. Clearly this also relates to differences in tuning. Because the violin is tuned in fifths, the repeat in mm. 63–78 involves physical transposition—down one string (−1, 0)—as well as pitch transposition (down a perfect fifth). On the lute, this repeated passage involves new fingering, since the instrument was typically tuned to a D-minor chord—to (A2, D3, F3, A3, D4, F4)—above unfingered diapason courses. BWV 1006a is typically played in F major to take advantage of the open-string $\hat{1}$ and $\hat{3}$. Even so, it is less idiomatic under the lutenist's hands—like most of Bach's lute works, it needs creative adjustments to work. (Though Bach owned a lute, he was not a skilled lutenist.)

Obviously these two versions have much in common—bariolage patterns change to fingerpicking patterns. At the same time, the lower register and bass make it sound typical of the lute. Toccata-like chord patterns over ringing pedal notes, for example, are particularly characteristic of this instrument. And David Ledbetter notes the prelude's resemblance to an undated caprice, possibly by Bach's lutenist friend Silvius Leopold Weiss (2009, 53–54) (see Figure 5.23).

In his BWV 29 cantata, Bach transcribes the piece for an ensemble. The featured organ part, however, is an idiomatic keyboard version of the piece. Here Bach changes the key—down a step to D major—to accommodate his three natural trumpets. And he emphasizes the original opposition between scalar and

Figure 5.22 Johann Sebastian Bach, excerpts from BWV 1006a Prelude for Lute: (a) mm. 125–30, with thumbed bass notes *added* to the violin's original melody; (b) mm. 43–50, with bass notes *extracted* from the violin's original melody.

string-crossing material by setting the former as tuttis and the latter as solos (see Figure 5.24).

The "string-crossing" pattern, however, works differently in the linear space of the keyboard: it becomes a back-and-forth turning of the hand that is anchored by a boundary digit, either thumb or little finger. In mm. 13–16, the same directed-stem notation Bach used to indicate string crossing, in this context, denotes the disposition of the keyboardist's hands (see Figure 5.25).[30] Instead of a single hand

30. Peter Williams (1994) discusses notation and hand distribution in the music of Bach and his contemporaries.

Figure 5.23 Silvius Leopold Weiss (?), Caprice for Lute (from Ledbetter 2009, 54).

moving along the strings (connected to a neighboring string by the movement of bow or plucking), the organist's hands intertwine in a kind of bimanual hocketing. With this passage, the keyboard—with its one-to-one place-to-pitch mapping—offers greater congruence between instrumental and sonic spaces. The repeated D5s occur in only one location.

From mm. 17–28, Bach makes more free translation to the organ idiom. Without the complication of the three-string bariolage pattern, m. 17 would simply present alternating thirds. Instead the composer refigures this passage. The chromatic passing tone (from the violin's D string) is lost as Bach introduces a more expansive dipping gesture, which resembles the original's triple-string-crossing movement more than its sound (see Figure 5.25). The following chain of suspensions (mm. 20–28) turns into Alberti-bass-like broken chords over a pulsing bass pedal.

While this section is translated more freely, the sinfonia as a whole bears traces of its violinistic origins. I find the solo organ part thrilling—with its constant linear motion, skipping across the keyboard—but it is hardly a typical texture for the instrument. It almost treats the organ as a monophonic instrument.[31] The performer's right hand plays no simultaneities, not even at the final cadence, where the violin

31. This resembles the BWV 964 keyboard arrangement of the Allegro from Bach's Second Sonata for Unaccompanied Violin in A minor (BWV 1003). Here the distribution of the melody between the hands would seem to affect performers' sense of grouping (if not listeners').

Figure 5.24 Johann Sebastian Bach, Sinfonia from *Wir danken dir, Gott, wir danken dir* (BWV 29), mm. 1–7. String-crossing passages from BWV 1006 become organ solos, while scalar passages become tutti passages.

Figure 5.25 Comparison of Prelude from BWV 1006 and organ part from Sinfonia BWV 29, mm. 13–29. In mm. 13–16, string crossing maps onto bimanual interlocking. After that, Bach writes an idiomatic keyboard figure for the organ.

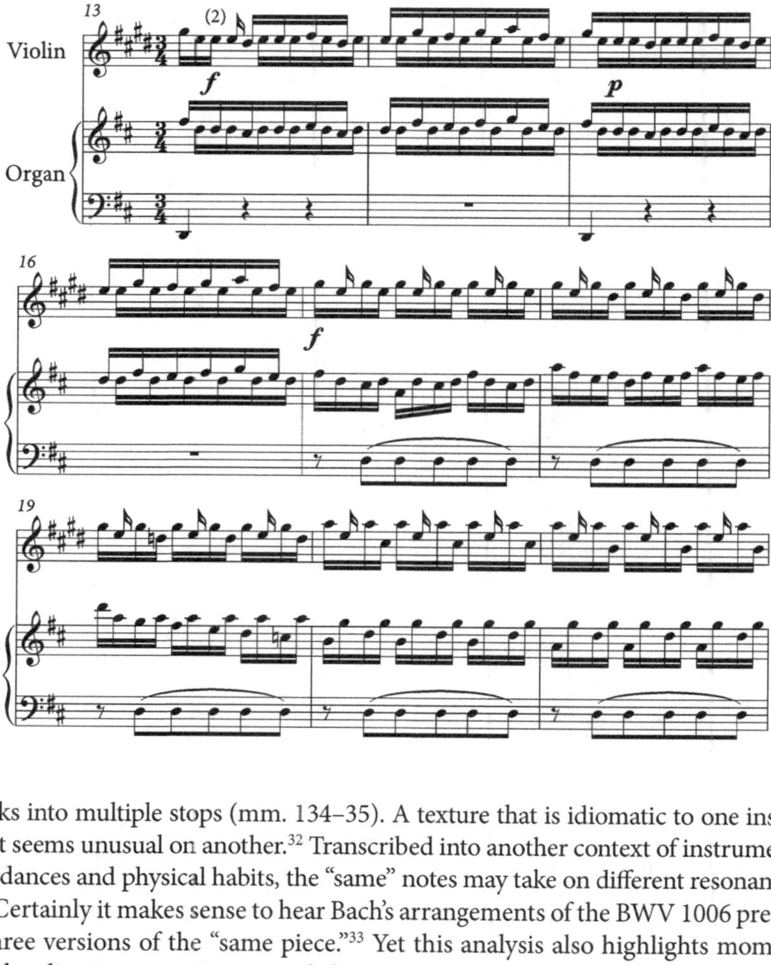

breaks into multiple stops (mm. 134–35). A texture that is idiomatic to one instrument seems unusual on another.[32] Transcribed into another context of instrumental affordances and physical habits, the "same" notes may take on different resonances.

Certainly it makes sense to hear Bach's arrangements of the BWV 1006 prelude as three versions of the "same piece."[33] Yet this analysis also highlights moments of delocalization, negotiation, and changing contexts—much like the processes of scientific generalization discussed by Galison. Sometimes Bach preserves aspects

32. Williams, for example, suggests that the famous Toccata in D minor (BWV 565) may reflect traces of another interface: "All the oddities one might hear in the piece disappear as soon as it is seen that the D minor Toccata may be a transcription of something else. The opening octaves, for instance, could well be a transcriber's way of making more rhetorical and effective on the organ a series of opening gestures that would have been solo on a melodic instrument (say viola da gamba, flute, or violin)" (1981, 335). Other authors suggest different sources, such as five-string cello (Argent 2000) or lute (Altschuler 2005).

33. Another notable version is created by Robert Schumann's piano accompaniment. Lester compares this arrangement to Bach's orchestra and organ version, emphasizing their different rhythmic profiles (1999, 117–22).

of body-instrument interaction, whether heard or felt. Listening to these arrangements together, for example, brings out similarities between affordances of the violin and lute and differences from the organ.[34] Other times Bach overwrites the original, engaging the unique affordances of the new medium—adding bass notes, changing figuration, and so on. With the lute version, the adjustments continue with performers, since Bach's version is not entirely idiomatic to the instrument. The largest change here is the shift in key from E major to F major. In fact, because E major clashes with the most common D-minor lute tuning, some believe that BWV 1006a is not a lute arrangement but a lute-inspired keyboard arrangement. Continuing along these lines, it has been suggested that this is Bach's only surviving work for the lute clavier, or *Lautenwerk* (Burguéte 1977, 52).

Playing Lute at the Keyboard

The *Lautenwerk* shows that Bach did not simply use existing instruments; he also helped develop new ones. According to Agricola, Bach designed a "lute harpsichord" (*Lautenclavicymbel*), which was built by the organ builder Zacharias Hildebrandt. This may have been one of the two lute claviers that Bach owned at the time of his death. The composer had been an early adopter of this experimental keyboard instrument. He facilitated the purchase of a *Lautenwerk* made by his elder cousin Johann Nicolaus Bach as early as 1715, only a few years after the first documented reference to the instrument.[35]

J. N. Bach's student Jacob Adlung claimed that "after the organ, the lute harpsichord is the most beautiful of the keyboard instruments" ([1768] 2011, 133). Yet *Lautenwerke* were never widely built or played, and no specimens survive. Organological details, however, are available from contemporaneous sources, including Adlung's *Musica mechanica organoedi* (*Musical Mechanics for the Organist*). The *Lautenwerk* was an undamped instrument, a clavier with ringing strings. To control this resonance it was equipped with a buff stop, which might be understood as the functional opposite of a piano's sustain pedal. Like lutes, *Lautenwerke* were strung with gut strings, with courses doubled at the octave in the lower range, doubled at the unison above that, and single courses in the highest register. (J. S. Bach's model, additionally, had single-strung theorbo-style bass strings made of brass.) J. N. Bach's *Lautenwerk* also offered dynamic and timbral variation through three manuals, each of which plucked strings at a different

34. Huron and Berec also note unexpected similarities between the violin's and the organ's affordances: "Bach's organ transcriptions of Vivaldi violin concertos reflect certain affinities between the organ and violin that are not immediately apparent— especially when compared to (say) hypothetical transcriptions of these same concertos for flute. Vivaldi's long melodic lines would leave a flautist struggling for air. Moreover, Vivaldi's frequent alternating figures (including unisons) between two violin strings are readily replicated using two organ manuals" (2009, 104).

35. Incidentally, this instrument was bought by Duke Ernst August of Saxe-Weimar, whose younger brother Johann Ernst composed the concerto discussed earlier in this chapter (Ledbetter 2002, 28; Williams 2004, 151).

distance from the nut. It is unclear how many manuals J. S. Bach's had, though it evidently included several stops (Ledbetter 2002, 29).

Peter Williams wonders about this instrument: "What the advantage of the *Lautenwerk* was other than a pretty sound is unclear: easier to tune or voice or restring, less sensitive to climate, less loud, good for accompanying?" (2004, 151). In my view, this "advantage" seems clear: the sound of the *Lautenwerk refers* to another instrument.[36] After all, it seems difficult to conceive of this instrument in isolation, to describe it—even to name it—without noting its organological hybridity. As the *Lautenwerk* combines the harpsichord's interface and basic mechanism with the lute's strings, it links playing techniques of the former and sonic textures of the latter. As Adlung puts it, the *Lautenwerk* makes it "possible to play the lute from a keyboard" (2011, 135).

Agricola reports that J. S. Bach's *Lautenwerk* sounded very much like a real lute:

> It is true that in its regular setting (that is, when only one stop was drawn) it sounded more like the theorbo than like the lute. But when the stop that on harpsichords is called the Lute stop … was drawn with the Cornet stop, it was almost possible to deceive even professional lute players. (*NBR*, 366)

Adlung's comments go further, recounting how Bach's cousin employed the instrument:

> Mr. J. N. Bach, in playing this instrument out of sight, [was able to] deceive the finest lutenist; one would have sworn that it was a regular lute. But it is necessary to keep playing rapidly and in arpeggios, as skilled lutenists are accustomed to play. It is also necessary to stay in the same key; any modulation will immediately be noticeable, since one cannot depart from the key on a lute without retuning it. (Adlung 2011, 137)

This effect, then, did not rely simply on the instrument's timbre but on idiomatic musical figures. It depends on evoking the lute's tonal affordances and manner of performance. While the *Lautenwerk*'s resonance would surely enhance this reference, its timbre can be separated from these other idiomatic features.

In fact, there was a long tradition of "playing lute at the keyboard." Harpsichord transcriptions from seventeenth-century France highlight the lute's characteristic features: low tessitura, broken or strummed chords, bass pedals, thin texture, irregular figuration, loose imitation, held notes (*tenues*), campanella (repeating note) figures.[37] Marin Mersenne recommended that keyboardists play such transcriptions "in order to transfer the beauties and riches of the lute to other instruments" (quoted in Ledbetter 1987, 30). Mersenne specifically links this to instrumental differences in action-sound coupling: the lute's dynamics reflect a

36. Of course, the organ contains such instrumental references too, with stops named for trumpet, oboe, viola da gamba, vox humana, and so on (see Yearsley 2012, 69–70).

37. This style is often referred to as the "style brisé" (broken style). Yet Buch (1985) shows that this term emerged in the twentieth century.

player's force of touch, where the harpsichord is insensitive to this aspect of performance. Keyboardists adopted such textural devices as a means to approach the lute's *expressivity* on the harpsichord (Ledbetter 1987, 26). This is to say that the lute clavier, before its invention as a material object, existed as a conceptual blend.

It is hardly surprising, then, that such keyboard arrangements of lute music led to new, original keyboard pieces in lute style. This hybrid style uses the means of the keyboard to imitate the sonority of the lute. Here the lute functions as a compositional instrument. It is not used to perform such works (say, lute-style pieces by François Couperin). Instead, the lute becomes a source of ideas. Its affordances inform composition for other instrumental means.[38]

In cognitive terms, this involves meshing or cross-domain mapping. Cross-domain mapping is a kind of conceptual metaphor, like the linking of pitch and vertical position discussed in Chapter 1. As Lawrence Zbikowski explains, "Cross-domain mapping is a process through which we structure our understanding of one domain (which is typically unfamiliar or abstract) in terms of another (which is most often familiar and concrete)" (2002, 13). Whereas Zbikowski illuminates mappings between musical and nonmusical domains—for example, between musical and bodily movement or between musical and poetic imagery—the lute style represents an "intra-musical" mapping, from one instrument to another. Like all metaphor, cross-domain mappings depend on some enabling similarity between source and target domains. This also shows how mappings are selective, partial. Lute and clavier share the standardized pitch materials of Western tonal culture; both afford polyphonic textures with bass, chords, and melody, played solo or in the continuo. Yet the mapping breaks down in terms of timbre and action-to-sound relationships: the lute has resonance and dynamic range, while the harpsichord has more piercing tone, allows for fuller chord voicings and so on.

If auditory-motor integration grounds modes of perception, my hearing of Bach's E-major prelude is colored by my experience as a violinist. I listen with my hands. The experiment by Drost, Rieger, and Prinz (2007), discussed at the beginning of Chapter 3, suggests that this is interface-specific, automatically activated through bottom-up processes. But the lute style further suggests that this may be driven from the top down: in other words, *musicians may creatively apply this hands-on style of listening to instruments that they themselves do not play*. Indeed, these complementary possibilities are central to Glenberg's theory of mesh: embodied conceptualization can respond to the environment, subconsciously integrating memories with perceived affordances; yet such conceptualization might also be consciously directed (1997, 10–11). I can distance myself from my current situation, contemplating objects or actions that are not present. When Bach listened to his friend Weiss improvise on the lute, for example, he could have imagined playing along on the keyboard.

38. Ledbetter notes an interesting conflict between these elements in Bach's Suite in E minor (BWV 996): "Paradoxically, it is the 'lute-like' low tessitura that makes for too much business on the diapason courses and is one of the main problems for playing this suite on the lute" (2009, 246). In a sense, the suite is more lutelike than actual lute music. It is perhaps unsurprising, then, that Johann Tobias Krebs marked this manuscript *aufs Lauten Werk*.

Figure 5.26 Johann Sebastian Bach, Prelude in E♭ major, *The Well-Tempered Clavier*, Book II, mm. 1–8.

Weiss's influence might be heard in Bach's Prelude, Fugue, and Allegro in E♭ (BWV 998)—whose autograph score is marked "for lute or keyboard"—but also in the Prelude in E♭-major from *The Well-Tempered Clavier*, Book II (see Figure 5.26). The two pieces' similarities go beyond their shared key and compound meter: the keyboard prelude's *arpeggiando* style (with sustained, broken chords, mm. 25–28), pedaling bass (mm. 5–8, 13–16), and open-voiced chords all recall the lute piece.

Such instrumental strategies can be found throughout Bach's work.[39] For example, the Prelude in E♭ major from the *first* book of *The Well-Tempered Clavier* recalls an organ style—with long sustained pedal, extensive ties, and so on—though it was unlikely to have been played on organ. (The C-major prelude from the second book shares such features.) More generally, this may help explain the stylistic blending and contrast that marks *The Well-Tempered Clavier*, with its alternation between preludes and fugues. The fugues exploit the keyboard's polyphonic affordances, often obscuring patterns of the hand by distributing independent voices among the fingers. The preludes, by contrast, may reference various genres, through dance forms or instrumental effects: these include the famous broken-chord preludes whose heritage can be traced back to the toccatas of seventeenth-century lutenist Johann Hieronymus Kapsberger. From this perspective, the interplay of Bach's preludes and fugues represents a negotiation of instrumental and contrapuntal elements, which are never fully separate but never identical.

Conclusions

Bach's compositional achievements, in sum, cannot be divorced from his activities as a keyboardist, transcriber, violinist, instrument designer, and so forth.

39. Ledbetter (2002) argues that this strategy of evoking one medium in terms of another is particularly prevalent in the second book of *The Well-Tempered Clavier*.

His music is grounded in embodied know-how, though not determined by it. Bach draws flexibly on instrumental idioms—with an original instrument, transcribed to another, or explored metaphorically in a process of cross-domain mapping. Examining these compositional strategies can help differentiate instruments' affordances, while also highlighting connections or references among instruments (and other musical technologies). Throughout Bach's music, instrumental and tonal levels mingle like the parts in *The Art of Fugue*'s Canon at the Twelfth, alternately leading or following, coupled or free, woven together in a larger whole.

Though this chapter has focused on Bach, "compositional instruments" appear in other milieus as well. For example, Jonathan Goldman has documented the influence of free-reed instruments—specifically, accordion and bandoneon (a large concertina associated with Argentinean tango)—on several twentieth-century composers. The Argentinean German composer Mauricio Kagel, who played bandoneon, exploited physical patterns on the instrument in his *Pandorasbox* (1960). The piece includes disjunct atonal lines, which move through adjacent buttons in the bandoneon's irregular interface (Goldman 2012, 34–35). The American pianist David Tudor, to whom *Pandorasbox* is dedicated, also used the bandoneon as he transitioned from performing to composing. His first public composition was the 1966 multimedia piece *Bandoneon! (a combine)*, which extended the instrument electronically. For Tudor, this collapsed the distinction between composition and instrumentation. "*Bandoneon! (a combine)* uses no composing means," he wrote, "since when activated it composes itself out of its own composite instrumental nature" (quoted in Goldman 2012, 54). Goldman (forthcoming) also shows how the music of the spectralist composer Gérard Grisey employs gestures associated with his first instrument, the accordion, as when multiple instrumental parts share an exact dynamic contour. (As mentioned in Chapter 2, simultaneously played notes on the accordion have the same dynamic because they are activated by the same bellows.) This would involve a kind of metaphorical transcription, almost treating the ensemble as a virtual accordion. Despite considerable historical distance from Bach, then, these composers respond to instruments in similar ways, taking them as sources of material, as compositional tools.

It is a small step, of course, from compositional instruments to theoretical ones. Though instruments like the monochord are used primarily for theoretical investigation rather than performance, I would suggest that any instrument may inform theoretical understanding. Historical examples here are numerous. When the medieval keyboard with its one-to-one place-to-pitch mapping gained prominence around 1500, Western theories of pitch shifted from a contextual model, based in the hexachord system, to an absolute model, where a note's name represented a measurable pitch (Bent 1984). Likewise, the popularity of strummed guitar music in seventeenth-century Europe contributed to emergent tonal thinking, since these guitarists (like many of their counterparts today) treated chords as objects, with little concern for issues of inversion and counterpoint so important for keyboardists (Christensen 1992). In fact, one of the most important concepts of tonal theory, the circle of fifths that is used to explain relations among keys and chords, first appeared in a 1596 guitar manual. It uses a kind of tablature that linked fretboard positions, finger placement, and sounding chords. Any musical instrument, then, can function as a theoretical instrument, an "epistemic tool."[40]

Even as I highlight instruments, I do not wish to overlook the significance of notation here. Just as writing lets language appear in the absence of a living speaker, notation productively distances music from its performance.[41] This suggests that any score is open to many possible realizations, that transcribability is built into notation from the start. Notation, then, is not simply a written copy of performance. After all, it is possible to write things that have never been performed and even things that are unplayable.[42] At the same time, insofar as consistent instruments facilitate musical repetition (as prostheses or artifacts of external memory), they represent a kind of proto-notation or proto-recording. And this repeatability, rather than notation itself, seems essential for the sense of musical objects in theory or composition.

Composers, like performers, are involved in poiesis. They make music. But what about listeners who neither perform nor write music? How might they relate to Bach's violinistic string crossing or his lutelike keyboard pieces? How, more generally, might instrumental technologies condition their musical perception and understanding? Such questions demand an account of musical listening that differentiates listeners from performers and composers—but also differentiates among lay listeners themselves. Such questions, in other words, require a musical aesthetics that is sensitive to musical technics.

40. While Magnusson (2009) discusses digital instruments as "epistemic tools," I take a broader view. Similarly, Lewin suggests that musical instruments with stable pitch affordances might make it possible to link pitch intervals "with *res extensae*, that is, with visible and tangible spatial distances outside the body-mind complex of the singer—distances between holes in a pipe, between points along a bow-string, between shorter and longer pipe lengths, etc." (1977, 234).

41. This compressed treatment of musical notation is inspired by Derrida's classic investigation of speech and writing. As Derrida puts it, "Writing is at the same time more exterior to speech, not being its 'image' or its 'symbol,' and more interior to speech, which is already in itself a writing" (1976, 46).

42. Of course, there is also music that can be played but not notated, that does not fit the symbolic representations of notation. As Friedrich Kittler argues, Western notation puts sound through an alphabetic filter, whereas phonography inscribes traces of sonic events that include noise (1999, 3–4, 23).

CHAPTER Six

Horns To Be Heard

The finale of Joseph Haydn's Symphony no. 73 starts with a jaunty tune played by the whole orchestra. Fast, loud, and rhythmically active, the music rushes, races ahead, and arrives at the dominant (mm. 26–29; see Figure 6.1). Then, a break. A pause. The silence defuses the rhythmic energy of the opening, and like the famous *subito forte* from Haydn's "Surprise" Symphony, it demands my attention. How should I describe what happens next? In mm. 30–37, I hear two melodic lines moving together; dyads that reassert the home key; a blend of sound colors, one brash, the other bright. Yes, I can hear these textural, tonal, and timbral features. But I might also say that I hear a pair of horns, doubled by oboes.

These alternative descriptions reflect different *modes of listening*—that is, different ways of experiencing or relating to sound. Where the first highlights sonic features, the second identifies sources of sound in the world. For some authors, there is a categorical difference between these modes (e.g., Jonas 1966; Gaver 1993, 1–2; Scruton 1997, 221). The former would represent "musical listening," and the latter ecological or everyday listening. One would be aestheticized, the other mundane. The philosopher Hans Jonas, for example, claims that musical hearing "refers not to an object other than the sensory contents but to their own order and interconnection" (1966, 138). This opposition, then, tends toward a metaphysics of listening in which musical experience would supposedly be cleansed of instrumental traces.

Yet instruments are not so easily hidden. They constantly reappear in experience, supplementing pure sound and revealing an interplay of musical and ecological listening strategies. The French composer Pierre Schaeffer refers to this interplay in terms of an "instrumental paradox" (1966, 43). "The musical phenomenon … has two correlative aspects," he writes, "a tendency to abstraction, insofar as play releases structures; and the adherence to the concrete, insofar as it remains attached to instrumental possibilities" (46).[1] For instrumentalists, the concrete aspect is bound up with their own bodily actions. But how does this paradox affect listening? How, in other words, do listeners relate to instruments they cannot play, instruments they never touch?

With these questions, the book turns from music-makers to audiences, from poiesis to aesthesis. Haydn's horn music forms a useful case study here, and not

1. "Le phénomène musical a donc deux aspects corrélatifs: une tendance à l'abstraction, dans la mesure où le jeu dégage des structures; l'adhérence au concret, dans la mesure où il reste attaché aux possibilités instrumentales." Translations from Schaeffer are my own.

Figure 6.1 Joseph Haydn, Symphony no. 73 in D major, "La chasse," mvt. iv, mm. 26–37.

31

Figure 6.2 Open notes of the natural horn. (Note the microtonal inflections at harmonics 7, 11, 13, and 14.)

only because of the composer's contributions to modern orchestration. The horns in Haydn's ensemble, like other instruments discussed in this book, have a distinctive idiom. By deploying this idiom in varied contexts, Haydn's music suggests several ways that contemporaneous audiences responded to horns. Ultimately, it shows how instrumental invariance shapes perception and understanding for listeners, much as it does for players. At certain points, this investigation will return to theories of grounded cognition and phenomenology, discussed in Chapter 1. But first it will be helpful to review the horn's affordances and its role in eighteenth-century European culture.

Haydn's Horns

In the aforementioned passage from Haydn's Symphony no. 73, the horn functions as a compositional instrument. That is, Haydn's melodic and harmonic choices are tied to his decision to feature the horns. Such connections are common in Haydn's music. As Emily Dolan has shown, his orchestration contributed to emerging discourses of instrumental character, by which each member of the orchestra was typecast in particular musical and expressive roles (2013, 148–68). Still, instrumentation and tonal design are especially entwined with the horns because of their distinctive pitch affordances.

Brass instruments—that is, wind instruments played with vibrating lips—afford a harmonic series above a fundamental pitch (see Figure 6.2).[2] Players move through the series by varying lip tension. Note that this overtone space is "irregular," as defined in Chapter 3. Its pitch collection may be reckoned in terms of a diatonic or chromatic scale, yet either way, there are both missing notes and added notes (such as the "out-of-tune" seventh partial). A "step" in this instrumental space corresponds to various pitch intervals, which become smaller as the player ascends through the series. The valves on a modern French horn expand the instrument's pitch affordances: pressing a valve (or a combination of valves) modifies the functional length of the instrument and thereby changes the fundamental.

2. Specific pitches vary from instrument to instrument and do not exactly match the mathematical harmonic series. The fundamental itself is generally weak. Of course, "brass" instruments need not be made out of metal. Indeed, the word "horn" indicates that such instruments have long been made from animal horns.

Haydn himself was indirectly involved in such technical developments: in 1796, he wrote a concerto for an experimental "keyed" trumpet. But the horns in his ensemble, valveless or "natural" horns, were more closely tied to the pattern of overtones.

That is not to say that hornists of the time could not play other notes. On the contrary, they developed techniques to bend pitches with the embouchure ("lipping") or putting a hand into the horn's bell ("stopping"). They also used these methods to adjust the "out-of-tune" harmonics. Still, stopping could be difficult, and it altered the instrument's timbre. While horn soloists were expected to master such techniques, orchestral horn parts typically stayed within the harmonic series.[3] The seventh harmonic's too-flat B♭ was usually avoided; the bright F-quarter-sharp, often accepted as is.

In many ways, the problems facing early horn players resemble those of harmonica players examined in Chapter 3: their instruments offer diatonic pitch collections with gaps, gaps that can be filled by the development of new techniques or alteration of the instrument. Where harmonica players carry an instrument in each key, horn players would have interchangeable crooks, each of which would set the instrument for a particular key. Just as the jazz harmonica player Howard Levy always thinks in C major, natural horn music was always notated in this key. Some of the technical solutions to these problems are strikingly similar. Much like the chromatic harmonica, the chromatic horn invented by John Clagget in 1788 effectively couples two instruments tuned a semitone apart, which are played through a single mouthpiece (Tuckwell 2002, 35). Another approach, closer to cross-harp harmonica playing, was the early-nineteenth-century *cor mixte* approach: here a hornist carried crooks only for F, E, E♭, and D, using them for closely related keys and faking or cutting the outside notes (Humphries 2000, 19–20). Neither of these approaches to the horn was very satisfactory, though, and neither caught on. Many preferred the sound of the natural horn long after its valved counterpart was widespread, particularly in France.[4]

The valveless horn's affordances gave rise to certain idiomatic figures, such as melodies that outline a major triad. Three examples of this phenomenon, taken from Haydn's symphonies, appear in Figures 6.3–6.5. In the first movement of his Symphony no. 6, the composer starts the cheery main theme with an unaccompanied horn, moments before the flute and strings initiate the recapitulation proper (see Figure 6.3).[5] Horns help create a different mood at the beginning of Haydn's Symphony no. 22, nicknamed "The Philosopher." As shown in Figure 6.4, this somber adagio begins with horns in octaves, moving in half notes against the muted strings' steady eighth notes (mm. 1–2). Symphony no. 31 also begins with

3. Composers typically used horns in pairs, where one player was a specialist in high-register playing (*cor alto*) and the other was a specialist in the lower register (*cor basse*).

4. The highly developed French tradition of valveless horn playing led to the instrument's common English name, the "French" horn (Tuckwell 2002, 17).

5. This moment, then, is a precedent for the famous "early" horn entry in Beethoven's "Eroica" Symphony.

Figure 6.3 Joseph Haydn, Symphony no. 6 in D major, "Le matin," mvt. i, mm. 85–90.

Figure 6.4 Joseph Haydn, Symphony no. 22 in E♭ major, "The Philosopher," mvt. i, mm. 1–4.

horns and strings—but its quicker tempo and rearticulated notes create a thrilling sense of momentum (see Figure 6.5). Although these excerpts are stylistically and affectively distinct, each of them prominently uses horns to outline the tonic triad.

In the latter two examples, the horns double each other at the unison or octave. The duet from Symphony no. 73 involves another kind of doubling. The

Figure 6.5 Joseph Haydn, Symphony no. 31 in D major, "Hornsignal," mvt. i, mm. 1–5.

Figure 6.6 Transformation network for the horn duet from Haydn's "La chasse" symphony, mvt. iv, mm. 30–31. The two horns make similar moves, above the same fundamental.

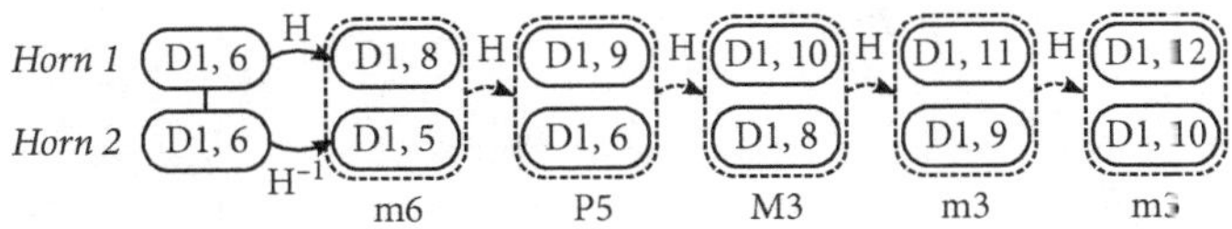

horns start on different harmonics, then make similar moves through the instrumental "scale" presented in Figure 6.2.[6] This motion can be represented via Kris Shaffer's transformational model of natural horn music. Shaffer (n.d.) represents the instrument's "overtone space" in terms of ordered pairs of the form (*f*, *p*), where *f* is the fundamental pitch and *p* is a numbered partial. For example, the first note of the horn duet would be (D1, 6), sounding as A3. Given the habitual avoidance of the seventh partial, it might make sense to define an operation H that skips this out-of-tune note. This can be achieved (somewhat artificially) by mapping 6 to 8, 7 to itself, and any other number x to $x + 1$. From this perspective, the horn duet would involve parallel motion in the instrumental space—even though the pitch intervals between the parts vary (see Figure 6.6).

In terms of pitches, the most distinctive part of this pattern is the similar-motion approach to the perfect fifth. This move, forbidden by contrapuntal tradition,

6. Again, Haydn avoids the seventh partial. This note, in fact, appears in only four of his symphonies (Bryan 1975, 214).

Figure 6.7 Joseph Haydn, Symphony no. 103 in E♭ major, "Drumroll," mvt. iv, mm. 1–4. (No other instruments play at this moment.)

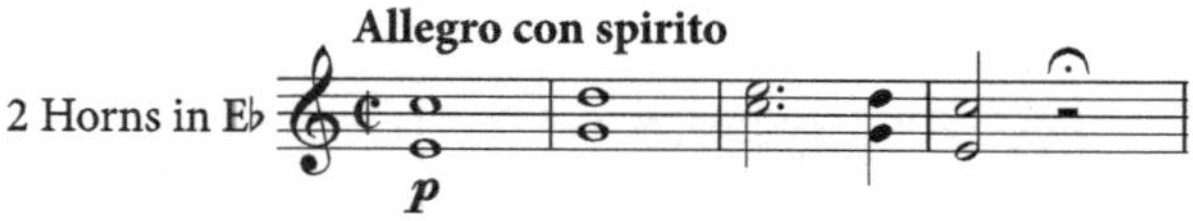

Figure 6.8 Joseph Haydn, Symphony no. 31 in D major, "Hornsignal," mvt. iii, mm. 41–44.

represents a clash between instrumental and tonal idioms. Haydn's corrections on students' exercises and annotations in his copy of *Gradus ad Parnassum* show that the composer's attitude toward "hidden" or "direct" fifths was even stricter than that of the textbook's author, Johann Joseph Fux (Mann 1970, 719). Yet these fifths are ubiquitous in Haydn's horn parts. As shown in Figure 6.7, unaccompanied horn fifths start the final movement of Symphony no. 103. They may also be woven into a thicker orchestral texture: for example, they accompany melodies in the oboes and strings throughout the trio from Symphony no. 31 (Figure 6.8).

These two-part figures have roots in an earlier tradition: hunters often played *cors de chasse* in pairs. Such duets appear in the first published collection of hunting calls, Jean de Serré de Rieux's *Les dons des enfans de Latone: La musique et la chasse du cerf* of 1734 (Monelle 2006, 51). Paired horns, then, recall the instrument's use outside of the concert hall. They reference the horn as *communication technology*. The instrument, in fact, was required equipment for hunters. A 1719 hunting manual notes that "by law every mounted member of a Parforce-hunt must wear his Parforce-horn round his neck, otherwise he will not be admitted to the field" (quoted in Fitzpatrick 1970, 18n2). Such practices were very much part of Haydn's world. His patron Prince Nikolaus Esterházy was an avid huntsman: he built the Esterháza summer palace at the remote site of his old hunting lodge and

Figure 6.9 "La sourcillade," as recorded by Serré de Rieux (1734).

founded a forestry school at Eisenstadt where all students learned how to play the horn (Fitzpatrick 1970, 18n2).

This tradition gives Symphony no. 73 its nickname, "La chasse." Though Haydn often writes in a generalized hunt style, the reference here is more precise. In mm. 30–37, the horns play an actual hunting call: the "sourcillade" or "vue," sounded when the quarry is first sighted (Ringer 1953, 150–51; Monelle 2006, 89–90). While Haydn likely knew the call from the hunting of his aristocratic patrons, his version is close to Serré de Rieux's, published nearly half a century earlier (see Figure 6.9).[7] This consistency across temporal and geographic distance speaks to the hunting tradition's strength—which relies on the horn itself, as an object of external memory.

This cultural significance made horns attractive for opera composers—who were the first to use the instruments orchestrally. In 1639, Francesco Cavalli added them for hunting scenes in his *Le Nozze di Teti e di Peleo* (Tuckwell 2002, 13). Horns here represented a kind of diegetic music—even diegetic sound or noise. The finale from Symphony no. 73 also derives from this theatrical tradition: it originated as the overture to Haydn's 1780 opera, *La fedeltà premiata*, which opens with a mythical hunt dedicated to the goddess Diana. At the same time, the hunt itself was highly aestheticized, and Raymond Monelle argues that the horn may have been borrowed from the theater: "The baroque hunting horn was poised between musical expression and practical utility. Less effective than the oxhorn as a signaling tool, it was more evocative of the splendor and exhilaration of the hunt. Thus, the signifier of the hunt topic was already halfway to being its own signified.… It may well have originated as a theatrical instrument. Such was baroque culture; the world was a stage" (2006, 41).

Haydn expected his audience to recognize common hunting calls—and to understand their meaning.[8] As Daniel Heartz puts it, hunting calls "came as close to universality as any musical language of the time" (1976, 529). The composer dramatizes this in no. 26 from his oratorio *The Seasons*. Here horn signals

7. Both versions are in D, which was associated with French hunting horns. German hunting horns were typically in E♭ (Monelle 2006, 42). Note that all of the horn solos cited in this section (plus the horn concertos attributed to Haydn) are written in one of those keys—and the hunting scene in *The Seasons* shifts from one to the other.

8. This recognition was not limited to human listeners: a German hunting manual published in 1783 (one year after the premiere of Symphony no. 73) notes that "the dogs must understand the calls as well as the huntsmen, and indeed they do understand them perfectly with some experience" (quoted in Heartz 1976, 526).

act out each stage of a hunt—from the "queste," which gathers the hunting party, to the "halili," which celebrates their victory. As the hunters and countryfolk comment on the action, they repeatedly direct attention to the instrument itself:

Hört! hört das laute Getön,	Hark! Hear the loud noise
Das dort im Walde klinget!	that rings there in the woods!
Welch' ein lautes Getön	What a loud noise
Durchklingt den ganzen Wald!	rings through all the wood!
Es ist der gellenden Hörner Schall …	It is the shrill sound of the horn …

Hearing Things, Hearing Tones

When Haydn's hunters and countryfolk hear the horns, they recognize them instantly. And their first word—the imperative "Hark!"—is an invitation to join in that hearing. The scene, then, stages a particular mode of listening. Heidegger calls this mode "hearkening." In it, I attend not to sounds themselves but to meaningful *things*, which the sounds reveal. "'Initially' we never hear noises and complexes of sound," the philosopher writes, "but the creaking wagon, the motorcycle. We hear the column on the march, the north wind, the woodpecker tapping, the crackling fire" (2010, 158). Hearkening to things in the world, Heidegger argues, is more primordial than "hearing" bits of sonic sense data. This argument situates aural perception in an environment from the start. As such, it resonates with work in ecological acoustics (discussed in Chapter 2), which examines sonic information about objects and events. It also fits with the results of an open-ended empirical study by Nicola Dibben (2001). In it, participants were asked to describe various audio clips, some musical and some nonmusical. Overall, the responses were diverse, mentioning the sounds' acoustic qualities and their associations with musical genres, emotions, or social contexts. Many descriptions, moreover, reflected an individual respondent's cultural and educational background. But by far the most common type of description—by participants with and without musical training—referred to physical sources of sound. As Figure 6.10 shows, more than 1,000 responses named a physical source, whereas fewer than 150 mentioned sonic characteristics.[9]

Of course, this does not mean that it is impossible to experience sound *as* sound, just that such an approach involves particular learned techniques. As Heidegger

9. Some ethnomusicologists have come to related conclusions through fieldwork. For example, Greg Downey explores such issues in an essay on *capoeira*, the Brazilian martial art–dance form: "When practitioners describe the berimbau's sound, they … do not say that they hear a changed pitch, for example, but that they hear the coin pressing on the string" (2002, 496). The berimbau is a kind of musical bow that accompanies *capoeira*. (See also Baily 1996, 172.)

Figure 6.10 Frequencies of sound-description categories from Dibben (2001, 179).

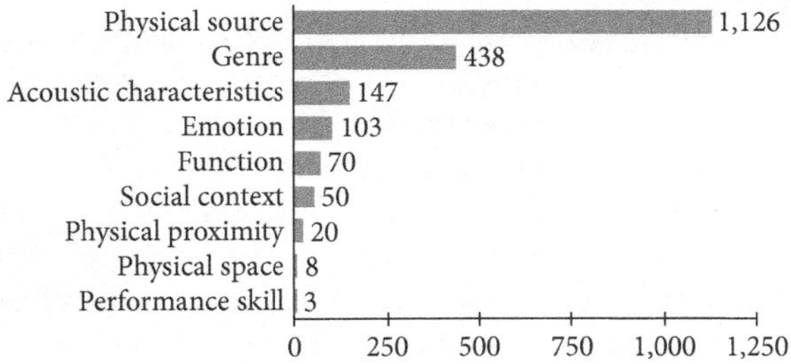

writes, "It requires a very artificial and complicated attitude in order to 'hear' a 'pure noise'" (2010, 153). This type of attitude might be found in the science of acoustics, where the horn's sound can be described in terms of resonance peaks and input impedance in a pressure-response curve (see Benade 1973). In light of Heidegger's ideas about technics (1977), it becomes clear that this acoustic description is made possible by scientific instruments, by a kind of technological enframing. For Pierre Schaeffer, radios and record players may perform a similar function.[10] Concealing sonic sources, he claims, can help reveal the sounds themselves.

In his *Traité des objets musicaux* (1966, 104), Schaeffer goes beyond the opposition of hearkening and hearing to propose four modes of listening:

(1) *Écouter* (listening), corresponding to hearkening, attends to a sound's source. For example, in the horn call, I hear an index of the instrument or the player's action.
(2) *Ouïr* (passive aural sensation) receives the sound unconsciously or indirectly. While I am in the car, driving and chatting with my wife, a horn might play quietly on the radio. Strictly speaking, I hear the sound (and this background music might even affect my mood), but I am not consciously aware of it.
(3) *Entendre* (hearing) focuses exclusively on sonic morphology. Here I would experience the horn call as a sound object out of context, as a particular timbre, rhythm, or pitch structure.
(4) *Comprendre* (understanding) interprets a sound's meaning. The horn call, at this level, is a symbol that might say, "The quarry has been sighted."

Each of Schaeffer's modes requires some kind of withdrawal. With *écouter* or *comprendre*, I do not listen *to* the sound. Instead, I listen *through* it to a physical source or a message. Like a written word, the horn call feels "transparent"; like a hammer, it is handy (*zuhanden*). With *entendre*, by contrast, I contemplate

10. Carlos Palombini (1998) draws parallels between Heidegger's and Schaeffer's approaches to technology, with particular attention to enframing (*Ge-stell*).

sounding patterns, while source and meaning withdraw. I seem to be concerned not with the instrument but with "the music itself."[11]

Though Schaeffer explores various tensions and relations among the four modes, he ultimately valorizes *entendre*. "*All music*," he proclaims, "*is made to be heard*" (1966, 133).[12] This resolves the instrumental paradox in favor of musical abstraction. For while *écouter* reveals things that can be seen or touched, *entendre* supposedly deals with sound alone. Here, Brian Kane (2014) has demonstrated, the composer faithfully employs Husserlian reduction techniques. *Entendre*, then, is often referred to as a "reduced listening." Setting aside the differences between sounds heard and sounds imagined, Schaeffer envisions an experience of pure hearing, of pure sound objects freed from their worldly origins. This accords with Husserl's own thoughts on music. "However much [Beethoven's 'Kreutzer' Sonata] itself consists of sounds, it is an ideal unity," Husserl writes, "and its constituent sounds are no less ideal. They are obviously not the sounds dealt with in physics; nor are they the sounds pertaining to sensuous acoustic perception, the sounds that come from things pertaining to the senses" (1969, 21; quoted in Schaeffer 1966, 132).[13] This is a radical view of musical autonomy, detaching music not only from its social function but even from its real existence as vibration. Moreover, if the sound object is to be constituted as an unchanging, self-grounded essence, then any trace of mediation or exteriority—any trace of technics—must be excluded.[14] Separating *écouter* from *entendre*, then, would theoretically sever the instrument from its sound.

Yet Heidegger's tool analysis teaches that withdrawal cannot always be sustained. When the horns' limited pitch affordances differentiate them from their orchestral companions, when they play direct fifths or a slightly sharp $\hat{4}$, when a performer of this notoriously difficult instrument botches a note—then horns become "present-to-hand" (*vorhanden*). Such disruptions draw attention to the instrument, shifting from *entendre* to *écouter*. (That pause in Haydn's Symphony no. 73 creates a similar effect. In it, Haydn orchestrates a moment of breakdown, directing attention to the horn call that follows.) Moreover, as discussed in Chapter 4, Levinas would emphasize that withdrawal is never complete, that handiness does not preclude enjoyment. From this perspective, Schaeffer's modes of listening are unstable at best. Each one may be dispelled by unfulfilled expectations; each one depends on a certain kind of habit or habituation. This connects listening, like the development of performance expertise, to instrumental invariance.

Listen again to the horn call. The melody emerges from pitch and rhythmic variance (which correlate, too, with a player's actions). The timbre, meanwhile, is

11. With *ouïr*, the sound would withdraw from consciousness more or less completely.
12. "*Toute musique est faite pour être entendre*" (emphasis in original). Similar arguments appear in other Husserlian treatments of sound and music, such as those of Jonas (1966) and Scruton (1997).
13. On the role of hearing—and, particularly, "hearing-oneself-speak"—in Husserl's metaphysics, see Derrida (2011).
14. For further discussion, see Gallope (2011, 59) and Kane (2014, ch. 4).

relatively stable, implying that these varied notes are produced by the same source. Because of this consistency, I may become habituated to the sound of the instrument, which facilitates its withdrawal. But instrumental timbre also affects the way that instrumental parts are grouped or divided (Bregman 1990, ch. 5; De Souza 2015). In other words, changing the instrumentation can change the music's perceived organization. Curiously, it seems that both timbral variance and timbral invariance may highlight the tension between structure and source. With Haydn's re-orchestration of repeated themes, the melody is more stable than its instrumental presentation. According to Dolan (2013, 134), this contributed to the idea of an abstract theme that transcends any single manifestation. Meanwhile, Thomas Christensen argues that four-hand piano transcriptions of orchestral music, by erasing differences in instrumental color, played into the nineteenth-century aesthetics of absolute music (1999, 290). The piano reduction, like a phenomenological reduction, was thought to reveal pure tone structures or spiritual essences.

As transcriptions changed performance medium and context—transforming an orchestral work, played in public, into a pianistic one, played at home—they blurred distinctions between genres. And this, too, could affect the perception of tonal structure. Research in music cognition indicates that tonal expectations are situated, contextual. Listeners develop different schemas—that is, different sets of expectations—for particular musical genres.[15] Even without formal musical training, they tune in to a genre's statistical regularities. So just as instrumental consistency grounds hand-ear connections for players, tonal consistency grounds style-specific expectations for listeners. Yet genre identification is so rapid that it must rely on timbre rather than harmonic information (Perrott and Gjerdingen 2008). In this case, instruments, whether heard or seen, may provide contextual cues, priming particular expectations or helping listeners learn new schemas (Huron 2006, 204–5). That is to say, Haydn's eighteenth-century audiences—and, to some extent, classical-music fans today—would be attuned to the relation between the horn's timbre and its idiomatic figures. Horn parts are far more predictable than, say, violin parts. As soon as I hear the horns' sixth at the opening of the "Drumroll" Symphony, I am primed for the possibility of direct motion to a perfect fifth. Here source identification informs tonal expectation. *Écouter* guides *entendre*.

For an experienced listener, the horn call might be heard to "sound good," imbued with a positive affect that rewards successful prediction.[16] But the instrumental-tonal expectations at play may be even clearer when they are denied. Carl Maria von Weber's 1821 opera, *Der Freischütz*, provides a striking example. The opera centers on hunting culture. Its protagonist, Max, is a gamekeeper, and the horn, as a tool of his trade, is an essential part of the opera's sound world. Desperate to win a shooting contest, Max decides to cast seven magic bullets in the Wolf's Glen at midnight—and unwittingly becomes involved in a demonic pact. Each bullet's production is accompanied by some

15. For example, a series of experiments by Bryn Hughes (2011) examines Western listeners' different harmonic expectations for classical music and the blues.
16. On musical expectation and emotion, see Huron (2006, 7–15).

disturbing supernatural event: nightbirds gather, a hurricane bends the trees, and wheels of fire cross the stage. After the fifth bullet has been cast, horns herald the imminent arrival of the devil Samiel (see Figure 6.11). But these horns outline a dissonant diminished-seventh chord rather than a consonant major

Figure 6.11 Carl Maria von Weber, *Der Freischütz*, no. 10 (Act II Finale), mm. 336–46.

triad.[17] They sound an augmented fourth in place of a perfect fourth, and minor thirds in place of major thirds. Moreover, the timbre makes it clear that none of the notes are stopped. That is, these horns appear to violate the laws of physics that ground the instrument's overtone space. They are not natural horns, then; they seem to be *unnatural* horns. Weber creates this illusion by combining horns in multiple keys: two in E, one in F, and one in B♭. In itself, this is not a new technique. It is particularly common in minor-mode works, such as Mozart's Symphony no. 40 in G minor, K. 550. Yet in the Wolf's Glen scene, the consistent timbre and aligned temporal attacks make it sound as though notes from multiple instruments come from a single, fictional source. The moment engages several modes of listening at once: the sound's source, its dissonant sonority, and its dramatic significance are all interrelated.

This example from Weber also suggests how instrumental sources may contribute to musical meaning. As I listen to the beginning of Haydn's Symphony no. 22 (see Figure 6.4), the horns might withdraw. I might be more aware of the piece's solemn, somewhat archaic character, its nickname "The Philosopher," or traditional interpretations that hear it as a dialogue between God and a sinner (Landon 1976, 566). But imagine how such experiences would change if the horns were replaced by electric guitars or kazoos.[18] Here, again, *écouter, entendre*, and *comprendre* are profoundly interconnected.

Phantom Horns

Let me return to Symphony no. 73, to an earlier section that has nothing to do with the hunt. In the second movement, Haydn's song "Gegenliebe" (Hob. XXVI:16) forms the refrain in a rondo-variation form.[19] Recognizing the song—or even its songlike character—represents another instance of handiness (*Zuhandenheit*). That is, the strings might be heard as relatively "neutral" instruments realizing the voice and piano parts from the original lied (see Figure 6.12a).

The rondo's first episode begins in m. 25. It presents the main theme in the parallel minor, G minor, then modulates to B♭ major. When the theme appears in this new key, though, I experience a moment of presence-to-hand (mm. 36–37; see Figure 6.12b). Something sticks out. As it happens, the upper strings have momentarily broken with their usual style of voice leading to accompany the tune with a horn-fifths figure. The actual horns in the ensemble are silent throughout this

17. The dramatic effect engages the diminished-seventh chord's inherent dissonance, as well as associations between the tritone and devils in Western art music generally and throughout this opera in particular. But, in my view, the distortion of the expected horn idiom is crucial here. The dissonance is more unpredictable, because of its instrumental context.
18. For an empirical study of instrumental affordances and emotion, see Schutz et al. (2008).
19. In *Haydn and the Classical Variation*, Elaine Sisman distinguishes between "rondo-variation" (variation form with contrasting periods) and "variation-rondo" (rondo form with incidental changes to the refrain) (1993, 72). She lists this movement as an instance of the former (268).

Figure 6.12 Joseph Haydn, excerpts from Symphony no. 73 in D major, "La chasse," mvt. ii.

(a) Main theme, derived from Haydn's song "Gegenliebe," mm. 1–4.

(b) Strings introduce horn fifths into the theme, mm. 35–37.

(c) Horns accompany the theme with direct fifths, mm. 55–56.

Figure 6.12 Continued

(d) The main theme, transformed into a horn figure, mm. 96–97.

episode, since its distance from the movement's home key makes it poorly suited to their tonal affordances. After the music returns to G major, though, the horns join the main theme for the first time, playing the direct fifth that the strings had introduced (mm. 55–56; see Figure 6.12c). And after another episode, at the main theme's final occurrence, the horns triumphantly take the complete tune (mm. 96–97; see Figure 6.12d). Now their distinctive fifths, doubled by the second violins, have become fully integrated into the theme. This movement, then, enacts a technique that is common in Haydn's slow movements—what Dolan calls "developing orchestration" (2013, 115). It seems that the strings in m. 36 were foreshadowing the horns' final arrival and the instrumental transformation of Haydn's song.

This horn-specific process of developing orchestration is found with other composers too. Monelle collects a few examples of this "hidden-reference" strategy, in which an idiomatic horn figure is presented initially by other instruments (2006, 100). Indeed, I briefly showed one earlier: the excerpt from Haydn's "Le matin" Symphony, where a solo horn anticipated the recapitulation (see Figure 6.3). In that movement, the triadic theme first appeared as a flute solo. Such pieces seem to emphasize other instruments' imitations of horns.

Yet horn idioms often appear without such confirmation. The most obvious examples reference the hunt, combining horn motion with lilting equestrian rhythms in six-eight time. For example, Haydn's first string quartet begins with a unison horn call, leading to its nickname, "La chasse" (see Figure 6.13). But imagined horns appear in other stylistic contexts too. In the "Emperor Hymn" from his String Quartet no. 62, Haydn harmonizes the first three notes of the melody with a triad in the second violin to create horn motion in the upper parts (see Figure 6.14). Whether the composer had horns or trumpets in mind, the direct fifth certainly echoes ceremonial brass and contributes to the music's stately character. Here, as in Bach's imitations of the lute style, Haydn puts an instrumental idiom in a new performative context.

In the nineteenth century, as valved brass instruments became more common, references to the natural horn took on new connotations, epitomized by the nostalgic horn fifths in Beethoven's Piano Sonata no. 26 in E♭ major, "Les adieux," and the slow movement from Johannes Brahms's 1865 Horn Trio, op. 40 (mvt. iii, mm. 59–65). Instruments like horns and bells—that is, instruments that can be heard far away—were particularly important for a Romantic aesthetics obsessed with distance, absence, and interiority (Hoeckner 1997, 61; Beller-McKenna 2005). All of this speaks to the historical significance of the horn topic, to the representation of an instrument that is not just distant, but actually *absent*. Such representations diverged from actual horn writing. The natural horn part for Brahms's trio goes beyond the instrument's open notes, requiring extensive stopping.[20] Passages *evoking* the horn, however, are more stereotypical, more schematic (for example, see the opening of Brahms's String Quartet in B♭-major in Figure 6.15).

This trend continues in the twentieth century with György Ligeti. His Hamburg Concerto (1998–2002) features four natural horns, using the "out-of-tune" upper harmonics that earlier composers avoided. These parts keep much from earlier horn idioms, even as they trade a triadic-diatonic profile for a spectral one. In the second movement, for example, Ligeti replicates the instrumental logic behind horn fifths: as two horns make parallel moves through the overtone series, the sounding intervals vary constantly (Shaffer, n.d.; see Figure 6.16). Yet in his piano étude "Fanfares," the composer uses a standard horn-fifths motif.[21] The imagined horns pop out of the texture, even in this nontonal context.

From Haydn to Ligeti, I have barely skimmed this tradition of instrumental reference. In these examples, horns seem to be simultaneously present and absent, real and ideal. They might thus be understood as virtual instruments, as phantoms haunting the music or its listeners.[22] Further examples could be provided ad nauseam, including examples that do not engage a conventionalized musical

20. Examining Brahms's manuscript, Peter Jost (2001) concludes that the part was originally written for valved horn, then modified.

21. This prelude is closely related to the manic second movement of Ligeti's Horn Trio (1982). Note, also, that the trio's final movement alludes to the horn fifths from Beethoven's "Les adieux" Sonata. (For an analysis, see Cuciurean 2000, 155–61.)

22. Here I would note that "phantom" and "phenomenon" both derive from the Greek verb *phanein* (to show).

Figure 6.13 Joseph Haydn, String Quartet no. 1 in B♭ major, "La chasse," mvt. i, mm. 1–4.

Figure 6.14 Joseph Haydn, String Quartet no. 62 in C major, "Emperor," mvt. ii, mm. 1–2.

Figure 6.15 Johannes Brahms, String Quartet no. 3 in B♭ major, op. 67, mvt. i, mm. 1–4.

Figure 6.16 Transformation network for György Ligeti, *Hamburg Concerto*, mvt. ii, m. 9 (adapted from Shaffer, n.d., figs. 4–6). Parallel moves in overtone space give rise to varied sonorities. (100c is equivalent to one equal-tempered semitone.)

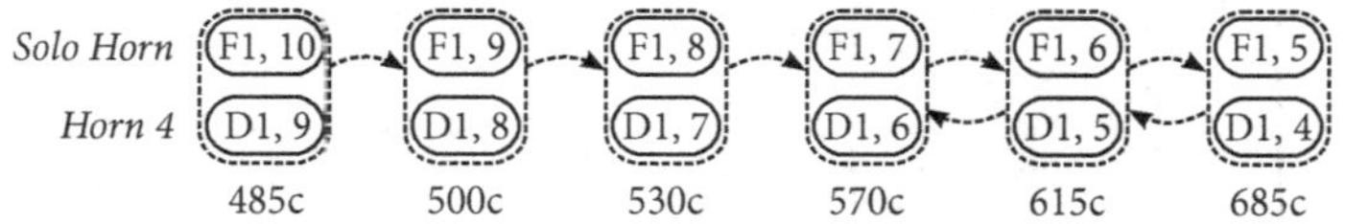

Figure 6.17 Pyotr Il'yich Tchaikovsky, *Album for the Young*, op. 39, no. 13.

topic. Briefly consider a short piano piece from Pyotr Il'yich Tchaikovsky's 1878 *Album for the Young* (see Figure 6.17). The piece is texturally and tonally constrained: right and left hands always move in the same rhythm, often doubling each other at the octave, and the harmonies simply alternate between close-position tonic and dominant chords. Here, again, the music is governed by a phantom source. Tchaikovsky is treating the piano as a virtual harmonica.[23]

Even without such examples, though, this section's survey provides enough context to launch a new set of questions. What do these phantom instruments presuppose, psychologically speaking? Which listeners can perceive them? And what might they show about the ways that audiences relate to instruments?

Instrumental Schemas

Since ecological listening responds to the physics of sound production, it is, to some degree, cross-cultural. For example, American listeners—including children—with no prior experience of Chinese music can hear how Chinese orchestral instruments are played and successfully group them into families (Palmer et al. 1989). And identifying sound sources often relies on visual cues.[24] Yet in these respects, a piano's "horn call" differs from a real horn call. Recognition of the absent instrument cannot rely on its timbre or its visual appearance. Instead, it depends on links between culturally situated sensorimotor experience and musical imagination.

Here I return to Lawrence Barsalou's theory of perceptual symbol systems. Recall how players' brains develop patterns of auditory-motor coactivation. Though listeners without instrumental training will not acquire these specific patterns, their engagement with music also combines multiple neural systems. Auditory perception coincides with vision, bodily states, emotions, and so on. And even a single note has various qualities—such as pitch, timbre, and loudness—that can stimulate distinct areas in the brain. Listening to music, then, cultivates sensory representations that are separate on the neural level but also dynamically interrelated. Once developed, such connections can be reactivated through bottom-up or top-down cognitive processes. Because these connections are bidirectional, horns can cue certain tonal schemas, and these same tonal schemas can evoke horns. To paraphrase Lawrence Zbikowski, references to the horn reactivate some of the same neural structures associated with actually listening to horn music, giving rise to an imperfect but still vivid simulation of that experience (2010, 48).[25]

23. Without the octave doubling, Tchaikovsky's piece is fairly easy to play on a harmonica, since it sticks to the tonal affordances presented in Figure 3.8. The final section of the piece does not require movement along the comb, only rhythmic breathing in and out (mm. 13–22). (In this respect, it resembles Bob Dylan's huffing and puffing, discussed in Chapter 3.) The last four bars of Tchaikovsky's piece might be the most taxing for a harmonica player, though, because they demand constant inhalation. That would explain the gradual diminuendo—the harmonica player is tiring, filling up with air. Although this breathing problem is foreign to the manual interface of the piano, it might be evoked in a pianist's interpretation.

24. Visual cues may shape listening in various ways. Jane Davidson (1993) has shown how performers' bodily movements visually communicate expressive features. Michael Schutz further shows how such gestures can affect perceived note duration (see Schutz and Manning 2012).

25. Zbikowski draws on perceptual symbol systems theory in an analysis of musical analogy in Louis Moreau Gottschalk's 1853 piano piece, "The Banjo," op. 15 (2010, 44–48).

Barsalou is careful to distinguish between conscious experience and its neural underpinnings (1999, 581–84). In experience, I encounter meaningful things situated in an environment.[26] But perceptual components, though integrated in conscious imagery, are processed and stored separately. Perceptual symbols are not holistic but componential and schematic. And this allows for the production of novel images and concepts:

> Productivity in perceptual symbol systems is approximately the symbol formation process run in reverse. During symbol formation, large amounts of information are filtered out of perceptual representations to form a schematic representation of a selected aspect. During productivity, small amounts of the information filtered out are added back. Thus, schematicity makes productivity possible. (Barsalou 1999, 593)

The horn call's tonal features can thus be separated from other sonic aspects, filled in with a different timbre. This allows me to recognize horn calls played by other instruments and also to imagine things that I have never heard (like the opening horn parts of Haydn's "Philosopher" Symphony played on kazoos). Because components are separate at the neural level, different musical elements—tone and timbre, source and meaning—are mutually irreducible; because they connect within and across modalities, they are also never fully autonomous.

Previous listening experience makes it possible for me to hear phantom horns, just as Beethoven's performing experience helped him hear phantasmal tones. The ability to notice horn calls thus depends on personal history, on an individual's immersion in a consistent cultural environment. This view, along with Barsalou's framework more generally, resonates with perspectives on historical modes of listening from musical schema theory (cf. Gjerdingen 2007a; Byros 2012). Indeed, idiomatic horn figures are readily interpreted as schemas. They are musical "constructions," pairing form and function, that appear at the musical surface (Gjerdingen and Bourne 2015). One of schema theory's main premises, derived from Leonard Meyer (1956, 60–62), is that the schemas that orient listening are acquired through social experience. As Meyer's bicycling analogy shows, this treats musical listening as a kind of know-how, habit, or skill. I cannot train my ears to notice horn fifths simply by reading a book about the cultural history of hunting in Europe. Instead, I learn to hear them though repeated listening. This perspective supplements a semiotic approach that would treat the string quartet's horn calls as signs representing some object. Instead it emphasizes how listeners attune to instrumental invariance, how instrumental idioms shape perceptual capacities. This is to say that listening, in its own way, is technical. Like performing, it is embodied, ecological, and historically specific.

26. Some of Barsalou's experimental research shows that categories and objects are situated against a background (see Yeh and Barsalou 2006; Wu and Barsalou 2009).

Conclusions

As I listen to Haydn's Symphony no. 73, I rely on previous experiences—hearing, studying, teaching, and playing classical music. What I have learned appears in the way the symphony shows up. The horns' entrance in the finale cues certain tonal expectations; in the second movement, direct fifths cue instrumental ones. In both cases, orchestration and tonal design are mutually implicated.

In the end, musical experience cannot be contained by any single mode of listening. Merleau-Ponty's assessment of Husserl thus applies to Schaeffer as well: "The most important lesson of the reduction is the impossibility of a complete reduction" (Merleau-Ponty 2012, lxxvii). Instead of being associated with one privileged mode, then, musical listening might be marked by the intertwining of *écouter, entendre*, and *comprendre*. Music, as Merleau-Ponty claims, would point to "an ideality that is not alien to the flesh, that gives it its axes, its depth, its dimensions" (1968, 152). That is, music would reveal ideas that cannot be disentangled from their sensible appearances, that can be accessed only through the lived body. From this perspective, Schaeffer's instrumental paradox cannot be resolved. A sound is never absolutely free of its source, yet never totally bound to it, because audition is never absolutely free of other corporeal powers, yet never reducible to them.

Even as an expert, I cannot recover the experiences of Haydn's contemporaries. My knowledge of the "sourcillade" is more declarative than procedural. I can only imagine its significance to an eighteenth-century hunter, for whom Haydn's quotation might summon memories of mornings in the woods, of animal sights and smells, of adrenaline. For such a listener, the horn call would be a call to action ("The quarry has been sighted," roughly meaning "Let's go!"). At best, I recognize this meaning at a distance. Here I enjoy Haydn's music without forgetting that it is a music of the past.

As Kane observes, Schaeffer's taxonomy includes no mode that can evaluate the recorded character of recorded sounds (Kane 2014, 126). Similar modes would be needed to register the symphony's historical character and other forms of mediation. If Haydn puts orchestral development "on display" (Dolan 2013, 135), this presumes a kind of listening that may reflect on that process. When the string quartet "samples" a horn call, playing it back in a different medium, I hear that the style is borrowed. Continuing along these lines, modes of listening would proliferate endlessly as a function of musical technics.

Indeed, that might be the central thesis of this book: Technics opens up possibilities for musical action and cognition. As I use instruments to make music, they also make me a musician. I come to sense hands at the keyboard in Beethoven's sonata, Chopin's prelude, or Lachenmann's study; fingers on strings in Rosenwinkel's waltz or Bach's partita; breath and reeds in Dylan's or Williamson's solos. The instruments call not only to my ear but also to my body. They alternately support and resist me, as partners or adversaries, implements or obstacles. Through technology and technique, then, this fleeting art is made tangible; through instruments, I come to encounter music at hand.

REFERENCES

Abbate, Carolyn. 1999. "Outside Ravel's Tomb." *Journal of the American Musicological Society* 52: 465–530.

Adelson, Steve. 2002. "Interview with Pat Metheny." *Twentieth-Century Guitar Magazine*, May. http://hepcat1950.com/pmiv02sa.html.

Adlington, Robert. 2003. "Moving Beyond Motion: Metaphors for Changing Sound." *Journal of the Royal Musical Association* 28: 297–318.

Adlung, Jacob. 2011. *Musica Mechanica Organoedi*. Translated by Quentin Faulkner. Lincoln, NE: Zea E-Books.

Adorno, Theodor W. 2002. *Aesthetic Theory*. Edited by Gretel Adorno and Rolf Tiedemann. Newly edited and translated by Robert Hullot-Kentor. London: Continuum.

Alibali, Martha W., Robert C. Spencer, Lucy Knox, and Sotaro Kita. 2011. "Spontaneous Gestures Influence Strategy Choices in Problem Solving." *Psychological Science* 22: 1138–44.

Altenmüller, Eckart, and Wilfried Gruhn. 2002. "Brain Mechanisms." In *The Science and Psychology of Music Performance*, edited by Richard Parncutt and Gary E. McPherson, 63–82. Oxford: Oxford University Press.

Altschuler, Eric Lewin. 2005. "Were Bach's Toccata and Fugue BWV565 and the Ciacconia from BWV1004 Lute Pieces?" *Musical Times* 146 (1893): 77–86.

Appleby, Amy. 1992. *The Harp Styles of Bob Dylan*. New York: Amsco Publications.

Aravena, Pia, Esteban Hurtado, Rodrigo Riveros, Juan Felipe Cardona, Facundo Manes, and Agustin Ibáñez. 2010. "Applauding with Closed Hands: Neural Signature of Action-Sentence Compatibility Effects." *PLoS ONE* 5: e11751.

Argent, Mark. 2000. "Decoding Bach 3. Stringing Along." *Musical Times* 141 (1872): 16–23.

Aschersleben, Gisa, Jörg Gehrke, and Wolfgang Prinz. 2001. "Tapping with Peripheral Nerve Block: A Role for Tactile Feedback in the Timing of Movements." *Experimental Brain Research* 136: 331–39.

Ashby, W. Ross. 1956. *An Introduction to Cybernetics*. London: Chapman & Hall.

Auerbach, Brent. 2008. "Tiered Polyphony and Its Determinative Role in the Piano Music of Johannes Brahms." *Journal of Music Theory* 52: 273–320.

Baber, Christopher. 2003. *Cognition and Tool Use: Forms of Engagement in Human and Animal Use of Tools*. London: Taylor & Francis.

Bach, Carl Philipp Emanuel. 1949. *Essay on the True Art of Playing Keyboard Instruments*. Translated by William J. Mitchell. New York: W. W. Norton.

Bailey, Derek. 1992. *Improvisation: Its Nature and Practice in Music*. Cambridge, MA: Da Capo.
Baily, John. 1977. "Movement Patterns in Playing the Herati Dutar." In *The Anthropology of the Body*, edited by John Blacking, 275–330. London: Academic Press.
———. 1996. "Using Tests of Sound Perception in Fieldwork." *Yearbook for Traditional Music* 28: 147–73.
———. 2006. "John Blacking and the 'Human/Musical Instrument Interface': Two Plucked Lutes from Afghanistan." In *The Musical Human: Rethinking John Blacking's Ethnomusicology in the Twenty-First Century*, edited by Suzel Ana Reily, 107–23. Aldershot: Ashgate.
Baily, John, and Peter Driver. 1992. "Spatio-Motor Thinking in Playing Folk Blues Guitar." *World of Music* 34: 57–71.
Bangert, Marc, and Eckart O. Altenmüller. 2003. "Mapping Perception to Action in Piano Practice: A Longitudinal DC-EEG Study." *BMC Neuroscience* 4: 26.
Bangert, Marc, Thomas Betzwieser, Gottfried Schlaug, Michael Rotte, Dieter Drescher, Hermann Hinrichs, Hans-Jochen Heinze, and Eckart Altenmüller. 2006. "Shared Networks for Auditory and Motor Processing in Professional Pianists: Evidence from fMRI Conjunction." *Neuroimage* 30: 917–26.
Bangert, Marc, Udo Haeusler, and Eckart Altenmüller. 2001. "On Practice: How the Brain Connects Piano Keys and Piano Sounds." *Annals of the New York Academy of Sciences* 930: 425–28.
Barolsky, Daniel, and Edward Klorman. 2016. "Performance and Analysis Today: New Horizons." *Music Theory Online* 22. http://mtosmt.org/issues/mto.16.22.2/mto.16.22.2.barolsky_klorman.html.
Barrett, David. 1995. *Mel Bay's Complete Classic Chicago Blues Harp*. Pacific, MO: Mel Bay.
Barsalou, Lawrence W. 1999. "Perceptual Symbol Systems." *Behavioral and Brain Sciences* 22: 577–660.
———. 2003. "Situated Simulation in the Human Conceptual System." *Language and Cognitive Processes* 18: 513–62.
———. 2008. "Grounded Cognition." *Annual Review of Psychology* 59: 617–45.
———. 2010. "Grounded Cognition: Past, Present, and Future." *Topics in Cognitive Science* 2: 716–24.
Barthes, Roland. 1977. *Image, Music, Text*. Translated by Stephen Heath. New York: Hill & Wang.
Bates, Eliot. 2012. "The Social Life of Musical Instruments." *Ethnomusicology* 56: 363–95.
Bateson, Gregory. 1972. *Steps to an Ecology of Mind*. New York: Ballantine Books.
Baudrillard, Jean. 1996. *The System of Objects*. Translated by James Benedict. London: Verso.
Behmer, Lawrence Paul, and Kelly J. Jantzen. 2011. "Reading Sheet Music Facilitates Sensorimotor Mu-Desynchronization in Musicians." *Clinical Neurophysiology* 122: 1342–47.
Beller-McKenna, Daniel. 2005. "Distance and Disembodiment: Harps, Horns, and the Requiem Idea in Schumann and Brahms." *Journal of Musicology* 22: 47–89.
Benade, Arthur H. 1973. "The Physics of Brasses." *Scientific American* 229 (1): 24–35.
Bent, Margaret. 1984. "Diatonic 'Ficta.'" *Early Music History* 4: 1–48.
Berliner, Paul F. 1993. *The Soul of Mbira: Music and Traditions of the Shona People of Zimbabwe*. Chicago: University of Chicago Press.
Bijsterveld, Karin, and Marten Schulp. 2004. "Breaking into a World of Perfection: Innovation in Today's Classical Musical Instruments." *Social Studies of Science* 34: 649–74.
Blacking, John. 1959. "Problems of Pitch, Pattern and Harmony in the Ocarina Music of the Venda." *African Music* 2: 15–23.
———. 1973. *How Musical Is Man?* Seattle: University of Washington Press.

Blasius, Leslie David. 1996. "The Mechanics of Sensation and the Construction of the Romantic Musical Experience." In *Music Theory in the Age of Romanticism*, edited by Ian Bent, 3–24. Cambridge: Cambridge University Press.

Borgo, David. 2005. *Sync or Swarm: Improvising Music in a Complex Age*. New York: Continuum.

Botvinick, Matthew, and Jonathan Cohen. 1998. "Rubber Hands 'Feel' Touch That Eyes See." *Nature* 391: 756.

Brauchli, Bernard. 1998. *The Clavichord*. Cambridge: Cambridge University Press.

Bregman, Albert S. 1990. *Auditory Scene Analysis: The Perceptual Organization of Sound*. Cambridge, MA: MIT Press.

Brower, Candace. 1997. "Pathway, Blockage, and Containment in Density 21.5." *Theory and Practice* 22/23: 35–54.

Brown, Roberta W. 1934. "A Preliminary Study of the Touch Method of Learning Piano Music." *Journal of Applied Psychology* 18: 516–27.

Bryan, Paul R. 1975. "The Horn in the Works of Mozart and Haydn: Some Observations and Comparisons." *Haydn Yearbook* 9: 189–255.

Buch, David J. 1985. "*Style brisé, Style luthé*, and the *Choses luthées*." *Musical Quarterly* 71: 52–67.

Bungert, James. 2015. "Bach and the Patterns of Transformation." *Music Theory Spectrum* 37: 98–119.

Burguéte, André. 1977. "Die Lautenkompositionen Johann Sebastian Bachs. Ein Beitrag zur Kritischen Wertung aus Spielpraktischer Sicht." *Bach-Jahrbuch* 63: 26–52.

Butler, Mark. 2014. *Playing with Something That Runs: Technology, Improvisation, and Composition in DJ and Laptop Performance*. New York: Oxford University Press.

Byros, Vasili. 2012. "Meyer's 'Anvil': Revisiting the Schema Concept." *Music Analysis* 31: 273–346.

Cage, John. 1961. *Silence*. Middletown, CT: Wesleyan University Press.

———. 1979. *Empty Words: Writings '73–'78*. Middletown, CT: Wesleyan University Press.

Calvo-Merino, Beatriz, Daniel E. Glaser, Julie Grèzes, Richard E. Passingham, and Patrick Haggard. 2005. "Action Observation and Acquired Motor Skills: An FMRI Study with Expert Dancers." *Cerebral Cortex* 15: 1243–49.

Canguilhem, Philippe. 2011. "Singing Upon the Book According to Vicente Lusitano." Translated by Alexander Stalarow. *Early Music History* 30: 55–103.

Cardinali, Lucilla, Francesca Frassinetti, Claudio Brozzoli, Christian Urquizar, Alice C. Roy, and Alessandro Farnè. 2009. "Tool-Use Induces Morphological Updating of the Body Schema." *Current Biology* 19: R478–79.

Chen, Jessie, Marjorie Woollacott, Steve Pologe, and George P. Moore. 2013. "Stochastic Aspects of Motor Behavior and Their Dependence on Auditory Feedback in Experienced Cellists." *Frontiers in Human Neuroscience* 7: 419.

Chen, Joyce L., Charlotte Rae, and Kate E. Watkins. 2011. "Learning to Play a Melody: An fMRI Study Examining the Formation of Auditory-Motor Associations" *Neuroimage* 59: 1200–1208.

Chopin, Frédéric. 1993. *Esquisses pour une méthode de piano*. Edited by Jean-Jacques Eigeldinger. Harmoniques. Paris: Flammarion.

Christensen, Thomas. 1992. "The Spanish Baroque Guitar and Seventeenth-Century Triadic Theory." *Journal of Music Theory* 36: 1–42.

———. 1999. "Four-Hand Piano Transcription and Geographies of Nineteenth-Century Musical Reception." *Journal of the American Musicological Society* 52: 255–98.

Chua, Daniel. 1999. *Absolute Music and the Construction of Meaning*. Cambridge: Cambridge University Press.

Cimini, Amy. 2012. "Vibrating Colors and Silent Bodies: Music, Sound, and Silence in Maurice Merleau-Ponty's Critique of Dualism." *Contemporary Music Review* 31: 353–70.

Clarke, Eric F. 2005. *Ways of Listening: An Ecological Approach to the Perception of Musical Meaning*. New York: Oxford University Press.

Clifton, Thomas. 1983. *Music as Heard: A Study in Applied Phenomenology*. New Haven, CT: Yale University Press.

Clough, John, and Jack Douthett. 1991. "Maximally Even Sets." *Journal of Music Theory* 35: 93–173.

Cohn, Richard. 2012. *Audacious Euphony: Chromatic Harmony and the Triad's Second Nature*. Oxford Studies in Music Theory. New York: Oxford University Press.

Cole, Jonathan, and Jacques Paillard. 1995. "Living without Touch and Peripheral Information about Body Position and Movement: Studies with Deafferented Subjects." In *The Body and the Self*, edited by Jose Luis Bermudez, Anthony J. Marcel, and Naomi M. Eilan, 245–66. Cambridge, MA: MIT Press.

Cook, Nicholas. 2014. *Beyond the Score: Music as Performance*. New York: Oxford University Press.

Couchman, Justin J., Robertson Beasley, and Peter Q. Pfordresher. 2012. "The Experience of Agency in Sequence Production with Altered Auditory Feedback." *Consciousness and Cognition* 21: 186–203.

Cox, Arnie. 1999. "The Metaphoric Logic of Musical Motion and Space." PhD dissertation, University of Oregon.

———. 2006. "Hearing, Feeling, Grasping Gestures." In *Music and Gesture*, edited by Anthony Gritten and Elaine King, 45–60. Aldershot: Ashgate.

———. 2011. "Embodying Music: Principles of the Mimetic Hypothesis." *Music Theory Online* 17. http://www.mtosmt.org/issues/mto.11.17.2/mto.11.17.2.cox.html.

Critchley, Simon. 2002. "Introduction." In *The Cambridge Companion to Levinas*, edited by Simon Critchley and Robert Bernasconi, 1–32. Cambridge: Cambridge University Press.

Cross, Ian. 2007. "Music and Cognitive Evolution." In *Oxford Handbook of Evolutionary Psychology*, edited by R. I. M. Dunbar and Louise Barrett, 649–68. Oxford: Oxford University Press.

Crump, Matthew J. C., Gordon D. Logan, and Jerry Kimbrough. 2012. "Keeping an Eye on Guitar Skill: Visual Representations of Guitar Chords." *Music Perception* 30: 37–47.

Csikszentmihalyi, Mihaly. 1990. *Flow: The Psychology of Optimal Experience*. New York: Harper & Row.

Cuciurean, John. 2000. "A Theory of Pitch, Rhythm, and Intertextual Allusion for the Late Music of György Ligeti." PhD dissertation, State University of New York at Buffalo.

Cusick, Suzanne G. 1994. "Feminist Theory, Music Theory, and the Mind/Body Problem." *Perspectives of New Music* 32: 8–27.

Czerny, Carl. 1851. *Letters to a Young Lady on the Art of Playing the Pianoforte*. Translated by J. A. Hamilton. New York: Firth, Pond & Co.

Dahlhaus, Carl. 1989. *The Idea of Absolute Music*. Translated by Roger Lustig. Chicago: University of Chicago Press.

Damasio, Antonio R. 1989. "Time-Locked Multiregional Retroactivation: A Systems-Level Proposal for the Neural Substrates of Recall and Recognition." *Cognition* 33: 25–62.

David, Hans T., and Arthur Mendel, eds. 1945. *The Bach Reader: A Life of Johann Sebastian Bach in Letters and Documents*. New York: W. W. Norton.

David, Hans T., Arthur Mendel, and Christoph Wolff, eds. 1998. *The New Bach Reader: A Life of Johann Sebastian Bach in Letters and Documents*. New York: W. W. Norton.

Davidson, Jane W. 1993. "Visual Perception of Performance Manner in the Movements of Solo Musicians." *Psychology of Music* 21: 103–13.

Dawe, Kevin. 2010. *The New Guitarscape in Critical Theory, Cultural Practice, and Musical Performance*. Farnham: Ashgate.

Demers, Joanna. 2010. *Listening through the Noise: The Aesthetics of Experimental Electronic Music*. New York: Oxford University Press.

Derrida, Jacques. 1976. *Of Grammatology*. Translated by Gayatri Chakravorty Spivak. Baltimore: Johns Hopkins University Press.

———. 1988. *Limited Inc*. Evanston, IL: Northwestern University Press.

———. 2011. *Voice and Phenomenon: Introduction to the Problem of the Sign in Husserl's Phenomenology*. Translated by Leonard Lawlor. Northwestern Studies in Phenomenology and Existential Philosophy. Evanston, IL: Northwestern University Press.

Descartes, René. 2001. *Discourse on Method, Optics, Geometry, and Meteorology*. Rev. ed. Translated by Paul J. Olscamp. Indianapolis: Hackett.

De Souza, Jonathan. 2013. "Musical Instruments, Bodies, and Cognition." PhD dissertation, University of Chicago.

———. 2014. "Voice and Instrument at the Origins of Music." *Current Musicology* 97: 21–36.

———. 2015. "Texture." In *The Oxford Handbook of Concepts in Music Theory*, edited by Alexander Rehding and Steven Rings [online]. New York: Oxford University Press.

———. 2016a. "'All Sights Were Perceived as Sounds': Pat Metheny and the Instrumental Image." In *Watching Jazz: Encounters with Jazz Performance on Screen*, edited by Björn Heile, Peter Elsdon, and Jenny Doctor, 147–68. Oxford: Oxford University Press.

———. 2016b. "Fretboard Transformations." Unpublished manuscript.

———. Forthcoming. "Timbral Thievery: Synthesizers and Sonic Materiality." In *The Oxford Handbook of Timbre*, edited by Alexander Rehding and Emily I. Dolan. New York: Oxford University Press.

Dibben, Nicola. 2001. "What Do We Hear, When We Hear Music? Music Perception and Musical Material." *Musicae Scientiae* 5: 161–94.

Dolan, Emily I. 2013. *The Orchestral Revolution: Haydn and the Technologies of Timbre*. Cambridge: Cambridge University Press.

Downey, Greg. 2002. "Listening to Capoeira: Phenomenology, Embodiment, and the Materiality of Music." *Ethnomusicology* 46: 487–509.

Dreyfus, Hubert L. 2002. "Intelligence without Representation—Merleau-Ponty's Critique of Mental Representation." *Phenomenology and the Cognitive Sciences* 1: 367–83.

Dreyfus, Laurence. 1996. *Bach and the Patterns of Invention*. Cambridge MA: Harvard University Press.

Drost, Ulrich C., Martina Rieger, Marcel Brass, Thomas C. Gunter, and Wolfgang Prinz. 2005. "Action-Effect Coupling in Pianists." *Psychological Research* 69: 233–41.

Drost, Ulrich C., Martina Rieger, and Wolfgang Prinz. 2007. "Instrument Specificity in Experienced Musicians." *Quarterly Journal of Experimental Psychology* 60: 527–33.

Dyson, Frances. 2009. *Sounding New Media: Immersion and Embodiment in the Arts and Culture*. Berkeley: University of California Press.

Ealy, George Thomas. 1994. "Of Ear Trumpets and a Resonance Plate: Early Hearing Aids and Beethoven's Hearing Perception." *19th-Century Music* 17: 262–73.

Edelman, Shimon, and Elise M. Breen. 1999. "On the Virtues of Going All the Way: A Commentary on Barsalou." *Behavioral and Brain Sciences* 22: 614.

Ehrsson, H. Henrik, Charles Spence, and Richard E. Passingham. 2004. "That's My Hand! Activity in Premotor Cortex Reflects Feeling of Ownership of a Limb." *Science* 305: 875–77.

Eigeldinger, Jean-Jacques. 1986. *Chopin: Pianist and Teacher as Seen by His Pupils*. Edited by Roy Howat. Translated by Naomi Shohet with Krysia Osostowicz and Roy Howat. Cambridge: Cambridge University Press.

Eitan, Zohar, and Renee Timmers. 2010. "Beethoven's Last Piano Sonata and Those Who Follow Crocodiles: Cross-Domain Mappings of Auditory Pitch in a Musical Context." *Cognition* 114: 405–22.

Elbert, Thomas, Christo Pantev, Christian Wienbruch, Brigitte Rockstroh, and Edward Taub. 1995. "Increased Cortical Representation of the Fingers of the Left Hand in String Players." *Science* 270: 305–7.

Emsley, Jason. 2011. *The Laptop DJ Handbook: Setups and Techniques of the Modern Performer*. Boston: Course Technology.

Erman, Britt, and Beatrice Warren. 2000. "The Idiom Principle and the Open Choice Principle." *Text* 20: 29–62.

Fazeli Fard, Maggie. 2012. "Harmonica-Playing Elephant Is National Zoo's Newest Star." *Washington Post*, May 2. http://www.washingtonpost.com/blogs/the-buzz/post/harmonica-playing-elephant-is-national-zoos-newest-star-video/2012/05/02/gIQABRf-pwT_blog.html.

Feldman, Martha. 2015. "The Interstitial Voice: An Opening." *Journal of the American Musicological Society* 68: 653–59.

Field, Kim. 2000. *Harmonicas, Harps, and Heavy Breathers: The Evolution of the People's Instrument*. Rev. ed. New York: Cooper Square.

Finney, Steven A. 1997. "Auditory Feedback and Musical Keyboard Performance." *Music Perception* 15: 153–74.

Fisher, George, and Judith Lochhead. 2002. "Analyzing from the Body." *Theory and Practice* 27: 37–67.

Fitzpatrick, Horace. 1970. *The Horn and Horn-Playing and the Austro-Bohemian Tradition from 1680 to 1830*. London: Oxford University Press.

Foucault, Michel. 1995. *Discipline and Punish: The Birth of the Prison*. Translated by Alan Sheridan. New York: Vintage Books.

Freed, D. 1990. "Auditory Correlates of Perceived Mallet Hardness for a Set of Recorded Percussive Sound Events." *Journal of the Acoustical Society of America* 87: 311–22.

Friedson, Steven M. 1996. *Dancing Prophets: Musical Experience in Tumbuka Healing*. Chicago: University of Chicago Press.

Frith, Chris. 2005. "The Self in Action: Lessons from Delusions of Control." *Consciousness and Cognition* 14: 752–70.

Frith, Fred. 2005. Liner notes for *The Compass, Log and Lead*, Fred Frith, Stevie Wishart, and Carla Kihlstedt. Intakt CD 103/2006, compact disc.

Fulton, Will. 2015. "Stevie Wonder's Tactile Keyboard Mediation, Black Key Compositional Development, and the Quest for Creative Autonomy." In *The Oxford Handbook of Music and Disability Studies*, edited by Blake Howe, Stephanie Jensen-Moulton, Neil Lerner, and Joseph Straus, 272–92. New York: Oxford University Press.

Galison, Peter. 2005. "Material Culture, Theoretical Culture, and Delocalization." In *Collection–Laboratory–Theater: Scenes of Knowledge in the 17th Century*, edited by Helmar Schramm, Ludger Schwarte, and Jan Lazardzig, English ed., 490–506. Theatrum Scientarum 1. Berlin: Walter de Gruyter.

Gallager, Robert G. 2001. "Claude E. Shannon: A Retrospective on His Life, Work, and Impact." *IEEE Transactions on Information Theory* 47: 2681–95.

Gallagher, Shaun. 1986. "Body Image and Body Schema: A Conceptual Clarification." *Journal of Mind and Behavior* 7: 541–54.

———. 2012. "Multiple Aspects in the Sense of Agency." *New Ideas in Psychology* 30: 15–31.

Gallagher, Shaun, and Mette Vaever. 2004. "Body: Disorders of Embodiment." In *The Philosophy of Psychiatry: A Companion*, edited by Jennifer Radden, 118–32. Oxford: Oxford University Press.

Gallope, Michael. 2011. "Technicity, Consciousness, and Musical Objects." In *Music and Consciousness: Philosophical, Psychological, and Cultural Perspectives*, edited by David Clarke and Eric F. Clarke, 47–64. Oxford: Oxford University Press.

Gaver, William W. 1988. "Everyday Listening and Auditory Icons." PhD dissertation, University of California, San Diego.

———. 1993. "What in the World Do We Hear?: An Ecological Approach to Auditory Event Perception." *Ecological Psychology* 5: 1–29.

Gawboy, Anna. 2009. "The Wheatstone Concertina and Symmetrical Arrangements of Tonal Space." *Journal of Music Theory* 53: 163–90.

Gibson, James J. 1966. *The Senses Considered as Perceptual Systems*. Boston: Houghton Mifflin.

———. 1979. *The Ecological Approach to Visual Perception*. Boston: Houghton Mifflin.

———. 1982. *Reasons for Realism: Selected Essays of James J. Gibson*. Edited by Edward Reed and Rebecca Jones. Hillsdale, NJ: Lawrence Erlbaum.

Gjerdingen, Robert O. 2007a. *Music in the Galant Style*. New York: Oxford University Press.

———. 2007b. "*Partimento, que me veux-tu?*" *Journal of Music Theory* 51: 85–135.

———. 2009. "The Price of (Perceived) Affordance: Commentary for Huron and Berec." *Empirical Musicology Review* 4: 123–25.

Gjerdingen, Robert O., and Janet Bourne. 2015. "Schema Theory as a Construction Grammar." *Music Theory Online* 21. http://www.mtosmt.org/issues/mto.15.21.2/mto.15.21.2.gjerdingen_bourne.html.

Glenberg, Arthur M. 1997. "What Memory Is For." *Behavioral and Brain Sciences* 20: 1–55.

Goebl, Werner, and Caroline Palmer. 2008. "Tactile Feedback and Timing Accuracy in Piano Performance." *Experimental Brain Research* 186: 471–79.

———. 2009. "Synchronization of Timing and Motion Among Performing Musicians." *Music Perception* 26: 427–38.

Goehr, Lydia. 1998. *The Quest for Voice: On Music, Politics, and the Limits of Philosophy*. Oxford: Clarendon Press.

Goldin-Meadow, Susan, and Sian L. Beilock. 2010. "Action's Influence on Thought: The Case of Gesture." *Perspectives on Psychological Science* 5: 664–74.

Goldman, Jonathan. 2012. "The Buttons on Pandora's Box: David Tudor and the Bandoneon." *American Music* 30: 30–60.

———. Forthcoming. "Gérard Grisey and the Accordion." *Twentieth-Century Music*.

Goldstone, Robert L., and Lawrence W. Barsalou. 1998. "Reuniting Perception and Conception." *Cognition* 65: 231–62.

Gollin, Edward. 2000. "Representations of Space and Conceptions of Distance in Transformational Music Theories." PhD dissertation, Harvard University.

Graham, Keith. n.d. "Sonny Boy Williamson II, Help Me Solo." *HarpTab.com*. http://www.harptab.com/helpme/helpme3.shtml.

Graham, Kyran T., Mathew T. Martin-Iverson, Nicholas P. Holmes, Assen Jablensky, and Flavie Waters. 2014. "Deficits in Agency in Schizophrenia, and Additional Deficits in Body Image, Body Schema, and Internal Timing, in Passivity Symptoms." *Frontiers in Psychiatry* 5: 126.

Grahn, Jessica A. 2009. "The Role of the Basal Ganglia in Beat Perception: Neuroimaging and Neuropsychological Investigations." *Annals of the New York Academy of Sciences* 1169: 35–45.

Graziano, Michael S. A., and Matthew Botvinick. 2002. "How the Brain Represents the Body: Insights from Neurophysiology and Psychology." In *Common Mechanisms in Perception and Action: Attention and Performance XIX*, edited by Wolfgang Prinz and Bernhard Hommel, 136–57. Oxford: Oxford University Press.

Greimas, Algirdas J., and François Rastier. 1968. "The Interaction of Semiotic Constraints." *Yale French Studies* 41: 86–105.

Guan, Connie Qun, Wanjin Meng, Ru Yao, and Arthur M. Glenberg. 2013. "The Motor System Contributes to Comprehension of Abstract Language." *PLoS ONE* 8: e75183.

Guterstam, Arvid, Giovanni Gentile, and H. Henrik Ehrsson. 2013. "The Invisible Hand Illusion: Multisensory Integration Leads to the Embodiment of a Discrete Volume of Empty Space." *Journal of Cognitive Neuroscience* 25: 1078–99.

Hafke-Dys, Honorata, Anna Preis, and David Trojan. 2016. "Violinists' Perceptions of and Motor Reactions to Fundamental Frequency Shifts Introduced in Auditory Feedback." *Acta Acustica United with Acustica* 102: 155–58.

Hall, Matthew J. 2015. "Keyboard Technique as Contrapuntal Structure in J. S. Bach's Clavier Works." *Understanding Bach* 10: 85–107.

Halwani, Gus F., Psyche Loui, Theodor Rüber, and Gottfried Schlaug. 2010. "Effects of Practice and Experience on the Arcuate Fasciculus: Comparing Singers, Instrumentalists, and Non-Musicians." *Frontiers in Psychology* 2: 156.

Harman, Graham. 2002. *Tool-Being: Heidegger and the Metaphysics of Objects*. Chicago: Open Court.

———. 2007. "Aesthetics as First Philosophy: Levinas and the Non-Human." *Naked Punch* 9: 21–30.

Harrison, Daniel. 1988. "Some Group Properties of Triple Counterpoint and Their Influence on Compositions by J. S. Bach." *Journal of Music Theory* 32: 23–49.

Hasegawa, Takehiro, Ken-Ichi Matsuki, Takashi Ueno, Yasuhiro Maeda, Yoshihiko Matsue, Yukuo Konishi, and Norihiro Sadato. 2004. "Learned Audio-Visual Cross-Modal Associations in Observed Piano Playing Activate the Left Planum Temporale: An fMRI Study." *Cognitive Brain Research* 20: 510–18.

Hatten, Robert S. 2004. *Interpreting Musical Gestures, Topics, and Tropes: Mozart, Beethoven, Schubert*. Bloomington: Indiana University Press.

Haueisen, Jens, and Thomas R. Knösche. 2001. "Involuntary Motor Activity in Pianists Evoked by Music Perception." *Journal of Cognitive Neuroscience* 13: 786–92.

Hayles, N. Katherine. 1999. *How We Became Posthuman: Virtual Bodies in Cybernetics, Literature, and Informatics*. Chicago: University of Chicago Press.

Head, Henry. 1920. *Studies in Neurology*. Vol. 2. London: Oxford University Press.

Heartz, Daniel. 1976. "The Hunting Chorus in Haydn's *Jahreszeiten* and the 'Airs de Chasse' in the *Encyclopédie*." *Eighteenth-Century Studies* 9: 523–39.

Heidegger, Martin. 1968. *What Is Called Thinking?* Translated by Fred D. Wieck and J. Glenn Gray. New York: Harper & Row.

———. 1977. *"The Question Concerning Technology" and Other Essays*. Translated by William Lovitt. New York: Harper & Row.

———. 2008. *Basic Writings*. Edited by David Farrell Krell. New York: HarperCollins.

———. 2010. *Being and Time*. Translated by Joan Stambaugh. Revised. Albany, NY: SUNY Press.

Heyde, Herbert. 1975. *Grundlagen des natürlichen Systems der Musikinstrumente*. Beiträge zur musikwissenschaftlichen Forschung in der DDR 7. Leipzig: VEB Deutscher Verlag für Musik.

———. 2001. "Methods of Organology and Proportions in Brass Wind Instrument Making." *Historic Brass Society Journal* 13: 1–51.

Hicks, Jonathan. 2014. "Aesthetics over a Barrel." Paper presented at the Eighteenth Biennial International Conference on Nineteenth-Century Music, University of Toronto, June 19.

Hoeckner, Berthold. 1997. "Schumann and Romantic Distance." *Journal of the American Musicological Society* 50: 55–132.

Holman, Bobby Joe. 2000. *The Hal Leonard Complete Harmonica Method*. Milwaukee, WI: Hal Leonard.

Holmes, Allen. 2002. "Bent over Overbends." *Harmonica Sessions eZine*.

Hook, Julian. 2002. "Uniform Triadic Transformations." *Journal of Music Theory* 46: 57–126.

———. 2014. "Key-Color Invariance". Paper presented at the Mathematics of Music Interest Group Meeting, Society for Music Theory Annual Meeting, Milwaukee, WI, November 7.

Hornbostel, Erich M. von, and Curt Sachs. 1961. "Classification of Musical Instruments." Translated by Anthony Baines and Klaus P. Wachsmann. *Galpin Society Journal* 14: 3–29.

Howell, Peter, David J. Powell, and Ian Khan. 1983. "Amplitude Contour of the Delayed Signal and Interference in Delayed Auditory Feedback Tasks." *Journal of Experimental Psychology: Human Perception and Performance* 9: 772–84.

Hughes, Bryn. 2011. "Harmonic Expectation in Twelve-Bar Blues Progressions." PhD dissertation, Florida State University, Tallahassee.

Humbert, Nicolas, and Werner Penzel. 1990. *Step Across the Border*. Cine Nomades Filmproduction, Munich; Res Balzli & Cie Filmproduktion, Nidau.

Humphries, John. 2000. *The Early Horn: A Practical Guide*. Cambridge Handbooks to the Historical Performance of Music. Cambridge: Cambridge University Press.

Huron, David. 2006. *Sweet Anticipation: Music and the Psychology of Expectation*. Cambridge, MA: MIT Press.

Huron, David, and Jonathon Berec. 2009. "Characterizing Idiomatic Organization in Music: A Theory and Case Study of Musical Affordances." *Empirical Musicology Review* 4: 103–22.

Husserl, Edmund. 1960. *Cartesian Meditations: An Introduction to Phenomenology*. Translated by Dorion Cairns. The Hague: Martinus Nijhoff.

———. 1969. *Formal and Transcendental Logic*. Translated by Dorion Cairns. The Hague: Martinus Nijhoff.

———. 1973. *Zur Phänomenologie der Intersubjektivität: Texte aus dem Nachlass*. Edited by Iso Kern. Vol. 1. Husserliana 13. The Hague: Martinus Nijhoff.

———. 2012. *Ideas: General Introduction to Pure Phenomenology*. Translated by W. R. Boyce Gibson. London: Routledge.

Hutchins, Edwin. 1995. *Cognition in the Wild*. Cambridge, MA: MIT Press.

Hyer, Brian. 2011. "What Is a Function?" In *The Oxford Handbook of Neo-Riemannian Music Theories*, edited by Edward Gollin and Alexander Rehding, 92–139. Oxford: Oxford University Press.

Ihde, Don. 1986. *Experimental Phenomenology: An Introduction*. Albany, NY: SUNY Press.

———. 1990. *Technology and the Lifeworld: From Garden to Earth*. Bloomington: Indiana University Press.

———. 2007. *Listening and Voice: Phenomenologies of Sound*. 2nd ed. Albany, NY: SUNY Press.

———. 2009. *Postphenomenology and Technoscience: The Peking University Lectures*. Albany, NY: SUNY Press.

Ingold, Tim. 2000. *The Perception of the Environment: Essays on Livelihood, Dwelling and Skill*. London: Routledge.

Jeannerod, Marc. 1997. *The Cognitive Neuroscience of Action*. Fundamentals of Cognitive Neuroscience 1. Oxford: Blackwell.

———. 2006. *Motor Cognition: What Actions Tell the Self.* Oxford Psychology Series 42. Oxford: Oxford University Press.

Johnson, Mark. 1987. *The Body in the Mind: The Bodily Basis of Meaning, Imagination, and Reason.* Chicago: University of Chicago Press.

Johnson, Mark, and Steve Larson. 2003. "'Something in the Way She Moves'—Metaphors of Musical Motion." *Metaphor and Symbol* 18: 63–84.

Johnston, Robert B. 1987. "Pitch Control in Harmonica Playing." *Acoustics Australia* 15: 69–75.

Jonas, Hans. 1966. "The Nobility of Sight: A Study in the Phenomenology of the Senses." In *The Phenomenon of Life: Toward a Philosophical Biology*, 135–52. New York: Harper & Row.

Jost, Peter. 2001. "Klang, Harmonik, und Form in Brahms' Horntrio Op. 40." In *Internationaler Brahms-Kongress Gmunden 1997: Kongreßbericht*, edited by Ingrid Fuchs, 59–71. Tutzing: Hans Schneider.

Kane, Brian. 2011. "Excavating Lewin's 'Phenomenology.'" *Music Theory Spectrum* 33: 27–36.

———. 2014. *Sound Unseen: Acousmatic Sound in Theory and Practice.* New York: Oxford University Press.

Kartomi, Margaret J. 1990. *On Concepts and Classifications of Musical Instruments.* Chicago: University of Chicago Press.

Kirsh, David. 2013. "Embodied Cognition and the Magical Future of Interaction Design." *ACM Transactions on Computer-Human Interaction* 20 (1), Article 3.

Kittler, Friedrich A. 1999. *Gramophone, Film, Typewriter.* Translated by Geoffrey Winthrop-Young and Michael Wutz. Stanford, CA: Stanford University Press.

Knittel, K. M. 1998. "Wagner, Deafness, and the Reception of Beethoven's Late Style." *Journal of the American Musicological Society* 51: 49–82.

Koozin, Timothy. 2011. "Guitar Voicing in Pop-Rock Music: A Performance-Based Analytical Approach." *Music Theory Online* 17. http://www.mtosmt.org/issues/mto.11.17.3/mto.11.17.3.koozin.html.

Kozak, Mariusz. 2015. "Listeners' Bodies in Music Analysis: Gestures, Motor Intentionality, and Models." *Music Theory Online* 21. http://www.mtosmt.org/issues/mto.15.21.3/mto.15.21.3.kozak.php.

Kramer, Lawrence. 1995. *Classical Music and Postmodern Knowledge.* Berkeley: University of California Press.

Lachenmann, Helmut. 1980. "The 'Beautiful' in Music Today." *Tempo*, n.s., 135: 20–24.

———. 1995. "On Structuralism." *Contemporary Music Review* 12: 93–102.

———. 1996. *Musik als existentielle Erfahrung: Schriften, 1966–1995.* Wiesbaden: Breitkopf & Härtel.

Laeng, Bruno, and A. Park. 1999. "Handedness Effects on Playing a Reversed or Normal Keyboard." *Laterality* 4: 363–77.

Lahav, Amir, Elliot Saltzman, and Gottfried Schlaug. 2007. "Action Representation of Sound: Audiomotor Recognition Network While Listening to Newly Acquired Actions." *Journal of Neuroscience* 27: 308–14.

Lakoff, George, and Mark Johnson. 1980. *Metaphors We Live By.* Chicago: University of Chicago Press.

Landon, H. C. Robbins. 1976. *Haydn: Chronicle and Works.* Vol. 1. 5 vols. Bloomington: Indiana University Press.

Lange, Oskar. 1965. *Wholes and Parts: A General Theory of System Behaviour.* Translated by Eugeniusz Lepa. Oxford: Pergamon Press.

Langwill, Lyndesay G., and Arthur W. J. G. Ord-Hume. 2001. "Barrel Organ." *Grove Music Online.* http://www.oxfordmusiconline.com/subscriber/article/grove/music/02111.

Larson, Steve. 2012. *Musical Forces: Motion, Metaphor, and Meaning in Music*. Musical Meaning and Interpretation. Bloomington: Indiana University Press.
Latour, Bruno. 1991. "Technology Is Society Made Durable." In *A Sociology of Monsters: Essays on Power, Technology, and Domination*, edited by John Law, 103–31. Sociological Review Monograph 38. London: Routledge.
Ledbetter, David. 1987. *Harpsichord and Lute Music in 17th-Century France*. Bloomington: Indiana University Press.
———. 2002. *Bach's Well-Tempered Clavier: The 48 Preludes and Fugues*. New Haven, CT: Yale University Press.
———. 2009. *Unaccompanied Bach: Performing the Solo Works*. New Haven, CT: Yale University Press.
Le Guin, Elisabeth. 2006. *Boccherini's Body: An Essay in Carnal Musicology*. Berkeley: University of California Press.
Leppert, Richard. 1993. *The Sight of Sound: Music, Representation, and the History of the Body*. Berkeley: University of California Press.
Lerdahl, Fred. 2001. *Tonal Pitch Space*. New York: Oxford University Press.
Lerdahl, Fred, and Ray Jackendoff. 1983. *A Generative Theory of Tonal Music*. Cambridge, MA: MIT Press.
Lester, Joel. 1999. *Bach's Works for Solo Violin: Style, Structure, Performance*. New York: Oxford University Press.
Levinas, Emmanuel. 1969. *Totality and Infinity: An Essay on Exteriority*. Translated by Alphonso Lingis. Pittsburgh: Duquesne University Press.
———. 1981. *Otherwise than Being, or Beyond Essence*. Translated by Alphonso Lingis. The Hague: Martinus Nijhoff.
———. 1989. *The Levinas Reader*. Edited by Seán Hand. Oxford: Blackwell.
Levy, Howard. 1992. *New Directions for Harmonica: Expanding Your Technique*. Woodstock, NY: Homespun Tapes.
Lewin, David. 1977. "Forte's Interval Vector, My Interval Function, and Regener's Common-Note Function." *Journal of Music Theory* 21: 194–237.
———. 1986. "Music Theory, Phenomenology, and Modes of Perception." *Music Perception* 3: 327–92.
———. 1987. *Generalized Musical Intervals and Transformations*. New Haven, CT: Yale University Press.
———. 1993. *Musical Form and Transformation: 4 Analytic Essays*. New Haven, CT: Yale University Press.
———. 1998. "Some Ideas about Voice-Leading between PCSets." *Journal of Music Theory* 42: 15–72.
Lidji, Pascale, Régine Kolinsky, Aliette Lochy, and José Morais. 2007. "Spatial Associations for Musical Stimuli: A Piano in the Head?" *Journal of Experimental Psychology: Human Perception and Performance* 33: 1189–1207.
Lingis, Alphonso. 1998. *The Imperative*. Studies in Continental Thought. Bloomington: Indiana University Press.
Lotze, M., G. Scheler, H.-R.M. Tan, C. Braun, and N. Birbaumer. 2003. "The Musician's Brain: Functional Imaging of Amateurs and Professionals During Performance and Imagery." *NeuroImage* 20: 1817–29.
Magnusson, Thor. 2009. "Of Epistemic Tools: Musical Instruments as Cognitive Extensions." *Organised Sound* 14: 168–76.
Mann, Alfred. 1970. "Beethoven's Contrapuntal Studies with Haydn." *Musical Quarterly* 56: 711–26.

Marcel, Anthony. 2003. "The Sense of Agency: Awareness and Ownership of Action." In *Agency and Self-Awareness: Issues in Philosophy and Psychology*, edited by Johannes Roessler and Naomi Eilan, 48–93. Oxford: Oxford University Press.

Margulis, Elizabeth Hellmuth, Lauren M. Mlsna, Ajith K. Uppunda, Todd B. Parrish, and Patrick C. M. Wong. 2009. "Selective Neurophysiologic Responses to Music in Instrumentalists with Different Listening Biographies." *Human Brain Mapping* 30: 267–75.

Marshall, Robert. 1972. *The Compositional Process of J. S. Bach: A Study of the Autograph Scores of the Vocal Works*. Princeton, NJ: Princeton University Press.

Maturana, Humberto R., and Francisco J. Varela. 1980. *Autopoiesis and Cognition: The Realization of the Living*. Boston Studies in the Philosophy of Science 42. Dordrecht: Reidel.

McClary, Susan. 1998. "Unruly Passions and Courtly Dances: Technologies of the Body in Baroque Music." In *From the Royal to the Republican Body: Incorporating the Political in Seventeenth- and Eighteenth-Century France*, edited by Sara E. Melzer and Kathryn Norberg, 85–112. Berkeley: University of California Press.

McClary, Susan, and Robert Walser. 1994. "Theorizing the Body in African-American Music." *Black Music Research Journal* 14: 75–84.

McLuhan, Marshall. 1994. *Understanding Media: The Extensions of Man*. Cambridge, MA: MIT Press.

McNeill, David. 1992. *Hand and Mind: What Gestures Reveal about Thought*. Chicago: University of Chicago Press.

Mead, Andrew. 1999. "Bodily Hearing: Physiological Metaphors and Musical Understanding." *Journal of Music Theory* 43: 1–19.

Merleau-Ponty, Maurice. 1963. *The Structure of Behavior*. Translated by Alden L. Fisher. Boston: Beacon Press.

———. 1964. *The Primacy of Perception*. Edited by James M. Edie. Evanston, IL: Northwestern University Press.

———. 1968. *The Visible and the Invisible*. Edited by Claude Lefort. Translated by Alphonso Lingis. Northwestern Studies in Phenomenology and Existential Philosophy. Evanston, IL: Northwestern University Press.

———. 2003. *Nature: Course Notes from the Collège de France*. Translated by Roger Vallier. Evanston, IL: Northwestern University Press.

———. 2012. *Phenomenology of Perception*. Translated by Donald A. Landes. London: Routledge.

Metheny, Pat. 2000. *Pat Metheny Song Book: The Complete Collection, 167 Compositions*. Milwaukee, WI: Hal Leonard.

Meyer, Leonard B. 1956. *Emotion and Meaning in Music*. Chicago: University of Chicago Press.

———. 1967. *Music, the Arts, and Ideas: Patterns and Predictions in Twentieth-Century Culture*. Chicago: University of Chicago Press.

———. 1973. "On the Nature and Limits of Critical Analysis." In *Explaining Music: Essays and Explorations*, 3–25. Berkeley: University of California Press.

Milkowski, Bill. 1983. "The Frith Factor: Exploration in Sound." *Downbeat* 50 (1): 22–25, 61.

Miller, Cherisse W. 2011. *Making Music with a Hearing Loss: Strategies and Stories*. Rockville, MD: AAMHL Publications.

Miner, Gregg. 2015. "What Is a Harp Guitar? The Definitive Organology of Historical and Modern Harp Guitars and Related Instruments." http://www.harpguitars.net/history/org/hgorg.htm.

Missin, Pat. n.d. "So Just Who Was This Richter Guy and What Exactly Did He Invent?" www.patmissin.com/ffaq/q37.html.

Monelle, Raymond. 2006. *The Musical Topic: Hunt, Military and Pastoral.* Bloomington: Indiana University Press.

Montague, Eugene. 2012. "Instrumental Gesture in Chopin's Étude in A-Flat Major, Op. 25, No. 1." *Music Theory Online* 18. http://www.mtosmt.org/issues/mto.12.18.4/mto.12.18.4.montague.php.

Moseley, Roger. 2015. "Digital Analogies: The Keyboard as Field of Musical Play." *Journal of the American Musicological Society* 68: 151–227.

Mumford, Lewis. 1934. *Technics and Civilization.* New York: Harcourt, Brace.

Musicians Professional Resource. n.d. "Howard Levy Interview." *Musicians Professional Resource.* http://www.musicians-professional-resource.com/interview3.html.

Nahmias, Eddy. 2005. "Agency, Authorship, and Illusion." *Consciousness and Cognition* 14: 771–85.

Nattiez, Jean Jacques. 1990. *Music and Discourse: Toward a Semiology of Music.* Princeton, NJ: Princeton University Press.

Nettl, Bruno. 1992. *The Radif of Persian Music: Studies of Structure and Cultural Context in the Classical Music of Iran.* Rev. ed. Champaign, IL: Elephant & Cat.

Novembre, Giacomo, and Peter E. Keller. 2011. "A Grammar of Action Generates Predictions in Skilled Musicians." *Consciousness and Cognition* 20: 1232–43.

Overy, Katie, and Istvan Molnar-Szakacs. 2009. "Being Together in Time: Musical Experience and the Mirror Neuron System." *Music Perception* 26: 489–504.

Pacherie, Elisabeth. 2008. "The Phenomenology of Action: A Conceptual Framework." *Cognition* 107: 179–219.

Palisca, Claude V. 1961. "Scientific Empiricism in Musical Thought." In *Seventeenth-Century Science and the Arts,* edited by H. H. Rhys, 91–137. Princeton, NJ: Princeton University Press.

Palmer, Caroline, and Simone Dalla Bella. 2004. "Movement Amplitude and Tempo Change in Piano Performance." *Journal of the Acoustical Society of America* 115: 2590.

Palmer, Caroline, Erik Koopmans, Janeen D. Loehr, and Christine Carter. 2009. "Movement-Related Feedback and Temporal Accuracy in Clarinet Performance." *Music Perception* 26: 439–49.

Palmer, Caroline, and Rosalee K. Meyer. 2000. "Conceptual and Motor Learning in Music Performance." *Psychological Science* 11: 63–68.

Palmer, Carolyn F., Rebecca K. Jones, Beth L. Hennessy, Marsha G. Unze, and Anne D. Pick. 1989. "How Is a Trumpet Known? The 'Basic Object Level' Concept and Perception of Musical Instruments." *American Journal of Psychology* 102: 17–37.

Palombini, Carlos. 1998. "Technology and Pierre Schaeffer: Pierre Schaeffer's *Art-Relais,* Walter Benjamin's *technische Reproduzierbarkeit* and Martin Heidegger's *Ge-stell.*" *Organised Sound* 3: 35–43.

Parry, Richard. 2007. "*Episteme* and *Techne.*" *Stanford Encyclopedia of Philosophy.* http://plato.stanford.edu/entries/episteme-techne/.

Paulson, Marcy. 2009. "Is Transposing on a Diatonic Harmonica Possible?" http://www.suite101.com/content/transposing-on-a-diatonic-harmonica-a137825.

Peled, Avi, Assaf Pressman, Amir B. Geva, and Ilan Modai. 2003. "Somatosensory Evoked Potentials during a Rubber-Hand Illusion in Schizophrenia." *Schizophrenia Research* 64: 157–63.

Perrott, David, and Robert O. Gjerdingen. 2008. "Scanning the Dial: The Rapid Recognition of Music Genres." *Journal of New Music Research* 37: 93–100.

Pfordresher, Peter Q. 2005. "Auditory Feedback in Music Performance: The Role of Melodic Structure and Musical Skill." *Journal of Experimental Psychology. Human Perception & Performance* 31: 1331–45.

———. 2006. "Coordination of Perception and Action in Music Performance." *Advances in Cognitive Psychology* 2: 183–98.

Pfordresher, Peter Q., and James T. Mantell. 2012. "Effects of Altered Auditory Feedback across Effector Systems: Production of Melodies by Keyboard and Singing." *Acta Psychologica* 139: 166–77.

Pfordresher, Peter Q., and Caroline Palmer. 2002. "Effects of Delayed Auditory Feedback on Timing of Music Performance." *Psychological Research* 66: 71–79.

———. 2006. "Effects of Hearing the Past, Present, or Future During Music Performance." *Perception & Psychophysics* 68: 362–76.

Phillips-Silver, Jessica, and Laurel J. Trainor. 2005. "Feeling the Beat: Movement Influences Infants' Rhythm Perception." *Science* 308: 1430.

———. 2007. "Hearing What the Body Feels: Auditory Encoding of Rhythmic Movement." *Cognition* 105: 533–46.

Pickering, Andrew. 2009. *The Cybernetic Brain: Sketches of Another Future*. Chicago: University of Chicago Press.

Pinch, Trevor, and Frank Trocco. 2002. "The Social Construction of the Early Electronic Music Synthesizer." In *Music and Technology in the Twentieth Century*, edited by Hans-Joachim Braun, 67–83. Baltimore: Johns Hopkins University Press.

Polanyi, Michael. 1958. *Personal Knowledge: Towards a Post-Critical Philosophy*. Chicago: University of Chicago Press.

Reichardt, Jasia, ed. 1968. *Cybernetic Serendipity: The Computer and the Arts*. London New York: Studio International.

Repp, Bruno H. 1987. "The Sound of Two Hands Clapping: An Exploratory Study." *Journal of the Acoustical Society of America* 81: 1100–1109.

———. 1999. "Effects of Auditory Feedback Deprivation on Expressive Piano Performance." *Music Perception* 16: 409–38.

Ringer, Alexander L. 1953. "The *Chasse* as a Musical Topic of the 18th Century." *Journal of the American Musicological Society* 6: 148–59.

Rings, Steven. 2011. *Tonality and Transformation*. Oxford Studies in Music Theory. New York: Oxford University Press.

———. 2012. "The Learned Self: Artifice in Brahms's Late Intermezzi." In *Expressive Intersections in Brahms: Essays in Analysis and Meaning*, edited by Heather Platt and Peter H. Smith, 19–50. Bloomington: Indiana University Press.

Riskin, Jessica. 2003. "The Defecating Duck, Or, The Ambiguous Origins of Artificial Life." *Critical Inquiry* 29: 599–633.

Rizzolatti, Giacomo, and Corrado Sinigaglia. 2008. *Mirrors in the Brain: How Our Minds Share Actions and Emotions*. Translated by Frances Anderson. Oxford: Oxford University Press.

Rockwell, Joti. 2007. "Drive, Lonesomeness, and the Genre of Bluegrass Music." PhD dissertation, University of Chicago.

———. 2009. "Banjo Transformations and Bluegrass Rhythm." *Journal of Music Theory* 53: 137–62.

Rodby, Steve. 2008. *Imaginary Day Live*. DVD. Eagle Eye Media.

Rohrer, Tim. 2005. "Image Schemata in the Brain." In *From Perception to Meaning: Image Schemas in Cognitive Linguistics*, edited by Beate Hampe and Joe Grady, 165–96. Berlin: Mouton de Gruyter.

Rosenwinkel, Kurt. 2007. "The Next Step—2001." http://www.kurtrosenwinkel.com/archives/144.

Rothstein, Edward. 1991. "Yo-Yo Ma and His New 'Hyper' Cello." *New York Times*, August 17. http://www.nytimes.com/1991/08/17/arts/review-music-yo-yo-ma-and-his-new-hyper-cello.html.

Rover, Christian. 2006. "Kurt Rosenwinkel: From a Guitarist's Perspective." http://www.christianrover.com/Englische%20Seiten/Rosenwinkelengl.html.

Rusconi, Elena, Bonnie Kwan, Bruno L. Giordano, Carlo Umiltà, and Brian Butterworth. 2006. "Spatial Representation of Pitch Height: The SMARC Effect." *Cognition* 99: 113–29.

Sacks, Oliver. 1989. *Seeing Voices: A Journey into the World of the Deaf*. Berkeley: University of California Press.

Saslaw, Janna. 1996. "Forces, Containers, and Paths: The Role of Body-Derived Image Schemas in the Conceptualization of Music." *Journal of Music Theory* 40: 217–43.

Schaeffer, Pierre. 1966. *Traité des objets musicaux*. Paris: Éditions du Seuil.

Schechner, Richard. 2013. *Performance Studies: An Introduction*. 3rd ed. London: Routledge.

Schindler, Anton F. 1841. *The Life of Beethoven*. Translated by Ignace Moscheles. Vol. 2. London: Henry Colburn.

———. 1966. *Beethoven as I Knew Him*. Edited by Donald W. MacArdle. Translated by Constance S. Jolly. Chapel Hill: University of North Carolina Press.

Schulz, Matthias, Bernhard Ross, and Christo Pantev. 2003. "Evidence for Training-Induced Crossmodal Reorganization of Cortical Functions in Trumpet Performance." *NeuroReport* 14: 157–61.

Schutz, Michael, David Huron, Kristopher Keeton, and Greg Loewer. 2008. "The Happy Xylophone: Acoustic Affordances Restrict an Emotional Palate." *Empirical Musicology Review* 3: 126–35.

Schutz, Michael, and Fiona Manning. 2012. "Looking Beyond the Score: The Musical Role of Percussionists' Ancillary Gestures." *Music Theory Online* 18. http://www.mtosmt.org/issues/mto.12.18.1/mto.12.18.1.schutz_manning.html.

Scruton, Roger. 1997. *The Aesthetics of Music*. New York: Oxford University Press.

Sebastian, John. 1992. *Blues Harmonica*. Woodstock, NY: Homespun Tapes.

Senna, Irene, Angelo Maravita, Nadia Bolognini, and Cesare V. Parise. 2014. "The Marble-Hand Illusion." *PLoS ONE* 9: e91688.

Serino, Andrea, Michela Bassolino, Alessandro Farnè, and Elisabetta Làdavas. 2007. "Extended Multisensory Space in Blind Cane Users." *Psychological Science* 18: 642–48.

Serré de Rieux, Jean de. 1734. *Les dons des enfans de Latone: La musique et la chasse du cerf*. Paris: Chés P. Prault. http://openlibrary.org/books/OL24194489M/Les_dons_des_enfanc_de_Latone.

Shaffer, Kris. n.d. "Overtones, Intervals, and Generative Transformations in György Ligeti's Hamburg Concerto." Unpublished manuscript. http://pushpullfork.com/media/ShafferHamburgConcertoPaper.pdf.

Shannon, Claude E. 1964. "The Mathematical Theory of Communication." In *The Mathematical Theory of Communication*, by Claude E. Shannon and Warren Weaver. Urbana: University of Illinois Press.

Sheets-Johnstone, Maxine. 2005. "What Are We Naming?" In *Body Image and Body Schema: Interdisciplinary Perspectives on the Body*, edited by Helena de Preester and Veroniek Knockaert, 211–32. Amsterdam: J. Benjamins.

Shikida, Leonardo K. 2007. "Honest Transcription, But No Style at All." Customer Review. *Amazon.com*. July 18. http://www.amazon.com/review/R2BYL49RBIQ1GA/ref=cm_cr_dp_title?ie=UTF8&ASIN=0825613418&nodeID=283155&store=books.

Sisman, Elaine R. 1993. *Haydn and the Classical Variation*. Studies in the History of Music 5. Cambridge, MA: Harvard University Press.

Solie, Ruth A. 2004. "'Girling' at the Parlor Piano." In *Music in Other Words: Victorian Conversations*, 85–117. Berkeley: University of California Press.

Spicer, Mark. 2011. "(Per)Form In(g) Rock: A Response." *Music Theory Online* 17. http://www.mtosmt.org/issues/mto.11.17.3/mto.11.17.3.spicer.html.

Sporns, Olaf. 2010. *Networks of the Brain*. Cambridge, MA: MIT Press.

Stewart, Lauren, Vincent Walsh, and Uta Frith. 2004. "Reading Music Modifies Spatial Mapping in Pianists." *Perception & Psychophysics* 66: 183–95.

Stiegler, Bernard. 1998. *Technics and Time, 1: The Fault of Epimetheus*. Translated by Richard Beardsworth and George Collins. Stanford, CA: Stanford University Press.

———. 2009. *Technics and Time, 2: Disorientation*. Translated by Stephen Barker. Stanford, CA: Stanford University Press.

———. 2011. *Technics and Time, 3: Cinematic Time and the Question of Malaise*. Translated by Stephen Barker. Stanford, CA: Stanford University Press.

Straus, Joseph N. 2003. "Uniformity, Balance, and Smoothness in Atonal Voice Leading." *Music Theory Spectrum* 25: 305–52.

———. 2011. *Extraordinary Measures: Disability in Music*. New York: Oxford University Press.

Sudnow, David. 1978. *Ways of the Hand: The Organization of Improvised Conduct*. Cambridge, MA: Harvard University Press.

Szendy, Peter. 2016. *Phantom Limbs: On Musical Bodies*. Translated by Will Bishop. New York: Fordham University Press.

Tallis, Raymond. 2003. *The Hand: A Philosophical Inquiry into Human Being*. Edinburgh: Edinburgh University Press.

Taub, Robert. 2002. *Playing the Beethoven Piano Sonatas*. Portland, OR: Amadeus Press.

Taylor, Timothy. 2001. *Strange Sounds: Music, Technology, and Culture*. New York: Routledge.

Temperley, David. 2007. "The Melodic-Harmonic 'Divorce' in Rock." *Popular Music* 26: 323–42.

Thakkar, Katharine N., Heathman S. Nichols, Lindsey G. McIntosh, and Sohee Park. 2011. "Disturbances in Body Ownership in Schizophrenia: Evidence from the Rubber Hand Illusion and Case Study of a Spontaneous Out-of-Body Experience." *PLoS ONE* 6: e27089.

Thayer, Alexander Wheelock. 1967. *Thayer's Life of Beethoven*. Edited by Forbes Elliot. Princeton, NJ: Princeton University Press.

Tresch, John, and Emily I. Dolan. 2013. "Toward a New Organology: Instruments of Music and Science." *Osiris* 28: 278–98.

Tsakiris, Manos, and Patrick Haggard. 2005. "The Rubber Hand Illusion Revisited: Visuotactile Integration and Self-Attribution." *Journal of Experimental Psychology: Human Perception and Performance* 31: 80–91.

Tucker, Mike, and Rob Ellis. 1998. "On the Relations Between Seen Objects and Components of Potential Actions." *Journal of Experimental Psychology: Human Perception and Performance* 24: 830–46.

———. 2001. "The Potentiation of Grasp Types During Visual Object Categorization." *Visual Cognition* 8: 769–800.

———. 2004. "Action Priming by Briefly Presented Objects." *Acta Psychologica* 116: 185–203.

Tuckwell, Barry. 2002. *Horn*. New ed. Yehudi Menuhin Music Guides. London: Kahn & Averill.

Tymoczko, Dmitri. 2011. *A Geometry of Music: Harmony and Counterpoint in the Extended Common Practice*. New York: Oxford University Press.

Varela, Francisco J., Evan Thompson, and Eleanor Rosch. 1991. *The Embodied Mind: Cognitive Science and Human Experience*. Cambridge, MA: MIT Press.

Verbalis, Jon. 2012. *Natural Fingering: A Topographical Approach to Pianism*. New York: Oxford University Press.

Vitale, Alessia Rita. 2008. "The Singing Lesson: Phenomenology of the Non-Verbal Dynamics Appearing in Studying the *Instrument-Voix*." *Musicae Scientiae*, Special issue: "Narrative in Music and Interaction," 111–28.

Waksman, Steve. 1999. *Instruments of Desire: The Electric Guitar and the Shaping of Musical Experience*. Cambridge, MA: Harvard University Press.

———. 2001. "Into the Arena: Edward Van Halen and the Cultural Contradictions of the Guitar Hero." In *Guitar Cultures*, edited by Andy Bennett and Kevin Dawe, 117–34. Oxford: Berg.

Walser, Robert. 1993. *Running with the Devil: Power, Gender, and Madness in Heavy Metal Music*. Hanover, NH: University Press of New England.

Webb, Nicholas. 1985. "Pat Metheny Interview." *Guitarist*, May. http://www.joness.com/gr300/metheny.htm.

Weber, Samuel. 1989. "Upsetting the Set Up: Remarks on Heidegger's Questing after Technics." *Modern Language Notes* 104: 977–92.

Wegman, Rob C. 1996. "From Maker to Composer: Improvisation and Musical Authorship in the Low Countries, 1450–1500." *Journal of the American Musicological Society* 49: 409–79.

Wenzel, Haik, and Martin Häffner. 2006. *Legende Hohner Harmonika: Mundharmonika und Akkordeon in der Welt der Musik*. Bergkirchen: PPVMedien/Edition Bochinsky.

Wiener, Norbert. 1948. *Cybernetics; Or, Control and Communication in the Animal and the Machine*. New York: John Wiley & Sons.

Williams, Peter. 1981. "BWV565: A Toccata in D Minor for Organ by J. S. Bach?" *Early Music* 9: 330–37.

———. 1994. "Two Case Studies in Performance Practice and the Details of Notation: 2. J. S. Bach and Left-Hand–Right-Hand Distribution." *Early Music* 22: 101–13.

———. 2004. *The Life of Bach*. Cambridge: Cambridge University Press.

Wiskus, Jessica. 2013. *The Rhythm of Thought: Art, Literature, and Music after Merleau-Ponty*. Chicago: University of Chicago Press.

Witt, Jessica K., and Michael A. Riley. 2014. "Discovering Your Inner Gibson: Reconciling Action-Specific and Ecological Approaches to Perception–Action." *Psychonomic Bulletin and Review* 21: 1353–70.

Wolff, Christoph. 2000. *Johann Sebastian Bach: The Learned Musician*. New York: W. W. Norton.

Wu, Ling-ling, and Lawrence W. Barsalou. 2009. "Perceptual Simulation in Conceptual Combination: Evidence from Property Generation." *Acta Psychologica* 132: 173–89.

Yamamoto, Shinya, and Shigeru Kitazawa. 2001. "Sensation at the Tips of Invisible Tools." *Nature Neuroscience* 4: 979–80.

Yearsley, David. 2002. *Bach and the Meanings of Counterpoint*. Cambridge Cambridge University Press.

———. 2012. *Bach's Feet: The Organ Pedals in European Culture*. Cambridge: Cambridge University Press.

Yeh, Wenchi, and Lawrence W. Barsalou. 2006. "The Situated Nature of Concepts." *American Journal of Psychology* 119: 349–84.

Yin, Henry H., and Barbara J. Knowlton. 2006. "The Role of the Basal Ganglia in Habit Formation." *Nature Reviews Neuroscience* 7: 464–76.

Yung, Bell. 1984. "Choreographic and Kinesthetic Elements in Performance on the Chinese Seven-String Zither." *Ethnomusicology* 28: 505–17.

Zanten, Wim van. 1986. "The Tone Material of the Kacapi in Tembang Sunda in West Java." *Ethnomusicology* 30: 84–112.

Zarlino, Gioseffo. 1588. *Sopplimenti Musicali*. Venice: Francesco dei Franceschi Senese.
Zbikowski, Lawrence M. 2002. *Conceptualizing Music: Cognitive Structure, Theory, and Analysis*. AMS Studies in Music. New York: Oxford University Press.
———. 2010. "Music, Emotion, Analysis." *Music Analysis* 29: 37–60.
Zheng, Zane Z., Ewen N. MacDonald, Kevin G. Munhall, and Ingrid S. Johnsrude. 2011. "Perceiving a Stranger's Voice as Being One's Own: A 'Rubber Voice' Illusion?" *PLoS ONE* 6: e18655.

INDEX